Praise
SAINT DEATH'S DAUGHTER

"Exemplifies what fantasy can do in the best of ways. Fans of cheeky and humorous prose, unreliable narrators, difficult topics and a story that makes you laugh and cry will find *Saint Death's Daughter* to be just the book to read."

Strange Horizons

"Cooney's stories include violence, abuse, death, ghosts, and the afterlife, but always infused with joy, lust for life, lighthearted humor, and hope; it is a surprisingly charming, poignant admixture. Grisly, dark, lovely, funny, heartfelt."

Kirkus Reviews

"*Gideon the Ninth* meets *The Addams Family* in this first book in a wildly inventive new fantasy series."

Buzzfeed

"Cooney's prose is beautiful and intricate and glowing, and I love it so. This book made me fall in love with her characters, too, in an emotional roller-coaster that had me crying and flinging the book across the room."

The Colorado Sun

"Every character arrives in a burst: fully-realized, dripping with detail and a fire in their heart."

Tor.com

"Lanie's journey is compelling; the world is intricate and beautifully realised. The story rewards the time invested in it."

The British Fantasy Society

"I can usually predict story beats, but the author managed to surprise me with the depth and complexity of the characters, especially the antagonists."

The Southern Bookseller Review

"This is the weirdest book I have read in a long time—
and yet its weirdness is charming. Somewhat reminiscent of *What
We Do in the Shadows* or *The Addams Family*."

Booknest

"The broad aesthetic here is 'whimsical gothic': a real
Ghormengast-y vibe, balanced with increasing nuance. *Saint
Death's Daughter* has gone straight to the favourites list."

Nerds of a Feather

"Strange and magical adventures in a colorful world
where most people are gender fluid, the gods are strange
and death is not an ending."

Thornwell Books

"The novel complicates and recomplicates, always to its benefit.
There's a puppy! And there is suspense, and twists, and a
satisfying resolution that gives no one all they want."

Black Gate

"A beautiful, stunning work of literature, more art than words,
and something that I recommend everyone reads."

Just Geeking By

"I don't *want* to tell you much about this book. I want you to
experience it as I did; a cake whose every layer is more delicious
than the last; a gemstone that always has another glittering
facet when you turn it over. This is a book you should go into
unprepared—and unarmed."

Every Book A Doorway

"I've never met a book that is so completely sure of itself. Cooney
could have gone off on any tangent and I would have completely
believed it. I loved *Saint Death's Daughter* for its complexities and
characters and chaos and I think this will remain one of my top
reads of the year."

FanFiAddict

"I loved *Saint Death's Daughter* to pieces: the world-building and the characters and the way that every time I thought I knew what kind of book it was, it changed. There was an ebullience to this book, in its world-building and its prose and its characters, that I found both delightful and compelling."

Katherine Addison

"A tumultuous, swaggering, cackling story, a gorgeous citrus orchard with bones for roots. Miscellaneous Stones's journey has an ocean's breadth and depth, its storms and sparkles and salt. Soaring with love and absolutely fizzing with tenderness and joy—I have never read anything so utterly *alive*."

Amal El-Mohtar

"Just as magical as I knew it would be. The compassion Cooney has for her characters, the ways in which she draws the reader deep into her world, are peerless and divine. I could go on about the wonder of her prose, but I'd rather readers just dive straight in and discover it for themselves."

Tiffany Trent

"Infused with brilliantly intricate world-building, dark humour, diverse characters and even a touch of whimsy. As Lanie navigates her world of familial strife, both natural and supernatural, and her own burgeoning powers, you can't help but learn to love death alongside her."

Rhianna Pratchett

"*Saint Death's Daughter* is marvellous: it strikes an expert balance between light and dark, serious and ludicrous, and always keeps a wonderful, strong, queer energy about itself."

Mike Brooks

"It feels like overhearing a conversation between Terry Pratchett and Susanna Clarke. A total must if you dig footnotes or fantasy."

Patty Templeton

"What happens if you are a necromancer born into a family of assassins—but you're literally allergic to death itself? *Saint Death's Daughter* is a whimsically gothy romp full of weird magic and intricate worldbuilding."

Nicole Kornher-Stace

"A luminous, chiming, bone-belled, ludicrous, austere, flamboyant, rhyming, reckless, affectionate novel; a giddy libation to a sly and shifting pantheon, a glittering ossuary-mosaic of incautious hope and over-generous loves, of gambling and falling and flying."

Kathleen Jennings

"Cooney's prose effervesces: each magnificent name, each glorious detail, each jig-and-reel phrase thrills like champagne bubbles on the tongue. Sumptuous, bawdy, and layered as a mille-feuille, this book is delicious, delectable, and impossible not to devour."

Lisa L. Hannett

"Gorgeous, sexy, cruel and compassionate and funny. Such rich, delicious world-building and frankly lovable characters (even the baddies are compelling!). I relished every word."

Liz Duffy Adams

"*Saint Death's Daughter* is filled with lavish world building, lyrical prose, and characters to die for. C. S. E. Cooney is a faerie queen barely trying to pass in the mundane world. This book is as luminous and flamboyant as she is."

Tina Jens

"A tantalizing hint at a fabulous backstory is followed by a mind-spinningly original bit of worldbuilding, and then that is in turn chased by an emotional arc so moving that I cried like a baby while reading at an airport gate, and nevermind all the people staring."

Caitlyn Paxson

First published 2025 by Solaris
an imprint of Rebellion Publishing Ltd,
Riverside House, Osney Mead,
Oxford, OX2 0ES, UK

www.solarisbooks.com

ISBN: 978-1-83786-449-2

10 9 8 7 6 5 4 3 2 1

A CIP catalogue record for this book is available from the British Library.

Designed & typeset by Rebellion Publishing

Printed in Denmark

MIX
Paper | Supporting
responsible forestry
FSC
www.fsc.org   FSC® C104608

SAINT DEATH'S HERALD

PART TWO OF THE SAINT DEATH TRILOGY

C. S. E. COONEY

SOLARIS

Dedicated to Zig Zag Claybourne, my brother

And I was alive in the blizzard of the blossoming pear,
Myself I stood in the storm of the bird-cherry tree.
It was all leaflife and starshower, unerring, self-
    shattering power,
And it was all aimed at me.
What is this dire delight flowering fleeing always earth?
What is being? What is truth?
Blossoms rupture and rapture the air,
All hover and hammer,
Time intensified and time intolerable, sweetness
    raveling rot.
It is now. It is not.

"And I Was Alive," Osip Mandelstam
(translated by Christian Wiman)

THE TWELFTH
SOTHAÍN SET

**The Twelve Attitudes of the Twelfth Sothaín Set
(Belonging to Doédenna, God of Death)**

And at the end of everything, I rest—
As all the corse exposed to birds of air
As all the corse in crypt and coffin kept
As all the corse surrendered to the sea
As all the corse for harvest sacrificed
As all the corse entangled in the trees
As all the corse preserved against decay
As all the corse on battlefields let lie
As all the corse who are to progress pledged
As all the corse made feast for other beasts
As all the corse cremated at the pyre
As all the corse who have been disappeared
So go we all, and go the gods besides—
who is my doorway that the dead walk through?

Part One

THE BORDERLANDS

In the marches of Damahrash and Leech...

CHAPTER ONE
The Ghost-Mounted Man

Year 4826 of Higher and Lower Quadiíb
On H'za, 24th of Jdeni: the Second Month
21 Days till Spring Equinox

IF THE MAN were a house, the ghost who possessed him would be the black mold spreading across his walls. No stopping it. No scrubbing it. Only enduring.

Except, he couldn't endure it. Not anymore.

"Just kill me," Cracchen Skrathmandan begged as he shoveled out the hanged man's grave with his bare hands.

"I *am* killing you!" the ghost of Irradiant Stones replied. "I'm just doing it at my own pace. Now dig!"

Useless to plead with the ghost. It only irritated him. So Cracchen prayed instead—to Erre'Elur, god of death and winter—for the blessing of death this winter's day.

But the ghost was a necromancer—or had been one in life—and a necromancer was a priest of death. Cracchen had himself dealt death in his day, plenty of it. Before the ghost had entered him, melting his left eyeball from his face and taking up residence in its empty socket, Cracchen had thought himself mighty. Warrior giant. Royal assassin. A ruthless killer in the prime of his life.

But he had never *worshipped* death. His dealings with Her had been transactional, a straightforward matter. That made all the difference now, when the only god who could help him would sooner bend Her ear to a ghost's demands than his own.

17

"Buck up!" cried the ghost, his nasal voice rattling through Cracchen's skull. "Put your back into it! You root out this gallows' meat for me, my oinker, or I'll seize control of your bone-bag again. Remember last time?" His sneer was palpable, like being spat on from the inside. "You don't want that, you dig, boyo. *Or else!*"

The ghost threatened, but held back, tucked smugly inside his eye socket. After all, Cracchen was well-trained, He'd been the ghost's mount for months now. For, perhaps, eternity.

A harsh, gray, late-winter day, edging into evening. Cracchen hardly remembered a time when the world held color or warmth, when he wasn't equal parts agony and numbness. A light but relentless precipitation waffled between liquid and solid states, resulting in gelid misery. Any bird or beast so fortunate as to not be possessed by the ghost of Irradiant Stones was tucked cozily away in bush or burrow, blissfully ignorant of necromancers or gods.

"Heave ho, boyo! Work those burly biceps! Think I chose you for your brains? Pah! Saint Death would gag on that paltry mouthful. Twelve Gods know it wasn't for your sorceries. A more gods-bereft sack of unmagical meat I never did lay eyes on."

As the ghost's regular pattern of complaints droned on and on, Cracchen heaved-ho.

And then—at last!—a sucking sound, and the grave's mud relinquished its buried treasure.

The corpse in Cracchen's cold grip glopped a few inches out of the half-frozen soup of earth and into the diffuse twilight.

"Again!" the ghost cried. "Heave!"

Cracchen bent his head to his breast, trying to breathe. He was dizzy. (He was always dizzy these days.) Each breath pinched a deep place between shoulder blade and spine, seized his sinuses, sealed his nostrils shut. His mouth and nose were blistered with sores.

But none of these, nor any of his multiple other hurts, were worse than the sensation in his empty left eye socket. The static shock of ever-present infection. The slow, corrosive crumble of invasion.

"Stop loitering! Do you think we have all the time in the world? Our foe is closing in!"

From inside his skull, the ghost set spur to his host body, sending a spike of disorienting pain straight into Cracchen's brain. With a sound that was half bellow, half groan, Cracchen hoisted himself, and the cadaver with him, out of the slickening grave in a gross parody of birth.

Cracchen thought: *I would give the world—I would give my mother's life—I would cut the heart out of my brother's body—if I could just lie back and make this grave my own.*

"Tsk tsk tsk," clicked the ghost. Tongueless, toothless, incorporeal, he was nonetheless still more than capable of clicking like a cicada. "Not on my watch, boyo."

Cracchen's vision grayed. One moment, he was backsliding into the mud with his hard-won corpse. The next, he was fully out of the grave, several yards away on solid ground, straddling the corpse, knife in hand, with the flesh of his arm already scored open.

Bewildered tears welled in his eyes. They fell, with his blood, onto the body beneath him.

"Every time I take control," the ghost growled, "it lights you up like a beacon, boyo. They can see you, clear as a signal fire in the darkest reaches of night. Think the foe won't tear *you* apart to get at *me*? You'd be wrong. And then you'd be dead."

As he wept and bled over the corpse, Cracchen felt the frosty breath of the upturned grave at his back, cold as Erre'Elur's kiss. Thank Her name, the corpse he'd just dug up must have been buried only recently—two or three days at most—for its flesh was blistered but not ruptured, and though its reek was foul, what of it? Everything stank. The corpse. The mud. Cracchen himself.

His breath rattled in his throat. He stared at the ropes still binding the corpse's wrists.

Criminal, the ropes accused.

So it doesn't matter, does it? he pleaded with Erre'Elur. *What we do to the corpse? Crimes committed upon the dead are no crimes at all. The dead will never know. And surely any criminal deserving of execution deserves whatever comes after. Don't they?*

The god did not answer. But for some reason, Cracchen did not think Her silence meant agreement.

At least praying (if it was praying) put his concentration elsewhere than his own nausea at the noxious stench. Not that his stomach had any contents left to vomit. His head spun as the ghost squirmed around inside of it, scanning the skies for enemies.

"You've done it now. Caught their attention. They're turning our way. Why isn't my ectenica catching? Your blood is useless! Cut again. We need more juice."

Cracchen's hand shook on the knife handle. He whimpered, uselessly, "Please. Kill me."

"Saint Death's sake, you nincompoop!" the ghost snapped. "Know this if you learn nothing else: before I move on to better accommodations, I'm going to squeeze every last minim of use out of you. Skaki trash. I gave my life destroying your kind, and Twelve Gods know I'll dedicate my undeath to it. Now. Cut me a good one and bleed on that corpse! Or I'll cut you myself!"

Trembling but obedient, Cracchen sawed into the soft crease of his elbow with the muddy, bloodied knife.

They had performed this ritual of resurrection dozens of times in the months since the ghost had first possessed him. Usually, the dead thing they would find was considerably smaller than a human: a bird smeared to feathers in the dirt, an incomplete set of fox bones tangled in some tree roots, a pony that had broken a leg and had been put down at the side of the road.

The ghost had a sense about the dead. He could sniff out a pile of old bones from a mile away, across water, cached beneath a stone. For days, he had been excitedly spurring Cracchen through the bush of western Damahrash, until, finally, late this afternoon, they had stumbled upon a crossroads marking the border between Damahrash and Leech. The gallows were not visible from the road. Both gallows tree and its garden of shallow graves were tucked behind a hill, where their presence would not distress passersby. Nevertheless, the ghost led them to the place unerringly. He had sniffed through Cracchen's nose, all the way up to a patch of freshly disturbed earth, positively gleeful.

Presently, the earth considerably more disturbed, the corpse exhumed, and Cracchen's new ragged cut now welling like a red spring, the ghost yelled, "That's enough!"

Cracchen dropped the knife into the mud. Ghost and host body both watched as their blood dripped down onto the cadaver. The ghost hissed when a few drops fell onto the ropes instead of dead flesh.

"Wasteful," he muttered. "Get out of my way! I'll do it!"

For the second time in a span of minutes, it happened. Cracchen's vision grayed. He felt his mind, like a kitten in a burlap sack, being thrust down into the darkest recesses of himself as the ghost took over. As he sank, he felt the ghost, that chewing-on-charged-metal presence, skitter out of his left eye socket, slide down the side of his neck, and hop into his shoulder.

Thence, it slipped into the open wounds of his left arm, where the ghost began to swell. He was pushing himself, pushing his magic—his *substance*, he called it, during his interminable lectures—into Cracchen's blood, mingling with it as it left his body and spattered on the corpse.

To make undeath required only three ingredients: living blood; dead flesh (or 'accident,' as the ghost designated it); and the substance, the *soul-stuff*, of a necromancer.

"Come on," the ghost muttered through Cracchen's lips. "Come on. Spark! Spark, my ectenica. *Before they find us.*"

The process was taking too long. It always took too long, according to the ghost.

Irradiant Stones was fond of telling his host that had Cracchen been blessed by *any* of the gods, with *any* magic whatsoever, he *might* at least have bent those mysterious sorceries to his purpose. And had Cracchen been that rarest and most coveted kind of sorcerer of all—a necromancer, priest of death—his blood would have been so charged with that particular magic, there was nothing the ghost might not have accomplished with his plenteous fluids.

Alas, Cracchen's utter lack of divinely blessed blood had been the cause of constant monologuing all their long months on the road.

Nor did the ghost stint now. Irradiant Radithor Stones was a ghost of many words. Many of them were the same words, over and over again. His obsessions were few but intense: how he had once been the world's greatest necromancer and would be once more; how he must complete his life's work in Northernmost Skakmaht, winning a war that the world had long moved on from; and how his foes would pay—*how* they would *pay!*—once he was at full strength again, and able to catapult upon their heads the fiery ordnance of his wrath.

Those foes, Cracchen had learned over long months of wearisome repetition, were a few dozen magically disembodied souls, all grouped together into some kind of single, uncanny entity, like a rack of storm clouds. This 'storm of souls' was pursuing the ghost with a single-minded fury.

At the very end of his life, Irradiant Stones had sundered the substances from the living accidents of hundreds of Skaki sky wizards in one mighty act of magic that ended the Northernmost War—and ended his own life. But even in death, he did not allow those souls to pass on into the god of death, but trapped them instead in a basalt sarcophagus. The shells of their bodies were abandoned in the far north, not dead but forever frozen, never to rot away, never to walk again.

Meanwhile, over the last century of his long afterlife, the ghost had been picking off his captive souls one by one, sucking their living substances dry to feed his undeath. Those who survived this had recently escaped their stone prison.

And now they wanted revenge.

For his part, Cracchen wished they would get on with it.

"All my life and after," the ghost droned, with honed-razor nasality, "I have had to contend with the shortcomings of my own kin. My own flesh and blood. *How* I suffered! But at least they were mine: my folly, my fruit. Their vanity, their vapidity and arrogance, their laziness and underhandedness and treachery, and worst of all," the ghost spat (he had to use Cracchen's mouth, lacking his own salivary glands), "their *ingratitude* I could endure, silently, nobly, and get on with my work. Because their blood ran with Saint Death's magic, and so, they were *somewhat* useful. But then, oh then, I was so accursed as to fall upon *your* useless husk as the instrument of my escape. Why, of all bodies on Athe, did it have to be you? Had you come with a fraction of *actual power...*"

Here the ghost seemed to lose his thread, and left off his complaints to growl at the blood-spattered corpse, "*Catch*, damn you duodecifold! *Give me my ectenica!*"

A moment later, it did.

Cracchen knew it did, because he heard the ghost hiss with pleasure through his own broken teeth.

Somewhere, in that mix of mud, blood, icy rain, and clay-cold flesh, a blue flame sparked.

Then two.

Then twenty.

And then the sparks became a shimmering throughout the surface of the skin. The corpse was glowing, as with foxfire.

"That's right," the ghost crooned. "There's my good ectenica. Go on. Open your eyes now."

The newly undead thing gummed open its eyes. These were not the worm-eaten remnants of the corpse's cold clay. No, these were the pure, radiant, blue-white beams of undeath, and they looked up at the ghost in Cracchen's skull with adoration and obeisance.

The ghost clucked Cracchen's tongue.

"Oh, no. No, no, no. There is *much* too much of you. I need a lot of speedy little pieces. I need decoys! Distractions! Break up!

Fall apart! Fly free! Fast as may be! My foes are almost upon us!" The corpse was no more corpse in truth, but full ectenica now—a semi-sentient phosphorescence, like the flash of a moonstone by moonlight, that listened attentively to the ghost's commands.

And obeyed.

The cadaver liquified itself into gelatinous chunks. The ectenical skull parted along its sutures. The ectenical arms dislocated from their torso, then snapped into pieces at elbows and wrists. (The ropes binding the wrists fell into the mud like discarded snake skins.) Thighs tore themselves from hips, lower legs from knees.

All pieces began to lose their former semblance to body parts. The ectenica became ever more amorphous, malleable. It flashed and flickered, bounced and slithered. And then, each ectenical blob began to hop away from the gravesite, fast as rabbits fleeing a fox.

"Off you go, my bugaboos!" sang the ghost, rubbing his host body's hands together. "Go ye, and keep my foes at bay! Take my magical signal and make them give chase! Send them scattering off in all directions! Buy me more time!"

Cracchen found himself floating back to the surface, somewhat to his regret. The dreary, deadening presence of the ghost receded back into his left eye socket.

Being back in his body disgusted him. The rain-that-wanted-to-be-snow was slicking down his filthy hair, plastering ragged clothes to clammy skin, turning his lips blue. His right eye kept wanting to droop closed—except that the ghost kept needling him to prop it back up.

"Get up." The ghost sounded weary, as he always did after performing an act of necromancy. "*Move*, boyo. We've got to keep going. Forward! Ahead! To Leech! While my foes are distracted."

The storm of souls, they both knew, would not be distracted for long. *They* didn't have bodies to feed and water. *They* needed no sleep.

"I'm running out," muttered the ghost. "Out of time. Out of blood. Out of *accident*. Need a new one. Something with *juice*. Plump me up. Give me back my edge. Something that will last me till my work up north is done. Finish what I started."

Cracchen wished him joy of his juicy new body, whoever it might be. So long as he, Cracchen, might finally be allowed to die, as he most ardently desired.

"No slumping now! We're too close! Heave-ho, boyo!"

A wave of gray tentacled over Cracchen's consciousness again as the ghost ascended. He piloted Cracchen's body away from gallows and grave, forcing him to climb that terrible hill once more. As soon as he prodded Cracchen over the crest and sent him stumbling down the scree on the far side, he loosed his host's reins and went dormant, leaving only the impression of his desired direction, and the compulsion to keep going.

AT THE BOTTOM of the hill, a ditch.

At the bottom of the ditch, a dead deer.

In his fog and rush, the ghost-mounted man tripped over her without noticing her. He picked himself up, scrambled out of the ditch on hands and knees, and pitched forward again at a lurching run down the stony road into Leech.

But as he passed over her, the dead deer opened her eyes.

They were filled with a swirling gray fog, and *they* marked *him*.

The dead deer studied Cracchen Skrathmandan carefully, memorizing every last detail of him: how his body was emaciated, his flesh cut in a hundred places; how most of those cuts had knitted badly, were swollen with pus and other rank fluids; how his feet and hands were bare even in this freezing wind, and missing several toes and fingers; how his veins showed black against his rosy flesh; how he shimmered with fever, shivered with cold.

The moment Cracchen vanished over the first hill of Leech, the deer picked herself up out of the ditch and trotted after him on rotting legs.

One of her four hooves was missing, but she didn't seem to heed that.

She didn't heed the holes in her head either, or the foulness on her fur, or the worms in her belly. Her torso was completely stripped, ribcage red and exposed, entrails long since become a feast for scavenger birds, rodents, and the bloom of blowflies that grew upon her carcass.

But she had no thought for that. She was focused on Cracchen's retreating form with an intensity far more befitting a predator than a ruminant—however undead that ruminant might be.

"*Grandpa Rad*," murmured the deer in the voice of Miscellaneous Stones, necromancer. "*Finally*."

CHAPTER TWO
The Yearling Doe

"GOT HIM, GOT him, got him!" Lanie snapped open her eyes and bounced in place. As she was seated on the ground, surrounded by bones she didn't want to disturb, she couldn't move much except to bob up and down, but she bobbed with enthusiasm and vigor.

Outside the open entrance flap of their traveling esh, Duantri was crouched beside a tiny cooking fire, her back to Lanie.

Lanie stopped bouncing, and glanced around, surprised. The esh was fully erected and lashed in place around her. Last she remembered, Duantri had staked out their campsite and announced she was going hunting. Lanie decided she would go hunting too—in her own way—and had flung Stripes the tiger rug down onto the cold, damp dirt, and arranged all the bits of bones she'd collected from her cache-traps in the hills hereabouts in a circle around her. She'd entered into communion with the bones, forgetting the light, icy rain falling on her head, forgetting the bone-chilling cold, forgetting everything.

Now, emerging from her meditations, she found she was warm and dry, sitting at the center of the bell-shaped womb of their esh. Where was all that toasty heat radiating from? Outside, she noticed, the sky was darkening, the rain worsening, the wind picking up.

Must be the socks, she decided, glancing around for them. Duantri always heated stones near the fire, then wrapped them in woolen socks, placing them at intervals around the canvas walls of their esh.

Duantri knew everything about living outdoors, from making rock socks to digging latrines to cooking over campfires. Without her, Lanie would have frozen or starved to death weeks ago. Probably both.

"How long was I out?" she called to her friend. "Did you do all this by yourself?"

Rhetorical questions. Lanie must have been meditating over the bones for at least two hours, for the light had changed, the esh was built, the stew smelled almost ready, and there was quite a lot of heat emanating from Duantri's rock socks. Rocks took a while to warm up.

The second answer was just as obvious. Of course Duantri had done all this by herself. There were only the two of them—not including Stripes, who considered flying his mistress through the air eighty or so miles a day to be his share of the manual labor, and besides, had no opposable thumbs to do any fiddly work—and Lanie knew *she'd* had nothing to do with it.

Smiling over her shoulder, Duantri answered the second question first, and in Quadic: "But no, my Lanie—'twas a little bird who built our esh and laid this fire for thee, and did it so without a moan or plaint, that all the gods do covet her for saint."

"You're the best," Lanie said in Lirian. "The best bird *ever*." She would have said it in Quadic, but that would have taken counting on her fingers and about seventeen more syllables.

"Mmn-hmn." Duantri turned back to the fire.

"I'll dig the latrine later," Lanie promised.

"Mmn-hmn." Duantri was expert at making agreeable sounds that had nothing to do with actually agreeing. Her over-the-shoulder grin flashed again. "Unless the phrase '*I got him*' thrice means else, methinks thou hast a different job to do." She broke the Quadic form to say in Lirian, "So get on with it!"

"The ghost tripped my deer trap!" Lanie crowed. "Walked right past her, never felt me in the deer. He's getting careless, maybe desperate. He knows better than to use all that magic off-surge—he's the one who taught *me!* Not only does it drain him, it exposes him—alerts whoever's looking to his magical stench."

"How do you know it's his?"

Lanie grimaced. "It's like... how you'd know if someone was standing behind you with a bludgeon and a grudge? Every time he uses death magic, I feel this awful tug. It sort of"—she waved her hands about—"pollutes the air in a certain direction."

"That seems a lot of power for a ghost," Duantri commented.

"It *is* a lot," Lanie agreed, "and he's drawing it from *himself*. The ghost is finite; his substance is not a renewable resource—and neither is his host's. The way he's draining him... Oh, Duantri!" she burst out. "I never liked Cracchen Skrathmandan, but I wouldn't treat an animal—a criminal—my *enemy*—that way. Grandpa Rad's barely feeding him. Cracchen's drinking out of ditches, sleeping cold. Doesn't the ghost remember what it's like to have a body?"

"Mayhap he thinks to find a new host soon." Duantri's voice was very dry. She cared about as much for Cracchen Skrathmandan as she would enjoy being shot in the face point-blank with a four-barreled blunderbuss, and had at other times expressed the opinion that whatever the ghost did to the man was justly, even richly, deserved.

"Duantri. We can't let that happen."

"I know," said the Gyrgardu, and if she sounded a bit wistful, Lanie did not remark on it.

Pushing her spectacles up the bridge of her nose, she bent at the waist and started pawing at her circle of bones until she found what she was looking for: a deer hoof, with dew claws and a bit of leg bone still attached. She drew it into her lap.

Thanks to both Stripes's and Duantri's air speeds, after weeks of travel, they'd finally managed to catch up with the ghost. They were coming all the way up from Quadiíb, but they had the advantage of a flying tiger rug, as well Duantri's other form. The ghost, despite his month-long head start, was on foot. His host body was ill, and had been hard used. The ghost also had to stop frequently and burrow into hiding from the storm of Skaki wizard-souls also in dogged pursuit. He was being harried on all sides.

As much as Duantri thought the ghost's possession of Cracchen was no more than the man deserved, Lanie believed otherwise. Her great-grandfather was pure poison, a blight upon the planet. She wanted Irradiant Stones eradicated from Athe, all memory of him erased. She wanted nothing to do with him.

Except, he was her *job*.

To exorcise the ghost, she'd need to be able to touch the host body. Reach, range, autonomy. Time to enter the deer more fully.

"Duantri?"

The Gyrgardu turned at the sound of Lanie's voice, eyebrows arching in inquiry. Lanie's heart panged. Here she was, warm and dry, while Duantri sat in the wind, cooking for the two of them, thoroughly wet and disheveled, her short black curls standing on end, her face streaked in soot and dirt.

Lanie swallowed. "I… I've got to go in deep for a bit."

Duantri rose quickly from her crouch. "I will be your eyes from on high."

"Oh, no! I mean," Lanie tried to protest, "you flew all day, then hunted, then set up the whole camp, then cooked, and—"

"Lanie." Duantri spread arms and legs wide, as if to show that she was strong enough to wrestle even Lanie's guilty conscience, a giantess. "It is what I am here for."

Lanie was silent for a long moment. One of Duantri's black brows crooked. They held each other's stares. It was a game they played, but Duantri always won, and Lanie knew it.

"All right," she said at last. "I hate to ask it, but… yes. Please be my eyes."

Duantri gave her an approving nod. She brushed off her clothes, ran a hand through her curls. Then she glanced at herself, snorted, and swiftly shucked off boots, socks, and heavy, travel-stained robe, and tossed them all into the esh.

One moment, the Gyrgardu was holding her woman-form.

She stood outside the esh, skin bare to the freezing rain, not seeming to feel the cold at all.

The next moment, she was a kestrel, hovering.

Rufous-backed, cream-breasted, wings barred in dark brown. She was no bigger than a mourning dove, her head a silvery blue. But the bright-dark eye, ringed all around in yellow, was a raptor's eye: wild and inscrutable, curious and keen. None of the gentle warmth of the human Duantri was left in it, only her intelligence, honed to a single purpose: the hunt.

A few light wing flaps above the low campfire, and she was gone.

THE WIND THWUPPED and whapped against the esh's canvas walls, sending a stiff chill through the open entrance flap. Campfire smoke twisted through the warm space, entering her nostrils, where it changed to the sharp tang of citrus.

Lanie's god was here.

The deer hoof in her hand twitched. She closed her fingers around it.

"Easy," she said. "I'm coming. Keep following, darling. Keep him in your sights."

She rested her left hand, balancing the deer hoof in its palm, on her left thigh. The wizard mark that turned her skin a cumulonimbus-gray from wrist to fingertips pulsed like a cloud about to break. A thin strand of silvery fog spiraled up from the center of her palm. It threaded through the hoof like silk through an ungainly needle, spun down over the mudcrack floor and made its egress. Thence, unfurling across the camp, it took to the road.

On it spun, following that rocky ribbon up and down the next few hills. The crossroads. That third hill: the gallows hill. There. The ditch where Lanie had found the yearling doe's body not a day before. Where she had set her cache-trap, as she had trapped many such remains in the area, knowing the ghost would be drawn to them, needing dead accident for his ectenica.

A pity Lanie hadn't bothered trapping the poor gallows corpse in his lonely grave; it hadn't occurred to her that the ghost would go digging for it. Usually, he was opportunistic and lazy.

Must be getting desperate, she thought. *Needed something large. Something fresh.*

On and on it ran, that thread of silver fog connecting Saint Death to Lanie to the dead deer whose hoof she held in the palm of her hand. A mile on, and a bit more, till it found terminus in the deer's remains. (The deer who, despite having only three hooves to walk on, and having been dead for weeks, was moving at a remarkably spry pace.)

Once the fog caught up with, moved into, the yearling doe, its silvery thread branched out into trillions of threads, each following the paths of a former nervous system, sending new robustness and vivacity into its limbs.

Lanie pushed herself through her left palm, sharing a bit more of her substance with the deer. Her substance—memory, identity, will—mingled with the deer's own memory of herself. The bond between them burgeoned, strengthened.

The deer picked up speed and purpose.

HUDDLED ON STRIPES the tiger rug, warm within her darkened esh, eyes shut, Lanie's boundaries of self grew fluid. She flew like fire along the thread: now Lanie, now the deer. Both at once. Lanie and a yearling doe, sharing two bodies, twin sets of memories.

Though no one but her god could see, Lanie's ears grew large as ostrich eggs. Her nose turned black, her chin as white as chickweed. Her neck stretched, thickened: too long and muscular for the small, delicate head that sat atop it.

Second by flashing second, Lanie was learning fine, new things about herself: the yearling doe.

Her brief life. The manner of her death.

Had she managed to survive her first year—had she lived till this coming summer—her rough charcoal coat would have burnished into a shining auburn. Eager in her early rut, she would have sought out her first stag in the grasslands, bid him follow to a place of her choosing, and in the nightshade-shade of the conifers, been covered by a stocky body only slightly larger than her own.

But that was not to be.

(Tears like quicksilver rolled unchecked down Lanie's furred face. She could not feel them.)

A wasting illness had done for her. She had withered, grown confused and listless, stumbled where once she had leapt.

And when at last she fell into the ditch, there the Doe-Her-Mother had found her.

How Lanie loved the Doe-Her-Mother.

How Lanie knew Her at once.

Like mist from a field She had risen. Softly, had stepped forward. Lightly, had nuzzled Lanie-doe beneath Her sheltering flank. Gray, too, the coat of the Doe-Her-Mother—but not the gray of fur. The gray of overlapping scales of bone. Her muzzle grizzled. Her ears so wide and high, taller than any antler rack, engulfing the sky. Her eyes, large and liquid brown, looked deeply into Lanie-doe's—

—and straight into Lanie herself.

Lanie.

Herself.

CONCENTRATE, MISCELLANEOUS STONES, adjured the Doe-Her-Mother, or as Lanie knew her: Doédenna, god of Death.

"Right," Lanie muttered, pulling back from the connection. "Right. Sorry."

Somewhat apologetically, she sent a quivering quop of love, a lolloping dollop of encouragement, to the dead deer whom she was steering from afar, and crooned, "Just a little further, sweetheart."

A few miles up the road from where the necromancer huddled in her esh, the deer told herself in a human voice:

"*Just a little further, sweetheart.*"

The deer felt only love and no fear. She picked up her pace. Her tongueless mouth flashed with lightning. Her wide, flat teeth grew new tips of silvered steel. From the matted fur on her skull burst a rack of smoky antlers like new growth from the wreckage of death. Her decaying haunches flexed. Her bony shoulders rippled. Her three hooves clicked as her legs quickened. Soon she began to bound, the frost on her pale caudal patch flashing like dew-fire on diamonds as the sun sank behind the hills.

Above her, the shadow of a kestrel crossed the deer's own shadow, and the deer knew it for a friend.

"*See anything, Duantri?*" asked the deer in Lanie's voice.

At first, she thought the bird too high to hear. Then came the *killy-killy-klee* of the kestrel's cry.

Warned in time, the deer saw a man come stumbling out from behind a yellow tower of flowering gorse, onto the road. In her decomposing throat, a human voice whispered urgently:

"*There he is, darling. Attack.*"

The deer knew her purpose and goal.

Dig it out, that small ball of blue flame sitting in the left eye socket of the man's skull, radiating malignity and spite. She would hook it out with her antlers. She would fling it aloft, expose it to the air, where, untethered, accident-less, it would unravel into motes that the Doe-Her-Mother would trample under-hoof.

The deer gathered speed, lowered her head—and rammed.

Right before she made impact, the man looked over his left shoulder, at her. He knew her. The blue fire in his left eye socket blazed.

The deer's forehead collided with the man's lower back. Her skull splintered wetly, minutely, at the impact. The man grunted. His large body crashed down like a wild almond tree in a windstorm and lay sprawled in the dirt. He moaned like a trunk splitting. He turned his head, pressing his right cheek into the stony ground. His left eye sparked, like light off a hunter's arrowhead.

The doe, trembling with victory, stood over his body. She grunted. Snorted. Sneezed. Rising up on her hind legs, she bore down with her forelegs, pinning him to the ground.

A wettish splat, as something in him gave. A rib, perhaps.

She bent her head.

The smoky, shadowy tip of one phantom antler dipped into the hollowed-out, scarred skin tissue of the left eye socket. It hooked that ball of radiant blue infection—that undead parasite, that fiend—and flung him far from his groaning host.

IRRADIANT WAS LUCKY.

No, not *lucky*. Luck was for feckless youths with no more brains than that maggot-rotted deer his treacherous great-granddaughter was piloting like a puppet master's drunken apprentice. Luck was for the gullible, the god-smote, the guileless.

It was not *luck* that he, newly extracted from his host, went flying in the direction of the gorse bush—and more particularly, toward the small, silvery brown, potbellied mistle thrush concealed in the gorse bush. The mistle thrush who, in the thick camouflage of yellow-laden branches, was industriously slamming a snail into a pebble to get at the meat.

Not *lucky* at all.

It was will. It was want. It was *aim*.

Not without purpose had Irradiant been driving his host body through Damahrash, making for the uplands of Leech— for *Leech*, he knew, was where the skinchangers dwelt, under the protection of their monstrous Witch Queen.

And a *skinchanger* was *precisely* what the ghost needed right now.

A skinchanger was a creature that fed on substance, not accident: souls, not flesh.[1] Ever since possessing the unmagical

---

1 The technical term was 'pneumaphage,' but Irradiant Stones was never pedantic to himself, only when he had a captive audience to torture with every instrument at his disposal, including (but not limited to) bombast.

wasteland that was Cracchen Skrathmandan, Irradiant had been pouring too much of his own substance into acts of necromancy. And though he was mighty, bloated with the substance of all those Skaki sky-wizards he'd captured and fed on for a hundred years—he was now running out of himself.

Dominating and draining a skinchanger's body would replenish him. The older the skinchanger, the more stored substance it would have to offer him. But in this particular moment, *any* skinchanger would do.

In Leech, there was a more-than-slim chance that any given mistle thrush in a gorse bush was no mere mistle thrush.

As the ghost rushed the gorse, he began to hear the faint noise the bird was emitting. Not the short, high-pitched call of a mistle thrush. Not at all. No, this was more like the long, sweet whistle of a finger-wetted crystal.

And there—was that a glimmering? An oil-slick effulgence clinging to the mistle thrush's shadowy underwings, imperceptible to mortal eyeballs, but to the likes of Irradiant Stones, a genius even among ghosts, obvious as the beacon of a lighthouse?

"Mine," said Irradiant, and took what was rightfully his—which was, in his opinion, anything he wanted.

As the yearling doe had rammed his prior host, so now the ghost rammed the mistle thrush.

For a moment, he was a confusion of feathers and desires. Small, soft body. Jealous for berries. Gloried in a coming storm. Loved high places, minor keys. Wanted that snail. Umbrage at the interruption.

But beneath all that avian instinct, another presence: older and wilder.

"Ah-ha!" cried Irradiant. "Can't hide from *me*."

From inside the body of the bird, the ghost opened his mouth and swallowed the thing that was more-than-bird.

A rush of new knowledge roiled through him as the skinchanger thrashed and fought, clawed and kicked. Parts of its feathered body bulged, other parts rippled, distended, as the thing shaped like a mistle thrush strove to expel the alien presence inside of it.

To no avail.

Though the skinchanger had been in its time, not only mistle thrush, but stoat, lizard, mountain hare, viper, giant hog, and various other local fauna, it had never once been *human*. All of its selves were animal selves, insect selves, going back and back to the first morn it had hatched, new and hungry, from its egg.

Having supped only on the wild things of these hills, all this skinchanger knew were the shapes it had consumed. The skinchanger had never ventured near enough to human civilization to suck the souls of mortals and learn to take *their* shapes, to consume their minds and memories and absorb them into its own identity. Its will was feral. Instinct, not intellect, ruled it.

It was no match for Irradiant Stones.

And so, Irradiant did unto the skinchanger as the skinchanger had done unto the thrush, the stoat, the lizard, the hare, the viper, and the hog before it.

He ravened through it. He chomped and chewed. He amassed its experiences. He absorbed.

Outside the bush, that duodecifold-damned deer was still screaming obscenities in his great-granddaughter's voice. She had seen him flee to the bush, curse her bifocals. Probably seen the skinchanger's darksome glimmering too, wizard that she was.

"*Duantri!*" The deer backed away from the body on the ground and shook herself out in a scattering of tiny, squirming insects. "*The bird! Get the bird! He's in the bird!*"

As she shouted, the deer ran headlong at the gorse, shaking the flowering branches with her shadowy antlers, startling the mistle thrush to flight. It fluttered in the air: white underwings, a cool brown back that was almost gray, a pale, spotted chest.

One eye was black and bright.

One eye was melting down its feathered face, filling with acidic blue light.

The kestrel plummeted from the sky, claws extended, ready to snatch the thrush from the air and break its neck with her bite.

"Not today, Gyrgardu," Irradiant growled.

Oh, how he hated those meddling Quadoni bitches. A foul day, when his great-granddaughter had fallen under their moralizing and old-fangled influence. Not to mention their protection. A Falcon Defender of Quadiíb more than made up for Miscellaneous's physical inadequacies, more's the pity.

He sifted around inside his new skinchanger host for the shape that would serve him best.

Something cunning. Something agile. Something that ate pesky birds for a living.

Ah.

That one.

The kestrel's talons brushed the feathers of his nape, and the mistle thrush exploded into fur.

Mid-air, what had once been mistle thrush now rounded on the kestrel, swiping at her with his claw. At the last second, the kestrel veered, bolted higher. Higher. A speck in the sky.

The catamount twisted to land on all four paws. On the ground, he turned, slowly, to face the yearling doe, whose fog-filled eyes locked with the catamount's glowing blue one.

"Hello, girlie," Irradiant Stones greeted his great-granddaughter. "Missed me, did you?"

Then the catamount pounced, and tore the little deer's rotting head from its spine.

Smoky antlers, silver fangs, fog-filled eyes vanished.

The deer collapsed, its undeath undone.

THE NECROMANCER MISCELLANEOUS Stones opened her eyes and shouted, "Fuck!"

CHAPTER THREE
All Due Rites

ALL SENSE OF being one with the yearling doe—*being* the doe—vanished. The delicate gray threads of Lanie's substance rebounded back upon her in a rolling wave, energizing and sickening her.

Too much. Too much!

"Up!" Gagging, Lanie rose to her knees. "Up, Stripes!"

She slapped her left palm against the dark trident marking Stripes's forehead, redirecting the tidal swell of her substance into him.

At the touch of her gray left hand, Stripes, who had been flopped, limp and demonstrably rug-like, on the ground, *pounced* straight up into the air. Lanie didn't have time to gasp before he was shooting them out of the esh, across the campsite, and into the sky.

The former-predator-now-rug had a tiger's instinct for carrion. Not that he ate it (or anything) anymore, but he could still *locate* it. No problem.

His lady necromancer wanted that maggoty sack of venison a few miles yonder? Easy peasy. All he had to do was follow the sort of gory smear overlaying those hills a little way down the road. A directional shimmer, like heat rising, or a lowering cloud, compounded with the taste of rot. One undead thing tracking another, formerly undead, thing.

Like called to like.

* * *

UNDEAD CREATURES, LIKE flying tiger rugs for example, were usually quite hard to kill. One sure way to do it—a messy one—was decapitation. Which, of course, the ghost of Irradiant Stones knew.

Not for the first time, Lanie wished her great-grandfather would anchor himself to something whose head she wouldn't *mind* lobbing off. Problem was, she was the *worst* head-lobber in history. Just thinking about decollation gave her a literal pain in the neck. She had a necromancer's innate allergy to violence: if she ever personally lobbed a limb in earnest, the echo-wound she'd get from it would probably make one of her own fall off.

Not really. Not exactly. Only, it would *feel* like it. Doing her own killing[2] would result in echo-wounds temporarily severing essential veins, arteries, nerves, tendons. She'd bleed copiously, if briefly.

The wounds would close right up. She'd likely heal fairly quickly, but...

Best not risk it. Not even to take care of Irradiant Stones once and for all.

While her great-grandfather seemed to have outgrown his own allergy during his lifetime (certainly, he showed no adverse reactions to violence during his undeath), Lanie was just learning to manage hers.

At least, she reflected, *I'm better off now than when I was little, and even the sound of Nita slapping a fly off a windowpane sent me into a three-day coma.*

She bent low over Stripes's head, the wind whipping her braids behind her, buffeting back her scarf and coat. Her spectacles, which protected her eyeballs from the freezing wind, were already fogging up and frosting over. She clutched her woolen hat to her head with one hand. Havoc had knitted her a new one when she'd lost the first. She loved this damned hat. It was big enough to fit all her braids inside it (when worn properly) and still cover her ears and neck. It was like a warm rainbow

---

2 In the parlance of the Stoneses who came before her, infamous assassins and executioners all, the 'wetwork.'

sack of love, and no way was she going to lose it to the freezing wind today.

Stripes lurched, gleefully.

Lanie burped a little, precursor to worse things her gorge could do, and flattened herself further against the flying rug's flapping length, white-knuckling his collar.

She *adored* Stripes. She just... couldn't seem to convince him that whatever new turbulence he encountered wasn't his very own delightful ribbon to bat around. Ten-foot length of unparalleled taxidermy he may have been; animated by necromancy he certainly was; but Stripes was still a big cat. Erratic pouncing was sort of his thing.

In Quadiíb, at the start of their journey, she and Duantri had come up with a system of straps and buckles to keep Lanie secured to the tiger rug in case of abrupt-onset zoomies. But back at the esh, when the ghost had severed her from the yearling doe, she'd been in too much of a hurry to bother with all that.

Well, she told herself, *live and regret, I suppose.*

Lanie hated speed. She hated heights.

Just, she hated her great-grandfather's ghost more.

Gulping down another wave of nausea, she whispered, "Faster, please," and pressed her cheek to Stripes's nape, squeezing her eyes shut.

Stripes's stiff ears twitched obediently. After all, he was as much *Lanie* as he was *tiger*. Her living substance was entwined with his every memory of having once been alive. This commingling, anchored to the corporeal accident of the rug (his skin), created the third of the three states: undeath.[3]

Stripes was willing to do *whatever* his lady necromancer asked. He was the first undead helpmeet whom Lanie had ever created off-surge, without the boost of the gods' fabulous All-Marvel to help her. He was the first she'd made by sharing her pure substance, instead of cutting herself open and bleeding

---

3 Undeath, in Stripes's opinion, was the greatest thing ever to have happened to him. He was *supremely* pleased to be operating on the z-axis after a lifetime of apex predatoring on the ground.

out her substance upon a piece of dead accident to make an ectenica. He was also the first who didn't crumble to ash once the potency in her blood faded. Whenever she spooled back her substance from his body and once more into her own, Stripes simply became a tiger rug again: inanimate but not *unmade*. But for him, Lanie never removed all of herself. They were always, lightly, connected. Even dormant, Stripes was always, just a little bit, undead.

The trick of sharing substance without having to bleed for it was one her great-grandfather had never learned in life. Lanie was determined he never would in undeath either. She wondered sometimes if he even could. This manner of resurrection left the undead creature with a bit too much... autonomy.

And Irradiant Stones liked *control*.

Patting Stripes's rough fur with her mittened fingers, Lanie took a fortifying breath.

"Okay"—she gritted her teeth—"fast enough. Thank you!"

"Aaaugghh!" shrieked the necromancer.

Stripes streaked past the crossroads and over the third hill— the gallows hill—like an orange and black and buff-colored rocket. Before becoming a rug, the tiger had occasionally been able to obtain speeds of up to forty-five miles per hour. In undeath, Stripes was happy to try and beat his record. For his lady necromancer's sake. Wheresoever she wished to go, there would Stripes, her gallant mount, convey her.

Faster and faster he flew, spurred on by his lady's dulcet encouragement, following that ribbon of gravel as it climbed the uplands.

Ah, it was an icicle-rose of an evening, luminous and gray. A fine time to fly.

In warmer seasons, the uplands would be perfumed with moss and meadowsweet and wild angelica. But in this last gasp of winter, only the scent of underwater springs, and the stony petrichor of earth locked in its hard frost, permeated the air.

Stripes appreciated it all, since it provided a neutral canvas for the undeath he was actually sniffing for.

Come to think of it, didn't he just catch a whiff of something utterly, unusually, *supernaturally* putrescent?

Yes.

Yes, he did.

Found it! Wouldn't his lady just *love* this?

Stripes stopped, mid-air. And dropped.

"Aaaugghh!" shrieked the necromancer.

BREATHE, LANIE REMINDED herself. *Can't do anything if puking. Breathe.*

Once the rug settled, holding itself still, about two feet off the ground, for her descent, she rolled off and stood on wobbly legs.

At least, that was the plan.

Her knees knocked. She held her breath, hoping.

No luck. They buckled, her legs gave out, and Lanie sank into the mud, gorge rising again as she fell.

Closing her eyes, she breathed in, held her breath, breathed out, held her breath again.

A sharp *killy-killy-klee* startled her head up from between her knees, just in time to see the kestrel come plummeting down. The moment she touched the ground, she exchanged her falcon form for her human one.

"I saw that mangy cat drop like a rock!" Duantri panted. "Hast thou a bruise or sprain, beloved friend?"

The Gyrgardu's face shone with concern and perspiration as she squatted in the gravel next to Lanie. Her black curls yet had a bluish-silver cast to them; her eyes had not faded from yellow-ringed brown to their true lustrous gray. Two vertical black marks streaked her brown cheeks. A plumy pattern of pale spots decorated her breast. These all began to fade as Lanie watched.

"I'm fine," she assured her, unable to keep from smiling at the miracle that was Duantri. "Just winded. Stripes really, just—*whew.*" She glanced at Stripes. "Thanks, you rascal."

Nodding graciously, Stripes began to lick his non-existent hindquarters with a tongue that wasn't there. Lanie returned her attention to the naked Gyrgardu. Her teeth began chattering in sympathy.

"Saint Death quakes, Duantri! I'm frozen just looking at you!"

Duantri, whose teeth were perfectly steady, replied, "It does not bother me as it does thee," but Lanie was already stumbling up from the ground, tugging off her coat, and handing it over.

Wordlessly, the Gyrgardu took it. She shrugged it on and belted it closed, saying nothing. She was not cold—it would take far worse than this mere winter spittle to rattle her—but she knew that Lanie, a machine of empathy, was growing goosebumps over her goosebumps the longer she stood there, watching her. But as soon as Duantri was covered, Lanie's teeth ceased chattering.

Chafing her arms and stomping her feet, Lanie asked, "So... the ghost got away?"

Such a look of fury sprang to Duantri's face that Lanie flinched back.

"He shifted into a godsdamned goshawk!" the Gyrgardu spat. She spoke in Lirian, as she always did when furious or disgusted. "After the catamount tore off your deer's head. Just sprang into the air—twice my size, with murder in his eye. Lucky it was his first flight in that body—he was awkward; I managed to shake him. Then he heard you come screaming in on your flying cat and made for the hills." She jerked a thumb in a northwesterly direction.

"Well"—Lanie tried to sound bright, cheerful, not too desperate—"that's a pity. But it can't be..."

She stopped mid-sentence. The gloaming uplands took on a tint of citrine, as though the lenses of her spectacles were ground of the pale-yellow crystal. Her nose twitched. She felt her mouth relaxing, her body flushing with heat and happiness.

"Do you smell," she asked dreamily, "orange rind?"

If Duantri answered, Lanie didn't hear her. She was already turning, toward the source of the citrus scent.

Her god was near. Her god was expectant. Her god was a perfumey sparkle of orange zest emanating from a small, headless deer lying in the road a few feet away.

"Oh, no!"

Dashing over to the dead doe's side, Lanie sank to her knees in the mud and laid a tender hand upon its flank.

"How could I neglect you?" she whispered. "You gave me everything. Thank you. Thank you."

Over her two woolen sweaters (one yellow, one pink), several shirts and a long-sleeved undergarment, Lanie wore an apron that was more pocket than canvas. From one of those pockets, she now withdrew the little hoof which had allowed her to steer the doe from afar—right up to its second death.

With all attendant rite and ritual, she returned the hoof to the rest of its accident, murmuring in Quadic, "O swift, bright light, I hold your memory; for whilst I live, thou livest on in me."

In Lirian, she added, "Farewell, darling. The Doe-Your-Mother awaits you in the shade."

On a soft sigh, she began to sing.

The Lahnessthanessar was the oldest of all spellsongs but one: the great lullaby, the song of Undreaming. It bid the undead to sleep—and in sleeping, forget the temporary dream of life granted them by necromancy.

All around the doe's body, frozen mud melted and rippled. It sprouted tendrils of itself, rich and mineral-scented, that reached around the discrete pieces of the corpse—head, body, hoof—like the kindliest of winding cloths. Once the mud was completely enshrouding the body, it began to suck the doe down into itself.

No noise. No flash. Only a final, sweet ripplet before the mud smoothed out again. Only a flat, glossy patch of earth, baked strangely dry, and in the air, the fading scent of citrus.

Lanie stopped singing, as she had started, on a sigh—

—and immediately gagged. The moment her perfect haze of orange rind vanished from her nostrils, a far worse smell besieged them.

"What," she gasped, clapping a hand over her nose, "is *that*?"

"Over here," Duantri called out.

Lanie looked over to where Duantri had been. She wasn't there. She swiveled on her heels, until her glance fell on the Gyrgardu.

"You moved!" she accused.

Duantri raised her eyebrows. "You were taking your time. This is urgent too."

Lanie dropped her gaze and beheld the source of the stench: the prone, emaciated form of Cracchen Skrathmandan.

"Oh."

Her voice came out small, but not because she felt chastened. Rage and disgust choked her. *Of course*, she thought, *of course—when the ghost jumped into a new body, he cast off the old. That's... just like him.*

"His pulse is thready," Duantri reported, gently rolling Cracchen onto his back. "His skin is colder than this slurry, and I do not like his color."

Lanie turned to Stripes, who was hovering near her thigh. His head tilted up to hers at the same time, and he fixed his amber glass eyes upon her. She saw in them the deep blue flash of Doédenna's magic, and nodded.

"Go, my vanguard," she told him. "Do what you can. I'll stay back and spare myself the echo-wounds." She could already feel Cracchen's debilitating, life-draining pain from where she stood; if she drew any closer, her body would start mirroring his many hurts.

Lazily, as if it were all his idea in the first place, Stripes undulated himself across the road. Before inspecting Cracchen, he first nosed around a few dead leaves and then explored a pile of scattered gravel, before, finally—still pretending utter uninterest—he stretched out his full ten-foot length of tanned tiger skin over the man's body, and draped himself over him, like a house cat the size of a capsized canoe. Duantri immediately started digging into one of her saddlebags for bandages and ointment, but looked up, startled, when Stripes began to purr.

She skewed a quick glance to Lanie. "I did not think big cats had the apparatus to purr?"

"They normally don't fly either," said Lanie, cheeks heating. "The perks of being undead, I guess."

The truth was, Stripes could purr because Lanie found the sensation comforting, just as he could fly because, at the moment of his initial re-animation, she had required a rapid means of transportation. Neither his capacity for flight nor his purring had been *conscious* decisions on her part, but strong desires that had instinctively manifested with her magic. Which she was only now realizing. Which was embarrassing.

As her face flushed hotter, Stripes redoubled his purring, and began emanating waves of smug heat, as if to say, *Look! I can do it all!*

Duantri, noting the rise in temperature, snorted. "Stripes is radiating like one of my rock socks."

"Is he?" Lanie asked faintly.

"Didst know," her friend demanded in Quadic, gray eyes dancing, "thy cat could generate such heat—enough to warm a travel esh or three? And I, who toil for hours to toast our rocks, might else be sprawling idle, clad in silk?" Her voice rose, trembling with suppressed laughter. "Thou grave-breath death-hag spawn of slothful bones! Didst thou *forget* to mention this wee trick?"

Lanie raised her hands in defense. "This is new. Brand new! Happened just now. First time ever. Didn't know I could do it. Would have done it earlier if…"

"If…" Duantri drawled in Lirian.

"If it had occurred to me."

At Duantri's bark of laughter, Lanie rushed on, "Well, you said he was cold. And I promised, I *swore* to his mother I wouldn't let him die. So…" She gestured helplessly at Cracchen.

"I'm just... trying. Something."

The laughter died from Duantri's face. "I... do not think anything we do will be enough. We can clean and bandage his external wounds, but *internally*..."

Lanie nodded grimly. "And invisibly. The ghost gouged him in more than just physical ways."

They stared at each other for a moment, Lanie shivering and coatless, but with more than just the cold. Then she shook her head fiercely, pushed up her sleeves, and marched across the road to squat at Cracchen's abraded head.

"I'm going deep," she told Duantri, who nodded, mouth tightening.

Lightly placing her fingertips on Cracchen's pottery-shard cheekbones, Lanie sent an exploratory strand of her substance into his body to feel out the extent of his damage.

It was *everywhere*.

Echo-wounds opened all over Lanie's body like tiny mouths, outside and in. Organ damage. Tissue degradation. Arrhythmia. Pneumonia. Her toes curled in her boots, sensation deadening in sympathy to the blackened stumps of his. Her fingers stiffened, swelled, turned the color of soot. Her skull cramped; her vision doubled with the clap of a concussion. Her lower back was all bruise; her ribs groaned with hairline fractures. Her left eye was on fire, mirroring Cracchen's burnt-out socket. Her right eye and her nostrils ran with mucus and blood.

Lanie's fingers flinched away from Cracchen's face.

The moment she wasn't touching him, her echo-wounds healed over—far more quickly than they would have done even a year ago.

"That's a relief," she murmured.

"What?" Duantri asked carefully.

"I'm getting stronger. But"—she sighed—"Cracchen is still dying."

Duantri paused in her ministrations to sit back on her heels. "You could brink him. You have done it before. Twice. Makkovian and the wolf."

Lanie nodded. "Sure. But neither instance was… comparable."

"How so?" As she asked, the Gyrgardu bent to her work again, her hands steady, her movements sure. Cleaning. Anointing. Bandaging. Lanie looked at her, and in her chest, her heart squeezed in sudden sympathy. This was a man that Duantri had once fought with no weapons but her hands. She had taken him down. She had no love for Cracchen Skrathmandan. And yet, she was doing whatever she could to extend his life for a few more measly minutes. There was this woman. And then there was Grandpa Rad. How could Athe have produced two such dissimilar people? Lanie would never know.

"A dying creature," she answered Duantri, "dies in *parts*—all of these microscopic, nigh-invisible parts—until the whole is gone. With brinking, I—with Saint Death's grace—can sort of *invite* those already-dead parts of a person to the dream of life once more. They become, in effect, undead. But a dying person is not *yet* dead. Their dream of life is not a dream, but a primal instinct to survive. That instinct reaches out to the undead parts for help. The undead parts of the body reinvigorate, re-set, and re-boost the living parts until life overwhelms death and the body heals itself of whatever was killing it. At that point, the person is resolutely alive again. Not dying, not partly dead, not undead. And because no piece of them belongs to death, they are no longer under my comm—my *invitation*."

When Lanie had set out to brink her niece's father Makkovian, who had ingested poison in his despair, he was still more alive than dead. She had, therefore, brinked him successfully. Makkovian lived. However, when it came to Datu's wolf cub, Undies had been more dead than alive when she'd reached him. Lanie had not succeeded. But failure wasn't an option, not with Datu sobbing next to her, and pleading for 'Auntie Lanie' to save the cub. So Lanie had invited more gods to the miracle, in addition to Doédenna, god of Death. In the end, the wolf cub had *survived*, but he was not exactly *alive*. But neither was he your average undead creature either. All in all, Lanie counted Mister Underwear Stones a victory, if an unusual one.

Unfortunately, neither of her previous experiences with brinking a dying body was remotely like this one.

Which meant she'd have to improvise.

Clearing her throat, Lanie leaned in again, and laid her hand against Cracchen's face. This time, when the wounds opened on and inside her body, she did not flinch away.

"Cracchen Skrathmandan!" She called his name with her doubled voice: the regular one that Duantri could hear, and her deep voice, which only the dead and the undead could hear. "It is Miscellaneous Stones. Your mother, Sari Skrathmandan, sent me to find you. Your brother, Haaken Skrathmandan, sent me to find you. Your god, Erre'Elur, whom I call Doédenna, sent me to find you. Come back to them. Wake. Wake and be whole."

As she spoke, the wizard mark on her gray left hand loosed a billowing cloud of starry fog. Lanie set it against his breastbone, keeping her right hand on his cheek. She pushed once more, pulsing out a silent toll of death magic. She had only her own substance as fuel. She poured herself *out* of herself and *into* Cracchen, seeking to patch his lack with her whole.

Stripes's purr quieted. The heat in his hide lessened. She borrowed her substance back from him first, attenuating that which animated him—but she did not take it all. They might need him again soon.

If today were a High Holy Fire Feast, those four days every quarter year when the twelve gods drew nearer to Athe, and their panthauma washed the human world like a tide, then magic would have been so abundant that every sorcerer and wizard and saint could work miracles from dawn to dusk to midnight, and it would never run out. Lanie could have snapped Cracchen upright and had him dancing the Nine Gallows Jig in no time. But they were almost a full month away from the surge at spring equinox, so Lanie had to draw magic from herself, her own life force—that which warmed her, kept her upright, let her thoughts be clear and her actions nimble. It wasn't an infinite resource. But at least, with time, it was renewable.

Lanie could just hear Tanaliín, her mentor and Duantri's beloved, scolding her for draining herself down to nothing when she found out. Which she would. Duantri concealed nothing from her gyrlady.

You strip-mine your own soul for this, leaving naught but a wasteland for your god to rest in.

For now, Lanie practiced her inevitable argument. *I can always replenish what I've surrendered with sleep and food and prayer and time—later. But unless I brink Cracchen now, there will be no later. Not for him.*

What if it is not enough?

I have all I need. Lanie willed herself to believe it. *Saint Death gives and gives, and so must I.*

The sparkling fog that flowered out of her fell in gray petals to cover Cracchen's body, overlaying his skin in gray scales, like the bone chips that made up Doédenna's endless cloak. Even after he was completely shrouded in it, the fog kept swirling about him, seeking entry.

Which it found. Too much entry. Lanie's substance seeped into the broken man, soaking and saturating him.

And then, it leaked right out again.

"Rarely have I seen thee look so grim." Duantri's melodic Quadic reached Lanie across the chasm of her concentration. "I gather that thy healing will not take?"

"He's like cheesecloth," Lanie managed to wheeze out. "The holes in his accident? Nothing compared to his substance. The ghost… made a *sieve* of him."

She sat back, shivering, dragging her fingers off Cracchen's skin. Her left hand was numb. Her right hand was shaking. She clenched them into fists, shook them out as vigorously as she could, and waited for the pins and needles to come. She breathed until the dizziness passed. Only when it did could she trust herself to press both palms flat against Cracchen's chest once more.

There. Right over his breastbone—where the bird of his soul dwelled.

Lanie's wizard mark pulsed; her fingers flexed with power. A gray mist swirling with stars flooded out of her and surrounded him once more, like an autumn graveyard lit with late fireflies. Cracchen did not twitch. He did not wake.

CHAPTER FOUR
Phantom Storm

"Stay thy touch!" Duantri gripped Lanie by the shoulder. "Thou art gone as gray as he."

Lanie's thoughts faltered with fatigue, her head tilting until her cheek brushed Duantri's knuckles.

If I don't stop, I'll pass out. By the time I come to, he'll be dead. What will I tell his mother?

Her eyeballs smarted in their sockets, her lids growing heavy. She caught Stripes's gaze. A blue flash, deep within the amber glass.

Saint Death's magic? Or a reflection of the oncoming storm?

A second later, the gloom-gray of twilight cracked. A sheer sheet of lightning illuminated the sky, horizon to horizon.

"Storm's here."

"What storm?" Duantri demanded in increasingly irate Lirian. "Lanie—are you falling asleep? *What storm?*"

"The lightning..." she mumbled, then stopped. "Wait..."

Was it lightning? She squinted at it. No, not *precisely* light. Not light Lanie perceived with her eyes—but with her deep senses. Which meant...

She groaned. "Oh, no."

Duantri shook her shoulder like a bell that wouldn't ring. "What? Talk!"

Lanie jerked her chin at the sky, sliding her spectacles to the tip of her nose. She rubbed the back of her neck, where the curly whorls of her hair prickled with sweat.

A second sheet of lightning overhead. No, *not* lightning.

Like it, but also unlike.

Lanie struggled to describe it aloud, as Tanaliín had taught her. *Most of magic is metaphorical, my dear.* When nothing occurred in Lirian, she attempted in her faltering Quadic, "The un-flash, void-bright, underside of light."

Her voice had doubled again, the presence of her deep voice surprising her.

Duantri uttered a frustrated growl. "I never thought I would say this. But—*in plain Lirian, please!*"

Lanie hesitated. Duantri was Gyrgardu, not necromancer. In her kestrel form, Duantri had *far* sense: she could spot a beetle in the grass fifty yards away, detect spiders disguised as pollen upon a flower petal, and discern patterns in the plumage of birds unseeable by the human eye. The urine trails of voles, mice, and shrews glowed to her vision like shooting stars, and even human skin sported stripes and spots like hunting cats. But she did not have the *deep* sense required to see the undead.

Lanie tried again, in plain Lirian, as the air turned dense, and the wind died off, as if the atmosphere were suddenly too cold and heavy to bear the weight of a breeze.

"It's... the storm of souls."

"Oh." Duantri's grip on her shoulder changed into a squeeze of warm understanding. She knew as well as Lanie what else was hunting the ghost, and what the defection of Irradiant Stones into a shapeshifter's host body would mean to it.

"They're probably angry. They might be coming for me. A Stones for a Stones."

Duantri bristled. "They'll have thee—only if they get through me!"

From bristling, she went straight to fluffing up and puffing out. Lanie watched the beginnings of a downy shimmer rippling just under her smooth brown skin. Her mouth, numb and strange as it felt, twitched involuntarily into a smile. She kept her voice calm but firm.

"Falcon Defender. I need you to *stay grounded*."

Above them, the sky cracked again. Duantri did not flinch or give any other indication that she had heard or seen it. To her, mere night was falling.

Lanie's shivers turned to full-body shudders. The Almasquin—Irradiant Stones's basalt sarcophagus, where he had stuffed the souls of all those Skaki sky wizards a hundred years ago—had felt cold like this. It leaked a life-leaching shadow. *Just* like this phantom storm.

Let it come, Lanie thought. She was sworn to her work. If the storm was determined to smite her on this dirt road, she might as well accomplish one last thing.

Bending over Cracchen, she whispered in his ear, "Irradiant Stones almost destroyed you. Help me help you live. Live, and return to your loved ones. Live, and outlast the undead. *Live, Cracchen Skrathmandan!*"

Her surface voice rang out, beseeching the living man. Her deep voice opened like a pit beneath it, commanding all the parts of Cracchen, most of him, that were dying.

But enough of Cracchen was sufficiently alive—sufficiently spiteful, fearful, untrusting—to refuse to obey the command of a Stones. *Any* Stones. Not now, when he had a choice about it. Instead of rising up in answer, his body remained limp and full of holes. His final breaths were beginning to rattle at the bottom of his lungs.

The sky cracked again.

Lanie ducked low—"Down, Duantri!"—and then, the storm of souls was upon them.

From the meager shelter of her arms, Lanie peered up. She perceived the storm with her deep sense as a raging, sparking soul-cyclone spinning dizzily overhead. It was not quite vaporous like fog, nor slinkily liquid like mercury, nor yet like a trillion pieces of shattered volcano glass. But it was a little like all these things, and limned withal in a dazzling blue-white glow like ionized plasma.

And it was *furious*.

Like thunder sheering the air itself, a voice sounded, far deeper than Lanie's own deep voice. Words made of pure substance, dozens of deep voices speaking together, all booming out a language Lanie understood not with her ears but with her bones.

Issue of ill-mage, heir of our arch-foe,
meet is our meeting, midst sky-road and soil!
Vengeance and vanquishment at last are upon us
Capitulate, craven—extinction ensues!

As soon as she processed the words, Lanie comprehended three things almost simultaneously, each of which she would have preferred more than a split second to contemplate:

1. The storm of souls did not grasp that she, the so-called 'issue of ill-mage,' was actually their ally. Thus;
2. it would probably not believe her if she told it that, as the only living necromancer (that she knew of) on Athe, she could help them:
   a) continue the hunt for said ill-mage, i.e., her great-grandfather's ghost, and;
   b) return what was left of their mangled, unhoused souls to the empty and frozen shells of their bodies up north. And finally;
3. the storm of souls was not speaking Lirian or Quadic, the only languages Lanie even remotely comprehended. It was speaking Old Skaki. But not only could Lanie understand every word, she could, if she wanted, scream right back at the storm in the same language—caesurae and all—because suddenly, a bright pink mist was drifting all about her, and her god was there, laying the gift of tongues upon her tongue. It tasted like grapefruit.

"Tits and pickles," she whispered.

Then, remembering herself, the necromancer Miscellaneous Stones bellowed in a voice to rival the raging hurricane:

Storm of the sundered, scourge of the Stoneses!
I work for the Woe-Woman, who wishes you well,
who seeks to send solace for the sorrows you suffer,
and advances Her aid, in exchange for your ears.

For a moment, all was silent, suspended. Lanie knew a moment of doubt. Had she just spewed nonsense? Had the storm even heard her?

It heard. Above the dirt road, the center mass of souls swirled like a vortex of liquid diamond: clear and dark, with an almost palpable gravity, so deep that its wellspring must be the heat death of the universe.

And then it lashed out—and down.

Seven arms of freezing, seething wind unfurled from the mass and whipped out at her.

Lanie threw herself over Cracchen and Stripes, sheltering them.

The storm was a thing of pure substance, a great working of death magic. Seven winds raked her, splitting the yarn of the two sweaters she wore, ripping through her several undershirts, and gouging her back. Seven lashes scored her skin. Her blood welled quickly, then flash-froze like a powerful, painful glue under the malice of the storm.

Then—oh, then, worst of all—she heard Duantri cry out. A second later, her body was covering Lanie's, strong arms pinning her to the gravel.

The Gyrgardu, Lanie realized, must be witnessing the mauling but not its source.

Poor Duantri, she thought, wry and squished. *A Falcon Defender who cannot defend. If it wins and I am killed, her life will be blighted with self-blame, just like Mak's was.*

Won't do, Miscellaneous Stones. Won't do at all. Upsy-daisy.

Gathering her wits, Lanie summoned all her old tricks of childhood. She had years of practice wriggling out of fierce grips and unbudging headlock holds. Her sister had been a pouncing predator, but Lanie had learned to be a very efficient prey animal.

Crackling pain blazed down her back, but she managed to eel out from underneath the Gyrgardu and squirm her way to her knees.

She winked at her friend.

Duantri, that doughty darling, looked tense and unhappy, but she jerked her chin in a nod, and didn't try to wrestle her back down.

Then Lanie stretched her neck to the sky and roared, in all her voices, surface and deep: "Back!"

The roiling mass of substance recoiled at her command. Those savage, seeking tentacles snapped up like sap cracking. The whole storm cell shrieked and keened, bulged and billowed, as if on the verge of bursting and disgorging something awful onto the onlookers below.

Lanie had bought herself a millisecond to think. She bit her tongue against another outpouring of reason and goodwill in ancient Skaki verse. The storm was in no mood to listen. In another moment, it would pull her apart with its tentacles. Duantri would grieve, Datu would be furious, and Lanie would have broken her word to Sari Skrathmandan.

So she did the only other thing she could think of.

Lifting her gaze beyond the storm, beyond the sky, Lanie threw her arms wide in a modified sothaín attitude. This was the sixth gesture of the fourth set, belonging to Brotquen, Four-Faced Harvest Goddess: *The Queen of Reaping Welcomes All to Feast*. It was a gesture of hospitality, of throwing open your door and letting a beloved guest inside.

"*Erre'Elur!*" she shouted.

Calling on her god was familiar, but Lanie mostly used the Quadic name, Doédenna, or the Lirian, Saint Death. The Skaki name for the god of Death burned like frostbite on her tongue. The pink mist turned to ice crystals in her mouth. Her esophagus ached with grapefruit-flavored snow.

The storm of souls recognized the name. A hundred years ago, those souls had been lodged inside the sky wizards of Skakmaht, ruling the northlands from their flying houses. Erre'Elur had been the god of all their winters and woes.

Now, upon hearing Her name in its enemy's mouth, the storm furled itself tighter, marshaling its tentacle winds and lightless lightnings back into its center mass, making to flee.

But Lanie reached out, left-handed, and yanked the storm back down. Down, and in.

Into herself.

And through her, into Cracchen Skrathmandan.

LANIE COULD NOT feel her body, only the cold sweat rolling off it. Too much. Too much at once. Tattered, angry substance poured through her in a magma stream—if magma could be the burning cold of frostbite. She could not tell where she ended and the storm of souls began.

These weren't even *whole* souls, she realized, honeycombed as they were—as Cracchen was—with Irradiant Stones's ghastly tooth marks. They were what remained of the thousands of souls that the necromancer had ripped free of their bodies, all terribly twisted up inside each other, as if, over the years, some of them had tried to staunch the soul-wounds of their fellows, but all they had to staunch *with* were themselves. And they were few. So few.

But they were those who had *survived*.

Their power and their rage, their memories and their wills, were so concentrated, so dense and intense, that Lanie felt as though her flesh were sloughing off under the onslaught of all that substance.

But one thing she could still feel: Cracchen Skrathmandan's thready heartbeat beneath her left hand.

Once again, she sent a strand of her substance unspooling into him. She opened herself to his wounds, allowing the echo-wounds to tear into her own body.

Only now, she was entwined with the storm.

The substance she sent into Cracchen wasn't just her substance.

And the body that opened to his pain was not her body alone, but shared out with all the surviving sky wizards of Skakmaht.

She let the storm feel what the ghost had done to Cracchen. How they were the same: they and he. Children of the north, devoured by a Stones.

"Help him," Lanie whispered. "Help me help him."

A hand clasped her shoulder. Through the love in that hand, Lanie remembered she had a shoulder; she could feel that part of her body again. Duantri was like a beacon of sunlight at her side: a gentle warmth to counteract all the scalding cold that thundered through her, loathingly lending her its strength.

"I'm here for thee," Duantri murmured into her ear (and suddenly, Lanie had an ear again), "and here is where I'll stay."

The words echoed with an old feeling. The most marvelous and awesomest and kindliest of feelings: Saint Death, appearing in Lanie's darkest hour, standing at her sickbed and opening Her arms.

I have such work for you, She had said.

Lanie, bent under the weight of the storm of souls, pressed her cheek to Cracchen's barely-there heartbeat. In the voices of all the sky wizards inside her, and in the words of Saint Death Herself, Lanie whispered:

"Cracchen Skrathmandan. Let us in. *We have such work for you!*"

Cracchen gasped a breath too huge for his deflated lungs. His one remaining eye flew open, rolled wildly, fixed on her. His hand shot up, flailed. Lanie did not know if he was trying to pull her closer or thrust her away. He did not have enough strength either way.

His hand fell, limp, to the ground. Beneath her weight, his spine arched, lifting off the ground until his only points of contact were the heels of his feet digging into the dirt and the sharps of his shoulders.

He made no noise at all. Lanie wasn't sure he was still breathing.

And yet, abruptly, his *will* changed—from refusal to welcome.

He did not welcome her. But somewhere inside himself, Cracchen Skrathmandan had agreed to receive what she carried.

The moment he let her in, Lanie released the storm of souls. A great burst of energy passed through her: bitterly cold and unbearably radiant. It pierced out from her chest in all directions like spiralized spikes of ice, then passed into Cracchen. Currents of lightning-like glister crackled across his broken body. All his wounds shone out at once, bright as starlight on snowflakes.

As the last of the storm left Lanie's body to enter Cracchen's, he bucked so hard, she was thrown back. Duantri caught her, hauled her away to safety. Lanie couldn't see; she had pressed her head to Duantri's shoulder, was shielding her eyes from the high white flare emanating from Cracchen that she was pretty sure the Gyrgardu herself could not see.

The no-longer-dying man screamed.

CHAPTER FIVE
Enemies to Allies

DUANTRI HANDED LANIE her wooden bowl of way-stew. She stayed crouched at her side until Lanie's cupped hands drifted the bowl to her mouth and she took a careful sip. She had removed her spectacles, and her tired brown eyes rolled with pleasure as the food passed her lips.

Duantri breathed out through her nose, satisfied. This was a good sign. On a normal night, Lanie suffered through her portion of way-stew. Its main staple was 'pocket soup,' which started out life as a strong venison broth, then was reduced over many hours to a stiff jelly, powdered in flour, sliced thinly, and sold in paper-wrapped lots. Most evenings, Duantri threw one of the slices into a cook pot full of hot water, added a handful of whey-fermented porridge balls, dried yogurt beads, some diced-up pemmican, and a bit of their precious salt—and that was dinner. It was also next morning's breakfast. Lunch was usually dried berries, nuts, more yogurt balls, and (for Duantri, who could stomach it) jerky.

When not on the road, with a wider choice of comestibles, Lanie rarely ate any animal protein that had been slaughtered by humans for human consumption. It gave her unhappy indigestion, and sometimes—depending on how fresh the kill—an allergic flare of echo-wounds. Experiencing how an animal died every time she ate its flesh had made Lanie a staunch consumer of beans, lentils, and other legumes for her protein sources.

In Quadiíb, with its long and illustrious history of vegetarian cuisine, this was easy. Out on the road, not so much. It hadn't taken Duantri long to observe that Lanie's digestion did much better if the animal proteins supplementing their way-stew came from small birds or rodents that a *kestrel* had killed. Small mercies. But her poor friend suffered the least nocturnal distress—flatulence, diarrhea, acidic burping, nightmares— on those nights they dug into their store of dried beans and foraged roots, avoiding the meat-based pocket-stew and fat-rich pemmican altogether.

Tonight, however, Lanie was slurping her way through the way-stew like it was the best invention since confectioner's sugar.

This relieved Duantri no end, for Lanie had poured out such a font of magic on the road earlier that she appeared to have halved herself. Her eyes were sunken in their sockets, and even her black travel braids seemed wispier.

Lanie needed to replenish. Tanaliín had assured Duantri that this could be done with food, rest, leisure, poetry, prayer, and had adjured her not to let Lanie deplete herself so wholly that she made herself sick again. *Your one job, my Gyrgardu*, she had said. *Your sacred duty. Defend her as you would defend me—especially from her own bad habits.*

Duantri was trying. If she could, she would steal the food from off the banquet tables of the Twelve Gods Themselves to feed Lanie. But here on Athe, after the end of the longest day of her life, all she could offer was way-stew.

"This is delicious," Lanie announced.

Duantri's eyebrows stretched for her hairline, each yearning for the other like two lovers parted by an infinite river. This was probably Lanie's twenty-somethingth time eating way-stew since setting off from Quadiíb in pursuit of the ghost. But it was the first time she had ever uttered those words.

"Oh?"

With one hand, Lanie pushed her glasses onto her head. With her other, she tipped her bowl to her mouth and slurped the remaining mouthful.

"I could eat that entire pot," she said, chewing on a tough bit of pemmican. "Also," she added thoughtfully, "the pot. But we have guests. I shan't be greedy." She glanced over at Cracchen. "How's yours?"

The man sitting opposite them on the other side of the fire neither answered nor moved, merely stared at Lanie like a rat watching a cobra. He had been like this since waking, covered in ice crystals that had come, not from the sky, but from within his own flesh. The crystals seemed to be knitting the broken bits of his flesh back together—which, if it were happening to Duantri, would have wholly occupied her attention. Instead, his focus was fixed elsewhere. Outside himself. On Lanie.

Which Duantri didn't like.

Lanie didn't seem bothered by his attention, but by his lack of appetite. Her look turned reproachful, the way she sometimes looked at Datu whenever the child was going through one of her occasional picky-eating phases, her voice positively aunt-like when she demanded, "Haven't you touched your way-stew yet? Cracchen, you need to eat!" She wagged her spoon like a scolding finger at the icicles growing from his skin. "You're eating for *multitudes* now! You—*all* of you—have been starving for too long already!"

Cracchen flinched at the reminder, or perhaps at the wooden spoon's wild gestures. He broke eye-contact and ducked his head to sip tentatively at his way-stew. Duantri had served it to him in her own clay cup, as she and Lanie only had two bowls and two cups between them.

Her eyes narrowed.

She did not like Cracchen Skrathmandan. The only other time she ever met him, back before the ghost had taken him for host, he had tried to shoot Lanie in the face with a blunderbuss.

Duantri had fought him then, and taken him down.

If called upon to do so, she would fight him again—no matter how many miracles he manifested. She would keep an eye on him. And on all the treacherous knives of ice jutting from his finger stumps. How easily his wounds could turn to weapons.

Watching him from under her lashes, she returned to her own food, now grown tepid.

Her belly was howling at her. She may not have been the one to call upon strange gods and storms of angry wizard souls to heal the broken body of a dying assassin—but *after* the miracle, it was Duantri who had manhandled both Lanie's and Cracchen's dead weights onto Stripes like two carcasses upon a cargo sled. It was Duantri who had dragged them both all the way back to the esh-site. A two-mile hike. In hill country.

It was a long, lonely walk, Duantri in the lead, grasping Stripes by the collar and hauling. The tiger rug had been so drained of his animating magic that he could not move of his own volition. He was barely able to maintain an inch or so of levitation above the bumpy ground. But Duantri was grateful for that much, for it meant that Lanie's magic—and therefore, her life-force—was yet still plentiful enough to help her, even while Lanie lay unconscious.

She took another bite of way-stew, fighting the urge to check if Lanie needed another serving. She had to care for herself, too, or she would be of no use to Lanie. If Tanaliín were here, she would make certain that Duantri rested, that the camp chores were shared, that no one person was doing too much. Lanie tried her best—she was a fast learner, eager to be of assistance, and most nights pulled her weight—but she could barely remember to feed herself most days. Her attentions were divided between this world and her deep senses, and tonight, more so than usual.

And so, the esh-site chores had fallen once again to Duantri. Someone had to do them, after all, and following their return to camp from the massive miracle on the road, Duantri had been the only one awake and capable of moving. She had reinvigorated the fire, melting their abandoned dinner, which had frozen in their absence, back into a semi-edible form. She had cleaned and bandaged Lanie's wind-raked wounds, wrapped both sleepers in blankets, and shook them awake once the food was hot and ready, forcing bowls and cups into their hands.

If you could call what now grew from the ends of Cracchen's wrists *hands*.

Not her god. Not her magic. Not her business.

Duantri hunched her shoulders against the lonesome, late-winter wind, and shoveled more stew into her mouth. A piece of dried cranberry sprang tart against her tongue. She rolled it around, savoring it, but a blast of campfire smoke blew directly into her face, suffusing her mouth with its acridity, overwhelming all other tastes.

If Tanaliín were here, she would say, "And lo, my kestrel hath invoked her curse." In most aspects of their lives, her gyrlady was the least superstitious person Duantri knew, but still Tanaliín claimed, only half-joking, that each human carried their own small curse about, to counter all their many blessings.

Duantri's curse was that, whenever they were camping out on the Caravan School Roads, no matter where she sat, she always managed to be in the direct line of smoke from the campfire. Tanaliín's was that, in any given line she happened to be standing in, at any given marketplace, it would always be the longest. Makkovian's: that whenever came his turn to run errands, the skies would inevitably open in a rainfall that lasted for precisely only as long as he needed to be outside. Datu's: that any new piece of underclothing she acquired would be immediately eaten by her wolf cub, Undies. He would not chew it so much as gulp it down whole. It would pass through his strange, undead body, unscathed by any of the acids or digestive filth that one expected in a living animal, and come out the other end in one piece. Datu would sigh, and wash it, and it would be good as new. But *still*.

Lanie's curse...

Duantri considered. Lanie did not do *small* anything. Her curses were cosmic, full worthy opponents in the gigantomachy against her many great blessings, and she bore them cheerfully. Perhaps, she mused, Lanie didn't think of them as curses, but as opportunities. Favors she might do her god.

A thin arm slipped around her waist, and squeezed, distracting her from her thoughts. She startled, glancing down at Lanie, who was beaming up at her.

"Thank you for dinner, Gyrgardu," said the greatest living necromancer on Athe.

Duantri felt her shoulders relax, her mouth soften and curve. She craved physical contact. She loved to be touched, hugged, caressed. She missed sleeping in Tanaliín's arms, waking to Makkovian's kisses. She missed Datu snuggling up for music lessons. She missed meeting her fellow gyrgardon and erophains for jam sessions every Rainday night. She missed playing her guitar. She missed singing. She missed *Quadiib*. She was very, very tired.

"You are not usually so fond of my way-stew, Lanie." How was it that her own voice always came out raspier when it spoke Lirian, as if the blunt language abraded her throat?

"You must be mistaken, Falcon Defender," Lanie protested. Her hugging arm squeezed harder until Duantri's involuntary smile began to spread. "I am righteously passionate about your way-stew! It is the ambrosia of the Twelve Gods. It is wedding banquet and hero's return and High Holy Fire Feast all rolled into one!"

"You *are* hungry."

"Yes!" Lanie agreed, so enthusiastically that Duantri actually laughed. The sensation opened up the tightness in her chest a bit, making room for the next mouthful of stew.

"And what of your... belly troubles?" They often started halfway through dinner and continued through the night, interrupting both their slumbers, for Duantri was a light sleeper, even if Lanie was not.

Scooting in, Lanie snuggled closer and whispered confidentially, "Tonight, Gyrgardu, I welcome my fetid umble-wambles. I don't care if they hear my farts all the way in Umrys-by-the-Sea! I hope they smell them in Rook!"

With a look so cheeky and cherubic that Duantri wanted to pinch her cheeks, Lanie abruptly swapped Lirian for Quadic.

"May farts waft out in praise of your fine stew—their perfume is my gift unto the world!"

Duantri's unexpected roar of laughter almost knocked her over, along with the rest of her stew. A release. A loud, explosive release. Lanie steadied her, patting her between the shoulder blades, chuckling along.

After a few minutes, they both wiped their streaming eyes. How good—how very good it was!—to laugh after such a day!

Grinning, Lanie stretched up to kiss Duantri on the cheek. "Thou surely art a doughty sparrowhawk," she exclaimed. "Tonight, whilst our mouths slumber, our butts talk."

Duantri groaned, ladling another helping into Lanie's bowl. "Forsake thine odes of praise," she adjured her in Quadic, "and eat thy fill." Winking, she added, "The airs thy body sounds are poems enow."

Lanie sprayed.

"Vengeance is... how does one say it in Lirian?" Duantri asked, in smug Lirian, slurping the last dregs from her bowl. "Vengeance is a bread best served stale? With, mayhap," she added, "a spit-take of stew."

But her mood plunged again when Lanie set down her own bowl, and said, grave and business-like, "So. The ghost has embedded himself inside a skinchanger host. He won't need roads anymore on his way north." She grimaced. "With wings at his disposal, he won't even need the *ground*."

At this, Cracchen spoke up unexpectedly. "He won't go north first."

Duantri's head snapped in his direction. Her eyes brought him sharply into focus, everything else fading around him. Behind her breastbone, Kestrel stirred, watchful. Ready to defend.

At her side, Lanie had gone preternaturally still, and was watching Cracchen with such intensity, Duantri wondered if she were using her deep senses to peer past his accident, into the very substance of him.

"No?" Lanie asked, too casually. "Why not? I thought for certain Skakmaht was his ultimate goal."

"It is. Oh, it is. But he wants"—Cracchen's voice was bitter, so bitterly cold that Duantri thought his tongue must have turned to ice like so many of his wounds—"a better body to take him there. One with *juice*."

How placid Lanie's face had become. How still, like the soil smoothed over a grave after the funeral was done. Everything about her was calm and restful: all but her wide brown eyes, which flickered with hints of yellow.

"He just got a new body," she remarked. "He used yours for months. Why would he change out again so soon?"

"I was his first." Here, Cracchen's voice deepened, seemed to take on an echo, an odd cadence. The skin between Duantri's shoulder blades twitched, like wings about to unfurl.

"Do you think, witch, now that he knows the way of it, that he will stop at some barely hatched skinchanger he found in a bush? Do you think *Irradiant Stones* will be satisfied with shaping only a few measly songbirds and a wild cat or two? No."

"No?" Lanie drawled, as if inquiring after the seating arrangements for a difficult family meal. "What is his plan, then, Cracchen?"

She placed a slight emphasis on his name, such that Duantri felt the feathering feeling beginning to crawl across her scalp. Kestrel's barbules, rising.

Cracchen snorted out a breath. His nostrils were frosting over. Fog poured from his nose like smoke.

"It is obvious, witch. Irradiant Stones will go deep into the uplands of Leech, to the capital—Witch Queen's City. There, he will wrestle a skinchanger elder for possession of its body, probably one of the kernelborn, who can take the fableforms. Perhaps even a gunugg. And that will just be the beginning."

"Ah. I see." Lanie carefully replaced her spectacles, all the while maintaining her mantle of placidity.

This only seemed to provoke Cracchen. "She doesn't believe us!"

Duantri cocked her head at his outcry. Once again, his voice sounded different, sans echo, full-Lirian in tone and timbre.

A terrible laughter cracked out of him, wild and broken, like sobbing.

At the sound, Duantri's body turned silky at the joints. Loose, easy. She rose to a crouch. Such laughter was unpredictable, unstable. This was a man who, in the next moments, might do anything. Fold down into a ball. Explode out like a bomb. Whatever happened, she would put her body between him and Lanie.

Lanie exuded a sort of calm exasperation, like a parent in the face of an overly tired child's tantrum.

"Of course I believe you, Cracchen," she told him, and then, more sternly, "I believe *all* of you, though we will do better going forward if you forego your insults and simply address me as Lanie. I have known Irradiant Stones all my life, but I daresay, between the... however many there are of you... you know him better. And if you say we need to adjust our course"—she shrugged—"then we will go to Witch Queen's City on the morrow."

Her words were like a hole punched in Duantri's lungs, sucking all the air out.

"No," she whispered.

Lanie looked her way.

Duantri tried to speak—*not there, not that place, not again*—but could not voice the words without the necessary breath to bolster them.

Lanie's mask of tranquility crimped into true concern. *What is it?* she mouthed.

Cracchen leaned forward, already talking before Duantri could recover, and the echo in his voice had redoubled, as if dozens of voices now spoke from within him.

"We must take him down in the city, before he jumps skins again. If Irradiant Stones leaves the capital in possession of a kernelborn, he will be too mighty to stop. He will go north. He will destroy what remains of Iskald, and the bodies he tore from us, so that we might never return. He will finish what he started a hundred years ago."

Duantri shivered, but not from the cold. Cracchen's empty left eye socket, once hollowed out by the ghost, was now filled with an orb of faceted ice, tracking and focusing just as his right eye did. In the depths of the ice danced tiny pinpricks of light—not unlike the yellow flames in Lanie's, but of a cold, strange blue-green hue.

"And when he has left Skakmaht in ruins, he will hunt *you* down, witch. And you will not be strong enough to bring him down." His gaze shifting from Lanie to Duantri, Cracchen finished in soft, perfect Quadic: "Though all the gyrgardon be at thy back."

CHAPTER SIX
Skinchangers

GRANDPA RAD WAS, in his way, predictable.

Other than that bit about going to Witch Queen's City for a powerful skinchanger host, nothing in Cracchen's dire predictions really surprised Lanie. It was Cracchen's *voice* she was interested in.

It kept changing.

Sometimes his voice was the way she remembered it: once big and brash—and now, like the rest of him, gone thin and cracked. And sometimes, it was something else entirely: a host of *other* voices, speaking as one. This latter voice was much deeper than the former, in both the substantial sense and the accidental. It echoed. The edges of his words curled like calligraphy.

Lanie recognized the strong Skaki dialect from notes and tones she'd heard buried in his mother's voice—though Sari had all but lost hers over the years she'd spent in the Rookish court, and then in Liriat. Cracchen's brother Haaken (who, Lanie suspected, studied Skaki daily, read and wrote it, thought in it, and probably dreamed in it) had a much stronger Skaki dialect. Almost as strong as Cracchen's second, newer voice.

Was Cracchen aware how the sky wizards were influencing his speech? His thoughts? He seemed to speak directly to them, as though they were all having a long conversation which neither she nor Duantri could hear. He had used the word 'us' when he cried, "She doesn't believe us," so Lanie did not think the sky wizards were suppressing his will, as the ghost had done.

But sometime, in the hours since his brinking, Cracchen

Skrathmandan and the storm of souls must have come to some sort of understanding.

What did this mean for her? For the work Saint Death had set her to?

She did not know. And so she watched, sunk in pensive silence. Plenty to watch, after all. All of it miraculous. None of it anything she could have imagined before tonight.

The last time she had met Cracchen in Liriat, just before the ghost seized him, Cracchen had been in possession of all his own teeth. A whole, mean, malicious mouthful of them, with a grin like a jackal. In the months since, Grandpa Rad had kept his host on such a diet of gutter wash and roadkill that Cracchen had lost most of his teeth to scurvy. Lanie had seen the state of his mouth as he lay dying on the roadside: inflamed gums; abscesses; only chips of shattered gray enamel remaining.

Now his mouth sparkled with icicles in the shapes of incisors, canines, molars, premolars. Every time he spoke, his teeth flashed and shimmered with foxfire: emerald and aquamarine, sullen ember-pink. The colors were gorgeous, distracting. His gums were silvered with frost. Erre'Elur had bejeweled him like a saint.

And his teeth were the least of it.

Every last one of his wounds was thusly repaired. Lustrous icicles grew from the stumps of his missing fingers and toes. Every few minutes, one or two digits would fall out, and chunk to the ground with a merry tinkle. Cracchen would startle at the sound, like a rabbit leaping at a stone shot from a shepherd's sling. But almost immediately, a new set of icicles would start growing from the wreckage of his hands and feet: this time finer, more detailed, and far more fingerlike than the last.

Soon, Lanie surmised, the magic would learn the ideal patterns of Cracchen's body, and how best to patch him. Once this pattern was perfected, the ice would lock in its spell, creating for Cracchen new, unmeltable, unbreakable appendages. These would probably last far longer than Cracchen's original bones.

Lanie imagined some future archeologist opening his tomb and cracking his casket, only to discover a heap of magical prosthetics, cold and shining like diamonds.

She had encountered such miraculous ice once before—when Haaken had preserved Makkovian's severed arm via some Skaki enchantment. That ice, too, had been impenetrable, sacrosanct. Lanie would never have been able to break it and get at the arm if Haaken had not advised her regarding the correct rites and words. When she did remove the spell, she had found Makkovian's arm untouched by rot, and was able to reattach it, and restore it to full use.

Apparently, Erre'Elur's ice could *itself* become a limb—if the original limb was gone for good.

Not something Haaken had seen fit to inform Lanie. If he'd even known. While Haaken had had none but himself to teach him, Cracchen now had at his disposal all the great minds of an entire generation of sky wizards. The ones who were left, anyway.

They do, she admitted to herself, *very good work*.

A starry splotch of frost overlayed Cracchen's temple, left cheekbone, and half his forehead. It twinkled like a delicate flower, its lines following the repaired fractures in his skull. Where a suppurating scratch had marred the right side of his face, a long scar of silver ice glistened. Cold, coruscant, crystalline armor had formed over his cracked ribs, and Lanie shivered, remembering the wounds she had felt echoed in her own body.

Cracchen did not shiver.

Lanie did not think he could feel the cold anymore. He *was* the cold. He was blessed of Erre'Elur. Woe-Woman. Winter-Crowned. Night-Outlasting-Day. Frost Queen of Skakmaht.

She was the Skaki god of death and winter, both like Doédenna and unlike her. Her magic, at once familiar and alien, sang in Lanie's bones: notes like needles-of-water; chords like calving-of-icebergs; progressions of thundersnow and sleet, of graupel and permafrost and salt-ice upon the shore.

She grew dizzy with the immensity of the symphony, absorbed in every tendril of frost creeping silver across Cracchen's scurvy rash and bruised skin.

As she watched, she realized the ice was clothing him in flexible crystal mail. Soon, his flesh would be entirely covered by interlocking chips of ice. White glitter and sparks of rainbows shot off his body every time he moved.

"You're just so lovely!" she blurted.

Loud. She'd been loud. Everybody jumped, including her. Cracchen's eyes widened, both frozen and flesh. She had surprised him: the man, and the sky wizards he carried inside him.

That gleam of deep green glinted again in Cracchen's icy left orb. A corner of his mouth twitched up—not Cracchen's old grin, but more like…

"*Lanie.*"

Duantri's voice, strained to the breaking point.

Duantri. Duantri was calling to her.

Lanie tore her gaze from Cracchen's rainbow sparkles, shifting it to her friend's face.

Also lovely. The loveliest.

"Hello," she said dreamily.

"He"—Duantri jabbed a finger in Cracchen's direction—"tells you that we must travel to Witch Queen's City—the heart of *Taquathura*—and that is all you have to say?"

Lanie frowned. Was it all she had to say? She cast her mind back to the last thing Cracchen—and Cracchen-adjacent—had told her.

Grandpa Rad. New body. The capital. Kernelborn. Something, something. Kill them all, et cetera.

Slowly, she began swimming her way out of her deep senses. "Wait," she said, licking her dry lips. "What did you say? What's 'Taquathura'?"

"Taquathura," Duantri reiterated. "This place." She pointed at the ground. "How the skinchangers appoint these lands they occupy: the Free Territories of Taquathura."

"Leech?" Lanie also pointed at the ground, just to make sure.

Duantri jerked her shoulders in a shrug. "Humans call it that—Leech, for a country full of soul-suckers."

Lanie bristled, offended on behalf of all skinchangers, though she'd never met one before Grandpa Rad possessed the mistle thrush. "Why didn't I know that?"

"If you had ever come close enough to a skinchanger to learn its ways," said Cracchen, still in his many-voiced voice, "the fiend would have first devoured, and then become you."

"Lanie—he is not wrong." Duantri lowered her voice, as if afraid to agree with Cracchen out loud. "Right now, we are but on the outskirts of Taquathura. Go much further in, and we will encounter such creatures as will suck out our souls as soon look at us. And then we will not be *us* anymore, but shambling husks without thought or name. Instead, some skinchanger will be walking the world in our stead, wearing our faces, bearing our memories—our magic—even the sacred bonds we hold with our..."

She stopped, swallowed, her golden-brown face taking on a gray cast even by the firelight. She shook her head, one hand at her throat, the knuckles of her other fist digging into her breastbone, where she felt the bond with her gyrlady, stretched almost to the snapping point.

Lanie stared at her, stricken.

Just that morning, they had hoped—both of them—so dearly, so desperately, to catch the ghost on the road today. To return him to Doédenna's cloak. To be rid of him, done with this chase, and to finally deliver Cracchen Skrathmandan back to his family in Liriat, so that they themselves could return to Quadiíb.

They had been so close. So close.

And Lanie had faltered. She had not only lost the ghost, she had set him on his path to still-greater power.

She had not failed her god. Not yet. There was still work to be done.

But she had failed Duantri.

A Gyrgardu was not meant to be so long apart from her gyrlady. Duantri had once described the pain of that separation like a nail driven daily through her heart, removed, mercifully, every night when she slept and shared dreams with Tanalíin, and then hammered back in upon waking.

How much more can she endure? Lanie thought. And then, to her secret shame: *What if she leaves me?*

She should never have allowed Duantri to accompany her in the first place, but her friends had left her no choice. Even Datu had said, *Auntie Lanie, you are not chasing after ghosts all by yourself. If no one else will go with you, I will. Me and Undies. We will be your Wolf Defenders,* at which point, Duantri had hastily interrupted with the plan that she and Tanalíin and Makkovian had already discussed.

"I know," she choked, "I know that you—"

Duantri shook her head. "We must go on. Thus have I sworn, and thus I swear again. Lanie, I will stay with you till the end. But I thought…" Her voice became more urgent. "Skirt the edges of Taquathura. Avoid touching down for more than a few nights. Ready Stripes to fly you to safety should danger befall. Let the ghost go to Witch Queen's City. Let him gather his paltry scraps of power. You are beloved of your god; what is his might to yours? Let us go north before him," she urged. "We can set a trap in Iskald—"

"Do that," Cracchen interrupted, still reverberant and ancient, "and it will be tantamount to trying to catch a dragon in a partridge snare. You must stop him *here*." And he, too, pointed to the ground.

Lanie touched Duantri's knee, letting her know that she had heard. Then she turned to Cracchen, whose face, with its asymmetric frost flower, was shimmering like indicolites.

"Cracchen… May I call you Cracchen?"

The thing that was Cracchen, and more than Cracchen, hesitated. Then nodded.

"Before we make any decisions, I think we have to start with the basics. It sounds like you've been here before, yes?"

Again, Cracchen hesitated. Then, he said, in his normal voice, "I was captain of a caravan guard unit in Lower Quadiíb. After Rook. Before Liriat. We would accompany merchants into Leech. Trade with the skinchangers."

"And you?" Lanie asked again, still looking at him.

His other voice replied, "We have had dealings with the skinchangers in the past."

"And…" she cleared her throat, glancing at Duantri. "You?"

Duantri ducked her head, nodded, but didn't say anything else.

"As for me," Lanie announced, "I didn't even know Leech had another *name* until, like, three seconds ago. I don't know from kernelborn or fableforms, or any of the rest of it. We had a book in Stones Library called *Cradle Tales and Spook Fables from the Uplands of Leech*. Children's fare. Amazing illustrations. I read it to *ribbons*."

The bridge of her nose throbbed. She pinched it.

"Correct me if I'm wrong—and I know I'm wrong—but I thought skinchangers were just… little hill monsters? Rare, shy. Not dangerous unless you happen on one alone. And if you do, then it's your fault if they eat you up, all but the skin, then walk around wearing it like a fancy new coat? Something like that?"

Next to her, Duantri had pulled up her knees and was hugging them to her chest, chin tucked into her arms. When Lanie looked to her, hoping for answers, she just shook her head, and hid her face. So Lanie glanced over at Cracchen, but he was staring into the distance, the expression on his face so remote, he might have been walking the lonely white wastes of Skakmaht.

Lost in some memory, Lanie thought. *Not a pleasant one.*

But whether the memory belonged to Cracchen or to one of a hundred other scraps of shared minds, she did not know.

"We're tired," she announced, pushing herself to her knees. "All of us. Cooked through like way-stew. We'll reconvene in the morning, make our decision then. Thank you." She bobbed a bow in Cracchen's direction, hands crossed over her chest

Quadoni-style. "You've been... You've *all* been extremely helpful. I am going to bed now."

When she looked up again, Duantri was already standing, holding a hand down to her.

"Come rest inside our esh, and let us sleep," she adjured Lanie in Quadic. "Doédenna, perhaps, will send thee dreams, advising us how best to steer our course. You"—she rounded on Cracchen, and flipped to Lirian, throwing her words like small, deadly knives—"bank the fire before you come in for the night. We will leave out a spare blanket."

"You've been here before," Lanie whispered. "To Taquathura."

She and Duantri were curled side by side under a shared blanket. Their 'spare' blanket was in fact Duantri's, folded in a corner for Cracchen, even though he still hadn't entered the esh.

Duantri took so long to reply that Lanie felt her thoughts turning to flotsam and starting to drift.

"Years ago," she whispered at last. "When Tanaliín and I first left Quadiíb, but before we settled in Liriat. You know my beloved: she wanted to open a school here, in the capital of Leech. Right in Witch Queen's City."

A soft giggle bubbled in Lanie's throat, the kind that only comes when one is overwrought, overwhelmed, and teetering on the last ledge of fatigue. Her skull effervesced with giddiness, even as her limbs grew heavy as sandbags.

"A Quadoni Waystation... but for skinchangers! That's *just* so Tanaliín!"

Duantri nodded. But when she didn't offer anything further, Lanie nudged her.

"What happened?"

"We were made welcome."

"How?"

"How not?" Duantri retorted. "They greeted us at the gates, the skinchangers of Madinatam. Dozens of them. Some of them so young, they still wore their coldfire forms."

Lanie flipped over to one side, facing Duantri. "Slower, please. Madinatam?"

"Their name for the capital. Not... not Witch Queen's City. All our human maps have mislabeled it—like we mislabeled the free territories of Taquathura as 'Leech.' Tanaliín was so embarrassed for our entire species when we found out." In the dark, Duantri sniffled when she spoke her gyrlady's name, and paused to wipe her nose and eyes.

Lanie waited, and squeezed Duantri's elbow for comfort. "I imagine so. And what, please, is a coldfire form?"

Duantri sighed. "The first shapes a young skinchanger takes are all very basic. Bioluminescent invertebrates, mostly. It is common for youths in Madinatam to volunteer service hours to the city by taking their coldfire forms, entering the municipal streetlamp system, and just... glowing."

"Glowing?"

"They take it in shifts, usually a few hours at a time. Lanie, it is truly uncanny, to see the lights of a city peering back at you from behind the glass."

"Extraordinary!"

"Not to them. To them, it is as normal as... as normal as a Lirian youth earning pocket change by mucking out a stable, or washing dishes in a scullery."

Lanie was not at all tired anymore. She was, in fact, delighted. "Wait till we tell Datu! How strange! How *wonderful!*"

"Not so wonderful," Duantri demurred, "when you are the glowworm that the newly hatched skinchanger devours."

At that somber thought, Lanie lost a few bubbles of her giddiness. "Is it just like in the cradle tales, then?" she asked softly. "Do skinchangers just... eat people—um, and glowworms—whole?"

A restless movement beside her as Duantri shook her head.

"Skinchangers do not eat flesh. They are... they call themselves 'pneumaphages.' What you refer to as 'substance,' Lanie, in your Lirian theology, they call 'pneuma.' Pneuma is their entire food source. Everything else, what you call 'accident' and they call 'durity'—the skin, the bones, the flesh—that is of no concern to them. What they eat is everything that makes a being *itself*. Their haecceity. Their *thisness*. *Thisness* is what they feed on."

Despite the gloom and doom in Duantri's voice, Lanie could feel some secret part of herself brightening at this new knowledge. She could not help it; she was half in love with the skinchangers of Taquathura already. How miraculous they were, how lovely, and how enviable! She wished *she* could survive on pneuma alone.

"All of us"—Lanie flung out her hands in the dark, gesturing to everything she could think of—"eat accident, one way or another. So, a skinchanger eats substance." She shrugged, both a mental gesture and a physical one. "No great difference. Everything eats something."

"Lanie, it is an enormous difference!" Duantri sounded frustrated at this philosophical approach. "They are our opposites in every way. Not just the opposite of *humans*, but of most creatures on Athe. Any sentient creature you can name is a being composed mostly of accident. We carry our radiant center of substance, here." Reaching across the blanket, Duantri tapped at Lanie's breastbone, where the bird of the soul was said to reside. "That is all of us—beast, bird, fish, and insect. That is what we are."

"And a skinchanger is… not?"

"A skinchanger is most definitely not."

"So they're made mostly of substance instead?" Lanie nodded to herself. "Makes sense, if substance is what they eat."

"They are mostly substance," Duantri agreed, "with an inverse amount of accident. The core of a skinchanger—its kernel—is pure pneuma: dense, compacted, layered like a pearl. Over this kernel is stretched the most delicate layer of durity. It is like skin, somewhat, but thin as a butterfly's wing. Flexible, supple. A living silk, changeable in color and texture. We think of skinchangers as swapping out skins when they change shape. But truly, it is their *pneuma* that changes shape; their durity merely reforms around it, providing an outer structure."

"How?" Lanie breathed.

The darkness was displaced above them as Duantri gestured, unseen, in the air.

"When a skinchanger sups of its prey, it leaves behind an empty husk. This husk can no longer feed itself, think for itself, act on any instinct or memory, for it has none. If not carefully tended to, it will remain wherever the skinchanger left it, performing the basic functions of life until all organs shut down. Meanwhile, the skinchanger, in devouring their pneuma, amasses it to their kernel, adding another layer."

"So when a skinchanger changes shape, what they're really shaping is a *memory*," Lanie said. "Their outer skin—the durity—conforms to the memory. Sort of... gives it dimension. Colors it in." She bit her lip. She would never, ever say it aloud, but the thought made Lanie love the skinchangers more, not less.

Duantri nodded. "And it is not only the *shape* the skinchanger steals. Each new pneuma it eats provides the skinchanger with new experiences to plumb, new languages to speak, new talents to exploit—all the better to help the skinchanger hunt and feed from its next, more sophisticated, source of pneuma."

"Is that all they are?" Lanie asked, turning over onto her side and propping up her cheek on her palm. "Mindless eating machines?"

"Not *mindless*." Duantri also turned, her hand sliding from Lanie's breastbone. "They have *all* the minds."

"So, when you two went to, to... Madinatam, what Tanaliín wanted was..."

"She wanted to teach the skinchangers. More, she wanted to learn from them. She sent letters ahead through a network of merchant caravans, and received word back from a citizen of Madinatam—one Mysalli—that we would be welcome to visit the capital. While we were there, we were to meet with representatives from the local government, and formalize arrangements for the school. Lanie," Duantri burst out, "we believed—Tanaliín *still* believes—that the skinchangers were in earnest! They would adore hosting a Quadoni Waystation, or even an outpost, in Madinatam."

This time, Lanie kept silent, loathe to interrupt again before the story was done.

"They greeted us with all due welcome and ceremony. Scarcely had we crossed the bridge into Madinatam, but there was a line of skinchangers to greet us. It was like a festival. They ushered us inside, and brought us to Plaza Inconi—their central square—where we met even more skinchangers, of all shapes and sizes. There were humans too, more than I would have thought."

Lanie perked up. "Can any human live there?"

Duantri was silent for a while, then seemed to change the subject. "Taquathuran merchants travel far and wide through the realm, disguised as humans so as not to be killed on sight. They trade the riches of the territories—alluvial jewels, ancient coins of such pure gold they leave pollen on the touchstones, bolts of nettle cloth, bolts of spider silk as yellow as amber—for the single import they truly want…"

"What?" Lanie whispered, when Duantri fell silent again. "What do they trade for?"

"Immigrants. They want humans to live in Madinatam. To become citizens of Taquathura. Their housing is free. Work is promised for any who want it, apprenticeships, education—though there are no formal institutions for that, as of yet. No one goes hungry. All are welcome. Of course, included in the new residency paperwork is a guarantee that, at the end of their lives—however that should arrive—the human citizens of Madinatam must agree to let their souls be consumed by their skinchanger neighbors. All of this is signed and notarized by a priest of Lan Satthi—in a binding blood oath."

Lanie thought about it, then loosed a low whistle. "Might be a good deal. For some."

She might have taken it herself, had a skinchanger approached her with such a contract at a certain point in her life. She could even imagine traveling to Taquathura, years from now, seeking out such citizenship on purpose. It would be something new. Something wildly exciting.

But not, she told herself, *something Duantri needs to hear right now*.

To her surprise, Duantri agreed with her. "For some, it seems a kind of heaven—to those oppressed, dispossessed, fleeing violence. For some, it is a perfectly valid choice. When it is a *choice*." She bit out the last word, a kestrel snapping the neck of a vole.

Lanie's breath quickened. "And when it isn't?"

This time, Duantri paused for so long that Lanie was afraid she wouldn't go on.

Finally, she continued with her story, as if the interruption had never occurred.

"The skinchangers took Tanaliín and me on a tour of Madinatam—not Leech Keep, the castle where the Witch Queen lives, but everywhere else. At the end of the night, we met Mysalli, the skinchanger with whom Tam had been exchanging letters. She hosted a feast for us at her nourisha."

"What's a nouri—"

"Oh, Lanie! I am getting to it! You are worse than Datu!" Her laugh was a strangled sound, not quite merriment, but wherever merriment goes to die. "First, I will say what the nourisha looked like. This is important."

Lanie waited.

"Think of your favorite tavern or tea house. The Lover's Complaint in Liriat Proper—or that open air cafe in Ylkazarra where you and Makkovian and Datu go for pastries each morning."

"Mmn." Lanie's stomach rumbled. It had been too many weeks since she'd eaten a pastry. Any pastry. Even a stale one. "Got it."

"A cozy place, clean and warm. The rafters were strung with little glass lamps like bubbles, where the coldfire forms of many skinchanger juveniles burned bright. The most delicious smells wafted in from the kitchen. Madinatam locals boasted of Mysalli's nourisha like it was legend: *It is where we all go to be nourished*, they said. And the food…! Tanaliín and I ate and drank our fill—and well beyond it. We chatted with a bevy of skinchangers. We even participated in one of their sacred rites, with Mysalli's consent and encouragement. She and Tanaliín were fast friends—it was like watching two long-lost sisters reunite when first they came together. Tanaliín adored her—and it seemed Mysalli felt the same. By the end of our meal, the two of them were already speaking of co-authoring a paper for the Judicial Colloquium. Tanaliín was happy. So happy. But then, when we tried to leave…"

Lanie felt like her eyes were drilling holes in the dark, trying to make out Duantri's expression.

"What?" she demanded. "What happened?"

"When we tried to leave… *the nourisha tried to eat us*."

Lanie bolted upright. "It *what* now?"

"Mysalli tried to eat us. *She* was the nourisha. The nourisha was a *skinchanger*."

Lanie stared down at their shared nest of bedding. Duantri flopped out a hand, groped for Lanie's thigh.

"I am not telling it right."

"You're telling it just fine," Lanie said faintly. "Only… *what?*"

"Mysalli was a skinchanger elder. Somehow, sometime, over the course of her long, long life, she had supped the pneuma of an entire building—and had become it."

"I…" Lanie cleared her throat. "I didn't know that buildings had… substance. Um. Pneuma."

She had never even *contemplated* such a thing before. As a sorceress of Doédenna, her very media was substance and accident. It was what she worked with, the stuff of which her magic was *made*. But Lanie had only ever considered that living creatures were possessed of it.

Yet… the god of death was the god of the death of *everything*. Everything that had mass, had accident, which must eventually perish. And if a thing had accident: the *matter* of what it was—then it must perforce also have substance: the *idea* of what it was.

Lanie's thoughts spun out in a ravelment of marvel. *If everything has substance and accident—if a* house *has it, for instance—might I resurrect a feral house from ruins, and re-animate it to its third state? What would an undead* house *look like?*

She would very much have liked to dwell in depth upon these novel thoughts, but Duantri's story wasn't yet done. And Lanie had a feeling—a premonition, really, bordering on prophecy—that she needed to hear the ending.

"The nourisha was the last thing Mysalli had ever intended to eat. It was her... her *fableform,* she called it. She was explaining all of this to us even as she began to feast on us. At first, we did not notice. There is a kind of spell—like Aganath's fascination magic—that lulls a skinchanger's prey to complacency. We were caught in her coils like rats caught by a constrictor."

Lanie found Duantri's hand and squeezed.

"Mysalli assured us that she had not invited us to Taquathura with any but the purest intentions. It would be in the city's best interest to host a Quadoni school. She wanted only to welcome us. But when she met us, over the hours we were conversing together, Mysalli decided that she had to have us. *Both* of us. To sup of the pneuma of a Quadoni gyrlady and her Gyrgardu *together!* We were a thing she had never tasted before. She would still start the school, she promised us. After consuming our pneuma, she would know precisely *how*—because all our knowledge would be hers. For anyone who came to attend our Waystation for an education, she would take the form of a Quadoni gyrlady—a proper professora—and do honor to our names."

"Oh," Lanie said.

Duantri huffed a scoff of dry laughter. "Yes. Oh. Later, after we escaped, Tanaliín hypothesized that the sharp awakening of Mysalli's long-dormant hunger must have caught her off-guard. A skinchanger elder rarely eats. As it approaches the end of its life-cycle, it can go years without supping off any pneuma at all. Tanaliín supposes that Mysalli's unexpected hunger made her heedless, irrational. Instinct took over. She wanted—*needed*—to consume us. To become what Tanaliín and I were to each other, god-bond and all."

"Skinchangers can eat a *god-bond?*"

"It is of the soul," Duantri said simply. "It is, therefore, food."

It is one thing, Lanie thought, *to offer up your soul to a skinchanger. It is quite another to have it ripped from you, by someone you consider a friend. This is where the cradle tales come from. This is where monsters are born.*

"So you fought her," Lanie said, with a firm nod.

Her skin crawled with repulsion for that necessity. If only Mysalli had *waited*. Tanaliín might have given herself freely, after years of service to Madinatam, as a bequest to her friend. It would be like Tanaliín to enter such a final union out of pure intellectual curiosity. Duantri might have gone, too, wherever her gyrlady decided to go.

It might have been so beautiful—had the skinchanger elder just been more patient.

"I fought her," Duantri said. "I fought all of them. The whole nourisha. Everyone inside. Even the young... young ones. The juveniles with, with... only a few... shapes to their names. Hurting them was so *easy!*" she burst out. "Like tearing through tissue paper! Their blood is white as milk, and it glows. It glows until the damage goes too deep... and then it turns black."

Lanie's knuckles grew sore with the memory of Duantri's violence. In the dark of the esh, her knuckles split, bled, healed, all unseen.

"I'm sorry."

Duantri hugged herself, trembling. Lanie could feel each tremor.

"Mysalli herself—she was so much stronger than the others. She was the size of a building. She *was* the building! She commanded its walls, its ceiling, its doors; it bent to her will as we bend our limbs. I... I managed to take our camping axe to the floorboards. Tanaliín was half-sunk inside it—she was *drowning*, Lanie—so I hacked and hacked and hacked at the floor until she came free. Black blood," she said. "Black blood everywhere. Only when I brought Mysalli to the very point of death did the nourisha spit us out, back onto the streets of Madinatam. And thus"—Duantri breathed out—"thus the great Gyrlady Tanaliín idden Fa'nim'wai and her Gyrgardu Duantri idden Ylkazarra fled in terror from Witch Queen's City, never to return again."

Lanie didn't say the obvious thing, but she thought it. *Until now.*

The esh's flap snapped open. Cracchen stumped in.

Immediately, Duantri turned her back to Lanie and curled on her side, her body solidly between Lanie's and Cracchen's, her face pointing toward the spot where he flung himself down against the wall of the esh.

Lanie listened as Cracchen wrapped himself in Duantri's blanket—for privacy, if not for the warmth he didn't need anymore—and balled himself up as far away from them as possible. His body radiated a steady cold that even the heat of Duantri's rock socks shrank from.

No one spoke.

All giddiness, curiosity, and horror drained out of Lanie's body, through Stripes the tiger rug, and into the packed floor. Her skin sagged, fatigued, against her flesh. Limply, she reached out for her satchel, the one with all the bones from her cache traps, and dragged it to her chest. From within her deep senses, the pearly caress of those sleeping bones tidal-tumbled through her, cuddling closer, memory-to-memory, sharing the sweetness of their ultimate rest.

Lanie loved every single bone in that bag, with a ferocity stronger than her fondness for pastries. But how she missed that little deer hoof, now buried in the mud of the hills beyond the gallows! How keenly she regretted the manner of the yearling doe's undreaming. How she longed to go back to that moment on the road, and pilot the doe's three-legged, blessed body out of the way of Grandpa Rad's vengeance.

How she wished... she wished...

Her eyes closed. Her breathing evened. The darkness behind her eyes, geometrically dividing and spilling into ever-flowering kaleidoscopic arrays—rose windows, portents, scatter jacks, constellations—melted into nothingness.

She slept.

Intermezzo

A VERY GOOD WOLF

Quadiíb

Year 4826 of Higher and Lower Quadiíb
On T'rahb, 25th of Jdeni: the Second Month

20 Days till Spring Equinox

DATU'S EYES OPENED in the semi-darkness.

She checked in with herself, because they were in a new place again, and sometimes she forgot which one it was. If she didn't remember to check in with herself, she might start breathing too hard, with a heartbeat like running away from a horde of blackbirds, and she'd get that whine in her ears, and feel like her eyes were two telescopes straining to focus on something too far away.

First: she was lying on her cot, in her and Didyi's travel esh.

Good, she told herself. *Familiar. Safe.*

In Ylkazarra, first among the twelve great Waystations on the Caravan School Road, the word 'esh' commonly referred to the enormous, circular, semi-permanent structures that made up the city's businesses, colleges, and housing developments. These eshes were all interconnected by a network of canvas-canopied corridors and open courtyards that went on for miles. Datu enjoyed the big city eshes, especially the restaurants and concert halls and libraries. (Especially the lending library of musical instruments). But out on the road like this, a small esh was better. The weatherproofed canvas walls wrapped her like a warm embrace.

Second: the road.

Yes. She squinted at the ceiling. *The Caravan School Road. That is where we are.*

She and Didyi and Gyrlady Tanalín were working their way across the Caravan School Road, which looped the entire desert of Higher Quadiíb. It connected each of the twelve Waystations like jewels on a golden strand more than a thousand miles long. It was the thriving trade route for all the precious goods moving through Quadiíb.

Third: why did her chest feel so heavy? It wasn't like panic. It was like some rotund, boulder-bottomed goblin was squatting on her ribcage.

"Oh," said Datu. "Good morning, Undies."

The wolf cub on her chest lolled out his tongue. He panted at her happily, as if he had every right to be there, which, of course, he did. His pupil-less eyes, the blue of hot-burning stars, shone with adoration. Undies never blinked. He did not need to, being mostly undead.

Datu reached up to scratch him under his chin. "What are you doing awake? It is too early for humans and wolves."

The cub opened his mouth, cleared his throat delicately, and said in Auntie Lanie's voice, "Hello, Datu."

Datu froze.

"I'm sorry," Undies/Auntie Lanie said. "Did I wake you?"

"Um. No, Auntie Lanie. I mean, yes, I was sleeping. But this is… better. Hello."

"Hello," Auntie Lanie said again, and Datu thought that if Undies wore spectacles, he'd be pushing them up his nose in a familiar gesture right now. She cleared Undies' throat again, which was an Auntie Lanie tic when she was feeling awkward or uncomfortable.

"Soooo," she said in a long-drawn out wolf-whine, "I've been trying this new thing where I throw my voice into the throat of an undead creature I've formed some kind of bond with. Yesterday I did it at a range of a couple miles with this deer I met. And when I woke, I got to wondering if I could extend that to, I don't know, fifteen, sixteen hundred miles or so. I thought I'd importune Mister Underwear Stones for the opportunity." She sounded a bit dazed. "I didn't think it would actually *work*. How do I sound?"

"Like you are right on top of me."

"Amazing!" Auntie Lanie cried. "Let's do this more often."

"Yes," Datu agreed. "But also, you could just come home. Did you catch the ghost yet?"

The wolf cub sighed.

Undies was a great sigher. He sighed when Datu refused to play with him because she had something far stupider to do, like schoolwork. He sighed when Didyi scolded him for eating yet another pair of undergarments.[4] He sighed when Gyrlady Tanaliín took him by the scruff of the neck and forcibly removed him from whichever midden or roadside dung heap he happened to be ecstatically rolling in.

But this sigh was not like his other sighs. This sigh was *patently* Auntie Lanie, like she was praying to Saint Death for patience.

Datu frowned. She wished she could read Auntie Lanie's expression on Undies' face. But the cub looked as he always looked: a little goofy, a lot good-natured, and entirely loving.

Her aunt, after a long moment, said, "Look, I have a lot to tell you all… where are you at on your journey?"

By now, Datu was awake enough to remember her precise geographical location. She made sure that Didyi and Gyrlady Tanaliín showed her every night on the map before she agreed to fall asleep.

She answered as promptly and as accurately as possible. "We just left Waystation Two, Zadiqai, yesterday, and are now on our way to Waystation Three, Nurr. Didyi says I will like Nurr. They have a music festival coming up for the High Holy Fire Feast of Spring Equinox. Didyi says, alas, we are scheduled to be well on our way by the time the festival starts, but Gyrlady

---

4 Named for his dietary preferences, Mister Underwear Stones, AKA "Undies," did not need to eat so long as Sacred Datura Stones, the living mistress to whom his afterlife was bound, kept herself well fed. He ate only for pleasure, and his pleasure was unmentionables.

Tanaliín says not to worry, there are street musicians in Nurr all year round, so we will be sure to hear some treats."

"And how is Makkovian's pilgrimage going?" Auntie Lanie asked when Datu fell silent.

"Complicated," Datu said cautiously, because that was what Didyi would say. She added, "And we must remain complex," which was another thing Didyi liked to say.

Gyrlady Tanaliín was sponsoring Didyi's pilgrimage, and since Duantri was gone with Auntie Lanie, Datu did not really have a choice about tagging along. Didyi would be walking—or rather, riding, on camelback—the entire circuit of the Caravan School Road in exactly one hundred twenty days. Of course, those one hundred twenty days did not count rest days, which they took every five days.

If Didyi kept to his set schedule, the journey should take him, on the whole, one hundred twenty days plus twenty-four rest days, the sum total neatly divisible by twelve—which pleased the Judicial Colloquium of Gyrveard, who had sentenced Didyi to this pilgrimage. (That's what Gyrlady Tanaliín called it: a sentence. Like a punishment. But the Judicial Colloquium called it 'Ritual Expiation and Reintegration of the Disenfranchised into Quadoni Society,' or something like that.)

It was Didyi's idea to present himself to the Judicial Colloquium for judgement. He was relieved to be sentenced to pilgrimage. His job, for the next one hundred forty-four days, was to stop at the major shrines at each of the twelve Waystations, and make his apologies to the gods for allowing his gyrlady to die when he, her gyrgardi, should have defended her with his life.

Didyi thought he had a lot to apologize for.

Gyrlady Tanaliín didn't agree with him—but the Judicial Colloquium's word was law in Higher Quadiíb, and he accepted it. Until he made his apologies to the twelve gods, Didyi would consider himself an abomination.

But the rule was, he'd assured Datu, that once he had done the walk and the work, he could stop thinking of himself that way.

Why not just stop right now, Didyi? Gyrlady Tanaliín says it is nonsense. Duantri says it is unfair. Auntie Lanie says you had no choice in the matter, because Mumyu ensorcelled you with her magic so that you could not stop her from murdering Gyrlady Gelethai.

But Didyi said, *Since before you were born, my plumula, I have considered myself an abomination. I, and no one else. It is just that the Judicial Colloquium are now offering me this ritual, so that I may come to know myself as human again.*

If Datu's mumyu, who was dead now, had been good at one thing, that thing was murder. Murder and magic. Two things.

Auntie Lanie liked to say that, in fact, Amanita Muscaria Stones *hadn't* been very talented at the latter; she was a one-trick magician, weaker than a hedge witch, but could wield what she had like a weapon.[5] Then again, Auntie Lanie's own talent for magic was so strong, it gave her an allergic reaction every time she so much as looked at a weapon.

Gyrlady Tanaliín said that Auntie Lanie's allergy to violence and her ability to raise the dead were two pieces of the same magic—not that Datu understood how. She was sure there was more to it, just like with Didyi and his pilgrimage.

There always was, with grown-ups.

"Datu." Auntie Lanie cleared Undies' throat again. "Do you think… do you think you could wake up Makkovian and Tanaliín? I'm not sure how long I can hold Undies. His mind is very… wiggly."

"So is his butt," Datu offered.

"I… can feel that. I think."

On her chest, the wolf cub was trembling with the urge to lick and jump, and jump and lick, and lick, and lick. Only Auntie Lanie's magic, from thousands of miles away, was holding him still.

Datu wanted to let him run around and play, so she said, "I

---

5 Stoneses throughout history were famous for their ability to weaponize anything, from tampons to bunny rabbits to cottonwood fluff, and on one occasion, all three of the aforementioned objects to the grievous slaughter of hundreds.

think Didyi is still sleeping. Apologizing to the gods is hard work, and he needs rest. Hold on, Auntie Lanie. I will wake Gyrlady Tanaliín first."

"Do not trouble yourself on my account, my plumula," came Didyi's dry voice from across the esh, where he sprawled upon his sleeping mat. "Didyi is not sleeping. Didyi does not sleep through the disembodied visitations of peripatetic necromancers. Didyi is awake, O my daughter. *Quite* awake."

Auntie Lanie was laughing in Undies' throat. "Good morning, Makkovian Covan!"

"Good morning, Mizka," Didyi said, in an even dryer voice, using his strange nickname for Auntie Lanie.

Datu smiled. When Didyi talked like that, he was only *pretending* to be annoyed. It was the way he talked to Undies, too—and Didyi loved Undies almost as much as Datu did. When Didyi was *really* annoyed, he was silent. For hours. Days, sometimes.

"Datu," Auntie Lanie said, "would you mind dashing over to get Tanaliín while I have a word with your father? I am charged by Duantri to convey some very specific words to him."

Datu nodded, wondering if her aunt could see her through Undies' eyes. Rolling to her feet from the sleeping mat, she padded over to the esh's entrance flap. Before she slipped out, she heard Auntie Lanie say, in a very dramatic voice:

"And I quote: 'O Prince of Peregrines, good morningtide; I miss thy mouth, thy hands, thy scent, thine eyes. I wish the day it soon would come to pass, that thou and I embrace again at last.'"

Datu spun around and marched back inside the esh. Even in the dim dawn light, she could see Didyi blushing.

Her own face aflame, she said, too loudly, "Auntie Lanie! No love-talk in *public!* Make Duantri write it down and send it to Didyi by *courier*. *Privately*. Like they do in *civilized* countries."

From the center of the esh, Undies cocked his head at her and winked. "Sacred Datura," said her aunt, "we must make allowances for new lovers." Undies' tongue lolled like a scarlet ribbon. "Yes, even we hard-hearted Stoneses have a solemn duty to regard such tender beings with lenience."

Datu huffed.

"My plumula," Didyi reminded her. "I believe your aunt has a task for you."

Datu narrowed her eyes. "No more love-talk," she warned, and turned to leave again.

"I make no promises!" Auntie Lanie sang out, or, rather, howled. "By the way, Makkovian Covan, I recently came into possession of a new language—Old Skaki, for my sins. It's all kennings and caesurae, not in the least practical—unless I happen to be bargaining with archaic entities or terrifying gods, which… never mind. But here's a piece of vocabulary I thought that you, a former Falcon Defender, would appreciate: the Old Skaki word for kestrel—or falcon, or eagle, or any raptor of size—is, and I do not jest, 'slay-pigeon'! Tell me you'll write a poem around it!"

"You are, as usual, incomprehensible, Mizka," said Didyi. "But you sound in good health and whole, so I forgive you. You would not be teasing if things were dire."

"Hmn."

Hmn, thought Datu as she ducked under the flap again, letting it fall shut behind her, *is not one of Auntie Lanie's reassuring noises.*

She lingered outside just long enough to overhear Didyi say in Lirian: "For Duantri's ears only, please, Mizka," and Auntie Lanie's laughing reply in Quadic: "I vow I'm but the vessel of thy voice."

But the moment Didyi started spouting love-talk—"*Bright kestrel, how I long for thy embrace. Thy touch, thy glance, the flower of thy face*"—Datu grimaced and dashed across their campsite to Gyrlady Tanaliín's scrape.

Two tiny bells were knotted beside the entrance flap by jesses of white horse hide. Datu slapped them a few times, shouting in Quadic, "Gyrlady Tanaliín, awake and see! Word comes at so miraculous a reach, we hear from friends who wander far in Leech!"

Three seconds later, Gyrlady Tanaliín burst from her esh

with the vigor of a geyser discovering a vent. She was barely dressed. Her bright, dyed-orange hair, the gray at its roots more pronounced every day since her Gyrgardu had left, was tousled and unkempt. Her face was frantic with joy.

"Where?"

Datu pointed, and Gyrlady Tanaliín bolted across camp to Didyi and Datu's scrape, disappearing beneath their esh's flap.

Even from where she stood, Datu could still hear the gyrlady's voice ring out: "Is that our Lanie? How clever of you to speak through Undies! This is new magic! Is Duantri well? Are you?"

Softly as she could, Datu tip-toed to their esh and crouched outside, moving the flap aside a scant half-inch, and watching the scene. Grown-ups interacted differently if they thought she was not among them, and though she might have to endure some more love-talk, she would also probably hear news that they might otherwise try to keep from her, or break to her in gentle roundaboutations that were more confusing—and therefore more anxiety-inducing—than plain speaking.

Datu preferred the latter. Especially when there was bad news. Like now.

Auntie Lanie was saying the *worst* news.

They hadn't caught the ghost yet. They weren't coming home.

Watching Gyrlady Tanaliín go slack in the circle of Didyi's protective arms, Datu felt sick. She was bound to Undies the way that Duantri and Tanaliín were bound to each other, in a rite so similar to the Rite of Bryddongard that, 'theologically speaking' (as Auntie Lanie would say), it was practically identical. As far as certain gods were concerned, Datu was Undies' gyrlady, and he was her Falcon Defender.

Therefore, Datu knew *exactly* how Gyrlady Tanaliín and Duantri felt, now that they were parted.

She shuddered. The one time she'd had to send Undies away had been awful, *terrible*, like trying to hold her breath for weeks on end. Like trying to make each of her heartbeats last twice as long. Like sitting with a crowd under a blazing sun, but only ever feeling chilled and alone.

She never wanted to do it again.

She didn't know how Gyrlady Tanaliín and Duantri could bear it.

Auntie Lanie finished explaining everything, talking too fast and using too many big words.

When she was done, everyone was silent for a long time.

"Well," Gyrlady Tanaliín said finally. "We... we knew the timing was uncertain, even with Stripes's flying speeds. We expected it. And we ourselves are... we are keeping quite busy on our pilgrimage. Are we not, Makkovian?"

Didyi agreed in a calm, even voice that belied the whiteness and tightness of his lips.

Datu's chest hurt to see it. Even with all his apologies and his sadness and his 'complexity,' it had been a long time since she had seen that look on his face. From her secret vantage point, she muttered the Quadic curse.

It was the worst word in any language. It rhymed with nothing, was ugly at its root, and was never meant to be spoken alongside any word but itself. She said it three times, fast, and felt both better and worse.

From inside the esh, another shocked silence. The grown-ups had heard.

Datu lifted her chin defiantly. She would accept any punishment. She'd do double camp chores, and practice her cavaquinho for an extra hour. She would ask pardon of all the gods. But she was *not* sorry.

Then all three grown-ups (if Undies could be considered a grown-up in this context) burst out laughing.

And when Gyrlady Tanaliín straightened up again, there was a light in her eyes and color in her face. Didyi's lips were full and smiling, red where he had tried to bite his laughter down. And Undies was making tail-chasing circles with delight, though Datu didn't know if it was him or Auntie Lanie in control at that moment.

"My very dear Lanie," said Gyrlady Tanaliín. "Just tell us how we can help."

In Auntie Lanie's pause, Undies sniffed himself. Then Auntie Lanie said, in a much lower voice than before, so low it sounded like her deep voice, "I need you to tell me a story."

Gyrlady Tanaliín and Didyi glanced at each other, confused. Datu's head was pressed so hard against the entrance flap that she was halfway through it.

"Tell me"—Auntie Lanie really was using both her voices now, although Datu didn't think Didyi or Gyrlady Tanaliín could hear the other one—"the most important story you know about the skinchangers of Taquathura."

IN OLDEN DAYS, *before the golden days, there was the first skinchanger of Athe, and she was dying.*

She was very old.

She had lived a hundred hundred hundred years.

She had seen her gods, the Three Lovers, call forth her people from the bed of lava where They made love, dreaming of a new kind of creature, different from all the rest who walked on Athe.

She had lain ten thousand eggs, which ten thousand other skinchangers had fertilized in passing.

She had witnessed ten-thousand hatchings, and the flourishing of her people.

She had roamed the uplands and the marshlands, the plains and dunes and mountains that were the territories of Taquathura, then ventured out into the realms beyond, even unto the far countries of the world, with a wild and wide-eyed curiosity.

Now, at the end of her life, she had a choice to make.

It is the same choice that every skinchanger thereafter, in their own time, is to be given.

To offer it, the Three Lovers appeared.

Yssimyss of Mysteries, Amahirra Mirage-Shaper, and Wykkyrri Who Is Ten-Thousand Beasts looked upon their firstborn daughter, aged in grace and wisdom, and smiled upon her with all Their many mouths and ways.

Daughter, *said They,* so many are the shapes you have amassed, so diverse in instinct and ability, in color, size, and durity, that now, at the end of your living, nothing on Athe is forbidden you.

From the unsounded depths of the ocean trenches to the heights of the unscalable peaks, the world is yours to explore.

You may spend the remainder of your days wandering, reveling in what We have made...

Or.

You may build yourself a hatchery, that you may lay one final egg.

A singular egg.

A special egg.

Your kernel egg.

You, who have lived an age and more, accreting pneuma to your kernel like a black hole accreting galaxies of stars, tell Us now: shall all this experience and wisdom and wonder die with you?

Or will you pass it on?

With those words, the Three Lovers left her to her choice.

The dying skinchanger chose to lay her kernel egg.

Not all skinchangers decide to do so. For those killed untimely, by accident or malice, this decision is ripped from them, and it is a loss like the loss of an ancient sun.

But there is grace even in this, for at the moment of their deaths, these beloved skinchangers are returned, with all their pneuma, to Doédenna: beloved sister of the Three Lovers.

For this first skinchanger, however—and for all those who followed in her path—her last long days were spent thus: in the hot sands of a hatchery, brooding her kernel egg.

From out of her own many-layered, high-souled mass of pneuma, she spun a new creation.

Herself alone fertilized it, of herself.

Herself alone fed it, of herself.

She sang the spellsong that the Three Lovers sang to her: a spellsong only skinchangers can know: the Kenosis Hymn, Last Outgiving, Pouring of Self from Self.

She sang and spelled, brooded and spun, fertilized and fed, until the kernel egg's shell shone clear as glass, until it glimmered like rainbows, and rang like silver bells.

Beneath the shell, within the yolk, a shadow moved and melted and changed.

A thousand thousand thousand remembered shapes would this kernelborn inherit, the moment it hatched into Athe.

A thousand thousand thousand desires and philosophies and instincts, but purified of its progenitor's personality, utterly itself alone, and new.

When the kernel egg was ready to hatch, the first skinchanger died.

Nothing remained of her.

All that she was, she had spent on her egg.

All that she left behind was the great husk of her empty durity: never to rot, never to crumble, but only, slowly, to petrify over the ages, into a hard black stone.

And so it was, and so it will be—until the olden days turn golden days, and are golden ever more.

DATU KNEW THE moment Auntie Lanie was gone from Undies' furry body. He scratched behind his ear with his least convenient paw, and panted up at them all, as if to say:

Behold! I am the very wonderful, beautiful, and best Mister Underwear Stones! Cuddle me, adore me, play games with me for all our waking hours! Especially thee, Mistress Sacred Datura, meat of my meat, blood of my blood, soul of my soul.

Datu opened her arms, allowing the wolf cub to leap into them—with a force that knocked her out of the esh, back on her behind in the dust. She sat still, letting Undies lick her face to his heart's content. His tongue was dry, as cool and smooth as suede.

In the esh, Gyrlady Tanalíin broke into a sob. "She's gone! Makkovian! I didn't get to say goodbye! I didn't ask her to tell, to tell Duantri…"

And she wept.

Datu stayed where she was, and did not try to peek inside again. She did not need to see. But she could hear Didyi saying, "If I miss her—so much my breath comes short each morning, and my heart slams hard at night, and every moment in between is stitching my skin with needles—then I can only imagine how hard, how very hard this is for you, my Tanaliín."

Tanaliín wailed, "I feel like I am dying!" and the sound chilled Datu so much that she crawled inside the esh, and wrapped her arms around the gyrlady's legs, and clung to them.

"Do not die, do not die," she chanted into Tanaliín's knees. "Please, please, please, do not die. Not when Auntie Lanie is gone and cannot raise you up again. Please, Gyrlady Tanaliín."

Eventually, the sobs and wailing slowed to a keening, and then to hiccups. Many minutes passed before Gyrlady Tanaliín patted the top of Datu's head, and tried to smile down at her.

It was terrible. A terrible smile. Red-rimmed, like she'd been weeping blood. Drowning in tears.

"Do not worry. Do not fear. Do not grieve," Gyrlady Tanaliín adjured Datu. Datu thought she was speaking not just to her, but to herself as well. "They *shall* triumph, my plumula, and soon."

Her voice was harsh, clotted with snot and grief, but the Quadic made it more beautiful when she said, "We'll see our loves again in happy throng, and meet in Ylkazarra when it's done."

Releasing the gyrlady's knees, Datu turned to bury her face in Undies' fur. She did not look up, or smile, or try to reassure anyone of anything. Nothing was certain—even if what Gyrlady Tanaliín said was true, and Duantri and Auntie Lanie were on the verge of laying the ghost to rest and coming home.

After all, Duantri was a Falcon Defender of Quadiíb. She had been teaching Datu some of her martial forms, each morning after they practiced their sothaín. Duantri was strong and graceful and powerful. She could probably fight off a whole army, naked, with her bare hands, then turn into a kestrel and leave all the corpses behind.

And then Auntie Lanie could *resurrect* the corpses, and turn them into an undead army, which would fall over itself to do whatever she wanted. Bones always danced for Auntie Lanie. She could do anything with them. *And* she talked to gods. *And* brought powerful sorcerers to their knees. *And* re-attached limbs that magic swords had severed—like she did with Didyi's arm.

Even when things were at their worst, and you were all alone, hanging from a crow's cage in the snow and cold, *and people were throwing spears at you*, Auntie Lanie would come and find you. She would not fail you. She would not fail.

So.

Duantri and Auntie Lanie *would* prevail. Of course they would. It was just…

Just… they were taking *so long*.

"I think," said Gyrlady Tanaliín, wearily, into the silence, "I shall take the remainder of our rest day alone."

"As you will, beloved," said Didyi. He let her go, but not before he kissed her with lingering kisses: on forehead, nose, mouth, and mouth again. "I will check on you at meal times, should you wish to eat."

"She *will* eat," Datu muttered direly into Undies' fur. "Or I will know the reason why."

If Auntie Lanie was here, and got sad, and forgot to eat like she sometimes did, Gyrlady Tanaliín would bring her food and sit by her bedroll all day until she remembered to put it in her mouth. And so would Datu do now. Or else.

Gyrlady Tanaliín loosed a watery laugh, and patted Datu's head one last time, her fingers tangling in the big, tangled puff of her uncombed hair, then shuffled like an old woman out of their esh.

Part Two

THE NETTLE-LANDS

Taquathura

CHAPTER SEVEN
Crystalskin

**Year 4826 of Higher and Lower Quadiíb
On Lasaqi, 1st of Anatha: the Third Month
19 Days till Spring Equinox**

CRACCHEN FOUND THE corpse at the foot of the bridge and knew immediately who it was, and who'd left it. Just like Irradiant Stones—to leave another gift in the dirt for his great-granddaughter to trip over. That's how he'd left Cracchen, after sucking him dry.

Will he not be surprised? asked his crystalskin, cold and amused. *That you did not stay where he put you? That you did not die like the filth he thought you? Nor did we remain, disembodied, howling for vengeance, in the sky. We are stronger now. All of us, together.*

Cracchen smiled to himself, crouching to inspect the corpse.

His left eye pulsed with cold, then flashed with an image: not of what lay before him, but of what stood behind him. One of the icicle shards currently mending a crack in his backbone was beaming a vision directly into his eye, like a mirror reflecting a mirror reflecting a mirror.

Behind his back, where she thought he could not see, the Falcon Defender of Quadiíb was glaring at him with suppressed loathing. Must've caught his smile, thought he was grinning at a corpse. Like the sight of it made him happy or something.

Let the birdie make an ass of herself, Cracchen thought. *She's earned nothing from me.*

His palm itched. He glanced at it. The skin there, no longer vulnerable but coated in frost, glimmered like a promise. Like it could push out a blade of ice sharp enough to rip her throat out. Let the Falcon Defender try to stab him in the back. She wasn't above cheating. Last time they'd fought, in Liriat, she'd fallen on him from the ceiling, completely naked. She'd gone from bird to girl in a second, and knocked him out flat without a fair fighting chance.

We will watch her for you, the crystalskin promised him. *But you must do nothing to compromise this alliance.*

Cracchen grunted.

"Lanie," called the Falcon Defender, still from behind him, still glaring. "Your pet wizard has found himself a plaything."

Pet, hissed his crystalskin.

Wizard, thought Cracchen, and his smile grew.

But as the Stones witch drew close, Cracchen lost control of his expression. Of his breath, too. Didn't feel like smiling anymore. Didn't know what his face was doing. For something—anything—to do, he pointed at the corpse. "Your grandpa left his trash in the road."

"I see that," said the Stones witch. Her eyes were wide and dark and soft, fixed on the corpse. She stripped off her glove, reached out her hand to touch it. Her left hand was an almost luminous gray, with iridescent undertones, like a black pearl. He'd noticed it before, but never like this. Never like his whole body was noticing. Never with *recognition*.

Cracchen watched her, frozen—and not just the icicle parts. Didn't know why she did this to him, or how to think of her, now that she was so different. Or maybe now that he was.

Miscellaneous Stones. Known her since she was a scrawny, acne-scrawled, frizzy-braided teenager, who dressed like an eyesore and bored on like a bookworm. Never *liked* her.

His brother, now... his dead brother, Scratten... Scratten'd always gone puppy-eyed and belly-up for the girl. Even back then. Before she was... this. His brother Haaken had always been more enigmatic about her. About everything, really—his magic or hers, power in general, the gods, their wizards, worldly politics, and the parts they all had to play.

But whatever it was that used to make Scratten blush like a debutante, that could make Haaken's opaque expression go, just for a second, translucent, Cracchen never got it. Sooner've shot the girl than look at her. She was Lirian. And a *Stones*. The enemy.

Then, she'd called the sky down into him.

Then she'd breathed winter into his wounds.

Power, she had granted him. Knowledge. The language of his forebears. And magic—magic such that Haaken himself might envy. She'd given him his fingers back, his toes. His left eye.

His crystalskin.

She'd exhausted herself sinking miracles into him—*him*, Cracchen Uthpansel Skrathmandan—who'd once tried to blow out her brains.

Never forget, said his crystalskin, with awe and wariness, *that she is a Stones*.

Ah, argued his crystalskin, for it was not one but many, *and yet—such a Stones!*

She almost married me, you know, Cracchen boasted internally, hoping to gain that reverence the crystalskin showed for her, for himself.

What he didn't tell them, because they already knew, because they were inside him, was that it had never come to anything, their potential union. At the time, his mordda had been plotting to secure the Stones bloodline—and its legendary death magic—for the Skrathmandan name. Sari had proposed marriage to Miscellaneous Stones on behalf of her triplet sons: Scratten, Cracchen, and Haaken, offering them to her on the grounds that the Blackbird Bride herself took multiple spouses in her great court of Rook. Said she'd forgive the Stoneses' family debt to House Skrathmandan if the little witch just cooperated.

Smart-ass fifteen-year-old that she was, Miscellaneous Stones refused. Refused all of them. Refused Scratten—who'd've adored her the rest of his dunderheaded days, and who shut himself away for weeks to write bad poetry. Refused Haaken—her equal in power, though she'd not have known that, since no one did except their family. Refused Cracchen, who'd been so relieved, he'd started a fistfight at a local public house.

Now, though…

What might we accomplish, with such a wife? She could lay the world at our feet.

His thought? The crystalskin's? All of them, somehow, in agreement?

Cracchen realized he was still kneeling in the mud, staring at the corpse, imagining marriage to the travel-stained necromancer squatting next to him. He glanced at her from the corner of his left eye.

She looked the same as ever. Her ostentatious spectacles—gold-gilt frames, enameled flowers and vines, little sparks of gems—sat askew on her nose. Her hair was scraped back in braids and stuffed under a fluffy knitted hat. She was bundled in so many colorful shawls and sweaters, she looked like some deranged effigy staked out in the barley fields to scare crows away.

"I…" the witch swallowed. Her left hand moved through the corpse's dry-as-hay hair like a silver rainbowfish through river weeds. Lurid colors, that hair. Unnatural. Purple as violets, green as ferns. It crackled under her touch. "I didn't know that skinchangers were so colorful."

Cracchen was surprised into a grunt. "Yeah. That's what they look like. In their natural forms. When not… flaunting a stolen shape."

He'd seen a fair few skinchangers while traveling as a guard with the merchant caravans of Lower Quadiíb. Mostly they appeared as humans when dealing with humans, but some had long-standing relationships with the merchants, and relaxed enough to show their true colors from time to time.

Now the crystalskin was whispering its collective knowledge to him. He cleared his throat and added, "The way they look, when they're like that, it's called their 'yolkform.' That's the shape they're born in. Hatched in," he corrected himself.

The witch's face brightened. She'd liked that. New words.

She leaned closer, asking, "Are the patterns on their skin to help them to blend in? Like camouflage?"

Encouraged by her interest, the crystalskin flooded him with images, vocabulary, lore. Apparently, it didn't want to speak through his mouth, as it had done that first night. Wanted to remain hidden, for now.

Fine by Cracchen. He didn't mind taking the credit.

"The opposite," he said and spouted one of his borrowed words. "Aposematism."

The witch glanced up sharply, searching his face.

Cracchen bristled. What? He couldn't know big words?

But all she said was, "Could you define that, please?" and he felt his chest puffing out a little. The mail that covered him expanded with his breath.

Felt good, knowing something the witch didn't.

"Bright colors and patterns," he explained, "to make them stand out. A warning. A skinchanger is like a venomous reptile or a poison dart frog. Doesn't profit a predator to approach her. She is at the apex. Has too many advantages."

This corpse was no apex predator now; Irradiant Stones had brought her low. She was shriveled like kindling, all plumpness sucked from her flesh. Her limbs were like twigs, the skin wrapping her alien internal structures like the leather of a hilt.

None of the bright colors of her yolkform, however, had faded. Her skin still gleamed like fresh paint: silver and indigo in a bold and swirling pattern. Her eyes were frozen open in death. Two different colors: white jade, green jade. Gemstone-hard. Petrified.

Heterochromatic, the crystalskin supplied for him.

"They're heterochromatic," Cracchen coughed. When the witch brought her curious gaze to him again, he blurted without thinking, "We had a cat like that once."

Exactly like that, the crystalskin approved.

"I like cats," the witch said wistfully. "We could never keep pets at Stones Manor because"—she shrugged—"Nita."

It took Cracchen a second to remember that 'Nita' was the late Amanita Muscaria Stones, noted contract killer, blood-courier to Erralierra Brackenwild, the (also late) Blood Royal of Liriat.

"Animals are fragile," he said gruffly. He'd pulled out his fair share of lizard tails, set fire to ants and beetles, plucked feathers from living birds. Not anymore. Much more satisfying to knock a man's teeth out. There was pleasure in a fair fight. He had killed for a living, though. Just another job. He'd liked captaining the caravan guard better.

The witch couldn't hear his thoughts—could she?—but for some reason, she scooted a few inches away from him. Her lips pushed briefly out, like she was running her tongue along her teeth, and the skin of her gray left hand went dull, patchy in places, and pimpled in sores.

But when he blinked and looked closer, the wounds were gone, her skin smooth, its pearly luster returned. Her face was bent over the dead skinchanger. She was tracing the patterned hide of the yolkform with her fingertips.

"It's the mistle thrush," she said, her voice hushed. "The one from the bush."

"Yes," the crystalskin agreed in Cracchen's mouth. The transition from his own voice to the one redoubled with echoes was so smooth, Cracchen almost felt like he was the one speaking. *Choosing* to speak. Never felt like this when the ghost was riding him. This was… easy.

"Irradiant Stones has jumped bodies," the crystalskin continued, "before crossing the bridge into Madinatam. Doubtless he ambushed an older skinchanger, one who had more pneuma amassed. He will need it to feed on."

The witch sighed, glancing up from the body to stare across the bridge, before lifting her gaze to the dark scarp rising up the other side, and to the city atop it, awaiting them.

"As you warned us," she whispered.

"As we warned you," said the crystalskin. It didn't sound smug, but Cracchen felt proud on its behalf.

Not a bad thing, sharing his voice with his crystalskin. Made him sound smarter. Made him *think* better, too. He'd hated all his teachers, growing up—Rookish sycophants, every last one, determined that their precious Blackbird Bride's Skaki chattel prove a useful investment.

Scratten ate it all up, that learning. Haaken was smarter: pretended to be stupid, then learned in secret. But Cracchen dug his heels in. The only thing he'd let them teach him was fighting. Learn that, he'd figured, and some day, he could fight his way free.

Now he was free. Reborn, even. Could learn whatever he wanted, from whomever he wanted. Even magic—previously Haaken's bailiwick.

We will teach you whatever you want to know, said his crystalskin. *Whatever we are is you. Is yours.*

"A most piteous sight," remarked the Falcon Defender, moving from her guard position behind him to crouch at the witch's other side. Her cursory examination fell upon the corpse, before she directed a longer, keener look at the witch. "Are you all right, Lanie?" She took that gray left hand, now utterly unmarked, and chafed it.

"Grandpa Rad... stripped her." The witch's voice was lullaby-quiet, like she was kneeling at a sleeping infant's creche. "He stripped the skinchanger's kernel, took all her pneuma. This is all that's left. It's just durity. I can't feel *her* anymore. Usually, with dead accident, I can feel the echo of the substance inside it. A link to Doédenna's cloak, where the memory of life is kept stitched. That's how I can sing the substance back, temporarily—through that link. But with this"—she gestured at the corpse—"there's nothing to call back. It's gone. He ate it. It's all *wrong*."

The witch glared from the husked skinchanger, first to the Falcon Defender, then to Cracchen, binding them to each other, and to her, through her rage. The pinpricks of yellow in her eyes flared to flames, which spread until the yellow light consumed both iris and whites.

Cracchen squinted. His nose stung like someone had zested lemon directly into his sinuses.

She is splendid, murmured the crystalskin. *She is a walking terror of Athe*.

"This is not how skinchangers are supposed to die," the Stones witch declared, standing up and brushing off her hands. "This is not how *anyone* is supposed to die. It's not *death* at all. It's just… emptiness."

LANIE WATCHED DUANTRI, in her kestrel form, circling the city on the scarp. With every gyre, she flew wider and higher, finally disappearing into the bluebell-blue of the late winter sky.

Stripes floated at Lanie's side, insistently butting his head into the palm of her hand. She scratched absently behind his ears, like Datu did with Undies, and at last lowered her gaze.

Better that Duantri stay above for now. Better not risk angering the skinchangers before they had a chance to make their case to the authorities.

Still, she hated being apart.

Lightly gnawing on one knuckle, Lanie contemplated the limestone bridge before her. Far below its triple arches, the River Fet rushed and roared.

The Fet was one of two rivers bounding Witch Queen's City, the other being the River Fragor on the far side of the scarp. Both rivers ran through Liriat as well, far to the southwest, though Lanie had known them by different names: the Poxbarge and the Whistlebelly.[6]

She could scarcely believe, looking down at the rushing river now, that they were same bodies of water. In the sea-level region of Liriat, the rivers meandered along, shallow and sluggish,

---

6 The Lirian nomenclature hints at a long history of communicable diseases spread through inland port cities, as well as the inadvisability of drinking river water without first thoroughly straining and boiling it.

warmish and wide, besmirched with sediment and sewage and other run-off. Here in the uplands, the Fet and Fragor ran swift in their slim, rocky beds, their waters tumultuous, cold and clear.

Across the river, on the other side of the bridge, the scarp rose steeply from a rocky embankment. At least a hundred fifty feet high, maybe three miles long, but barely a hundred yards wide, the scarp was like the carcass of some rough leviathan, turned to stone in its final slumber. It rested between the two silver serpents of its river guardians, the waters continuously carving away at the bedrock.

This idiosyncrasy of geography, Lanie knew from the reading she'd done on the area, was due to overlapping lava flows from a time before history. Religious texts referred to those lava flows as the divine couch where once the Three Lovers had slept: where Yssimyss of Mysteries, Amahirra Mirage-Shaper, and Wykkyrri Who Is Ten Thousand Beasts had all bedded each other in love; and where, in the molten heat of Their mutual desire, they had created the first skinchangers of Athe.

Sometime later, humans came and built a city on the scarp.

Sometime after that, the skinchangers took it back for themselves.

Lanie wasn't clear on the details or the timeline. If she ever made it back to Quadiíb, she would seek out a gyrlady specializing in Taquathuran history, and take an independent study with her.

At the top of the scarp, she could barely make out the squat structures crowding the narrow ridge. Built with an eye for defense over beauty, the blunt buildings jutted like bad teeth, ground down by the meteorological caprice of centuries. A dismal sight indeed, were it not for the glowing flora running rampant over the old, umbrageous buildings.

Scarlet lichens tapestried the basalt walls and streets, interspersed with vibrant patchworks of tangerine, marmalade, velvety saffron, and all threaded through with startling veins of viridian. From the baked red clay of the rooftops spilled enthusiastic fountains of star-shaped ivy, the pointed purple lobes of the leaves all limned in rusty orange. It flowed down the dour defensive walls, covered the narrow streets and alleys, and flooded the edges of the scarp. From there, it frothed and fizzed over the sheer cliffside in lusty profusion, falling like draping hair all the way into the River Fet.

Lanie was surprised the ivy hadn't completely overtaken the bridge. But, though it had smothered the gatehouse on the far side, the ivy stopped just short of the granite outcropping where the bridge was anchored, as if someone had made it their business to regularly, and brutally, chop it back.

Or chomp it back, Lanie considered, imagining a skinchanger with the appropriate-sized teeth.

"At least it'd be an herbivore," she muttered.

"What?" asked Cracchen.

"Nothing. Ready to cross?"

Gleaming in the creamy morning light, the limestone bridge leapt the River Fet like a long-legged hare in three graceful bounds.

Lanie gestured for Stripes to proceed her. He nipped at her wrist, his always-bared teeth lightly grazing her skin, and began zipping across the long ivory path, never once touching down. Though they had wrapped the skinchanger corpse in blankets and strapped her to him, and loaded him down with all their goods and equipment, Stripes did not sag even a little under the weight.

Watching him fly straight and true, Lanie grinned fondly. Stripes was full of pep this morning: a measure by which she could gauge her own vigor. A relief, after her prodigious outpouring of magic the day before yesterday, to have bounced back so quickly. For the work ahead, she would need all her power.

And what better embodies power, she thought, *than an undead, airborne tiger rug, grinning down at all he surveys?*

Cracchen cleared his throat.

Lanie glanced at him. What she could see of his face under the

118

cowl of Duantri's extra robe glittered like snow by moonlight. His skin was overlaid with a delicate veil of interlocking ice mail. Lanie hoped, after all he'd endured, that the sky wizards would protect him against any further torment, and keep him safe from Grandpa Rad.

She hoped that, once he felt safe, he would not turn against her.

Cracchen jerked his chin toward the bridge. "What are we waiting for? Want me to hold your hand?" His lip curled in derision.

Lanie almost rolled her eyes—but stopped when she saw that his gaze cut away from her to the bridge. A current of sparkling color rolled through the patchwork of him, lighting up the various frost flowers and icicle parts in a fireworks display he seemed to have no control over.

Something about the bridge was frightening him.

No, not him.

The sky wizards.

Lanie stepped closer. She did, in fact, take his hand. It was cold, and it clung to her own, with a sort of unconscious helplessness. She brought her other hand up to cover their entwined fingers, asking softly, "Cracchen. What were Skakmaht and Taquathura to each other a hundred years ago?"

There. That flashing fear again. Panicked lights, moving through his prosthetics. Deep green. Cold blue. A hint of pink.

But Cracchen snapped, "How should I know?" and jerked his hand out from between hers. Then, for good measure, he crossed his arms over his chest, hiding his fingers in his armpits, and lifting his chin with the belligerence of a bull. All the strange, swirling lights in his skin dimmed and darkened.

Did the sky wizards go into hiding? Lanie wondered. *Or did Cracchen stuff them down?*

"Hmn," she said.

Cracchen huffed in response, and stomped onto the bridge.

Lanie hesitated. But what other course was open to them? The sky wizards themselves had insisted on going to Witch

Queen's City. The ghost was here. They had found one corpse already. There would be others, if she didn't move, and quickly.

Rolling her shoulders, Lanie stepped onto the bridge, and—

—and—

—and then, the moment her feet touched the limestone, her anxieties, her doubts, the aches in her muscles and joints, her guilt and hunger and mind-eating fear, her flame-white fury at Grandpa Rad, the murders he'd committed, the mockery he'd made of his victims—all of it, *everything*—drained away through the bottoms of her feet.

Lambent pleasure licked up from the limestone itself. It suckled and lapped and nibbled, absorbing anything back into it that was not delight. Lanie entered an ecstatic focus, her consciousness expanding all the way into the bridge—pier, point, and arch barrel. The limestone pressed up through her boots and entered her pulse, shocking her with its alertness and purpose, its vigorous welcome. The stones themselves seemed to be wafting her aloft, lending her their strength, so that they, not she, should bear the weight of her woes for a while.

Limestone! Wonderstruck, Lanie slowed her steps, picking up and placing each foot as if walking on air-buoyed silk. Thoughts frisked through her mind like gems through a tumbler.

Limestone! It's hardly stone *at all, but animal made mineral. A symphony of skeletons. Microscopic once-life. The dead as architecture. The dead as a bridge from the known into the unknown...*

All she wanted was to sprawl across the center keystone and pray. The Three Lovers may have built Witch Queen's City, but Saint Death was in this bridge, as She was everywhere. Lanie could feel Her love in every step.

Her toes twinkled. Her heels hummed. The bridge thrummed. All the tiny fossils caught in the limestone beamed their nummulite-shaped memories up through her legs. Like walking on radiant coins. They sang to her, chimed and belled and hummed the tales of their tiny lives and tiny deaths. Millions of them. Millions and millions.

Limestone! Her new favorite rock!

Rapturous, Lanie-as-bridge moved through the ages of Athe—now-bone, now-stone, now-structure, now-bone again—until she smashed face-first into Cracchen.

She bounced off his back, her nose smarting, and cussed in Quadic. It was Datu's favorite word. She said it again.

Now-Lanie, she thought morosely, rubbing her nose. *Lanie, not bridge.*

It was only when her boundaries were reasserting themselves, as she readjusted her spectacles—dangling off one ear like a drunken tightrope walker—that her wits returned enough to wonder: *What on Athe stopped him in his tracks like that?*

Stepping on the heels of that thought, Lanie darted around Cracchen's rigid body, looking ahead for signs of danger.

She froze.

She backed up a step. Backed, yes, right up into Cracchen. His hands grasped her shoulders, steadying her. But also keeping her still—in front of him.

At the end of the bridge, blocking their exit to the gatehouse, stood the most enormous creature Lanie had ever seen.

CHAPTER EIGHT
God~Beasts

YOU COULD SAY *it's human-shaped*, Lanie thought, *if the human were gigantic. And a rhinoceros. A sort of giant-like, rhino-like, human-like hodgepodge of a person with heterochromatic eyes.*

One round eye was a pale amber, the other dark brown.

Skinchanger.

"But," she breathed, "what kind is it?" It was so huge. *So huge.*

"Gunugg." Cracchen muttered the word, a puff of bitter breath against her ear. Lanie rubbed the delicate lobe, knocking frost into the bright air. The echo under his voice meant it was the sky wizards, not the man, who spoke.

"Gunugg," Lanie repeated.

"God-beast. One of the Witch Queen's personal guard."

God-beast, she mouthed but did not vocalize. An apt description.

The creature was twice Cracchen's height—and Cracchen already towered over her—and thrice his width, round-jowled and wrinkle-whittled and *slabbed* with muscle. It—*they?*—wore their hair in two, thick, clay-dark braids that wrapped their elongated brow like a tholobate. Their skin was the color of dust and dead lace, with a bruise-like mottled pattern. Two bony protrusions jutted from the front of their face: one from the bridge of their nose, another from their brow. Their ears were like rolled-up leaves, twitching along the sides of their skull.

They held Stripes by the scruff of his neck. He dangled, looking kittenish and pathetic.

This was a ruse, Lanie was sure.

Almost sure.

She swallowed, wet her lips. She tried to summon the authority of an Erralierra Brackenwild or a Bran Fiakhna, that she might leave the gunugg in no doubt of her right to walk this bridge. But thoughts of the late Blood Royal and the still-living Rook of Rook did nothing but give her tongue the taste of dirty wool. At the last second, she switched to channeling Tanaliín instead. Tanaliín always tempered command with kindness, power with humor.

"Greetings, gunugg of Madinatam," she began. Good. Her voice was loud and clear, not too quivery or abrasive. "We are strangers to your city, though my companion has had dealings with Taquathuran merchants in the past. Tell me, please—why have you detained my mount?"

"Wherefore, wizard," the gunugg demanded, "does your mount fly before you, bearing one of our dead on its back like a trophy? Is it for sport?"

"Oh, no!" Lanie cried, distressed, losing her tether to Tanaliín's assured tranquility. "No—it's not like that. We found her at the foot of the bridge. We were bringing her to... to your authorities. We know what killed her. We're hunting her murderer—have been, for months. It's... there's... your city is in danger," she finished, and if her voice quavered a little, at least it sounded completely earnest.

The gunugg's gaze shifted to Cracchen. Their lashes were long and curling, pale beige in color.

"You bring danger into our city," they agreed, "when you walk in the company of criminals."

"C-criminals?"

Lanie knew that Cracchen had been, for a time, Royal Assassin of Liriat, and had no doubt butchered *reams* of people, just like Nita. But surely he'd've mentioned it—before insisting they all traipse into the capital—if he'd murdered a few skinchangers. Twisting to look over her shoulder at him, she asked, "Care to expl—"

She stopped so hard she bit her tongue.

A glimmering helm of bespelled ice now covered Cracchen's entire skull. Its thick, blue-hued visor distorted his features, and the lace-mail-veil overlaying his skin was beginning to goosebump up into nubby piles of hoarfrost. She watched as the newest layer hardened into wicked little points and spikes.

She grasped his arm. Her palm seared with cold.

"Cracchen." She shook him. "Talk to me. Tell me what's going on."

Cracchen did not move. She could not tell if he could hear or see her from behind his helmet, or if it was even he who was peering out from his own eyes. When she tried to tighten her grip, the ice itself repelled her, shooting slender needles into her hand that melted the moment she withdrew.

Behind her, the bridge began to tremble. Lanie whipped about to see the gunugg marching closer, each footstep like thunder.

"Let the criminal turn himself in. We will escort you into the city, that you may lay your case before Tam."

Lanie held up her gray left hand. "Stop." Both her voices boomed out of her, deep and surface.

The gunugg did stop, their alien features expressing wariness and surprise.

"Release my mount, and move aside," Lanie said. "We mean no harm. We will come with you peacefully. But I will not let you detain any of my companions without cause. Step back."

"Without cause?" the gunugg bellowed. "You have brought an egg-stealer into our midst!"

"I don't know what that mea—" but before Lanie could finish, the gunugg lowered its horned head and stampeded forward, the limestone shaking with each bound.

Three things happened then.

Lanie's left hand clenched.

Stripes turned his head and bit the arm holding him.

And the bridge bucked.

Once again, Lanie became the limestone, and the limestone became her. Each, sharing in the other, creating the third of the three states: ectenica, the immaterial material of undeath. Fluid, malleable, ready to be shaped to her hand.

The limestone willed her to use it, use all of it, every lost fossil, every forgotten coral, shell, and shard of bone.

It writhed, greedy to please.

How does she want us will us need us? Unspooled into the thinnest ribbon? Shattered to a cloud of dust? Rising to defend her like the tail of a scorpion—metasoma, telson, vesicle and venom glands? At her word, we sting!

Oh, dear. Saint Death help her. The bridge was a little *too* eager, perhaps.

Lanie flattened her hand, tilted it, sent soothing thoughts into the limestone. When the bridge was calm enough to listen, she had but to hint at what she truly wanted from it, and it leapt to obey.

Like a long-time dance partner who could foretell her every mood, her every move, the bridge rose sharply in the middle, with Lanie and Cracchen riding the stable center of the keystone. From the pinnacle, the two sides slanted down, steep and smooth. The gunugg tried to keep their purchase, but the limestone slide was inexorable. Scrambling and slipping, the gunugg clawed for a handhold, but gently and dreamily, the limestone slid the great god-beast all the way back down to the gatehouse, where they landed in a massive heap.

Stripes did a quick loop over their head, batting at one of their sensitive ears with a paw, but Lanie whistled sharply through her teeth, calling him off. He flew to her as she stepped down off the keystone.

The ectenica rose to greet her feet, forming stairs where she walked. Slowly, she moved toward the gunugg, who was still sprawled in a confused heap of itself upon the dead ivy detritus. Left hand still outstretched, Lanie allowed her fingers to relax. She opened her palm and turned it up.

"Suhm'sda, se'qa, sihesh," she said, speaking three of the twelve Quadic apologies with both her voices. "Truly, good gunugg, I do not mean you, or any of the skinchangers of

Taquathura, any harm. I am Miscellaneous Immiscible Stones, priest of Doédenna, friend to the Three Lovers. Please. Let us come peaceably into your city—for I must speak with your Witch Queen about the peril stalking your people."

At her words, the gunugg lifted their head, the spooked panic fading from their face. Their leaf-like ears twitched.

"Stones?" they asked, slowly rising to their three-toed feet. "But why... why did you not say so from the start?"

LANIE WASN'T SURE *what* she was expecting the Witch Queen of Leech to look like—but this twiggy-limbed skinchanger, with the face of a child and the eyes of a crone, wasn't it.

The Witch Queen wore her yolkform to receive her audience. The patterns on her skin were striking. Her entire dextral side, starting at the hairline and running to her bare right foot, was the gleaming black of pitch. Her sinistral side was the brilliant crimson of flame. Her right eye was a great golden moon, her left eye a well for drowning in. Her hair was blacker than Lanie's, fine as silk, longer than she was tall. It spilled around her body like blackwater cascades, clothing her more modestly than did her plain homespun robe, ragged and abbreviated, and tied carelessly at the waist.

She was squatting on an enormous egg.

This, unless Lanie missed her guess, was her kernel egg.

Which meant that Tam, the great Witch Queen of Leech, after four centuries of ruling the uplands and the monsters who roamed them, was dying.

The kernel egg was about the size of a large globe, similar to one that used to spin in solitary splendor in Stones Library. As a child, Lanie used to play with the globe, standing barefoot on Stripes the tiger rug (not yet animate at that time, nor, for that matter, yet named Stripes) and rotating the sphere in its free-standing cradle mount. She would polish the titanwood stand with her sleeve, trace the numbers etched into the haloing brass of the meridian, and try to imagine a world outside the walls of her home.

Like the globe,[7] the kernel egg was many-colored. But instead of bearing latitude lines in gold, longitude lines in silver, oceans of blue jasper, continents limned in mother of pearl, and nations cut from lapis lazuli, pink quartz, white jade, red jasper, tiger's eye, abalone, amethyst, turquoise, and various marbles, all the bejeweled and gemlike colors of the Witch Queen's kernel egg were constantly moving and shifting. From time to time, the eggshell would shimmer and go opaque, a slick liquid-mercury surface in which Lanie could see her own curious expression reflected back. Then, slowly, this opacity would fade until the shell was translucent—not like glass, but like an opalized fossil, and she could peer through the shell to the restless shadow of the embryo within.

The shadow flickered like a heartbeat. With each flicker, it changed into another shape, more than Lanie could count, no two shapes repeated, for as long as she watched.

All of the Witch Queen's long life of amassed pneuma, poured into this newly made thing.

How much life does she have left? Lanie wondered. *How long does she have left?*

The heady scent of honeysuckle, lavender, lilac, and lily wafted off the Witch Queen's skin and from the mottled cuticle of the kernel egg she brooded. Skinchanger magic, Lanie was rapidly learning, smelled like wildflowers: a bridal bouquet for her deep senses.

The Witch Queen had not blinked once since Lanie had entered her hatchery, floating on Stripes's back with the skinchanger in her arms. She had lowered the body gently at the foot of the egg, and waited for the Witch Queen to speak.

But the Witch Queen did not speak.

Scratching the side of her neck, Lanie asked, "Do I address you as Blood Royal? Your Majesty? Your Resplendence? Some other title?"

---

7 An heirloom piece of the Stones family, modeled after the famous 'Faht'affaal,' or 'Stone Fruit': the first known to-scale globe of Athe in existence, currently kept under glass in the Rare Collections room at the University Library of Ylkazarra.

The Witch Queen, still without blinking, replied, "I am Tam."

"Tam?"

No reply.

"As in," Lanie ventured, "Madinatam?"

A slow nod.

Lanie found herself nodding back. The Quadic word 'Mahthhyna,' often written 'Madina' by non-Quadic speakers, could be translated as 'city' or 'principality.' Perhaps the capital of Taquathura had been called 'Tam's City' for as long as Tam had ruled it. Perhaps, after Tam was gone, the capital would be called Madina-something-else. When this was a human city, when Taquathura was occupied by the humans who called it 'Leech,' this place had just been called King's City. She remembered that from the old maps in Stones Library.

The gunugg at the bridge had also called the Witch Queen 'Tam.' Just Tam, no honorific. Now Lanie wondered if the title 'Witch Queen,' like the name 'Leech,' was a human appellation, divorced from the reality of the denizens of Taquathura.

"Hello, Tam," she said. "Thank you for agreeing to meet with me. You can call me Lanie."

"Lanie." Tam's head slowly tilted to one side. The edges of her lips curled: half scarlet, half ebony. "As in, Miscellaneous Stones?"

Lanie sat up straighter on Stripes's back. "Yes. As I told your... your gunugg."

She was glad now that Stripes had insisted on maintaining a strict levitating height of three feet above the hatchery's sandy floor. It put Lanie and Tam, perched atop her kernel egg, eye level with each other. (Stripes obviously considered Lanie to be the equal of any queen, and opined she deserved a seat of power worthy of her: namely, himself.)

"Tam, tell me," Lanie said, "what reason did your gunugg have for attacking my companion at the bridge? Why was he not allowed to accompany me into your presence?"

She had left Cracchen, guarded by the nervous gunugg, in the antechamber to the hatchery. She didn't want to leave him—

not least because she could see the poor gunugg was half out of their mind with dread and loathing, and from the look of it, poor Cracchen and his poor sky wizards obviously felt the same.

Each time she'd glanced back at him, as they'd processed through Madinatam's narrow streets—navigating the crowded Plaza Inconi to the stares of many strange onlookers, passing through a heavy portcullis that was more ivy and rust than gate, and moving deeper into the heart of the keep—she'd noticed that Cracchen's gloss of ice had piled a new layer onto itself.

As each new layer melted over the last one, it re-froze, hardened, and smoothed out. By the time she had left him in the antechamber, Cracchen was completely covered in a panoply of heavy plate armor. Every piece of it—sallet to sabaton, greave, gauntlet, cuisse and cuirass, vambrace, pauldron, helmet, and so forth—was the same sapphirine blue of his helmet: a pure, deep, magical ice that only magic could break.

When she'd asked if he'd be all right, left on his own with the gunugg while she sought audience with the Witch Queen, he'd made no reply. Not out loud anyway. But his helmet did grow a few more spikes.

The gunugg had tried to reassure her: "No harm will come to him. But under no circumstances will an egg-stealer be allowed access to the hatchery."

Egg-stealer. That was the second time the gunugg had used those words.

Lanie wanted to ask Tam about it—if Tam ever deigned to answer her first question.

The Witch Queen's pauses were extremely long, as disconcerting as her unblinking eyes. Lanie wondered if this was a tactic to make her feel uncomfortable, or if it was merely a symptom of Tam's old age.

Or both.

She opened her mouth to repeat her first question, just in case Tam did not comprehend it the first time.

Then, in a blur of movement so fast Lanie could barely track it, Tam slithered out of her squat. She sprawled, belly-down, over the curvature of the kernel egg, and slid arms-first almost all the way to the floor. But before she smashed down completely, she braked herself, bare feet clutching the sides of the kernel egg, and paused to scoop up a handful of sand. Treasure secured, Tam slithered upright again and crossed her legs neatly, like a child at sothaín.

In one graceful gesture, she extended her arm, offering her handful of sand to Lanie.

Bewildered, Lanie scooted forward on Stripes, and opened up her palm to receive it. Silken stuff, fine and faintly golden. The sand shirred lightly under the stir of her breath. It was *baking*-hot.

"It's shells," she blurted in surprise. "Egg shells. Right?"

Lanie looked up and around, seeing the hatchery with new eyes. The sand, knee-deep in some places, breast-high in others, covered the length of the vast room, which had probably been some kind of great hall or throne room back when humans had first built this keep. How many egg-shells, pulverized to particulate, did it take to make such dunes? Tens of thousands? Hundreds of thousands?

Only the Witch Queen's kernel egg was visible at present, but Lanie wondered if other eggs were buried here, in the simmering, shimmering heat. She met Tam's glorious, golden-midnight gaze.

"In Madinatam," Tam explained in her slow, low voice, "we come here"—she tilted her head again, indicating the great ruined hall, full of nothing but sand and ivy leaves—"to lay our eggs. We incubate them till emergence. Elsewhere in the uplands, we lay our eggs under bush, in cave. We keep them concealed, hoping the egg-stealers will not come. Hoping they will not take our eggs, and murder our young. For many years, we have been let in peace. But we remember."

Diffuse light fell from the high windows. They were empty of glazing, fringed only with the stained-glass teeth of centuries past. Remnants of the enormous tapestries that had once draped the stone walls were now rotting in the ubiquitous ivy. Scraps of silk and wool snarled the star-shaped leaves like embroidery floss. The handsome hammer-beam ceiling was carved with wooden faces, each one wearing a far more human expression than the one on Tam's.

Tam's face was smooth, almost insectile in its lack of changeability. Human words came out of it, and other than the coloring, it might be mistaken for a human face. It just... didn't *move* right.

Humans, Lanie knew, had a tendency to conjure human faces out of anything—from a piece of toast to a passing cloud. Mountains became mimetoliths;[8] moons stared down with cratered eyes and crescent smiles.

Skinchangers, she thought, *must use that to their advantage.*

But lack of expression did not mean lack of *awareness*. More than Tam seemed to be aware of Lanie: the ivy, the stone walls and wooden rafters, the rippling sand underfoot, the kernel egg itself—all seemed bristlingly attuned to her. Awake. Wary. Waiting for her reaction.

"I," swore Lanie, "have not come to take your eggs." Her hand touched her heart, which ached at the thought. "I am here for one thing only. There is a ghost who... who I must return to Saint Death's cloak. He is my responsibility. He came to Madinatam for skinchanger bodies. He wants to... to mine them for their pneuma."

She tried to keep her voice calm but firm. "We mean to extract him and be on our way. Your eggs will be safe as soon as I can get him away from this city. Soon, I hope. In time for... for your great rite."

Tam nodded acknowledgement. The egg beneath her bare legs pulsed and glowed.

---

8 In the uplands of Taquathura, any massive face emerging from a hillside might be a trick of the light, or a passing whimsy of the imagination. Or it could be an actual skinchanger who had supped the pneuma of the landscape and was now bound to its shape. You never knew, with skinchangers.

"On Izmeerya," she murmured, "my hymn is done. At dusk, when night comes equal to the day. That is when she shall hatch. And I shall be no more."

Izmeerya, Lanie thought. *The High Holy Fire Feast of Spring Equinox.* The hour Tam had chosen for her death.

"Please," she said, "give me permission to do my work. I can see that my companion has disturbed your peace. I can ask him to wait outside the city. Please do not detain him, or... or hurt him."

Tam raised her red left hand in response. She flicked her index finger straight up, and a sharp black nail, half as long as her finger, gleamed like a jet blade aimed at the ceiling.

"And what," she asked, "of her?"

From the furthest broken window at the end of the hatchery, high up near the hammerbeam ceiling, there came a piercing *killy-killy-klee*.

A mob of birds dove into the room in pursuit of one—a kestrel, desperately fleeing the rest.

CHAPTER NINE
Egg-Stealers

KESTREL PLUMMETED. BIRDS everywhere.

No escape. Not ivy. Not rafters. Not shadow. Eyes everywhere.

Motley flock. Squawking. Shrieking. Defecating. Driving. Herding.

Not birds. Alter-birds. No show-offs. Not mating. Too varied. All sizes.

Focused. Raucous. Not real.

Skinchangers.

Break necks? Kill some? Small ones? Starlings? Sparrows?

No. Alter-birds. Not real. Skinchangers. Consequences.

Hide. Hide. Nowhere to hide. Nowhere to fly.

Not ivy. Alter-ivy. More-than-alive.

There. Below. Familiar. Bright hat. Glass-flash. Human. Friend.

Lanie.

Kestrel, desperate, dropped.

TAM'S RED ARM stretched out. Her robe slipped down a bare scarlet shoulder.

Her shoulder bulged once, then flared out into an enormous, gelatinous bell, orange-amber in color, with eight pointed lobes like a star. From where her arm had been now unspooled hundreds of hair-like tentacles, each more than a hundred feet long, whipping out to snatch the kestrel from the air.

"No!" Lanie surged forward at the same time that Stripes,

133

responding to her distress, lunged at the Witch Queen. Jarred, Lanie rocked forward on his neck. Her teeth clamped her tongue, drew blood. She clutched the tiger rug's ears to stabilize herself.

Stripes never made it. He slammed nose-first into a curtain of ivy, which had shaken loose from the ceiling and fallen upon him, tangling them in rust-edged, purple leaves.

Vines twisted around Lanie's arms and waist. She struggled, tearing at them, crying out, "Duantri! Duantri!" frantic to pry the Gyrgardu loose from Tam's stinging tentacles.

At the tumult, the door to the hatchery burst open and the gunugg with the rhinoceros features rushed in. On heavy legs and three-toed feet, they thundered for the kernel egg, putting their body between it and danger. But their flickering gaze seemed to perceive danger approaching from all directions, and they flung back their head and loosed a bellow that Lanie recognized as a call.

Reinforcements were coming.

Realizing this, her heart beat all the faster, and her mouth went dry, but she bit back her next shout, forcing herself to go limp in the ivy. With each fraught breath she sought for *sothain*, *sothain* until she could rasp out: "Stripes. Stop. Just… stop. Duantri. Duantri—be calm. Please, be calm."

In Tam's grip, the kestrel continued to struggle and shriek. Echo-wounds lashed Lanie's arms and face. Stinging burns no wider than a thread. So many of them. So many and everywhere, covering her in all the places Tam's jelly-like arm was wrapping the kestrel.

"Tam," Lanie gasped as her throat swelled. "Please. She won't harm you. None of us will harm you. By Saint Death, I swe—"

Then Cracchen, enormous in his panoply of ice, crashed into the room.

Even from behind his distorting visor, Lanie felt the moment his frantic gaze landed on her. He turned toward her, chinking and clinking, moving eerily fast, as if the ice itself were somehow mechanized like an automaton—or like a miller's wheel, powered by forces of wind and river.

He sprinted for Lanie.

Lanie, who was on Stripes, tangled in the ivy. Lanie, who hung in the air, between him and the kernel egg.

He never made it either.

Two enormous creatures came bursting through the doorless arches leading into the hatchery hall. Snarling and roaring, they cleared the dunes in a few bounds, and leapt at him, tackling him to the ground.

Or, they tried.

Like the rhino, these were enormous beasts—gunuggs, Lanie guessed from their size, but such a blur of fur and fang and claw that she was left with only an impression of something bear-like, something ape-like—but Cracchen's armor made him immoveable. They managed to halt his momentum—raining blows on him with meaty arms and thick legs. But with each strike against Cracchen's wizard ice, the layers of it grew, redoubling and expanding ever out from his body until the gunuggs were pounding on a pillar of ice.

From the center of the pillar, Cracchen watched the giant god-beasts rage at him. His eyes were wide, his hands splayed against the ice as if against a window.

His gaze shifted and met Lanie's again, even through the ice, even through the ivy leaves.

So much fear.

Fear, she perceived, that was commingled with absolute confusion (Cracchen), and too much understanding (the sky wizards).

She narrowed her eyes. She needed more information. She'd needed it hours ago, before they'd ever set foot on the bridge. She'd needed it yesterday, or the day before yesterday, when the sky wizards encouraged her to pursue the ghost into Madinatam.

They would have *words*, she and Cracchen. In the alliterate verse of his ancestors, if need be.

Another ivy vine looped her throat, but she scarcely paid it heed, or acknowledged the echo-wounds still welting her skin and squeezing her breath. She stared into Cracchen's left eye, the eye of ice, and asked in her deep voice, "*What did you do?*"

The rustling leaves grew still, slackening. Her echo-wounds vanished as Tam's arm un-jellied itself, became her yolkform arm again: uniformly red and tipped in lacquered black claws. She still held Duantri, inexorable still, but now with a gentleness, cradling the kestrel to her breast as Saint Death cradled the bird of the soul. Her other hand, jet-black with golden talons, rested in her lap, quiet as a blown rose.

"He is a sky wizard," Tam answered Lanie's deep-voiced question. "A war criminal."

Lanie's gaze snapped from Duantri to Tam. "You heard me?"

Not a twitch of expression, not a restless movement betrayed any hint of perturbation. Tam's eyes did not narrow, her lips did not tense, no furrow appeared in her brow. And yet, Lanie thought Tam was furious—in some massive, elemental way, the way a landslide might be furious. A landslide able to direct its ire where-so-e'er it pleased.

"Give us the wizard," said Tam, still so calm and still, "and I will give you the bird."

"Oh." And Lanie felt a landslide in her own chest, waiting to be directed.

Tam's golden claws lightly combed the kestrel's feathers. "*Her* past crime in Madinatam resulted in no deaths. Those she fought recovered. Eventually. I will overlook her presence here. Return her to you. But give me the wizard."

In the time it took Tam to speak those words, Lanie breathed. Deeper into sotháin. Stillness. Stillness. Deeper into her deep senses. Into her own substance, and the substance of all things. Plasmatic, malleable, ectenical. Everything was easier here. Easy, to slip the greater part of her own substance into Stripes, boosting the thread of her soul that already powered him.

That thread widened into a channel. Lanie entered Stripes, feeding him her substance—and this time, *just* this once, unspooling some of her accident out with it.

Stripes returned the favor, lending her his substance in

return. Stripes's *stripesness* infused her, gleeful to share itself with her living body. The striking black marks of his disruptive coloration sprang to the surface of Lanie's skin like newly inked tattoos. Her teeth grew, curved, sharpened. Tufted ears sprang up behind her human ears, and from the back of her trousers sprouted a black-ringed tail, more shadow than flesh.

She gave more of herself to Stripes—substance bolstered with a thread of accident—and pulled more of Stripes's ectenica into herself.

Not too much, not too much, Lanie cautioned herself.

She'd once doused herself entirely in ectenica, covered her whole body in it, in an attempt to become invisible. It had worked—but it had made her feel more dead than alive, untethered to Athe, ill and indifferent. She'd vowed never to do that again.

But it *worked*.

She needed just a little of that. Just for a moment. One final push-pull, push-pull, and then...

For a moment, nothing more, Lanie became more ectenical than accidental.

In that moment, the ivy clasping her limbs found no flesh to grasp. She slipped through the vines, and fell to the sand. She didn't feel the thud of the ground jarring her body. She seemed to stop a bare centimeter above it, floating gently.

But above her, Stripes swayed in the ivy, grown suddenly heavier: the weight of his own accident briefly doubled.

She prepared to swap back with Stripes, letting themselves become their own beings again: flesh and hide respectively. Separate and discrete. Mostly.

"Tam." Lanie found that, in this form, she was only able to use her deep voice, as if her lungs had become silk and tissue paper. "I am willing to parley. But I need—"

One of the shaggy, snarling gunuggs who had been attacking Cracchen now spun like a top and sprang at her. Lanie stood from the sand, bracing for impact with muscles that no longer obeyed like muscles, and the god-beast smashed into her.

And fell through her.

It rounded again, confused, and Lanie reached out her gray left hand, more like silver mist than flesh, and bopped it on the nose.

Her hand passed through the skinchanger's paper-thin accident, and connected with the dense, bright substance—pneuma—beneath.

How easy, Lanie thought, *to take it. All of it. Just like the ghost would take it.*

"Stop," she said. "I'm not your enemy."

The gunugg sat back on her haunches, careful to convey that she was not flinching back from a fight, oh no, she was merely awaiting orders from Tam. That was all. Really.

She was like a gorilla, Lanie saw. But also like a human woman. Grand as a caryatid, heavy-breasted and heavy-hipped. Her skull sloped up and back from her thick brow, humped like a burial mound. Her face was more skinchanger than gorilla: bare of fur and faintly reflective, as if it carved from cabochon onyx. Her massive body was covered in a blur of hair the color of smoke and silver and shadow. She was everywhere thick with muscle, her canines sharp and black as glass. She wore a braid down her back, black and silver, streaked with rust. Her eyes were brown topaz and yellow topaz: intelligent and oddly sardonic as they rolled from Lanie to Tam in an unspoken question.

Tam lifted her jet-black hand. "Leave her be, Elkinzirra. The egg-stealer is our concern."

The moment the gorilla gunugg turned away, Lanie released Stripes's ectenica. Her own substance, with its infusion of accident, slammed back into her. She became fully incarnate again, the stripes fading from her arms, along with her second set of ears, her tail. She regretted that, a little.

For a brief, dizzy second, as her body solidified, and her heels sunk into the sand, and her lungs remembered their original intent, Lanie wondered if there were some Quadoni tattoo artist back home who could paint her arms with permanent stripes, and how long such an endeavor would take, and how much would it cost?

Her daydream shattered as a sound cracked out from the pillar of ice.

Lanie whipped her head about in time to see a half dozen—a dozen—twenty—forty—a hundred—long spikes push themselves out of the crystal surface of the pillar. The sharpened ice radiated in all directions like a morning star,[9] thin and sharp and jagged as teeth. Inside the ice, Cracchen's silhouette spread its arms and legs, and braced itself against the semi-opaque walls. He thumped the internal crystal of the pillar like it was a prison cell. He cried out.

Or Lanie thought that he did; the sound was so muffled she might have imagined it.

She stumbled to the pillar, still unaccustomed to her own weight, to the slog of moving through sand, and laid both palms against the ice.

"I swore," she whispered, in both her voices, "I swore by Saint Death I would get you home. I swear it now by Erre'Elur. Cracchen, keep your head. Don't hurt yourself or anyone else. Let me try to fix this."

When the Woe Woman's name passed her lips, the spikes of ice stopped growing. A few cracked off and fell into the sand. The others retracted, shrinking back into the pillar, leaving only smooth, cold crystal behind.

Lanie turned around, set her shoulders to the ice. The three gunuggs in the room had all drawn closer to the Witch Queen, were crouched in the sand, as ready as any of the gyrgardon sworn to protect a gyrveard. Even Tam had changed positions. Now she was perched upon her egg, leaning far forward on the balls of her feet, toes gripping the shell, the kestrel still helpless in her grip.

Lanie wanted to snatch Duantri back, tuck her away, keep her safe. She forced herself to stay still, waiting for the Witch Queen's next move.

Tam's glossy, smooth features seemed as unreadable as ever.

9 The weapon, not the celestial object. If one is not a Stones, or Stones-adjacent, the martial metaphor might not be immediately apparent.

But then, as she glared into the ice, the two ends of her half-scarlet, half-ebony mouth curled like fern fronds. Her teeth gleamed like tiny, perfect, abalone needles.

"She does not know." Tam seemed to be speaking to Cracchen, who gaped through the pillar as one witnessing an advancing avalanche. "Tell her."

After a long silence, Tam shook her head. "No? Cowards. All of you. Still. After all this time."

"Why don't you tell me?" Lanie asked softly.

CRACCHEN HATED THIS.

He hated it.

Miscellaneous couldn't hear him, but he could hear her as if she were standing right next to him. He could feel her too, where her shoulders pressed the ice. Her warmth suffused his chest, the pillar but an extension of his flesh, sensitive as if it were as full of veins and nerves as his body. He could hear her breathe, like she was close enough to kiss.

He could hear the Witch Queen too, telling a story of the crystalskin.

How the sky wizards, in their day, had wronged her and her people.

How she now wanted to kill *him*, Cracchen, for deeds he hadn't done.

The crystalskin whispered back to him in counterpoint:

When a skinchanger lays an egg that cannot carry life, one that will never hatch, it is a wind egg. They pass them like kidney stones, it said dismissively. *Like fewmets dropped on the side of the road. Wind eggs mean nothing to them.*

Then why did you want them? Cracchen demanded.

Because to us—to humans—a wind egg is invaluable. While it is not the bejeweled, singing thing that is the kernel egg, a wind egg is made of solid gold. It can be melted down and repurposed for anything inert gold may be used for—and more, for no mountain-born metal, no, nor the ore that falls from the stars, can hold enchantment half as well as the gold of a skinchanger's wind egg.

Cracchen grumbled. *Should've left them alone. Weren't yours.* But he felt like a hypocrite saying so, since he surely would've pocketed any golden egg he saw lying on the side of the road.

The crystalskin pressed: *Our home was at stake, Cracchen Skrathmandan. Iskald, Skakmaht, the sky houses—all we held precious. We were fighting a war with the rest of the human realms who were jealous of our sky houses. Liriat, Rook, Damahrash—they would stop at nothing to bring our great country crashing down. Funds were needed. Enchantments were needed. Why not take what no one in Taquathura wanted?*

Cracchen had no answer. He would have done the same. But he wouldn't tell the crystalskin that.

Unfortunately, he didn't have to tell the crystalskin anything. It already knew all his thoughts and feelings.

Outside the pillar, he heard Miscellaneous ask, her voice still intimately close: "Why didn't Quadiíb come—you have trade relations with them?"

The crystalskin said, self-satisfied, *They would not have dared. The gyrveard knew how fragile was even the great Ylkazarra—a collapsible city, a city of canopy and esh. Fire and stone falling from our sky houses could have burned Higher Quadiíb to the ground.*

The Witch Queen made her own reply to Miscellaneous's inquiry in that garbled tongue she and the Falcon Defender sometimes spoke in front of him, when they wanted to discuss matters not for his ears. Cracchen almost stopped listening, his cue to sulk, a wholly automatic response.

But then he realized the crystalskin was already translating for him.

Quadic. He could understand the *Quadic*.

"Our lands invaded, and our clutches snatched—but lo, in High Quadiíb, the falcons slept, their jesses slack and leathern hoods affixed. While Skakmaht's Guilded Council ruled on high, the gyrladies trembled in their esh. They feared to break the balance of the Twelve in answering the rally of the Three—and so they sat in silence and did nought. But one in Liriat was unafraid. One came from Liriat to offer aid. And but for him, our skies would yet be dark with all the fearful shadows of the north."

"But"—Miscellaneous still sounded bewildered—"why? Why did Irradiant care? Why did he come and no one else?"

For his own ends, said the crystalskin. *His own and no other's.*

That, Cracchen could've guessed for himself. He'd been fettered body and mind to the ghost for months, had tasted the bile-bitter urgency that drove Irradiant ever north. Obsessed, selfish, tyrannical. He thought and spoke and acted as if he and he alone had a right to exist.

The Witch Queen made an animal noise. To Cracchen it sounded like several noises at once: a hunting cat's cough, a rattle in the grass, a hiss.

"He cared that Skakmaht was powerful. He cared that their winter god had lifted their great houses aloft. Set them above him. Above Liriat. He cared that Liriat could not rival their trade routes. Their resources. He wanted what the north had. For his own. For his Blood Royal, whom he loved."

Miscellaneous was shaking her head. Cracchen could feel the brush of her hat against his collarbones.

"I had no idea… no idea Taquathura was involved in the Northernmost War. Grandpa Ra—the ghost never spoke of it. What *happened* here?" Her voice was so soft, so soft it made Cracchen shiver, the way the cold no longer could.

His crystalskin was crawling too, uneasy with her line of questioning. Hairline fractures in the ice, instantly mended.

"The egg-stealers came. Those who writhe inside your companion like maggots in carrion. They stole into Madinatam from the sky. Their great icicle houses swooped down on us like dragons. Even when I took a dragon's shape, I could not fight them all."

You fought a dragon? Cracchen asked the crystalskin, impressed despite himself.

What is one dragon, against the jaws of winter? the crystalskin returned. *We were many. But few are the fableforms in Taquathura. Fewer now—for we killed most.*

Aren't that many of you *left either*, Cracchen retorted.

But not, said the crystalskin, *because of the skinchangers. It was Irradiant Stones who reduced us to this.*

This, thought Cracchen. *Me.*

The Witch Queen was still talking. "They wounded me grievously. I fell. The river swept me deep. While I bled in the caves beneath the scarp, the egg-stealers ravaged Taquathura. They gathered their sky houses into one great clot. A dirty comet of snow suspended over Madinatam."

The crystalskin rushed to expound on this, eager to correct any bad impression Cracchen might be receiving from the enemy.

We assembled the Guilded Council above Madinatam. Our shadow darkened their shambles of a city. The skinchangers trembled in their dens and burrows like beasts, like fiends crawled up from the hells, who do not know how to live in a civilized society.

"From the craters of their dirty comet flew ships of ice," said the Witch Queen. "Small vessels, but fast. Faster than our fastest falcon shapes. Faster than our bat shapes and our cheetah shapes. Their ships ranged abroad. Combed our territories, searching for eggs. They stole our wind eggs to melt for war gold. They stole our natural eggs to suck their pneuma dry. They stole our kernel eggs..."

"Eggs? Why?" Miscellaneous whispered. "What could they possibly want with... with eggs?"

The kernel eggs, the crystalskin whispered, with such longing that Cracchen felt a magnetic jolt in his belly. It was something like hunger, something like sexual desire, something like the balked ambition he'd felt as a child to shake free the shackles of Rook and be his own man. He shuddered with it. He pressed his front against the pillar of ice, leaned his forehead against its smooth surface, hoping to slake the feeling.

"Sky houses," said Tam, "are powered by the dead. Skaki ancestors, encased in engines of ice. But generations of power made the wizards arrogant. They thought they were above death. So they sucked yolkforms from our natural eggs. Extended their lives with our unhatched pneuma. But with no more wizard dead, they needed new fuel to power their houses. So they stole our kernel eggs. Our amassed pneuma of centuries. These they stuck in their corpse engines instead. Used them up."

Cracchen flinched. *You did?*

We did, the crystalskin crooned, a sweetness and triumph in the echoing voice that filled Cracchen with renewed longing. *And how we flew. How fast and how high.*

Miscellaneous took a pause that seemed to progress at the pace of glaciers. Cracchen could still feel her there, against him, rigid. Her fists were clenched. She was locked in some kind of staring contest with the Witch Queen.

"They stole your eggs—wind, natural, kernel," she repeated slowly. "Just like… Just like Irradiant Stones is now stealing your skinchangers, and using their pneuma to extend his undeath."

Stubborn little thing, wasn't she. She was so obviously disgusted by what she'd heard, but she had an agenda and was sticking to it. Cracchen didn't doubt he and the crystalskin'd be getting an earful later. If there was a later.

An even longer pause. Then Tam said, "Just. Like."

The odd note in her voice—clipped and bitter—had Cracchen turning his reluctant gaze her way again. The Witch Queen's far-forward, toe-tip perch on her kernel egg granted him a brief view of the shadowy trail moving beneath her. Dark, with a soap-bubble iridescence. It connected Tam to the kernel egg like an umbilicus: the cord through which she was feeding the flickering embryo ever more of her pneuma.

The crystalskin made a keening noise within him. It wanted that egg.

Visions of a towering, many-sided palace, turrets and towers and battlements glittering with ice crystals, besieged him. It hung suspended in the air, inert. Its windows were dark.

The kernel egg, Cracchen knew, could make it fly again.

Outside the ice, Miscellaneous sighed.

"Tam of Madinatam. I promise you. I mean you and your kernel egg no harm. Duantri idden Ylkazarra means you no harm. Cracchen Skrathmandan means you no harm. We are all here at the behest of Saint Death. The ghost who once helped you now means to injure you—has already done so."

The Witch Queen's head tilted. She said nothing, but shifted positions again, sitting on her bottom with legs crossed at the knees. Her golden eye and her black eye were like twin suns from two different universes, piercing the fabric of existence to shine on Miscellaneous Stones.

The crystalskin whispered: *The Witch Queen likes her. She is listening. She wants to trust her. She fears her old ally. This is good. This is very good.*

"You speak of cowards?" Miscellaneous lifted her voice. "Irradiant Stones is a coward—hiding in your city, murdering your people instead of facing me. And through me, facing his god."

She gestured toward the skinchanger corpse in the sand, lonely and forgotten.

"Look at his work. Irradiant Stones is no skinchanger. He is a ghost, ravenous for pneuma. But he will not consolidate what he devours with his kernel, and live in sympathy with it. No— he will use it up until it is no more. And at the end of days, when even the dead stars are stitched into Saint Death's cloak, there will be nothing left of her. No memory. No imprint. No thread of the pneuma that was hers alone. She will be forgotten, as even the smallest grain of sand is not forgotten. The god does not want this. The god *hates* this."

"You speak for your god?" the Witch Queen asked.

Lanie lifted her chin. "I do."

"That is what Irradiant Stones said, too.

Cracchen felt Miscellaneous flinch. He reached out, wanting to comfort her. Touch her shoulder. Draw her into his arms. But his fingers met ice.

"He... he is lying," was all she had to say.

"A riddle, then," said the Witch Queen. "Two necromancers of a death god come knocking at my door. Family, no less. Of a blessed bloodline. One of them, I do not know. She comes trailing enemies of Madinatam. She demands my help. The other one, though undead, is my ally from a century back. He aided me when the egg-stealers came. When they kidnapped us and murdered us. So. Two necromancers. Both claiming the love of their god. Whom do I trust?"

Silence.

Then Miscellaneous asked, almost inaudibly, "Can't you... ask *your* gods?"

The Witch Queen smiled again, with all her nacreous, needle teeth.

The crystalskin cursed.

CHAPTER TEN
Nettle Coat

THE PRIEST OF the Three Lovers was another gunugg—and the strangest, so far, that Lanie had seen.

His god-beast was a crab. A giant, crimson, spider crab.

Parts of his torso were less crustacean and more human, if a bit spiny and pear-shaped. There was also something vaguely human about his face, suggested by a forest of spiky protrusions and stubby eye stalks. Spindly and delicate and the color of flame, with an arterial orange undertone, the crab gunugg was at least three times as tall as the next tallest gunugg—the bearish-looking one, who'd rushed into the hatchery alongside gorilla-like Elkinzirra—so tall that the top of his carapace brushed the ivy hanging from the ceiling beams.

He had ten legs. Eight for walking, two front chelipeds. The chelipeds were much longer than his other legs, and tipped in nippers that could double as lopping shears.

His name, he told her, was "Karramorra."

The gorilla gunugg's name she already knew, but he pointed her out anyway, with a cheliped larger than Lanie's head. He introduced the grizzly gunugg as 'Medyeved,' who gave her a cursory glance, then ignored her in favor of keeping his narrowed gaze fixed on the ice pillar. The rhino gunugg, who still seemed nervous with the whole situation in the hatchery, stayed close to Tam's kernel egg, but muttered at Lanie that their name was 'Zerrinoa.'

When Lanie looked at Karramorra, she felt a warmth in her chest like a small sun. The crab gunugg was so beautiful, so aglow with the love of his gods, and so incredibly polite that she wondered, briefly, if gunugg priests of the Three Lovers were anything like the fire priests of Sappacor.[10]

"I like you," she told him impulsively.

"My gods know you," he replied in a confidential undertone. His voice was light and crisp, his eye stalks alive with curiosity, and, she thought, kindness. She'd never imagined kindly eye stalks before.

"They helped me when I needed them," Lanie confessed, rubbing at the affectionate glow in her chest, trying not to let it overtake her reason. "They helped my niece with her... her wolf cub."

"They remember," said the crab gunugg, whose face could not smile—and yet it did.

But these niceties were brief. All too soon Karramorra was tasked to beseech the Three Lovers for Their guidance.

He took a moment apart, standing in one of the shafts of floating dust motes that drifted down from the high, empty windows. His mouth parts moved in prayer. These were many and layered: arm-like, teeth-like, hair-like. His great mandibles, with their comb-edged setae for scraping food off rocky surfaces in the aquatic abyss, opened and shut, opened and shut. If he was speaking in a deep voice, Lanie could not hear it.

A flash of violet light—definitely not sunlight but some internal glow—lit up a mark on his neck, set between antennae and eye stalks. It was as uncanny as the gray mark on Lanie's left hand, or the triple flame that marked every fire priest's face beneath their cosmetics.

She recognized it instantly: Karramorra's wizard mark.

She'd seen the shape before, in old religious texts, particularly ones that concentrated on the ancient heraldry and vexillology of the holy orders devoted to the twelve gods of Quadiíb.

The wizard mark was a triskeles of three bent legs: one each for the Three Lovers, connecting at a central symbol. This symbol was a symmetrical tangle of flowing lava threads,

---

10 i.e., generous with their affections and curious to explore all sensual options at any given buffet of fleshly delights.

forming an 'eternal' knot, representing Their mutual passion for each other. One foot sported a striped stocking—for the Trickster God, Amahirra Mirage-Shaper; one foot was a claw—for Wykkyrri Who Is Ten Thousand-Beasts; the third, a spiral of smoke—for Yssimyss of Mysteries.

Her deep senses swept her up in a fascination for Karramorra's wizard mark. Her nostrils tingled with the smell of wildflowers, and the strong animal musk underlying it. There were overtones, as well, of the musty sweetness of ruffled feathers, and a base note of cool mist and petrichor. Lanie swam in sensation, wholly lost to her surroundings.

Therefore, when Karramorra stirred from his contemplations, she jumped a little.

And when he said, "The Three Lovers have given us Their answer," and picked his way on delicate legs to stand before Tam, Lanie had to struggle to make sense of the words.

The gods are in the hatchery, she thought with a pang of loss. *But They are not talking to me.*

"There must be a Hastiludes," Karramorra told the Witch Queen.

"A what?" Lanie asked, inserting herself into the small crowd of large skinchangers. Karramorra shifted a leg to make room for her, though the other gunuggs didn't budge.

"A Hastiludes," said Tam. "A series of trials." Her hands, scarlet and jet, absently caressed the kestrel she held.

Lanie twitched. Duantri was quiet and still, all signs that her little bird body was stressed beyond endurance.

Soon, she thought as loudly as she could. *As soon as these negotiations are over.*

Oh, she owed Duantri the world. She owed her the moon, and a meteor shower, and whatever comet happened to be streaking by. She *would* make this up to her.

"In a full Taquathura Hastiludes," said Karramorra, "there is a total of twelve games: the tournament we hold for our coming-of-age rites. But the necromancer Stoneses, so spake the Three Lovers, are well past any jejune demonstration of their skills.

The Three Lovers require you to compete in only *two* games to determine which of you is favored by your god: the Game of Changes and the Game of Favors. We have adjusted the rules, this once, to allow the inclusion of the death god's miracles by the contestants. Normally, only magics of the Three Lovers are allowed. But all the gods agree that this is a fair division of devotion. Do you accept?"

Lanie's heart kicked up to a quick march, but she lifted her chin, rolled back her shoulders, and asked, "What's the win condition?"

The grizzly gunugg—Medyeved—grunted. "Whoever's left standing wins."

Elkinzirra flipped her braid over her shoulder. "Or you mutually destroy each other. In which case, Taquathura wins."

Lanie felt her eyebrows take wing. If she weren't wearing a hat, they'd've flown right off her forehead. "But what if he… what if one of us cheats?"

Because Irradiant Stones would cheat.

Karramorra waved his chelipeds. "Never fear, cousin. The Three Lovers and the death god have petitioned Their sibling for aid. The god of trials sends Her notary priest as referee for us."

Tongue and throat turned temporarily into sandpaper, Lanie swallowed. "The god of… do you mean… *Lan Satthi?*"

"Lan Satthi." Karramorra seemed pleased to confirm it—though again, Lanie could not pinpoint how, exactly, she could read pleasure in his alien body language.

She shoved her hands in her pockets, bowed her head. Of all the gods, Lan Satthi was never one of her favorites. All the same, Her mediating presence—an infamously fair one—at the Hastiludes was reassuring. Lan Satthi would be hard to hoodwink, even for Irradiant Stones. Not that he wouldn't try. But a blood oath, signed in Lan Satthi's name, and notarized by one of Her priests, was one of the most binding spells on Athe.[11]

---

11 Miscellaneous Stones had lost house, lands, and most of her possessions as a result of the blood oath her parents had sworn to their debtors in Lan Satthi's name. That loss was not the god's fault. But when everyone else is dead, only the gods remain to blame.

Nodding to herself, she scuffed a boot in the sand. Her boots were golden with the radiant dust of egg shells.

"And, Tam"—she looked up suddenly—"what of the Gyrgardu? Will you at least release her and let her linger outside the city gates, awaiting the results of the trials?"

At that, the kestrel let loose a series of shrieking *klee klee klee klees* and struggled in Tam's grip such that those long-taloned hands tightened briefly.

"No," Tam said. "She must remain with you. Where we can see her. We will permit you to choose her shape: human or bird. But once you choose, we will bind her to it—for howsoever long you remain in Madinatam."

Lanie swallowed. "And what if… what if I lose the Hastiludes? Will you let her leave Taquathura unmolested?"

"How can you lose?" Tam asked. "You are favored by your god."

There seemed to be no answer to that.

At last, the gunugg priest took mercy on Lanie. "The gyrgardon are blessed of Wykkyrri and Amahirra. The gods watch over her. Do you trust Them?"

Lanie swallowed again, nodding.

"Then choose," said Tam, "her fixed form."

THE PLAIN, UNDYED robe of homespun nettle cloth burned Duantri as if it were the stinging nettle leaves themselves she wore raw against her skin.

Inside her chest, kestrel was inert. Heavy. An iron urn, shaped like a bird, but containing the ashes of the bird she once was.

Nettles didn't commonly grow in Quadiíb, but every fledgling gyrgardon training at the academy knew it was best to avoid purchasing nettle cloth from traveling merchants, for to wear it meant losing their connection to their gyrveard—and thus losing the ability to change into their falcon form.

Of course, one *might* purchase it to prank some other fledgling in the academy—should that fledging have done something, or somethings, to torment one in one's first year…

But one only did that once, and then was put on latrine duty for the next three months.

Fibers from stinging nettles spun up into no ordinary linen—at least, not if you were any kind of skinchanger. Harvested from forest edge and fallow fields, or places of waste, like graveyards and barnyards and stock yards, the stalks were stripped of leaves, then soaked and scutched and heckled, and spun into yarn. But whether or not the yarn was woven with any intended enchantments in the name of the Three Lovers, there was always, inherent in the nettle cloth itself, a binding charm that kept a skinchanger—be they Taquathuran-born, or a Quadoni fledgling new-promised to the Rite of Bryddongard—fixed in their present form for however long they wore it.

The skinchangers of Madinatam, Duantri had learned on her first, disastrous visit to this city, always clothed their juveniles in nettle robes, at least until such time as they learned to control their appetites, and select their meals with thoughtfulness, discretion and—when dealing with more sophisticated life forms—consent. (This consent being fully documented, signed and notarized by the priests of Lan Satthi, who kept a small temple office in Plaza Inconi, right next to Immigration Affairs.) A juvenile skinchanger was only able to shuck their nettle robes upon the successful completion of a full Hastiludes, which was undertaken in the company of a cohort of like-matured juveniles.

How did the skinchanger young bear it?

The robe itched and burned her.

But worse than this—far worse—Duantri could not feel Tanaliín anymore.

It was like death. Like her gyrlady had died.

And what if Tanaliín *did* die, while she, Duantri, was not able to feel it? What if the abrupt shock of their severance killed her, or sent her into a crashing panic that caused some accident, or left her so ill with sadness that she could not eat—as had happened when Tanaliín had lost her first gyrgardi to cancer, before Duantri came to her, and demanded to belong to her, or to no one?

Anything could be happening in Quadiíb—but Duantri *could not know it*, for the taut thread of their shared substance, knotted under her ribcage, and stretching more than a thousand miles to find its twinned knot in Tanaliín, was as deadened and dark as the kestrel in her chest.

She stood, shivering, itching, numb, but not numb *enough*, as Tam's gunugg—the gorilla, Duantri did not catch her name—circled her, cinching the robe's belt with a rope of twisted nettle yarn.

When she was done, she stood in front of Duantri and studied her face for a long moment.

"It will not kill you," she said softly, as one who knew. "By tonight, it will all be over."

Duantri stared. She stared until the gunugg left her, and then she stared at nothing, at the far wall of the hatchery, where ivy and rotted tapestries stared back with eyes that were not eyes.

Then Lanie was there.

"Duantri," she said. "Duantri, I'm sorry. Was I wrong? Did I choose wrong? Would you rather have stayed a kestrel? Please! Talk to me!" She seized Duantri's hands, then gasped, her own flesh suddenly rippling with a bumpy pinkish nettle rash. But she did not let go.

"Defender, falcon, daughter of Quadiíb," Lanie said in Quadic. "O speak, that I may know thy senses sound, that thou hast ta'en no harm nor ill in this, the choice I thrust on thee without consent."

"I," Duantri rasped, "I…"

She wanted to say *I am fine* as she had done all these months of travel, of camp chores and ghost-hunting, of keeping busy and keeping Lanie safe, so that the pain of Tanaliín's absence did not incapacitate her. But she could not force the words out.

"I cannot feel her," she finished. "Lanie… she is gone."

Lanie laid her gray left hand upon Duantri's chest. "No, no," she whispered. "I promise you. The bond is strong and well. It's the nettle cloth that's muffling it. I promise you—"

"The kestrel in my breast is dead and done!"

"Thy kestrel sleeps," Lanie soothed, "a falcon in her mews. And as for news of Tanaliín, but soft—I'll sing through Stripes a message thou hast made, and wait for her reply, which I'll convey. I promise thee, my friend, I'll mend thy hurts. I'll see this right, I'll—"

"It is time," said the great crimson monster, whose legs were almost as tall as the ceiling, and whose claws could take Duantri's neck in one, Lanie's in the other, and finish them with a single snip. "Are you ready for your Hastiludes, Miscellaneous Stones?"

Lanie was still looking at her anxiously, as if she had no attention to spare for the monster. Her frown deepened, however, scrunching the bridge of her nose so fiercely that her spectacles slipped down to the very tip. Her eyes lost their focus, most likely now seeing a blur where Duantri's face had been. But she did not loose her hold on Duantri's hands to fix them.

Duantri opened her mouth. She wanted to say, *O Lanie, please have mercy of thy friend; I cannot, cannot, cannot wear this cloth. I fear my heart, my breath, my blood shall end.*

She wanted to say, *Move not until we send my message forth; I need to know my Tanaliín yet lives. Thou owe'st me this and more—a debt unpaid, that digs me ever deeper in my grave.*

She wanted to say, *Can we not leave this place, forsake the ghost? Do not these monsters rate his ravages? Let them become his victims, them his hosts—and live our lives whilst we have lives to live—away from here, where naught is as it seems, where lamplight meditates and ivy dreams.*

She closed her mouth.

She removed her hands from Lanie's, and breathed deep, and entered sotháin. The fifth set—Makkovian's favorite—dedicated to Kywit the Captured God. Tenth attitude: 'Captured god cries out, but goes unheeded.' Arms crossed over breast, head tilted back, mouth open wide in a silent scream.

As far as sotháin gestures went, a scream was very like a yawn; it stretched the muscles and awakened the skin, and when relaxed back to a neutral expression, brought new blood rushing into the face. Duantri held sothaín for a long stretch, and then returned, more quiet in mind and spirit, to a neutral stance.

She still could not speak. Did not think she could say, *I am ready. Let us do thy will.* But she nodded once at Lanie, and moved one corner of her mouth into something near enough to a smile that her far-sighted friend sniffed, pushed her spectacles back up her nose, and nodded back.

Lanie turned to the crimson monster, an armored spider-like, crab-like thing with just enough of a human in its form and face to make it wholly eerie to look upon, and said, "We're ready."

She took Duantri, gently, by the hand, and led her to a pillar made of ice.

"This is Cracchen," Lanie said. "He's trapped too. Will you watch out for him?"

Duantri cleared her throat, forcing her mouth to form words—Lirian ones. Lirian was all she could manage, raw and ugly as she felt. "I will watch out for *you*."

Lanie started to protest, but the crimson monster's shadow fell over them. His claws clicked.

And then, the floor began to move.

The sand dunes that were heaped throughout the hatchery shook loose their mounded forms and rose into the air, parting into veils, strands, particulate, no longer bound by gravity. Finer than glitter. Silkier than soil.

A wind whipped up from the center of the room, a swirling spiral with an unseen eye, sweeping the sand in eddies and currents throughout the cavernous space until the walls, ceiling, and floor all began to disappear. The ivy, where the tiger rug still hung suspended, vanished from Duantri's view. The cold blue crystal of Skrathmandan's ice pillar was now dusted in a layer of golden darkness, or her eyes were dusted in the same. Either way, though not three feet from where she stood, she could no longer see it.

Even Lanie, who never loosed her hand, was lost to her in the seethe.

But Duantri could still perceive a pair of eyes—one black, one gold—suspended in the fine particulate, watching her from the center of the storm.

Then they, too, disintegrated into dust.

And the sand pulled them all under.

Intermezzo

PEREGRINE SHADE

Quadiíb

Year 4826 of Higher and Lower Quadiíb
On Lasaqi, 1st of Anatha: the Third Month

That same hour...

GYRLADY TANALIÍN IDDEN Fa'nim'wai passed into a terrible green dream.

She was walking a lonely road and high, carved along a cliffside. She held out her right arm, fingers stroking some of the glossy verdure flourishing along the solid rock wall. To her left, the road dropped off into a steep gorge, filled with more leafy growth at the bottom. She was humming to herself, a lullaby she had never heard before.

No lullaby—but the Kenosis Hymn, Tanaliín thought, with a dreamer's certainty of her received knowledge. *How beautiful the melody, how bright. How bright and right the spellsong burns its tune.*

Not only did the melody burn, but her right hand was starting to burn as well. Her humming faltered.

The serrated leaves she had been caressing were, Tanaliín noticed, covered in nearly invisible stinging hairs, thin as needles, hollow as straws, filled with the fiery acid of a thousand ant bites. Her palm felt as if she had purposefully thrust it into an open flame.

She snatched her hand back and stumbled away from the leaves—which she recognized now as nettles.

But she stepped too far. She stepped right off the narrow road, into the air.

Her foot caught a slant of scree. She slipped on it, went sliding, the scree hailing down along with her.

Soon enough, she landed—far more softly than she had dreaded—but winded, the impact broken by a patch of nettles so thick they blanketed her. When she stirred, groaning, they stirred in response.

When she tried to sit up, the nettles reached up and swallowed her.

GASPING AWAKE, TANALIÍN reached, as she always did, for her Bryddongard.

One touch of the silver-chased bracer, and through the grace of Amahirra and Wykkyrri, she would feel Duantri's substance entwined with hers. The braid of their souls was gossamer-thin these days, stressed by distance and time apart, but for all of that, enduring. She tried not to pluck at it too often, lest her attentions distract Duantri when she was needed elsewhere.

Sometimes, though...

Sometimes Tanaliín needed to reach out, to know Duantri was alive, and sound, and aware that Tanaliín adored her, always. Missed her, always.

But when she touched her Bryddongard, entering its braided bond, she did not find Duantri there. She found nothing but a stinging green darkness.

Tanaliín screamed.

She was still screaming when Makkovian slapped open the entrance flap of her esh and sprang to her pallet. He knelt beside her, rumpled, efficient, wild-eyed, and laid a hand against her cheek.

His fingers were warm and rough, gentle as every gyrgardon was when touching a gyrveard. His was not Duantri's touch, but Tanaliín had been learning to lean into his love and draw strength from it.

She stopped screaming.

When he brought water, she swallowed it until she could croak out, "She is gone. The Bryddongard—the bond—is silent. Snapped."

"Show me." Makkovian held out his right hand. Her screams must have woken him, for he was shirtless, the way he always slept. He smelled of the sweet oils he always anointed himself with at night: frankincense, black pepper, and vetiver tonight. Tanalíin could see all of his new wizard marks, stark as tattoos. They branded his right arm, which the Blackbird Bride had severed, and which Lanie had reattached with Haaken Skrathmandan's help, and the aid of several gods—including the Skaki god of winter, Erre'Elur.

Anfractuous and iridescent, the dark markings wrapped his right arm, wrist to elbow, like an alphabet written in grackle feathers. Where the marks ended, a thick band of scar tissue encircled his flesh at the attachment site. The scar itself was strange: an aquamarine color, with the glister of frost about it. It was always cold to the touch, which Tanalíin knew from many caresses, even when the rest of Makkovian burned.

She set her right arm, heavy with its Bryddongard, palm up, in his. He bent to examine her forearm, lightly touching her skin where it showed beneath the leather lacings.

"What is this rash?" he asked softly.

Tanalíin hissed as Makkovian's fingertips brushed her itchy and swollen skin. Hard red bumps pushed up from her epidermis along the bracer's edges. From the way her arm throbbed, she knew the rash had spread beneath the bracer's tooled leather.

Makkovian frowned. "My skin did not react like this when... when Gelethai... when she died.[12] But once"—his voice slowed as he went on—"when she spilled hot wax on her hand, my own hand formed a blister. Might this"—gently, he replaced Tanalíin's hand in her lap—"be ought else than death? Some

---

12 Before Makkovian Covan committed himself to his gyrlady at the Rite of Bryddongard, and long before her murder by Amanita Muscaria Stones, Gelethai was a star pupil of the Judicial Colloquium, and one of Tanalíin's mentees.

kind of allergic reaction, such as Mizka has when she comes too near a thing of violence?"

"Then why can I not feel her?" Tanaliín wailed. "There is nothing but a green and burning darkness."

Makkovian cupped her face, caught her gaze, and looked deeply into her eyes. "A green and burning darkness is not null. Thou know'st the pain of null loss. As do I."

Makkovian, because he had lived through Gelethai's murder. Tanaliín knew, because she had survived her first gyrgardi's death. Every day that he sickened in body, she had sickened in soul. At first, he grew too weak to hold his flute—and Tanaliín had no heart to sing the spell-songs that she knew. Then, he grew too weak to pick up a quill—and Tanaliín took leave of absence from teaching at the Caravan School. When he grew too weak to speak, to eat, or to stay awake for more than a few minutes a day—Tanaliín gave up bathing, clothing herself, cooking food, doing most anything but sitting by his pallet, holding his hand. By the end, he was almost translucent, and so was she.

And when he died, she tried to die as well.

And yet, she did not die. Duantri had pulled her from her despair. Duantri, her luminous tether to life ever since.

Makkovian was correct. The null of death and that green darkness were not the same. And where there was *something*, there might be something else behind it. Hidden, perhaps wounded. But not dead.

Heart rate slowing, panic receding, Tanaliín bent her head to examine the rash.

"Do you…" At Makkovian's pause, Tanaliín glanced up from her Bryddongard—just in time to see the leftward saccade of Makkovian's eyes as he mentally phrased his next question. His expression was neutral, almost stony; he was pushing down all of his own dread, striving for calm clarity.

She waited, lifting her brows in welcome.

Makkovian settled next to her on the pallet. "Do you have any idea what happened? Did you notice anything peculiar prior to the… rash?" His thumbs came up to brush her cheeks, wiping her tears away.

"They're leaking," Tanaliín said, surprised. "Old, weak eyes."

"They are black and keen," Makkovian whispered. "They are wise and sharp. Gods-blessed eyes, love-bright eyes, and I will not hear a word against them."

Sighing, Tanaliín cradled her head on his shoulder, thinking back to the moment before she snapped awake. "I was dreaming," she remembered. "A cliff full of nettles. They stung me. I fell a great height, into more nettles below."

"Leech," Makkovian commented, "is sometimes called the Nettle-Lands."

"What is happening over there? Why does Lanie not speak to us through Undies, as she did before? Why is Duantri… why is she, is she…"

"I do not know." His voice was hushed but no longer strained, his stony calm giving way to excitement. "But we need neither Mizka nor Undies for this. I can discover for myself what stirs abroad."

Tanaliín clutched at him. "Your peregrine shade! You would—"

"We will lay a dwalming ring together." Makkovian nodded, threading his fingers with hers like a small basket. "You and Mizka have done this for me many times, watching over my body while I practiced sending my peregrine shade to explore the skies. It always knows where to find Mizka. It was her magic that made it possible. So," he decided, "I will fly my shade to her, and then return to my body to report back whatever has happened. At least then we will know."

"Sacred Datura," Tanaliín murmured. "What will she—"

"Datu will not like it." Makkovian sighed, explosive but silent. Then he raised his voice, casting it from his body to the far wall of the esh, where anyone with an ear to the canvas wall could hear it. "But I believe, if we explain our great need to her, my plumula will be brave."

Tanaliín followed Makkovian's gaze to the flap of the esh.

Nothing stirred beyond it. Not a peep. Not a tremble. That meant nothing. The child was sothaín-trained, the daughter of a Falcon Defender of Quadiíb and the assassin Amanita Muscaria Stones. Moving quietly was her birthright. She, too, raised her voice.

"Sacred Datura will help me with the dwalming ritual. She will take her Auntie Lanie's part and lay the ring with me. We will both watch over your body while you fly free of it. Surely Sacred Datura would do anything for our Duantri—and for her Auntie Lanie, who might need our help as well. Our plumula's heart is as valiant as Engoloth's own champion. She will not fail us."

Makkovian's glass-green eyes searched hers. Keeping his next words between the two of them, he whispered, "Once I am gone to shade, Datu will need you here. Focused. Present. I must trust you to stay with her—no matter how worried you are about Duantri, or how ardently you wish to be elsewhere. Can you do this?"

Tanaliín understood his concern. But oh! It stung, that tone of forward reprimand, as if he scolded her for future inattention to his child. At least the sting was clean, like cold rain on fevered flesh. It refreshed her, and put strength into her spine.

Sitting up straighter, Tanaliín smoothed her sleeping robes and pushed her frazzled hair out of her face. Her right arm still throbbed, but she welcomed the pain, for it was not nothing.

"You may trust me. And I trust you to bring us back the information we seek."

Makkovian cleared his throat, then raised his voice again. "Sacred Datura! I know you are outside, listening. You might as well come in. Bring your infernal hell-cub with you."

Looking more defiant than chagrined, Datu ducked into the esh. One of her hands rested on Undies' head. Her other hand was half-dragging, half-lugging a leather bag filled with smooth river rocks, which Makkovian had collected over the weeks of their long journey from Liriat to Quadiíb.

"I brought your dwalming rocks, Didyi." Datu's green eyes

were big with bravery and terror, but her voice held no tremor, nor any apology or shame for eavesdropping. "Do we lay the ring right here in Gyrlady Tanaliín's esh?"

A rush of love moving through her, Tanaliín stretched out her arms for the child. "Thank you, my plumula! How thoughtful you are, and how quick you were to perceive what was needed." Her heart was so full, it overflowed into Quadic. "We'll set the circle here, just as you say, and in the river stones thy father lay—then dwalm his flesh, invoke his shade, and pray."

Undies took Tanaliín's open arms for invitation. Tail a-wag, he trotted up to her and flopped onto her pallet, plopping his head into her lap. His star-blue eyes rolled up in doleful solicitation, begging for scritches.

Tanaliín bestowed them, allowing the act of comfort to soothe herself as well. Datu, on the other hand, was in no mood to be soothed—not by Tanaliín, and not by her didyi. But she did haul the bag of rocks into the esh, and when Makkovian took it from her, she gave him a long, disapproving look, which he returned with one of calm neutrality.

"Take care of Tanaliín, my plumula," he murmured. "I trust her health to thee—and thine to her—and hope that both shall thrive whilst I am bird."

Datu put her fists on her hips. Then, in perfect mimicry of the Umrysian peasant dialect, she commanded, "Don't fret yer knickers into knots, lover. I got me hatches battened down all right and tight."

This was not the first time that Datu had slipped into another person's speech when she felt stressed. It was as if, by doing so, she donned some kind of armor against the world: a new persona, with a new set of skills and strengths, whatever she felt she needed at the time. At the moment, it seemed, Datu needed to be their mutual friend from Liriat, Havoc Dreadnought, proprietress of the Lover's Complaint.

This did not surprise Tanaliín. There was little in the way of woes that Havoc had not weathered—yet had lived to spin the grandest of yarns about the weathering.

"Clip, clip," Datu admonished her didyi, still in full-Havoc mode. "Get yon shadybird a-gonner. Me and Tanaliín'll guard yer front like you was our own brassiere."

Makkovian laughed like a dog shaking off water, making Datu huff in response. Tanaliín herself could not manage a smile; even trying invited a fresh wave of tears.

No matter. What were tears between friends?

Letting her arms fall from her Engoloth-like stance, Datu patted Tanaliín on the head, almost absently, as if she were Undies instead of a gyrlady of Quadiíb. "Do not worry, Gyrlady Tanaliín," she said, this time in her own voice. "If Duantri is lost, Auntie Lanie will find her. If Duantri needs rescuing, Auntie Lanie will raise an undead army to dance down her foe. And if"—her gaze met Tanaliín's directly, a freezing look, cold but very clear—"*if* Duantri is dead, she will not be dead for long. You will see."

Dropping her gaze from this child who had suffered too much, Tanaliín nodded. "We will all see, my plumula."

Datu thrust her hand into the bag of river rocks and removed the top stone, slipping it into Tanaliín's palm and clasping it for a long moment. For Datu in this mood, that was tantamount to a bear hug.

The stone was large and pale gray, cool as the walls of a mausoleum. It had endured decades, perhaps centuries, of relentless water. It would endure, in one form or another, long after Tanaliín was dust.

The burning in her arm had faded now to a low wash of itchy prickling. She stood up, walked to the center of the room, and set it in its place. The first stone of twelve in the dwalming ring, just where the one o' clock hour would reside on a timepiece.

Eleven more stones followed, and then Tanaliín handed Makkovian into the circle, like a parent handing off their child to the gyrveard on their first day walking the Caravan School Road.

He squeezed her hand, smiled at Datu, and settled on the ground on his back, hands crossed over his breast, hooked at the thumbs, like wings.

Datu sat on the floor at his head, Undies beside her. Tanalíin set a cushion near his feet and curled herself upon it.

Makkovian closed his eyes. He inhaled and exhaled slowly, entering sotháin. His stillness deepened, as he fell through the fathoms of himself into his deep senses.

The hoarfrost scar ringing his upper forearm glittered in the low light of the esh. The blue-black wizard marks on his skin writhed like living writing. His skin drained of its golden vitality.

"And now," he murmured, his voice slow and low and echoing from far away, "I lay me down into my dwalm."

Tanalíin and Datu replied together, "Twelve gods to speed thy wings and keep thee safe."

The scars on his face stood out like thorns. His body went slack. Tanalíin glanced at Datu, whose cheeks were as ashen as her didyi's.

"Breathe, my plumula."

Undies, underscoring her command, licked Datu's wrist. The child shook herself, and sighed.

Not a breath later, the twelve gray river stones that were surrounding Makkovian in a circle rose up from the floor and hung in the air—all but the stones at his head and feet, which remained where they had been placed. The rest floated wide, and re-formed in the shape of wings flaring out behind him.

A pulse—not of air or sound but *something*—rippled out from his body. The ten floating rocks clattered back down to the rugs in their new winged shape, just as a bird of shadow and smoke emerged from Makkovian's chest.

On wings of sweet, translucent dark, it flew through the roof of the esh, and away.

CHAPTER ELEVEN
Blood Oaths

THE GHOST GLARED from his side of the stage across the great hypogeum of Madinatam.

Godsdamn it all, god-beasts were massive brutes. Massive and unnaturally still. Every movement must cost them so much in terms of energy, they were reluctant to waste any. But when they moved, air displaced and light unfocused, and whatever they moved upon, never moved again. Silent sentinels, they stood below the lip of the stage, on the wide pavement surrounding it, and watched with their creepy, reflective, two-toned eyes as the players pacing the stone platform.

The Witch Queen had explained the rules to him before bringing him down here to play her games. He'd agreed. Irradiant would've promised anything. Otherwise, she might have kept him in that cell, where every chink in the stone and every gap in the bars was so stuffed with repellent ivy leaves that not even the smallest shapes his stolen host could take would fit between them.

Rule one: If either of the players attempted to cross from their side of the stage to the other before the Hastiludes began, intending to harass their opponent, the god-beasts were there to stop them.

Rule two: Likewise, if either player attempted to leave the stage at any time *during* the Hastiludes, there would be several tons of rhino, grizzly, gorilla, and crab meat in their way.

Not that Irradiant would let such a paltry thing like a god-beast prevent him from doing anything he wanted to do.

But everything in its time. First things first. He had to annihilate that traitor, his great-granddaughter.

Ratty old backpack in her lap, she sat on her side of the stage, opposite his. Facing him.

Heh. Doesn't dare turn her back, does she? Scared, is she? Good. Got reason to be.

But for all that she was facing him, she was not *looking* at him. A puerile tactic. Hoped to irritate him—was that her game?

Irradiant grinned, unfazed. His secret was, he was always irritated. He'd been born irritated, had died irritated, and had been irritated with *her* in particular ever since she was born with Saint Death's favor so bright upon her that even the sight of a squished fly gave her weeks of colic. So that was nothing new.

What was she covered in? *Sand?*

The girl looked as if she'd just burrowed like a worm from the top of the city all the way down through the solid basalt of the scarp, finally reaching this underground chamber at the bottom of the cliff with a new crust of phenocryst clinging to her. She sparkled with flecks of olivine, feldspar, and mica, and kept brushing off her jacket and trousers, removing her knitted cap to whack it against her legs, and shaking out her braids. Iridescent sand fluttered around her, glassy as fragments of dragonfly wings. Every so often, she'd turn and spit out a mouthful of glitter and dirt. Vulgar.

Her friend, the Quadoni birdie, seemed to have fared no better. Filthy as his great-granddaughter, she sat cross-legged on the floor at the Witch Queen's right side, like a favored handmaiden. Her attitude, however, wasn't that of a favorite but a prisoner. Her rigid spine did not lean against the back of the stage, where a blank sheet of rock rose up to the highest point of the cavern. Also, she was wearing a nettle robe and nothing else. He knew what *that* meant.

Heh. Falcon Defender got herself some proper jesses. Look at her, all shackled in nettle. Bet that shocked her—and her hag of a gyrlady too, wherever she is. Serves 'em right.

"Hey, birdie!" he called out to her. "Nice robe!"

Her eyes cut his way, murder in them. Irradiant snickered, then continued his perusal of the stage. His battlefield.

His gaze fell to the hump of bags and camping equipment near the birdie's feet, where a tattered, battered, completely filthy tiger rug was curled up, watching him with amber glass eyes.

Irradiant stirred, irritated all over again. *That's my tiger rug! Mine! A Stones heirloom—not some beast of burden for traitors and birdie bitches to drag across the realms at whim!*

But no. No, if he let himself get worked up now, he'd be fair dancing with rage, stomping across the stone floor, screaming. Needed to save that juice for the Hastiludes. Rage was a great engine—and not one that his gumptionless, garden-loving, bread-making, soft-bellied dabbler of a great-granddaughter had any interest in or access to.

Irradiant slid his eyes away from the tiger rug, but avoided looking directly up at the Witch Queen.

A quick peripheral glance couldn't hurt, though. She was perched, as ever, on top of her big shiny egg, which was now set on a heap of sand centerstage near the back wall. Dragged that egg everywhere she went, and the sand pile with it. The whole apparatus seemed to move with her, wherever she went—or else she kept rearranging all of Leech Keep around herself to suit her purposes.

The Witch Queen held herself as still as her god-beasts, still as an effigy, the sharps of her elbows digging into the sharps of her knees. Her brooding gaze pierced the darkness of the hypogeum. It was like she was awaiting some signal only she would recognize.

Her egg, half-buried in an enormous drift of glowing sand, pulsed at him.

Irradiant had to concentrate *not* to stare at it. The power it was putting out would have made him salivate—if his host's mouth hadn't lacked the appropriate glands. The gleam of the eggshell was currently a carmine sheen, the juicy red of raspberries and rubies. In another moment, it would turn a different color entirely, lighting up the stage and throwing strange shadows onto floor and wall.

Nope.

Nothing to see there. Don't look at the egg. Don't look at the Witch Queen.

Moving on.

To the left of the Witch Queen (and her great, gorgeous eggy) rose a pillar of crystal. It extended from the black roof of the hypogeum all the way down to the stage floor, like a stalactite of antiquity that had formed its complex structures in secret and alone, down here in the dark.

Which would have been mildly impressive if Irradiant didn't know for a fact that that pillar hadn't even been here an hour before. And that it wasn't made of crystal—or, at least, not of quartz. It was ice.

Wizard ice.

Irradiant would recognize the vile, nostril-pinching, midnight-and-wintergreen scent of Skaki magic anywhere—even sniffing after it with this nose that wasn't really a nose. (Not a proper, *human* nose.) (Skinchanger accident—or whatever they called it, *durity*—produced incredible simulacra, sure. But it couldn't mimic *function*. Which made possessing one… irritating.)

Within the pillar of ice, a shadowy figure moved.

Those bastards. They dared. They dared take my used-up, dried-out, meat-sack of a host and puppet him all over Leech in pursuit of me. In Madinatam, at least, I thought I'd lose 'em. Infernal pests. Why didn't the Witch Queen execute the lot of 'em?

The injustice of it made him want to transfer his glare back to her. But he didn't. He wouldn't. He needed to save his rage. Wouldn't do for the Witch Queen to feel threatened by him in any way. Quite the opposite. Lull's the word. Ease. Old friendship. Alliance. Trust. Nice and smooth.

He'd just glare at his great-granddaughter instead. She deserved it.

Look at her, just *sitting* there, sifting through the contents of her backpack like a child at her blocks. She'd been like that as a baby. Played by herself for hours, because… there'd been no one else to play with. Except for Goody Graves, who didn't count, because that was tantamount to playing with a barely sentient tombstone. And Amanita Muscaria, of course. Nita thought every good game included pinching her little sister or setting fire to her eyebrows.

The ghost chuckled. He didn't *miss* Nita, exactly, but she'd been fun while she lasted.

What is *that little ingrate doing now?*

Apparently, she was selecting certain objects—scant bits of bone: skulls and claws and a scattering of vertebrae from a variety of small animals—from her backpack and methodically placing them within arm's reach. She was, what? Forming some sort of sorcery circle? She hardly seemed conscious of doing it, whatever she was trying to do.

Girlie always was absent-minded. Took about three times as long as she should to whip up an ectenica—every single time. To others, it probably looked like deep focus. To him, it looked like shoddy workmanship.

Irradiant rolled his stolen eyes. At least they *could* roll. The least that eyes should be able to do, in his opinion.

Skinchanger eyes could see in the dark, even if they weren't eyes like *people* had them. They perceived things pretty much as someone, say, of an undead state might do: wherein the accidents of living beings appeared in a sort of spiritual grayscale, but their *substances*—the deep, juicy, shiny stuff—really popped, all colors and sparks.

However alien his depth perception, he did have a fairly good view of the hypogeum. The whole place was a piece of work. Some addled architect of Madinatam must have carved it from the heart of scarp—or built it out of a naturally existing underground cavern. The amphitheater featured a vast stage, surrounded on three sides by tiered seating, all of it chiseled from the same black basalt. Three sets of stairs ran from the pavement at the bottom of the stage into the tiers: left, right, and center.

At the top of the hypogeum, above the last tier of seating,

another wide pavement hugged the space in a crescent, opening into a series of arched tunnels that conducted back to the top of the scarp, where the visible city of Madinatam, much like its Witch Queen, squatted and preened upon the cliff. At the bottom pavement, built into the basalt beneath the bottommost tier, mirroring the arched openings on top, was another set of tunnels. A breeze wafted out of these from time to time, carrying on it the scent of petrichor.

Somewhere close, somewhere deep, rivers under stone: the Fet and Fragor, meeting in secret caverns and waterfalls in the blackness below.

The ghost rubbed his hands together, as if to ward off the chill. (Not that he could feel the cold.) (Not that these were really hands. They just *looked* like hands.) (Duodecifold-damned skinchangers. Possessing them made him, made him... *itchy!*) (Completely unfair, since neither he nor the cursed fiends had any itchable nerves to speak of!)

To distract himself from the urge to scratch, Irradiant yelled across the stage, "What do you say, girlie? Ready to play?"

She didn't look at him, but her shoulders hunched. He grinned again. *Won that round—and the games haven't even begun!*

Then, rolling her shoulders back, she removed her spectacles, wiped a thin film of sand from their lenses, and replaced them. Took a deep breath.

Envy panged at him.

Oh, for breath. To have lungs again! To have muscles and bones and blood—real blood, *red* blood—again! His *own*.

Irradiant was working his way through his second skinchanger host now, blowing through its densely packed substance—or whatever they called it, *pneuma*—and even so, wearing it *still* felt wrong. It wasn't getting any *righter*. This chitinous exterior with its origami mimicry of organs lacked the sympathetic resonance to his own substance that possessing one of his own species would have provided to him.

But the juice!

The juice was worth it. He wanted more. Bigger. Deeper.

Denser. Those god-beasts on the pavement. He wanted them. A worthy snack. Or better yet—

Nope.

Don't think it. Don't look for it.

Never know who's listening. Worshippers of Yssimyss have mysterious powers, and who knows if reading minds is one of them?

The ghost glowered at his great-granddaughter. If she turned on her deep peepers and directed her gaze his way, he wouldn't put it past *her* either to try and pry his thoughts right out of him—for what were thoughts but substance? What was he, but substance?

But no. No, thank Saint Death. She was still ignoring him.

Heh. Her fault, then. Whatever happens next.

The next item she pulled out of her backpack was a hornet's nest. She handled it reverently, like it was Queen Ynyssyll's coronation regalia or something.

What's that for? She can't mean to use it for ectenica?

Ridiculous! Embarrassing! Insects had notoriously poor accident for ectenica. It lasted only seconds. What could she hope to do with it? Had she forgotten *everything* he'd ever taught her? All those years, all that effort, and this—*this!*—was her arsenal against him?

Girlie wouldn't last long if all she had to work with were bone fragments and winter-withered wasp corpses. Which would reflect poorly on *him*.

Then again, if he won this rigamarole in the first round, he could get on with his work in the north much faster. That's what really mattered, after all.

Rankled, though. Rankled right in the Stonesish pride— which his great-granddaughter obviously had none of.

Over on her side of the stage, the girlie blinked, looking up and out, peering into the amphitheater's tiered seating. He followed her gaze.

The empty darkness of the hypogeum... wasn't. It was, in fact, growing steadily lighter and less empty as more and more skinchangers came pouring through the tunnels at the top of the tiers.

Ah! thought the ghost. *We have an audience!*

The light, of course, came from the juvenile skinchangers, who were wearing their coldfire forms: beetles, glowworms, fireflies, millipedes—but also anglerfish, jellies and jellyfish, and several varieties of squid. No skinchanger was bound to the same proportions (or laws of physics) that had circumscribed their original prey. Jellies and jellyfish that had been, in their brief lives, no bigger than biscuits, were rendered enormous when skinchangers took their shapes. Their sizes ranged from that of small piglets to large carthorses—if said pigs and horses were amorphous, gelatinous, undulating monsters who glowed in the dark. Hundreds of jellies were floating into the hypogeum, fluctuating in color from purple-violet to violent green to fiery orange to a pale, sunshiny yellow. They were casting their brazen hues around the place like lights through the panes of a stained-glass lamp.

The *squids* were even larger than the jellyfish, and even more absurd. Irradiant knew that an average adult firefly squid, native to the Glistring Sea off the coast of Rook, might grow to about three inches, no more. But a skinchanger who'd supped the pneuma of a firefly squid could scale it up, stretch its size to one more befitting a *colossus* squid.

From his place on the stage, the ghost scowled up at the grotesque thing as it undulated blubberingly through one of the tunnels, swimming through the air as if it were water, its luminous photophores the silvery blue of moonlight on water. The skinchanger squid must've felt the lance of his gaze, for it turned to stare down at him. Its large yellow eye, round as a wheel and glowing like a brand—and, the ghost noted, sporting *nothing* like an eyelid—winked at him.

It *winked!*

Come what may, Irradiant decided, after the Hastiludes, he would hunt down that saucy young'un, and devour its soul to boost his own substance. *Wink* at him, indeed!

Through the upper tunnels more skinchangers were still entering the hypogeum. Down the tiers they flowed: trickles of twinkling lights that bobbed on the air, scaled figures that slunk down the stairs, furry things that hopped, leathery or feathered things that flew, things that looked like normal people, walking on normal legs. But they were *all* skinchangers. His stolen eyes told him that much. They were positively *alight* with substance.

Many, upon selecting their seats (or perches) started chattering with their friends, for all the world like they were there to enjoy a night at the theatre.

Well, Irradiant was gonna give 'em a show.

With each new addition of a coldfire form, the amphitheater took on the telltale underwater glow that Madinatam's famed Plaza Inconi was known for. The ghost could now account for hundreds, if not thousands, of skinchangers. A veritable smorgasbord. All here for him. Because they felt the need to watch him play their paltry games to win the favor of his god.

Should've stayed home. Stayed safe. The ghost already knew the outcome of the games. It was inevitable. He'd doubted maybe a half dozen things over the course of his life and undeath—but he'd never doubted himself, and never the love of his god.

It was She, after all, who'd given him the power to raise armies of the undead for Blood Royal Sosha Brackenwild. She, who'd guided his hand when he'd pulled the very souls from the sky wizards of Skakmaht. She, who'd helped him stop their flying houses dead in the sky.

Competing with his skinny, dizzy, hyperopic, tender-hearted great-granddaughter in a Hastiludes built for skinchanger juveniles not yet out of their nettle coats?

All too easy.

THE HASTILUDES OFFICIALLY began the moment the referee took the stage.

Lanie watched her ascend the stairs, from pavement to platform. She was bent over two canes, and wore a loose Taquathuran robe, dyed green for Lan Satthi. She took her time, placing one green-shod foot on a step, then one snake-headed cane on the same step, then her other foot, then her other cane, moving deliberately, making sure of her footing.

She was old, silvered, pared down to essentials. She moved slowly, with authority and decisiveness, chin up, eyes bright. The smell of her god was strong on her, green as her robes. It wafted off her skin so stingingly that Lanie's eyes smarted behind her lenses.

How long had this referee been working in Madinatam for the Witch Queen? What did she do all day? Process contracts for the human immigrants coming into the city hoping to find sanctuary? Notarize any and all blood oaths that promised their bodies in trade at death to the skinchangers, in exchange for a lifetime of safety and opportunity?

Was she happy in her work? Cozy in her notarial atelier up in Plaza Inconi? Did she preside over every single Hastiludes that played out down here in the hypogeum, the official witness to the skinchanger juveniles at their moment of maturation? Was it she who declared them fully adult entities of their species, signed and sealed by the sibling god of the Three Lovers?

Or had she been brought in special for this? For *them*?

When the referee reached centerstage, at a point equally distant from both Lanie and Grandpa Rad, she unslung a great book from a strap over her shoulder and lowered it to the floor. From a long steel chain around her neck, she withdrew a shining steel stylus—her notarial amulet of office—and looked first at Lanie, then at the ghost.

"Come," she said. "Sign your blood oath. The gunuggs, your witnesses. I, your notary."

Lanie glanced at Duantri at the back of the stage, who looked tense and miserable and was clutching Stripes's tail like a friend's hand for support. Mouthing "Don't worry," Lanie flashed the Gyrgardu a thumbs up. The withering expression Duantri returned her made Lanie feel much more cheerful, because for that one moment at least, the Gyrgardu wasn't embodying abject wretchedness and defeat.

"Come now," the referee called to Lanie. "You're first."

Walking up to the green-robed woman, and holding out her left arm, Lanie repeated cheerfully, "Me first? Kywit's luck, I guess."[13]

The referee held her gaze. Her eyes were a very dark, very glossy black.

There's something about them, Lanie thought. *They're so interesting. What makes them so interesting?*

She was so fascinated by the referee's eyes, she scarcely felt it when the steel stylus cut into her arm: a small incision, just below the elbow. The referee dipped her tip of the stylus into Lanie's blood, then indicated that she should kneel on the floor, and sign at the bottom of the open page of her great book.

Lanie scanned the text quickly. "*An Instrument to Compete as a non-Citizen in the Taquathuran Hastiludes.* Instrument, interesting. I like that. *The undersigned contestants Miscellaneous Immiscible Stones and Irradiant Radithor...* yes, yes, we all have ridiculous names... *shall compete in two of twelve possible games, as assigned by consensus of the following deities...* Right, well, we already know the gods involved."

She cleared her throat. "*...1. Contests. A. The Game of Changes. This first contest is a variation of the traditional Taquathuran challenge of the same name, wherein the undersigned face off against each other in a series of mock battles, each taking whatever shape they think will dominate, outmaneuver, or outwit the other. This continues until one of the two opponents surrenders, perishes, or the referee calls the end of the game.*"

Puffing out a breath, she fast-read the addendum in a mutter. "*Use of magics blessed by the death god is permitted in this special Hastiludes only.* Thank Doédenna."

The next lines, she had to read twice. "*B. The Game of Favors. Should the outcome of The Game of Changes prove unclear, the contestants progress to the Game of Favors, a variation of the traditional Taquathuran challenge of the same name, wherein the gunuggs of Madinatam [Elkinzirra, Zerrinoa, Medyeved,*

---

13 Kywit, the most unfortunate god, did not have any.

and Karramorra] pit their might, enhanced by the magics of the Three Lovers, against the contestants, in order to test the strength of their alleged bond with the death god. The nature of this secondary game shall be determined in situ, at the improvisational discretion of the gunuggs. The game continues until one of the two opponents surrenders, perishes, or the referee calls the end of the game."

Lanie paused. Frowned. Said, "Mmn." Glanced at the referee. Said, "Mmn," again.

The referee said nothing.

Sighing, she continued, "*2. Anti-Cheating Measures. Should the contestants obtain a victory by any fraudulent, dishonest, or deceptive means, the god of law and trials has the right to enact punitive measures up to and including... including...*"

Lanie scowled at the referee. "This says Lan Satthi will 'zap' us if we cheat."

"So," said the referee, "don't."

"What does 'zapping' mean?"

The referee smiled, ominously. "I hope you never know."

"How will we know if we're cheating? The rules"—Lanie pointed to the large book—"are fairly vague."

"You will know," the referee told her. "And so will the god. And so, therefore, will I."

"So *intention* to cheat counts as cheating?" Lanie hoped Grandpa Rad was hearing this.

"Cheating is an action, not an intention," the referee clarified.

"Mmn." What else was there to say? Lanie finished scanning the text, but knew she'd sign it anyway, whatever the clauses and subclauses. It was her fault any of them were here at all. She was the one who'd asked Tam to ask her gods for guidance. She'd stood there in the hatchery, watching Karramorra pray for and receive his answer. Delaying the paperwork wouldn't do any good.

"All right," she decided. Before her blood could dry on the stylus, she scrawled her name at the bottom of the book, under the 'Witness the Following Seals and Signatures of the Party' section, and underlined it twice, with a panache that she was not feeling today. Duantri had once teased her that she had a 'famous' sort of signature—a few capital letters, some jabs, stabs, and squiggles. Really, it was more flourish than alphabet.

She needn't have worried about her blood drying out, either on the stylus or on the page. The red ink of her name gleamed up from the book as it would gleam in perpetuity—as wet and fresh as it was now. The smell of blood mingled with the creamy richness of heavy parchment, and the leather, and the cucumber scent of reptile musk.

"What's this thing called anyway?" Lanie asked the referee, rising to her feet and pointing at the great book on the floor.

The referee's stern face almost—very nearly—warmed at that. "All notary priests of Lan Satthi receive their own cartulary upon ordination. In the beginning, it is a plain book, blank of any contracts. The first blood-sworn contract that appears is always our own, with our god."

"Huh." Lanie reflected back the referee's almost-smile. It was not every day she got to interact with a holy object. A holy object *not* belonging to her own god, that was. *Those* she handled all the time. She had a whole sack of holy bones with her right now.

And, of course, there was Duantri. Duantri could count as a holy object, being one half a Bryddongard-bonded pair.

And Cracchen, blessed by Erre'Elur.

And Cracchen's pillar of ice, likewise.

And Stripes.

Really, Lanie thought, *they're everywhere, holy objects. Once you start thinking about it.*

Now came Grandpa Rad's turn.

Lanie stepped back as the ghost approached, wearing his stolen skin. His current shape seemed to be some sort of human merchant or tradesman. Possibly originally from Damahrash: people of that region often wore their facial hair just so, in flowing mustaches that spiraled up at the ends like ferns. His curly brown hair stuck up all around his head like dandelion fluff, and his cheeks blushed pink as pomegranates. His broad brow was written with the wear of five or so decades, and he exuded a robustness that Lanie envied.

That robustness is only durity-deep, she reminded herself. *A skinchanger's skin is less substantial than a dried flower petal. This is no human, but the memory of a shape that once a human wore in life. Other shapes lie beneath, within, concealed. They might burst forth at any moment.*

When the ghost caught her gaze, his grin was all Grandpa Rad. "Girlie!" he sang out. "Look at us, together again! It's a regular Stones reunion."[14]

Lanie did not reply, only held the ghost's mocking gaze. One of his eyes was a warm, raisin-brown. The other blazed a sickly, static blue.

Grandpa Rad bent his host's knee and, with an elegant flourish, offered his forearm to the referee, like a knight offering his sword to his queen. The referee snorted softly, and gripped his elbow with one hand. Then she took her steel stylus and sliced his papery skinchanger skin.

The blood that welled from the crease of his elbow was not red but some milky, luminous liquid.

Lanie recalled Duantri telling her about skinchanger blood: pale white at the surface, but darkening to a tarry, viscous black if the durity took too much damage.

But no black blood was coming up now from the referee's shallow cut. She dabbed the very tip of her steel stylus into his fresh wound, handed the stylus to the ghost, and indicated the line on which he should sign.

Grandpa Rad didn't bother to read the instrument at all; he merely scrawled his name at the bottom of the cartulary's page with the bombastic self-assurance of a man who'd once destroyed cities as a hobby. Due to the plethora of curlicues,

---

14 The phrase 'a Stones reunion' is a common Lirian euphemism for 'bloodbath.' Its roots date back to the infamous 'Battle of the Poxbarge,' wherein Ham-Handed Stones led his battalion of Direwolves against Umrysian river pirates who were laying siege to Liriat Proper. On the eve of their decisive battle, his speech to the troops consisted of a single sentence: "Tomorrow, we're gonna give those Umi fish-shits a real Stones reunion, ain't we, fellas?"

embellishments, and underscores he felt it necessary to add, this took much longer than the length of his name warranted.

Watching this gleeful process, Lanie shifted from foot to foot. She felt an old, familiar discomfort, like a too-full bladder, or an impending cold sore. Lately, she'd had to unlearn *many* of the lessons the ghost had impressed upon her during her long apprenticeship with him at Stones Manor. Did she now have to change the way she signed her name too?

But Lanie *liked* her signature. She liked how fancy it looked, how thoroughly and unmistakably her own it was. Hers and no one else's. Indecipherable but unmistakable. And, after all, Irradiant Stones didn't get to have the monopoly on curlicues.

White blood on a white page, Irradiant's name next to her own was yet luminous enough to be legible. Like Lanie's, it would remain forever bright and wet, for the ink upon a Lan Satthi contract never dried.

The ghost arose from his genuflection, bowed to the referee, flashed another grin at Lanie, and sauntered back to his side of the stage.

It was the gunuggs' turn to sign. One by one, Tam's god-beasts leapt onto the stage, signing on as witnesses and, if need be, participants in the second game. That done, Karramorra took up the cartulary in one of his great chelipeds and carried it over to the back of the stage for Tam to sign.

Tam's blood oath was needed at Clause B, labeled *Non-interference by invested parties*. The Witch Queen was here to witness the Hastiludes only, not meddle with their outcome, whomever her personal preference for a winner might be.

Lastly, the referee herself carefully appended her signature to the instrument. She then handed her canes to Karramorra, lifted the cartulary in both hands, and raised it to the ceiling. Her eyes closed in an expression that, to Lanie, was as familiar as the smell of citrus.

This was the face of ecstasy. The face of a priest communicating with her god.

The cartulary's pages flashed a deep, glade-light green. Lurid veins of viridian scrawled themselves across the brown leather covers, lashing them in secret script. Then, the cartulary hoisted itself out of the referee's hands and up into the air, its heavy pages fluttering like wings.

Higher and higher it soared, until it could rise no further. On its way up, the cartulary slowly rotated itself until its spine faced the dark ivy and stone of the ceiling and its pages were facing the floor. Lanie could still make out the red wink of her signature, all the way from her place on the stage.

The book was a long way up.

The audience clapped (and clomped and stomped and buzzed and hummed and roared) in ritual appreciation, but the energy that filled the hypogeum wasn't one of awe-filled excitement, or dread at the unexpected—just a sort of interested, appreciative attention. None of this, then, came as a surprise to the skinchangers. Perhaps all their juveniles signed such instruments before competing in their own Hastiludes. Perhaps the citizens of Madinatam had seen this kind of display a thousand times before—but, like fireworks, it was a sight that never palled.

A beaming aquamarine light shone down, undimmed, from the pages, lighting the surface of the stage in a bright, summery green. The red of Karramorra's carapace appeared lacquer-black in this light, Elkinzirra's silver fur shone like emeralds, and Zerrinoa's mottled markings looked more like bruises and blemishes than ever.

Lanie stepped back further, into the circle of bone she had made. The moment she was standing among them again, she felt safe. The bones sang to her, as she had been singing to them when removing them from her backpack. They were singing to each other the Maranathasseth Anthem—the Dreamcalling.

All in all, the circle of bones consisted of:

Three sheep spines, like the curvy boning of a strange corsetry, remnants of a freak lightning accident in the hills of western Damahrash that took out an entire flock.

One boar tusk, the color of a crescent moon, warm and smooth, larger than what she could close her fist over.

One turtle shell, brown and amber, the size of a teacup.

A handful of coyote teeth, all sickles and triangles.

One fox paw, bleached white and delicate as lace, tipped in amber claws.

The bottom jaws of two fitch weasels, each found a hundred miles apart.

One wing, barred russet and orange, of a 'dimmet owl,' native to the uplands.

A complete set of tapestry viper vertebrae, subspecies of the saw-scaled viper, delicate as a millipede, and purchased at a horn-and-bone stall in Ylkazarra.

And three hundred seventy-six dead hornets.

All here, all a-buzz, and all attending her. All present and darling and *awake*. They had joined her, joined with her, ready for whatever would happen next.

Just in time, too—because something else was arriving.

Here it came—hurtling.

Fast.

Now.

From out of the cartulary, the god Lan Satthi rushed down.

Her notary priest opened her mouth in a shriek of ecstatic welcome. Her feet lifted a few inches off the floor.

Overhead, the cartulary sparked like an iron wheel turning on an iron rail in the dark. The smell of ozone seared the air. All around the edges of the stage, a thin barrier of nephrite jade appeared, slim as a wire, flush with the floor, and as impenetrable as a mountain fortress. For the duration of the Hastiludes, this milky green line would seal all the players standing on the stage within it. It glowed faintly by the lagoon-light that was shining down from the cartulary above.

Lan Satthi, god of Law, Memory, and Commerce had manifested the barrier and entered it: this stage was Her holy ground; these Hastiludes, Her games.

Raising her left hand in acknowledgement, Lanie made the first attitude, modified, of the eighth set of sothaín, belonging to Lan Satthi: *Praise the serpent, praise Her scutes and scales.*

Still suspended in the air, lips and teeth and tongue flashing like sunlight off malachite, the referee began to speak, holding her god in her mouth. "Behold! The Game of Changes begins in—"

"Now," said Grandpa Rad.

And lunged.

CHAPTER TWELVE
The Game of Changes

As HE CHARGED, he cackled.

As he cackled, he changed.

Dominate her. Make her grovel. Make her submit.

He'd make her submit all right. He'd make her submit with his teeth in her belly, her skull underfoot, her heart in his fist. Perforated meat was the *most* submissive meat. He'd make her *offal* submit.

Hemorrhage her.

Nothing in Lan Satthi's ridiculous rulebook said Irradiant couldn't gore his opponent till her tripes came out her ears.

His host's onionskin body juddered and crawled. The layer of pneuma that had been the Damahrashian merchant melted like wax against the flame of his will. Burned off. Smoked away. Gone entirely. Nothing left for Saint Death. Not that She would grudge it to Irradiant—he was doing *Her* work, after all.

Irradiant was pretty sure that skinchangers didn't lose pneuma every time *they* changed shape, but whatever their trick was, he didn't have it. Didn't want it. Just wanted to dig right down to the good stuff.

Somewhere in this pantry-suit of goodies he was wearing—stuffed full of mythic shapes and ancient shapes and shapes of creatures he had only read about in books—was the one he wanted. He'd felt it in there. Knew it at once, for he'd seen its like before.

Back when he was alive, in his prime, he'd visited a so-called 'wonder-room' in the private museum of some Lirian baron's

186

son (*Morissthiss barony, perhaps? Or Nahathiss?*). There he came across, among many other oddments collected under glass, the elongated skull of a prehistoric cat. The snot-nosed, snide-eyed baron's son saw Irradiant studying it and boasted how he wasn't surprised 'Sosha Brackenwild's pet necromancer' admired the item, "knowing how you like your bones."

How that boy had preened and purred as Irradiant strove with himself not to stave in the glass and take the pretty skull for his own. Of course he wanted it. Of course he did.

It sported a double sagittal crest: two razor-thin discs of bone, stained arterial red by a previous collector to emphasize their striking shapes. The crests arced back from the frontal bone like war-quoits. The brow sloped down into a rounded muzzle, forming a pair of canines more like tusks than teeth.

Double-crowned sickle-cat, proclaimed the label on the vitrine.

Now, a whole lifetime and deathtime later, Irradiant had found it again. But far better than some shard of antiquity, *this* double-crowned sickle-cat was perfectly preserved within his host body's kernel; its shape was whole, its memory was intact—and all of it was his for the claiming.

Surprise, girlie! Guess what toothsome snack some primordial soul-sucker supped on, back in the days before days, when such creatures still walked Athe? Guess what got passed on, kernel to kernel, till I gobbled up a skinchanger kernelborn—just like I'll gobble you!

Irradiant gathered the prehistoric sickle-cat from the depths of his host body. Called it up. Called it to the surface. Big as a tiger, burly as a bear, with lightly spotted fur, and a leathery belly. Massive shoulders. Robust forelegs ending in huge paws and deadlier claws—four inches when fully extended. Less appealing were the underdeveloped hindquarters and stubby tail—thick, hairless, and rat-like, with a short tuft of bony spikes at the end.

But the teeth! Ah, fangs like stalactites, serrated and spear-sharp! True, they were made of the same flimsy-feeling skinchanger stuff as the rest of his host. He hated that his teeth were the same texture as his tongue, the roof of his mouth, his throat. But one thing he was sure of: whatever they were made of, these teeth were yet strong enough to maul his great-granddaughter. And that, after all, was what really counted.

Irradiant's host body solidified into its sickle cat shape. He instantly felt heavier—also slower, a bit stupider—but ready to take on the world. Take on the girl. He caught her eye. She was staring at him, slack-jawed.

His whole body stilled, but not on purpose. Not by his will. The sickle-cat, whose will now marched alongside his own, seemed wary of attacking her—thwarting Irradiant's intentions.

Not like this, the sickle cat advised. *Not while the prey is watching us.*

The cat seemed to want her unaware of his presence, weak, lagging. He wanted to attack her from ambush, with his fellow hunters to aid him. Wanted to surround her, separate her from her herd. *Then* he would grapple her. Pin her to the ground. Make sure she was belly up so that he could stab and stab and stab her dead with the jutting spears of his long, long teeth.

The huge muscles at the back of his neck (*stabbing muscles,* Irradiant thought) tensed with hunger. But he could not urge the sickle-cat forward. Irradiant wrestled with the shape, trying to bend it to his will.

His first soul-sucker? The one he'd gobbled up in the gorse bush when his great-granddaughter had sicced her undead deer on him? *She'd* taken seconds to consume. First, he'd taken her mistle thrush shape, and then he took the rest of her shapes—of which there had been a fair few, though not by any means a fabulous amount. When he'd left her corpse by the bridge for his great-granddaughter to find, that skinchanger had been husked right down to her yolkform.

She'd been *easy.*

But this sickle-cat? He was an ancient pneuma. His memory of himself was powerful and true.

Irradiant wanted to hunt the girl? Fine. The cat knew how to hunt. Who better? Certainly not an undead tick riding along in his memory like an itch he couldn't scratch. Puny thing. How dare the *ghost* of a *naked ape* attempt to subvert his own unwavering instincts?

Then again, Irradiant suggested, sidling and sibilant, cat-like, *is not our prey standing right in front of us? Unmoving? Paralyzed with fright? No herd to protect her. Easy food. Take her now, before she runs.*

Finally, the sickle-cat took his first padded step toward her. Irradiant almost howled in triumph.

But then he stopped again, shying back as the prey adjusted her spectacles.

She wasn't goggling anymore. She didn't look a bit afraid. No, she was calmly lifting her hands in (*what's that? a stupid sothaín attitude? at a time like this? The little heathen!*) some kind of gesture.

A summons.

The circle of bones she'd arranged on the floor at her feet floated up. Slowly, the pieces began to orbit the space around her, like moons around their primary planet.

The sickle-cat backed up a pace, startled.

What poppycock is this, girlie? Think a bit of roadside detritus can harm Irradiant Radithor Stones? I was made to eat such meat as you!

His will proved stronger than the sickle-cat's wariness. He pounced.

But his prey snapped out her left hand. One of her orbiting carcass fragments flew into her palm. Something curved... Some kind of tusk?

Didn't matter. Too little, too late. *Heh.*

A groan exploded from her as the sickle-cat knocked her onto her back, his great paws stomping the breath from her lungs. He reared his head. He would gore her. Right in the belly. Right there in her gamey, gooey sweetbreads. *Delicious.*

He started to bring his head down, his teeth like two pikemen finishing off fallen soldiers on the battlefield. Under his crushing paws, his inept, inert prey once more raised her weak left hand.

Irradiant, triumphantly mounted inside the sickle-cat's left eye, expected to see her trembling human fist clutching the broken tusk like a dagger in some last-ditch effort to stab him.

But that was not what he saw.

What he saw instead was his great-granddaughter's entire left arm ripple and fatten, until it no longer bore any resemblance to a human limb. From the joint of her elbow to the tips of where her fingers had been, her arm had transformed into the rankly foaming head of a wild boar.

The boar's head squealed as the sickle-cat struck down. Its bristle-thick neck twisted with a muscular velocity that almost jerked the rest of her non-boar body right out from under the sickle-cat's grapple. Tusks caught canines, twisting them away from the targeted sweetmeats. Dentine scraped dentine. Blue-white sparks sprayed. A smell of burning hair.

One of the sickle-cat's long front teeth snapped off at the tip. Thwarted, he yowled, straining back his neck and slamming his great paw down on his prey's elbow joint in that soft crease right where her human arm thickened into boar muscle and boar fat, a double layer of iron-and-rust fur, and a stiff black mane.

The boar squealed again as the sickle-cat's paw pinned it to the floor. Its shovel-shaped head slammed onto stone and went limp, its curving tusks useless to prevent a second attack.

Ha! thought Irradiant. *This time, we'll go for the throat!*

Once more, the sickle-cat reared, aching with ancient hunger and bloodlust, about to thrust again with his long, no longer perfectly paired teeth. A swarm of ectenical hornets rose up and dove for his head, stinging his nose and the insides of his ears, but they were hardly more distracting than raindrops. He took a second to shake them off—but it was one second too many. He noticed too late his prey's hand—her right one this time—closing over another bone shard from her floating orbit. It snapped to her palm like steel shavings to a magnet.

A small bone. Nothing of moment. Nothing that could bring him down.

But then, faster than he could think, faster than he could *blink*, a sinuous S-shape spiraled out of the flesh of his prey's right shoulder.

Coils upon coils, grown directly from her skin and bone. Roughly keeled scales, painted a sort of sandstone coral with dark brown edgings. Stoutish body, thin tail. A pear-shaped head with rounded snout. Bulbous amber eyes, an elliptical pupil.

The viper was small. But the wicked sizzle of its stridulating scales sounded a clear warning.

The sickle-cat had just enough time to glimpse it, hear it, recognize the danger for what it was, before the tapestry viper struck at him—right below his left eye.

As LANIE SHARED her substance with the tapestry viper's vertebra, it shared its memories with her.

My thisness to your thisness. We are sisters. We are snakes. We are not prey.

In the moment of their sharing, Lanie knew, without a doubt, that while the viper's venom was powerful enough to cause hemorrhaging and blood clots in a *human*, a cat of this size (*what even* is *that thing?*) wouldn't suffer many ill effects—or at least not for long. Her bite might sting him a bit, maybe even confuse him, but the echo-wound that would splash back on her from her allergy would hurt Lanie a lot more.

Yet—the viper bone was what had come to hand. So Lanie hoped it would distract the ghost for a little while longer at least.

The viper struck.

The echo-wound from the bite site swelled her face so fast that her left eye ballooned shut immediately. All the skin surrounding it began to itch and burn. Blisters burgeoned in a protective barricade along her cheekbone, her inner eye, and the soft flesh of her lower eyelid.

But almost as soon as the blisters bloomed, they burst, and the ruptured skin began to seep.

Or maybe Lanie was just weeping blood out of her left eye now, and she would never stop, not ever, because the anticoagulants in a tapestry viper's venom were awful. *Awful.*

A wave of nausea hit her, just as—*all praise and thanks due to Saint Death*—the weight of the big cat also rolled off her chest. Ignoring, for the present, her bleeding eye and roiling guts, Lanie rolled too—in the opposite direction of the cat. The greater the distance she put between herself and an act of violence (*my act of violence, my doing, my fault*), the fainter her echo-wounds would clamor to be its mirror. Blinking grit from her eyes, Lanie scuttled to the furthest edge of the stage.

The pain in her face was getting fainter... fainter...

Gone.

Blisters, sickness, blood, fluid... gone.

She was now up against the slim jade barrier, which flashed as she brushed it. The dome that contained the players on the stage, invisible until that moment, went a hard and opaque green. The audience made various sounds of protest, but when Lanie scooted back an inch, the dome went invisible again, except for that thin line of green limning the edge of the stage.

For better or worse, she thought, *it won't let me tumble off— no matter how hard someone hurls me at it.*

Her left arm was still heavy with wild boar's head, her right shoulder still wound 'round with stridulating tapestry viper. Lanie pushed herself up to a crouch. She watched as Grandpa Rad, still wearing his big cat's shape, pawed at the bite site under his left eye with an overdeveloped forelimb. Making an eerie coughing sound, he paced in a graceless half-circle before collapsing to his haunches, tumbling to his side, and batting at his eye again.

Shock, Lanie thought. *More that than pain. I think.*

The big cat shook his bone-crested head from side to side, and rubbed his furred cheek against the stone floor. Lanie knew that the tapestry viper's venom couldn't kill the ghost's host body; a skinchanger's actual yolkform wouldn't be affected by venom or poison or anything of that nature. Only the particular stratum of pneuma that bore the big cat's shape, that remembered its instincts and responses, its hungers and what worked upon its body, harming or healing it, would be affected.

So Grandpa Rad had two choices. One: wait out the symptoms in his present shape, then resume pursuing her. Or, two: assume a new shape—one that had not been bitten by a tapestry viper.

So, basically, she'd bought herself a few seconds. She'd take them. Absolutely. They were seconds Grandpa Rad would've otherwise spent making a cheese grater out of her with his *face*.

Concentrating hard, Lanie flexed and released both of her fists. The fist that had been a boar's head spat out a tusk, then turned back into a hand. The arm with the viper attached released its scrap of vertebra back into the orbit of bone still whirling merrily around her.

Lanie sent her deep voice towards the tusk and bone, using the sweet and soothing croon she always assumed with the undead. *Thank you for sharing your memories. You kept me alive.*

As the tusk rejoined its fellow satellites, it smiled at her like a crescent moon, olden-golden and inspiriting. The vertebra fragment cracked back into position with the string of its sistren, completing the delicately fringed serpent that undulated past her face with the grace of dancing lace.

Lanie pushed herself out of her crouch and back onto her feet. Her body having resumed its natural shape, she took a moment to reacquaint herself with it. She was glad she had seen Tam turn her arm into a lion's mane jellyfish, for it had taught her something of how skinchanger magic worked.

The way that Lanie could share her substance temporarily with a chosen piece of dead accident, becoming part of that accident as it temporarily became a part of *her*—so too could a skinchanger choose any part of all the pneuma it had amassed, and embody it. A skinchanger did not burn her kernel for fuel (the way the sky wizards used the stolen eggs, and how Grandpa Rad was obviously burning through his hosts). Instead, she shared herself with the pneuma she had amassed. Once she consumed it, she became it. It was all one creature.

Grandpa Rad had never learned how to share his substance with dead accident. He'd always done as he taught Lanie to do: cut himself, bleed on the dead, mingle their matter together, and create ectenica. This blood sacrifice invoked a powerful death magic, but it destroyed the original dead accident in the process, and drained the necromancer as well.

That's what the ghost was *still* doing—only he was cutting open *other* people's bodies to do it, burning through other people's magic. His power wasn't as stable as Lanie's, and it wasn't as sustainable.

But then again, he didn't care who he killed. His pool of resources was potentially much larger than her own.

Lanie considered her options. Her left arm was sore where the cat had stepped on it, in the exact same spot where the referee had cut her for her blood oath.

Across the stage, the big cat was rolling to his feet again, a trifle unsteady but furious.

Time's up.

Lanie flung out both her hands and snatched two more little satellites from the circle of bone whirling around her. She didn't even look to see what she had grabbed; as soon as she touched them, she knew what she was working with.

A dimmet owl's wing feathers. Soft and silent. Pure pleasure.

A tiny spark of pain. Fitch weasel jawbone. It bit her, not maliciously—a love bite.

Perfect.

Jawbone and wing pulsed as Lanie partitioned off strands of her substance, sending them spinning out through her palms, reinforcing the bond between herself, the wing, and the jawbone. She beckoned them in, invited their memories into her accident, opening up her mind like throwing wide the doors of her house to her friends.

Some part of herself also rushed out of those same unbolted doors, into the pieces of owl and fitch weasel that she held, where they, in turn, made her most welcome.

Thy temple, I—and thou my temple, too. Cathedrals of Doédenna we be.

The dimmet wing flooded Lanie with a rush of shushed memory: noiseless gliding, slow flight, how to comb the evening air with velvet-fringed wings. It wanted to teach her all the delights of flying. Oh, it knew that she had flown *before*—on the back of a tiger rug. But it would teach her how to fly *properly*. Like an owl.

Lanie clutched the fragile accident of feather and dried sinew in her fist.

Another gentle pulse of shared substance passed between them, and a pair of ectenical owl wings burst from each of her ankles, the dimmet colors of copper and rose-gold and rust.

The wings growing from her ankles flapped in unison, and with a soundless whoosh, Lanie was lifted up and up and off the stage. She was airborne, she was aloft, she was...

She was sick.

She was very, very sick.

Her stomach lurched all the way up to her eyeballs. Her eyeballs rolled all the way down to her knees. Something in her ears did a double somersault and didn't know where it landed.

Heights. Speed. Flight. She'd *never* been any good at any of it. Not with Stripes and not now, with her darling owl friend.

One time, when she was little, her sister Nita had pushed her out of a window.

This was like that, only she never hit the ground. It was worse, not hitting the ground. Flying was just like falling, only it went in any direction.

Burping up violent hiccups, her mouth filling with the worst kind of saliva, Lanie tried not to retch as her ectenical ankle wings swept her up, higher and higher, toward the ceiling. She tried to halt her progress, go slower, steady herself. She succeeded only in lurching to a stop mid-air, then abruptly dropping down about a yard, her feet sliding out from under her like a child wearing ice skates for the first time.

Twelve gods, please, if only she could puke.

If she could puke, she could clear her head, and then, and then...

A great bounding *something* leapt at her from below.

Sharp hooks sank into her foot, just beneath the wings in her ankle joints, and yanked her down.

IF IRRADIANT EVER met the Three Lovers, the so-called gods of Leech, he'd rip them a few new holes to propagate their illogical, ill-conceived, soul-sucking skinchanger babies with.

This body. Was Such. A bad design.

It made a *terrible* host for ghostly possession. What had the gods been *thinking*?

There was hardly anything to it. This body was like a sac of spider silk stuffed with the dreams of dead things. Its blood was the wrong color. None of its internal systems worked the way they ought. When something struck it, it was like being struck in a dream: impact without sensation.

And yet, when a fatuous, brattish, traitorous quacksalver of a half-baked necromancer came at this body with some kind of weird undead viper shooting out of her shoulder to sink a fang into one of its eyes, somehow this nonsensical host body of his still managed to get *envenomated*. Not because the body was physically responding to the venom, but because the shape it was wearing *remembered* how it would have responded to venom.

Saint Death snipe it all. He'd been so close. So close.

The sickle-cat would've crushed her, pierced her, gored her, then eaten her innards while she watched—not necessarily in that order. He'd've done it all with a jubilant panache and an inordinate amount of splash, with guts flying and arteries shooting arcs of blood, and a lot of delicious screaming.

Not that skinchangers ever ate flesh of any sort. But Irradiant would've forced some of his great-granddaughter down his gullet anyway, all the way into his host body's mockery of guts—just on principle.

Oh, well. Better luck next time.

In a snap, he burnt through the sickle-cat's shape, laving up its last juices, and then, stood naked in his host's yolkform, peering around for wherever his great-granddaughter had got to.

His yolkform was a handsome specimen, at least as Taquathuran soul-leeches went. It was slight, like all of its kind, human-like enough in appearance, but lighter than desiccated leaves, like a stick figure painted in bright, glossy enamels. Blue abdomen, black limbs with alternating orange and red bands, a red throat and face. First thing upon possessing him, Irradiant had sucked the skinchanger dry of his centermost substance, so that there would be no primary personality left to fight him for ascendency of the host. (He'd learned *that* lesson after his months spent riding around in the skull of a Skaki lunkhead, whose milquetoast whingeing utterly annoyed him.)

On reflection, perhaps this yolkform would have felt less brittle had a skinchanger's soul still inhabited it. But, still, the partly-husked yolkform held enormous amounts of substance, like a bank vault whose owner was murdered while counting his coins, and Irradiant wasn't shy about using what he found.

Annoyingly, he didn't spot the girlie right away.

Nowhere on the stage, damn her duodecifold. He had to glance out into the hypogeum, stare into his audience's innumerable and incomprehensible faces, and follow the trajectory of their focus in order to find his quarry.

And he did—just in time to see her go flying over his head.

Was her face a bit greenish, or was that just the light from the cartulary?

No, no. That was a bit of frothy puke dribbling from her mouth. *Heh.* Girl couldn't hold her heights, could she?

He'd have to take advantage of her queasiness. Couldn't let her recover and get the drop on him.

Now, what shape did his host body have tucked away in its cupboard of curiosities that had *reach*? What had *pull*? What could bring down a flying necromancer—and teach her that showing off with a bit of owl fluff for ectenica was really too pathetic for words?

Oh.

He found something.

Ha.

It was glorious.

Now, thought the ghost, almost in awe, *isn't this interesting?*

Not an extinct predator this time, more's the pity. Definitely a grass-eater by its teeth, though an unusual one. Fairly large, which was good. Better yet, it came equipped with defenses.

That tail, for instance. Thick and long, prehensile. A tail like a third limb, perfect for balancing. Could free up his powerful hind legs for what they were truly good for. Hind legs like rubber bands. Hind legs for days. Hind legs enough to kick a girl across the room again and again and again. And such clever little hands, with the most cruelly clawed tips! More than one way to rip a girl's stomach out after all.

Oh, thought Irradiant exultantly, *this will be a very fun shape indeed.*

When he glanced up again, his great-granddaughter had come down a bit and was now hovering only about ten feet or so above the stage. The wings on her ankles seemed to be urging her higher, into the cover of the ivy, far beyond his reach. But she, the idiot creature that she was, was resisting, sinking, slipping, looking biliouser and biliouser.

Just ten feet. A grass-eater of this size should be able to make that jump. Easy. Those legs? Those haunches? Jumping was what it was *made* for.

Irradiant shimmied.

The outer durity of his host solidified around his newly chosen shape. He'd never seen one before, only read about them. It was a kind of marsupial called a roo, which inhabited only certain islands in the southern equator.

Very satisfying.

He leapt, claws extended.

IF LANIE HIT the floor, the basalt surface would break every bone in her body. She had a split second to act.

The dimmet owl's wing pulsed in Lanie's sweaty palm. Their shared substances flowed back and forth, an open channel between them.

The split-second split again, a water droplet dividing on a windowpane.

Within that infinitesimal chasm of time, in an extraordinary burst of power, and instinct, and shared memory, clouds of ectenical owl wings erupted all over Lanie's body. Dozens of them. From her upper and lower arms. From her shoulder blades, her ribcage, her thighs, her spine. From behind her ears and the top of her head.

All her wings flared open, beating against gravity, in that sliver of a single second before she smacked down—just long enough to soften the guillotine-shock of impact.

Then every wing winked out.

Lanie hit the floor. The wing and the jaw bone flew from her grip. But her landing, though clumsy, was soft. She was not shattered.

But, if she didn't move—*right now*—Grandpa Rad was going to leap at her again with those huge legs and those... those tiny claws?

What even *was* he?

Some sort of bipedal mammal. A small head, large ears, fox-colored fur, and a tail almost as long as its body was tall, as thick as one of its legs. It was such an unlikely shape as to be memorable, and Lanie recalled coming across a few fanciful sketches of a similar creature in a dog-eared travelogue back in Stones Library.[15] A roo, she thought it was? Judging by its size

---

15 The title was: *The Unluckiest Voyage of the Merchant Vessel* Acquisition: *A Tale of Mayhem, Murder, and Marvelous Marsupials.*

and color, Grandpa Rad's roo was male, so it would be called a flying copper jack. It was a bit like a deer, if a deer stood on hind legs.

Lanie scrambled to her feet. She did not want to be leapt on.

But neither did she want to harm a single copper hair of that beautiful jack-roo. She didn't want the echo-wounds, or the sorrow of seeing Grandpa Rad burn another rare and gorgeous stratum of pneuma to best her. She didn't want him to waste the host body he had ambushed, stolen, and murdered outside of Madinatam. She was tired of it. She was tired. She wanted the Game of Changes over and done.

How to finish it?

Lan Satthi's light beamed down from the cartulary, emanating its zealous contractual glow. She could almost feel the light acid-etching its terms upon her exposed skin. According to the rules, Lanie didn't have to hurt the other contestant at all. That was just Grandpa Rad's interpretation of the game. He'd been putting her on the defensive ever since the Hastiludes began.

Lanie had already outwitted his sickle-cat with her tapestry viper. Grandpa Rad, in turn, had outmaneuvered her dimmet owl with his flying copper jack. All that was left in the game was for one of them to dominate the other.

What did she have on hand, in her circle of bones, that might dominate a large marsupial? She didn't even know what a roo's natural predators were, for all that she'd read about them, years ago, and traced the abalone contours of their native islands on the gemstone globe in Stones Library.

Right. She'd just have to improvise. Again.

Lanie snapped the gray fingers of her left hand.

Forty-two coyote teeth dropped out of her orbit and zipped toward her. Incisors, canines, premolars, molars: all swarmed her head like a cloud of gnats at dusk, creating a secondary inner orbit around her head much smaller than the outer one. Soon, the teeth were clustered together so tightly, they had formed a kind of large, prickly bolus.

Opening up her stance, Lanie flung back her head and

stretched her mouth wide, thinking, *Please, Saint Death, let me live long enough to tell Datu about this day—even though she'll never believe me anyway.*

The bolus crammed itself between her lips.

Lanie gagged.

Inside her mouth, the coyote teeth took root in her gums, crowding aside her human teeth. Her face and neck fluffed out in fur: first, a soft underfur; then, a layer of stiffer, coarser guard hairs, pale gray in color but with a handsome deal of butterscotch mixed in. Her ears grew long, round-tipped and forward-facing. Her new coyote eyes quickly adjusted to the lagoon-lit dimness of the hypogeum, much keener than her human eyes had ever been—despite the spectacles still perched on her nose.

Not her *nose*. Her... muzzle? Her slender, pointed muzzle.

O my good god of Death, Lanie thought. That was all she had time to think—before she grew a second head.

And a third.

Three coyote heads—one fulvous, one cinereous, one sable— bloomed from the single stock of her throat like three furred flowers. Lanie could suddenly see out of three sets of eyes, hear from three sets of ears. A jumble of desires crowded her. Information flooded her: secrets and surprises and scents and appetites and joys that she had never experienced before.

One of her heads wanted nothing but to eat berries all day. The other longed to dig a burrow alongside a friendly badger companion, and see what tasty rodents they could ferret out together and chase across a sunny prairie. The third head only desired to den down in the hollow of an uprooted tree, and nap in its darkness.

But when her three coyote heads beheld the flying copper jack, all their desires instantly contracted into a single, focused want. They began barking the alarm: *Tell the others. Warn them. Aggressor.*

Pulling back from the substantial connection she shared with the coyote teeth in her mouth, Lanie reaffirmed her own boundaries. She reminded herself who she was, who the coyotes were, and what they could be to each other. Friends. Allies. Pack.

We are *the others*, she reassured them. *All three of us.*

The jack-roo swayed on his hind legs, pugnacious as a boxer in the ring. Lanie hesitated. Much like herself, the coyotes would by far rather flee a jack-roo than fight it.

But, she reminded them, and herself, *it's not really a jack-roo, is it? It's a pack-threat. Destroyer of dens. Killer of friends. Poisoner of berries. And we must* dominate *him. Drive him from our territory. Frighten him off.*

The coyotes understood. They bared their triple muzzles, and Lanie rushed at the jack-roo, though her steps were slow and staggering, her center of mass unsure, and her body top-heavy.

The jack-roo was ready for her—but only for one of her. He punched her left-facing face with a sharp-clawed fist, fast and hard. From her throat yelped a coyote's sharp yip of pain.

But her center face, unfazed, bore down upon the jack-roo, closing its muzzle all the way around his mouth, and clamping it shut.

A COYOTE? IRRADIANT thought. *Coyotes don't prey on jack-roos. They aren't native to the same hemisphere!*

He could have howled! *Would* have howled—except he wasn't wearing a howling sort of shape.

She was, though. Not that she was howling, just biting his jaw shut with a pair of bone-crushers he was coming to envy and regret.

That triple-faced cheating little cheater. How *dare* she use pack tactics on him, with only *herself* for a pack? She was *cheating!* Lan Satthi should *smite* her!

Irradiant tried dropping the jack-roo shape, but found himself struggling to let it go. Its desires were too much in line with his own—and besides, the pneuma itself was denser than any of the other shapes he'd worn. It was as if his skinchanger host had spent many years inhabiting this shape in particular, had enfolded several strata of lesser pneuma into it, reinforcing the shape, swelling it, making it *more*. The jack-roo was not yet a gunugg, nor yet a fableform. But the process to make it so—before Irradiant had wrecked it with his possession—had obviously begun.

This jack-roo *wanted* to fight. It wanted to box its foe, to bounce her, to balance back upon its tail and bring up its hind legs and *kick* her!

Kick his skinny, defective, perfidious, mutant-headed monster of a great-granddaughter! Kick her right in the chest. Scratch her up. Disembowel her. Mark her. Bleed her. Punch her in all her coyote faces. Kick and kick and...

But he couldn't breathe.

Irradiant—the jack-roo—they *couldn't breathe*.

Skinchangers didn't breathe, did they? They didn't have lungs! *Irradiant* didn't have them either! He was dead! The dead don't need oxygen! One of the best things about being dead was *not* blacking out from paltry things like a sudden lack of it.

But the jack-roo, the jack-roo remembered being alive, remembered breathing, remembered what it felt like to die for lack of breathing, and, and...

THE JACK-ROO SLUMPED, its shape evanescing off the skinchanger's body like vapor, leaving only the unconscious yolkform on the ground.

Lanie stood back from it, panting, and spat out of mouthful of sharp little teeth. Three coyote heads blurred back into one human head, looking weary and mournful and a bit bewildered.

From her high stool at the foot of Tam's sand mound, the referee raised her snake-headed canes and thundered: "*The Game of Changes is done! I declare the winner Miscellaneous Immiscible Stones!*"

CHAPTER THIRTEEN
The First Death of Irradiant Stones

WHEN IRRADIANT RADITHOR Stones was young, and alive, he used to pray regularly.

Friends from the start, him and the death god. Back then, Saint Death appeared as a skinny kid in spectacles, just like him. Never minded stretching out on the floor and reading over his shoulder—whatever book he was hooked on at the time. Sometimes he chatted at Her, because he liked thinking out loud, and She? She always listened.

Saint Death followed his early necromantic experiments with interest. She closely observed Irradiant as he swept flies from windowsills, collected fish bones from the midden, and ripped silk-wrapped insects from entrapping webs, in order that he might experiment upon them for his ectenica. She never once left his side all those times he methodically drew blood from his arm with a syringe, squirted it onto his dead things, and (once they'd come undead) put his ectenical constructs through their paces, scribbling field notes for as long as they lasted, and then, when the ectenica burnt away, scrubbed the charred, gooey remains off his workbench.

If, as years passed, Saint Death's smile of approval turned into a frown of disapprobation, well, what of it? Irradiant had never invited Her opinion. He never invited anyone's opinion. He was intent on perfecting his ectenical process, and that was all.

But as the years passed, he wanted more.

He hated waiting for things to die so he could continue his

work. He needed more practice; he needed variety; he needed a consistent source of accident for his ectenica.

Around age thirteen, it finally dawned on him that sourcing his supplies from naturally occurring corpses was an inefficient means of acquisition. There was just too much competition for carrion. The Diesmali Woods swarmed with scavengers, and Irradiant was weary of scouring the lands about Stones Manor for a few meager bones.

And so, he took to scavenging his supply from more domestic elements.

Those kittens? Would've been drowned the next day anyway. Those broke-neck rats the household terriers shook to death? Who wanted 'em? Those terriers, too battered and rat-bit to be of any use anymore? Better use 'em than burn 'em or bury 'em. Maggot-riddled sheep. Diseased horses. Chickens with prolapsed cloacas. All ripe for his harvest. (And in most cases, he really did mean *ripe*.)

Things died out in the country. All the time. You just had to be paying attention.

And sometimes, you had to help them along.

Soon, Irradiant was rearing his own farm animals for the purpose of slaughtering them and raising them up again. A kind of glorified husbandry, really. He wasn't ashamed of it, though his gaggle of bullying siblings mocked him for mucking about in the barns and fields, calling him 'Old Farmer Raddy.' He was the youngest of them, and—they thought—the weakest. An easy target. Soft.

A few years into his great ectenical animal husbandry experiment, and Irradiant began to crave an ectenica derived from a more complex animal: the human being.

Now, he had more siblings than anyone but himself had probably ever bothered tallying. With both parents dead, there was no responsible adult around to ride herd on the horde of wild Stones kids—except for a few drunk uncles and spendthrift aunts, and they didn't count. (Well, Irradiant *did* count them, but only as prospective accidents for his ectenica.)

So there they were, his literal *flock* of siblings. Near at hand, easy to catch, fully matured. Cattle fatted for the slaughter. A massive resource, just waiting to be tapped.

And they all underestimated him.[16]

As he labored and sweated, plotted and recorded—working himself to a thread to create the most incredible, sophisticated, ectenical constructs that Athe had ever known—Irradiant somehow lost the chummy closeness with his god that had so defined his childhood.

In fact, he began to find his god's companionship superfluous. Furthermore, he hated the way She'd come to regard him with that expression of appalled disappointment. He hated how She crouched in one corner of his underground laboratory in Stones Ossuary, and hid Her face in Her hands, not even trying to admire his labors—as if his great vocation didn't matter, *as if he were doing it all wrong*. She was like an anchor too heavy for the boat. She was dragging him down.

One afternoon, frustrated with the capricious brevity of his latest batch of ectenica's undeathspan, Irradiant marched across his lab to where Saint Death squatted like a spider on a rickety stool, and reached out, meaning to snatch the spectacles from Her face and dash them to the floor.

His hand passed through Her face instead.

Unbalanced, Irradiant staggered, knocking over the stool and then tripping over it, before falling to his hands and knees. By the time he clambered upright again, She was gone.

After that, Saint Death never turned up to visit him at random hours, not even on a surge day. By this sign Irradiant knew that She was no *true* friend: stalwart to the end, whatever tests of loyalty he tossed Her way. She was just like the others: backstabbing, unreliable, judgmental.

He didn't need Her. He didn't need anyone.

But not long after that, he met Sosha Brackenwild.

---

16 To this day, no one knows where Lackadaisical "Daisy" Stones, Pulchritudinous "Trudi" Stones, and Pugilistic "Gili" Stones are buried—if any part of them was buried at all. Depleted ectenica leaves very little trace.

And Irradiant realized he *did* need someone—just not a god. He needed a friend. A playmate. A true companion of the soul. And this was, he knew from the first moment of their meeting, the young Blood Royal Brackenwild of Liriat, direct descendent of the Founding Queen, and blessed of the god Sappacor.

Only Sosha. Always Sosha. Forever.

Later, Irradiant married, sired children, and presided over an endless parade of dinners and hunts and dances like a true Stones patriarch, all with Sosha's blessing and approval. He kept his residence at Stones Manor, the rest of his siblings all having either moved elsewhere, or else having died in secret and been buried (or otherwise disposed of) on the grounds.

Nothing Irradiant ever did in life served any purpose but to please himself and his Blood Royal. He would have burned every last one of his supposed friends in fire and acid had Sosha required it of him.[17] Saint Death might have been the god of his youth, but Irradiant had a new idol in the fullness of his maturity: one who grew with him, approved of him, and provoked and piqued his interests with new and exciting challenges every time ennui set in.

Decades passed in an idyll of entertainment and employment. Irradiant's ability to raise the dead, paired with Sosha's supreme reign over Liriat, made the two of them the most feared and respected men of their place and time.

And Irradiant was happy.

UNTIL THE NORTHERNMOST War.

Until the last night of Irradiant's life, in Iskald, capital city of Skakmaht.

KNEE-DEEP IN A pile of broken skinchanger eggshells, Irradiant trembled.

The night-drenched capital lay in silent ruins all around him.

---

17 Which, occasionally, he did.

Overhead, hovering like a cloud-wrack of colossal consequence: the mountainous mass of the Guilded Council. It was all of the flying sky houses of the Skaki wizard elite that had been called home for the war, combined to form a single great fortress of icicle and crystal and stone. It blotted out the starlight.

The opposing armies of Liriat and Skakmaht had fought to a standstill in the city below. Irradiant's undead army had ravaged Iskald, but the sky wizards had reigned down horrors upon Sosha's living army from above.

The Lirians couldn't reach the sky wizards.

The sky wizards couldn't stop the Lirians from destroying Iskald and its civilians.

Now, in the dead of winter, Irradiant was sick, starving, and so sapped from all the magic he had been expending off-surge on his ectenical constructs that he could barely make a dead worm flop on the hook.

And so, out of options, he stood alone, and called the name of his god for the first time in years.

The eggshell refuse beneath his feet splintered and snapped. Brittle and cracked as they were, still the empty luster of their cuticles flashed with a pale phosphorescence. No moon shone that night, yet the eggshells—even drained of pneuma, even kernel-sapped and sucked dry—glimmered in the bleak blackness.

He had chosen his platform with the utmost care.

Shard-dust coating his throat, Irradiant shouted into the darkness.

He told Saint Death all about the crimes committed by the sky wizards of Skakmaht. He demanded that She show them Her justice, in his name. Lend him, Irradiant Radithor Stones, the power to imprison his enemies *inside* a stone, as *they* had driven Tam of Madinatam into the dark heart of her own scarp. Let *them* be shucked of their shells, like the kernel eggs had been, and borne to some distant land, there to be sucked dry of their pneuma, robbed of all their bright potential—slowly—over the span of countless years. Irradiant would see to it.

He would give his own life, he promised, to keep the sky wizards locked away. He would ravel out the whole length of his undeath to ensure that they would never, *ever* hurt anyone again. Or invade their countries. Or steal their young.

Do it for Your sibling gods, Irradiant adjured Saint Death. *Do it for the Three Lovers, who lost a generation of skinchangers to Skaki avarice. Only see what these sky wizards did in Your name—changing even that, corrupting it with their tongue, degrading You, conflating You with their demon Erre'Elur, walking death at the heart of winter.*

How he talked and talked, a lone, middle-aged man, standing amongst a thousand thousand thousand shattered eggs.

And when his words ran out, Irradiant took up a sharp shard of shell and slashed open his arms, first his right arm, then his left, to show his faith in Her, his god.

He bled upon the shattered eggs, swearing himself to their vengeance, binding himself as an instrument to his god's will. He prayed to Saint Death, poised like an ant beneath the anvil of the Guilded Council. He directed all of his formidable thought, will, and attention to his all-but-forgotten god.

And, in that moment, Saint Death became everything to him.

She was his last hope as the life bled out of him. As the seconds ticked and dripped from the broken hourglass of his body, Irradiant prayed for Sosha—his beautiful Sosha—sick from some ailment of the lungs that Irradiant couldn't brink him back from. If Irradiant didn't win this war now, if the armies didn't return home to Liriat soon, Sosha would die.

He prayed as he had never prayed before.

"Saint Death, my friend," he begged, vulnerable and genuine as he had never been, even as a child, "hear me. Let me see Your face once more, before the end."

And before the end, She answered him, appearing to him right there on the mound of eggshells.

But She was not as She had been before.

The bespectacled face that Irradiant used to love, and had grown to despise, was gone. In its place, within Her hood of interlocking bone, was an oval of pure void: bereft of friendship, bereft of judgement. It merely... presided... silent, as his blood drained out onto the skinchanger eggshells.

But just when Irradiant thought She would do nothing to help him, that he would die without knowing his prayers realized, Saint Death reached out and put Her hand upon him.

In that moment, the mound of shining, blood-spattered shards of shell that he was standing on liquified. The soles of his boots slipped on the surface of a pool of new magma—then steadied.

He did not sink. He did not burn.

Irradiant's boots, however, did begin to smoke. His trousers smoldered. Angry cinders snapped from his wools and furs like incandescent moths. White-hot eggshell glass flowed beneath him, a circular current within the glowing orange pool. At the pool's heart, a shadowy shape began to form: darker than the lava, a hot, angry red. The shape began to push itself free, shedding magma and thrusting Irradiant up beneath it until he stood ten feet in the air, a man upon a molten altar.

He was dizzy from blood loss. His breath was coming short. Despite the heat, which kept away the bitter bite of winter night, his flesh was cooling from the inside. He was done for. He was almost gone.

But not quite.

His platform of magma began to harden. White ashes fell from it like snowfall. The final shape of Saint Death's miracle emerged: a sarcophagus carved of shining black basalt. Basalt: for the scarp-stone of Madinatam, sacred rock of the Three Lovers. By this sign, Irradiant knew that not only the death god of Liriat, but also the Three Lovers of Leech, had bent Their will and power towards Irradiant's demand for justice.

But atop the sarcophagus, Irradiant could sense only the presence of Saint Death. She stood just behind his left shoulder. Her left hand supported his arm, raising it for him when he was too weak to raise it himself.

She pointed his hand straight up, right at the Guilded Council of Skakmaht.

Impregnable fortress. Mocking edifice. Citadel that for so long had eluded the worst of what the Lirian armies could throw at it.

And then, for the first time, he heard Her speak. *For Madinatam.*

And lo—Saint Death called out the very souls of every living sky wizard inside that floating mountain. She drew them down. She sealed them in. She bound them to the sarcophagus of the gods' own making.

The Skaki sky wizards did not go gently. The lightning of their passing obliterated Irradiant's body as they moved through him and into the stone. Nothing of his accident remained, not a scrap, not a cinder. Irradiant would have been affronted at this indignity—him, a necromancer and a Stones without even a corpse to leave behind to display with all pomp in Stones Ossuary!—except, at the moment of his body's death, he was no longer *inside* it.

Saint Death had taken him at his word. She dedicated his undeath to the wardenship of the imprisoned wizards. Irradiant remembered the first sensations of his undeath so clearly: the purity of his own substance, chaotic and borderless but for the safety and solidity of the iron padlock that surrounded him, sealing shut the Sarcophagus of Souls and providing him with a home.

Later, when the Skaki sky wizards awoke inside their prison, husked of their bodies, shivering and unanchored and alone, the ghost of Irradiant Stones addressed them from his padlock.

He told them exactly where they were, and who had put them there, and his plans for them. He let them know that they were his to snack on for the foreseeable future, courtesy of the gods they had angered.

How sweet they tasted, swollen with their stolen skinchanger power. How they fed him, engorging him, prolonging his own undeath.

* * *

"*THE GAME OF Favors*," shouted Lan Satthi's notary bitch in her souped-up voice, "*has begun!*"

A hundred and some years later, and here he was, back in Madinatam. In a next-to-useless host body, on the floor of some stupid hypogeum, after getting the glowing white skinchanger snot kicked out of him by his cheating great-granddaughter.

But here too, now, was Saint Death, once again answering his bitter prayer for Her aid.

Her presence spilled over Irradiant like the cool, stale breath of a tomb. She didn't want his great-granddaughter to beat him at the Hastiludes, any more than She'd wanted the Skaki sky wizards to win the war.

His great-granddaughter—who'd stupidly allied herself with the *enemy*—could not win. Saint Death would *never* favor a traitor to Liriat. No, She would help Irradiant break these brutish god-beasts in this second trial, the so-called Game of Favors. And together, they would show Madinatam, worshippers of lesser gods, who the greatest of the Twelve really was.

Turning his host's papier-mâché head on the cold stone floor to stare into the void of Saint Death's face, Irradiant whispered, "You were *my* friend first."

Saint Death did not reply.

"She's weak," he reminded Her, his mouth barely moving, speaking not with his surface voice but his deep. "Runt of the litter. Nothing to either of us. You and I, we've done great things before. Now we will again."

Since She wasn't wearing any kind of face, Irradiant could almost imagine he was talking to Sosha again, instead of the death god. He couldn't remember Sosha's face very well anymore. He could barely remember his own.

Saint Death leaned down, and pressed Her hand to his left shoulder. Her fingers were not skeletal, though they were covered with overlapping scales of bone. Her nails were long and curved, the color of horn, and limned in a pallid, crawling foxfire. This close, Her bone-plated cloak exhaled the aching cold of quarry water.

Irradiant's host body recognized the sensation of cold, but was numb to it. His host was just a shell, after all. A thin, dead skin. It couldn't *feel*, and Irradiant couldn't *make* it feel.

He never thought he would miss the cold.

He raised his host's limp left hand, thrust it towards the god, and closed its fingers around Her bone-wrapped wrist.

"Come," he dared Her. "Favor me in this Game of Favors. Let's show these skinchangers what You and I can do together."

Saint Death reached down and hauled him to his feet. He landed lightly, as if gravity meant nothing to him. Keeping hold of his left hand, the god sent Her answer flowing down his arm, from his shoulder and through his fingers like a current, like a dam breaking. He knew this sensation. He knew what She was helping him to do.

"I want to go"—Irradiant pointed their entwined fingers—"*there.*"

CHAPTER FOURTEEN
The Game of Favors

WHEN THE GHOST, puppeting the bright parody of his yolkform, lifted his arm and pointed to the cluster of gunuggs who were standing centerstage, the audience of skinchangers, each in their flexible, floppy, or furry forms, like a single organism, leaned forward.

When the ghost opened his mouth and spoke unhearable words to the empty but somehow *dense* space behind his left shoulder, the whole auditorium seemed to hold its breath, waiting for whatever happened next.

When a bolt of green lightning shot from the pages of the hanging cartulary and blew a hole through the center of the ghost's host body, the collective flinch from the onlookers was so uniform, it seemed the entire hypogeum had suffered a seismic shift.

A second later, the yolkform's corpse crumpled to the stage floor, like a hock of ham cut from the rafters of a smokehouse.

A second after that, Duantri leapt from her position of resigned patience at the foot of the Witch Queen's mound, and rushed to meet Lanie where the corpse had fallen.

The moment the ghost had lifted its arm and pointed, she had seen Lanie dash across the stage and throw herself at the host body. When it collapsed, she was already there, scraping her knees as she crashed down to catch it, cradling it in her lap, like she wanted to shelter it from harm, but knew she was too late. Now Lanie was bent nearly nose to nose with the thing, studying the yolkform's dead scarlet face: dry-red, wine-red mouth in a mantis rictus; a vivid sapphire abdomen; a large smoking hole right in the crunched-out center of its chest.

"Husked," Lanie said.

"What happened?" Duantri asked.

"Cheated his contract." Lanie sat back on her haunches. "Abandoned the body he'd sworn to compete in the Hastiludes. Since the ghost used his host's blood to sign the contract, it was the host who took Lan Satthi's punishment, not he. Not," she added, "that there was anything left to smite. This skinchanger was long gone. Irradiant ate the rest."

She closed the yolkform's staring right eye. The left was a burnt-out socket, blackened and puckered where it had cradled the orb of the ghost's sickly substance.

"And the ghost?" Duantri asked. "Where is he?"

Lanie's mouth twisted. "Oh, he's still around somewhere. He can't exist long without… an anchor, be it a person or an object. Some kind of accident to latch onto. Something, preferably, he feels a modicum of sympathy with—or his hold on it will be tenuous. Stay close?"

"I will," Duantri swore. "I am. I would fight now, at your side, if you asked." She cast an uneasy glance at the gunuggs gathered centerstage, their great heads bent in consultation. Was Lanie now to fight them all on her own, *and* the ghost besides? The Hastiludes were still ongoing, the second game already begun. Lan Satthi's notary priest and the Witch Queen were looking on, apparently not at all surprised by the turn of events.

They knew the ghost would cheat before the end, she thought. *And counted on my friend to turn his tide.*

But Lanie seemed distracted, almost insouciant about the game to come. "I know you'd fight, Duantri. But we don't want that big green book to smite *us* next. The contract specifies the contestants and the nature of the magic we may use. Which does not include Falcon Defenders, alas." She snapped her fingers in disappointment, or tried. Duantri saw her hand was shaking badly. "If only."

Duantri placed a hand to her chest, where her kestrel still did not stir. Her chest itched. Her whole body itched. Her skin was crawling, as if her nettle robe were alive with stinging ants. She pressed her hand harder to her breastbone, until the reassurance of her heartbeat reminded her she was alive. Then, she reached out her other hand to Lanie's chest, just to feel their hearts beating together: the closest she could come to connecting with another person like she should have been connected to Tanaliín.

"An thou but ask it," she whispered. "I will risk the book."

Lanie shook her head, replying in Quadic as well, "I'll risk thee not. But bide; thy time will come. Burn vigilant, Gyrgardu, bright as flame—thine is mine only candle in this dark."

"I—"

Suddenly, Lanie's attention snapped elsewhere, her soft brown eyes flaring a bright, hard yellow. She cracked out one word in Lirian: "*Go.*"

Duantri went. She returned to crouch at the Witch Queen's feet, skin on fire with nettles and shame, like an alley dog slinking from a volley of sticks and stones, into her midden to hide.

A GHOST IS *a tiny thing*, Lanie thought, trying to locate the small static flicker she'd caught at the edge of her periphery, like sensing a tick drop from a leaf to a baby's arm from twenty feet away.

She stood at the edge of the stage, right by the corpse. Her back was to the audience.

A ghost is an invisible knot of hate. A necrotic point in space.

She scanned each of Tam's four god-beasts. The ghost was there, somewhere, in their midst. He had pointed at them, spoken to the thing standing at his left shoulder, and that thing—that awful Saint Death, with Her stench of rotting oranges, and Her shadow-shroud face of pure void—had obligingly sent him forth out of his host body.

A ghost can worm its way in. And it can burrow.

The gunuggs hulked towards each other in an in-folded rose of protection directly beneath the cartulary at the center of the stage, communicating... something.

Communicating... and *examining?*

Thoughts buzzing like bees in her skull, Lanie slow-walked the edge of the stage, keeping her attention on the gunuggs. Searching for that flicker. That tick. From time to time, one of the gunuggs would glance over at her, tracking her movements, but mostly they concerned themselves with each other: sniffing at one another's pulse points, grooming through fur and hair, peering deeply into eyes and ears and noses and mouths, searching for...

The ghost, Lanie realized. *Scanning for signs of possession.*

So they *knew*. They knew Irradiant Stones could already be in any one of them, gone stealthy but latched on.

That was a relief—that she wouldn't have to convince them. They had not been caught unawares.

Had the gunugg priest Karramorra seen Saint Death appear to the ghost, as Lanie had? Did he know why She had freed the ghost from his host body and flung him into the dark to find purchase where he would? Had he interpreted this as a sign of Saint Death's favor? Had the referee? If so, why not just call the game right now? Why prolong it, when it was so clear to everyone with a deep sense whom the god had appeared to, whom She had bent Her ear to, whom She had acted for— without even once turning to acknowledge Lanie's presence?

Don't get distracted, Lanie scolded herself. *Where did he land?*

Thus far in his possessions, Grandpa Rad had always made his ingress from the front: specifically, through a host's left eye. Lanie didn't know if there was some ectenical reason for this, or if the ghost did it because there was something so mockingly *in your face* about it. Irradiant was not subtle.

But what if, with the help of Saint Death, he was able to establish his burrow in the *back* of a host instead? What if he had somehow made his way inside a fold of flesh, a tuck of skin? An armpit? The sole of a foot? He could be anywhere, in any of the god-beasts.

That was a *lot* of gunugg to examine.

Karramorra, taking point on the investigation, was scrutinizing one of the lily-belled ears of Zerrinoa, who trembled at his attentions like a rhinoceros calf in captivity. Their ivory braids were still in disarray from Elkinzirra's careful combing. Their homespun robe, untied during Medyeved's brusque examinations, was now as carelessly knotted as Tam's. As Zerrinoa waited for the priest to pronounce them haunt-free, they lumbered from foot to anxious foot, until Karramorra placed a calming cheliped upon their broad gray shoulder and bobbed his head-body in benediction.

Zerrinoa sagged in relief. Unbalanced by their sudden weight, Karramorra's legs tapped out a dainty dance, trying to keep them both upright. His kindly cheliped descended again, giving the rhino gunugg another comforting pat.

Lanie's heart cracked a little. That simple gesture reminded her of Makkovian Covan—how willingly and well he older-brothered the whole world, and Lanie first and foremost. She wished the former gyrgardi and the gunugg priest might one day meet.

I'll introduce them, she decided. *If I survive this*.

If Karramorra were not himself already corrupted.

The idea that Grandpa Rad might even now be drilling a path through the gunugg priest chilled her like a splash of yesterday's hoozzaplo.[18]

What if Karramorra were only going through the motions? What if Grandpa Rad was puppeting *him*, making a pretense of inspecting everyone for possession, but none of the other gunuggs had any idea? Lanie had to be sure.

Unfurling her deep senses, she spooled them out in the direction of the gunugg priest, tasting for corruption, for any slight acid taint of spoilage in his gorgeously dense substance.

---

18 Originally the Lirian contraction for 'Hoods up below,' 'Hoozzaplo' has since become a euphemism for any of the contents in a chamberpot being tossed out the window as the phrase is shouted, as well as a vulgar term of endearment for nearest and dearest friends, or, on occasion, a deadly insult answerable only by a duel at dawn. A useful and versatile word, like much Lirian slang.

The moment she did so, a furnace-blast of magic flared off Karramorra's mighty carapace like heat from a forge. A heart-stopping flood of wildflowers-in-a-sunlit-meadow fragrance accompanied it: honeysuckle, lilies, lilac, pansies, hyssop, milkweed, and aster. His pneuma shone abalone-rainbow-dark, denser than diamonds, and he directed it like the beam of a lighthouse, flashing it straight through his fellow gunuggs, seeking out the ghost who dared to dock his unclean barque in their sweet harbors.

Karramorra turned his eyestalks in her direction. *Know me*.

In her deep voice, Lanie answered, *I know you*, and respectfully withdrew her seeking senses. She took a moment to fan herself. *Not Karramorra*, she decided.

And so, when he declared that Zerrinoa and Elkinzirra were clean of possession, Lanie was satisfied as well. Which left Medyeved.

Karramorra minced over to the grizzly gunugg, dignified and business-like, as if crossing a bit of continental shelf to explore a crop of algae on the other side. Seeing the priest's attention turn to him, Medyeved puffed out his chest, rolled back his shoulders, and rose to the tips of his clawed feet, as if trying to match Karramorra's towering height. A futile attempt—for though the grizzly gunugg stood a good ten feet tall, he could have passed under the priest's abdomen with room to spare.

Medyeved's body was more man-like than bear-like in shape, and covered in fur the color of hammered bronze, except for his shoulders, which were splashed with cream, and a single blond streak in the middle of his brow. His furred face, unlike Elkinzirra's, bore little of the smooth symmetry of his yolkform, but had taken on the ursine aspects of his god-beast. His nose was flat and black, huge nostrils wet to the world. His sulfur-crystal teeth bristled, bright yellow, from a protruding lower jaw, and his neck was thick and shaggy.

Karramorra stooped lower to peer into his eyes. At the last second, Medyeved shied away. Every spine, antenna, and eyestalk on Karramorra's strangely human face twitched in dismay.

Medyeved lowered his head. His jaw swung open with a cracking pop. A quantity of luminous ivory fluid—not saliva, but something—foamed from his mouth.

Recognition washed over Lanie. She caught her breath. Every wizard mark on her body—from her gray left hand, to the silvery leaf pattern on her thigh, to the three middle toes on her right foot, and the big toe on her left—thrilled with cold, as she watched Medyeved's ale-colored eyes cloud in confusion. He raised one great forepaw alongside his muzzle and gave it a light smack, followed by a much harder smack, as if trying to jar loose a carpenter bee from his skull.

Lanie concentrated on the grave ache in her wizard marks. A familiar frozen numbness was awaking in them, tingling and sluggish, remnants of the magical damage she'd taken last year.

Was this just her old wounds griping, the way migraines served some people as a painful warning of a storm about to hit? Or was this freezing feeling, perhaps, not just a warning—but an offering of aid?

Doédenna? Lanie whispered in her deep voice. *Is that You?*

The cold spots contracted, growing denser, bitterer: an answer and a riddle.

Saint Death had manifested for Grandpa Rad in the faceless form he had assigned to Her, an aspect of Doédenna that Lanie had never seen before and was repulsed by. But the ghost, great with death, swollen with it, murderous and insatiable, had prayed to his god for Her favor, asking Her to direct him to a source of greater power than the host he currently possessed. He'd probably demanded that She fling him towards the gunuggs, that he might wrestle with a god-beast for its pneuma and grow greater still.

Saint Death had done this for him, because he'd asked it. But in doing so, She had also *destabilized* him. It took time for a ghost to overpower a host body. The stronger its substance, the longer it would take. Grandpa Rad's vacating one host for another had opened up an opportunity for Lanie and the gunuggs to join forces and overwhelm him.

And now her god—*her* Saint Death—was prodding at Lanie's old ectenical scars, the cold of them gnawing at her from the inside, and she knew that Saint Death was urging her to *use* them. Somehow.

You can't favor us both, she muttered, but the only answer was the sharp twinge in her wizard marks.

Gritting her teeth, Lanie willed the huddled cold spots out of their hiding places and compelled them to travel up her limbs like little lead pellets with tadpole pretensions. Gathering up all of that dense, freezing, disheartening feeling—the memory of how she'd failed Saint Death before, how her family had abandoned her, how she'd starved herself, how she'd nearly destroyed herself trying to make it all right again—Lanie concentrated it into a single pool at her center. Then, mentally heaving, she forced the pooled numbness up through her shoulder, down her arm, and into the palm of her left hand.

Mist started seeping from the palm of her hand, taking the shape of a long gray pole with a silver hook at one end.

Saint Death's guisarme, Lanie thought.

The weapon was not physical but ectenical, yet she could feel both coolness and solidity in her grip, as if she had closed her hand over a strong current of wind or water. When she opened her hand, or even imagined dropping the handle, she couldn't feel the guisarme anymore. But when she curled her fingers into a fist once more, and wanted it—*willed* it—back, there it was, waiting for her.

A guisarme is what happens when farmers go to war, Lanie thought. *When the only weapons they have are pruning hooks and weeding irons. Let this be Saint Death's weeding iron, then, and I Her farmer. We'll harvest the ghost out of Medyeved's durity, like we would a grub intent on gnawing at his roots.*

Sweat popped out on the bridge of her nose, causing her spectacles to slip. Her scalp prickled, releasing a drench of sweat. She kept half her concentration on her left hand, the other half on Medyeved, as she moved from the edge of the stage to its center.

Tried to move. Almost immediately, she had to skitter out of the way to avoid being knocked down by Elkinzirra and Zerrinoa, who had both leapt back from Medyeved as he flung himself belly-down to the floor. His big body started thrashing: legs kicking, arms flailing, his torso twisting and torquing. He knocked his head against the basalt—*bang! bang! bang!*— fighting the ghost for sovereignty over his own skull.

Dodging the gunuggs, Lanie darted in closer, the silver-and-mist guisarme hardening like an icicle in her grip. She flung her deep senses out in Medyeved's direction, trying to zero in on her target.

But Irradiant remained hidden to her, still buried deep inside the grizzly gunugg. She could not detect his substance anywhere near enough to the surface to hook him out. He was burrowed in, but not yet *latched on*.

The audience outside the jade barrier leaned in to follow the progress of the players, murmuring amongst themselves. They seemed unsettled by this turn of events. By the rules of all former Hastiludes, the game should have ended when one of the contestants was smote to the ground. But the cartulary remained aglow, and even though the skinchanger audience couldn't follow the ghost's movements, they could sense the distress among the gunuggs.

The silver hook of Lanie's guisarme winked like a star. The weapon was a sign of her god's favor, but what *that* meant in light of all the prior events, Lanie didn't know. Nevertheless, she tightened her grip on the pole as she walked into Karramorra's spiny black shadow. He must have noticed her, for he shifted his forest of legs to allow her through, and hovered over her as she advanced towards Medyeved, who had risen up on all fours, his back arched high, his head hanging limply between his shoulders.

Something crawled beneath the skin of his left eyelid.

"There he is!" Lanie cried, and sprang forward, guisarme poised to thrust.

Except, she didn't get a chance. Karramorra's cheliped shot

out, snagging the back of her coat. He hauled her back under his abdomen, and dumped her down gently. Several of his legs danced around her, not so much in a cage as in a protective embrace.

At a sharp gesture from his other cheliped, Elkinzirra and Zerrinoa rushed in to throw themselves atop Medyeved, flattening him out of his arch and pinning him to the floor. A new froth of foamy ivory fluid spurted from his mouth. The grizzly gunugg heaved and thrashed, snapped and swiped, no longer fighting the thing inside him but his fellow god-beasts.

Still holding onto Lanie, like a mother preventing her tiny child from rushing into a carriage-choked thoroughfare, Karramorra lowered his jointed legs until he was straddling the struggling knot of his sibling god-beasts. He stretched out a cheliped, letting it hover in front of Medyeved's left eye. Its large claw opened and closed, opened, closed, as if feeling for some kind of invisible wire in the air.

Then his claw opened again—and snipped.

A blue spark snapped from Medyeved's left eye. The grizzly gunugg groaned and slumped to the floor. Lanie spun inside her cage of crab legs, scanning the stage, searching for any traces of the ghost's bright mote.

No sign. No trail. Just a smell: that terrible, olid stench of singed hair, bad eggs, and rotting teeth, the stuff that grows under curling yellow toenails. Of citrus gone to spore.

High above her head, Karramorra raised his voice and addressed the audience. His voice was light and thin, with a sibilant 's' that reminded her of Datu as a toddler, but it filled the whole hypogeum, magically augmented, like he wore one of those Damahrashian theatre masks made of wood and stiffened linen that actors wore to amplify their voices in large spaces.

"THE SHADE IS SEVERED!"

Lanie shivered at the words, but the crowd of skinchangers made a great noise: a flapping, a hooting, a thunder. She flinched from it, her whole left side a blockish bar of ache. The pain was large and dull in some places, sharp and spiky in others, and it spread across her ribcage, extending all the way down her left arm, and past it—into the guisarme, right to the hook's very tip. It was as if she'd stripped her nerve cells to forge this instrument, like it was some long, exposed axon, naked and electric.

Turning away from the applauding audience to the back wall, Lanie sought out one face like a heliotrope seeking sunlight. There. Duantri. Gold-lit from the glimmer of the Witch Queen's eggshell mound. Green-touched by the glow of Lan Satthi's cartulary.

Duantri had been waiting for Lanie to look at her. The moment their eyes met, her black brows flew up in a question. *What is happening?*

Frowning, Lanie returned an uneasy shrug. *Not sure.*

Centerstage, Medyeved had regained his feet with the help of Elkinzirra and Zerrinoa. Elkinzirra raised both arms in the air, and ran to the very edge of the stage—until the jade barrier threatened to spark up again—pumping her fists at the audience. The skinchangers screamed back in appreciation. Scuffing his clawed foot, Medyeved swayed, looking chagrined at the part he'd almost played, but too relieved to mind his rescue.

Duantri's gaze met Lanie's again. *Is it over?*

Lanie jerked her chin to where the referee presided over the Hastiludes at the foot of the Witch Queen's mound. *Not my decision.*

Duantri made a shooing gesture. *Go ask!*

Lanie's numb face spasmed. She realized the sensation might be a smile. Rubbing her lips, she limped her way over to Tam's mound, still clutching her immaterial guisarme. By the weird light of the cartulary, the referee's high tripod stool cast an insectile shadow upon the floor. The referee herself sat very still, her snake-headed canes crossed over her lap, her attention, like Tam's, fixed on the gunuggs.

"Lady Referee," Lanie called up to her. "Is the game forfeit? Are the Hastiludes done? What does Lan Satthi have to say?"

The gray-haired referee started, as if jerking awake. Her hands twitched in her lap and her head turned—a sharp movement, like scissors snicking. Her face, which until that moment had been as fixed and waxen as a doll's, stretched in two directions, like taffy torn apart by sharks.

She was, Lanie realized, grinning.

"*The Game of Favors is done!*" the referee announced, not in answer to Lanie's question, but to the audience at large. The applause in the hypogeum quieted. The skinchangers settled, ready for the ritual conclusion of the Hastiludes and the final ruling of Lan Satthi.

Lanie shook her head in disbelief as she stared into the referee's eyes. The dead right eye was dull and dusty as an old black mirror. The left eye was a charred hole, where at the very bottom burned a single spark, blue as poison.

Still grinning, the referee clambered to stand atop her stool. She was almost supernaturally nimble—despite her bilateral clubfeet, the impedimenta of her skirts and robes, her age, her canes. When she was standing, she raised both canes high over her head.

"I declare the winner… *Irradiant Radithor Stones!*"

CHAPTER FIFTEEN
Phantom Feast

WITHIN HIS CHRYSALIS, Cracchen Skrathmandan listened to the crystalskin. It was singing to him of the nature of crystals. How the seeds had been planted, and dropped into the holes of him. How he nurtured them with his blood and heat and flesh and breath. How, if he but allowed them to do what they would, they would nourish him as well, with their power and wisdom and riches. All the wealth of the Skaki sky houses for him alone—because he and the crystalskin would finally be one. Not just a shared body, sheltering a cluster of minds in conversation, but a complete integration.

The shreds and tatters of substances that composed the crystalskin were willing, they sang, to surrender their individual scraps in the service of a greater, single-minded, single-bodied being. Was Cracchen?

Of course he was. Cracchen was alone and afraid. The only thing that had been keeping four monstrous god-beasts and the Witch Queen herself from ripping him apart was the ice that his crystalskin extruded. The crystalskin loathed the ghost as much, if not more, than he did, and what's more, would protect him from any further possessions, eat whatever tried to eat him, or pierce it through with a spear of ice, or entomb it in a glacier.

How could it even be a question? (Though he loved the crystalskin for asking.) He'd be a fool not to integrate.

Of course, he told his crystalskin. *Do what you will. I am yours.*

He did not know it then, but those were to be the last words he spoke as himself.

226

And we, said the crystalskin, *are you.*

From seed to crystal, from crystal to lattice, what the god of winter had planted inside him began to propagate. His crystalskin doubled and redoubled, twinned and mirrored, replicated and spread. All throughout him, under his skin, over it, expanding through his organs, his heart, his brain, the ice advanced and increased, plaiting and pleaching him, braiding and lacing him. It went on like this, and on and on.

Until Cracchen Skrathmandan and the severed sky wizards of Skakmaht were one and each other: individual, inviolate.

IRRADIANT SURVEYED THE hypogeum, lord of all he looked upon.

He'd had a plan. A good one. Take the bear. Husk the rest. Kill the girl. Kill the witch. Get what he came here for. Leave.

And then... *then*, that pietistic ogre-sized *crustacean* of a soul-sucking leech-priest just... *snipped* him. Just fucking snipped him! *Him!* Irradiant Radithor Stones!

Time to pivot.

(Irradiant hated pivoting.)

And a long dark pivot of the soul it was too—three minutes at least, as he floated around the stage under the law god's invisible dome, untethered, discombobulated, undignified, trying to latch onto something—*anything*—before his dastardly defector of a great-granddaughter caught him on her silver hook. Three minutes of being nakedly aware of everything outside his own indomitable existence. Three infinite and terrible minutes of void tearing at him from all directions, wanting to peel him away from himself, like lunar winds blasting the regolith of a bald, blank-faced moon.

He'd tried to steer. Couldn't. Could only float, directionless, until he came up against Lan Satthi's boundary line.

And wouldn't you know it? She'd done Her work too well, that Serpent Lawyer, that Snake of Memory. Her jade wall was so strong and smooth and high that when he came up against it, instead of passing through and dissipating into the aether of Athe, Irradiant had bounced off.

And ricocheted.

Right into the referee's left eye—like a magician's cups and balls routine: ref, the cup; Irradiant the ball. He'd snugged right in.

And oh, the power! Oh, the wallop! Oh, the surprise!

This host body, this referee of Lan Satthi, was no *ordinary* human. It was *too* delicious, too funny! Was nothing in this accursed country what it seemed? No, she was *not* a human— but she *had* been. Right up until some skinchanger walked up and ate her, god-bond and all. That old skinchanger must've loved this brittle, twisted shape, too—enough for it to have taken the notary priest as one of its fableforms.

Fableforms were different than gunuggs, who sacrificed the rest of their shapes to engorge and empower their god-beasts, all to serve Madinatam. Fableforms were simply a selection of the most powerful of a skinchanger's shapes, the ones lavished with any extra pneuma they accumulated, the ones the skinchangers favored over all others.

This skinchanger must have planned to live in the notary priest's shape all the rest of its days, lavishing its attention on every human detail: the twisted feet and curved spine, the loose skin and wet-paper wrinkles, the hag-gray hair, the arthritis-gnarled hands. Mimesis at its finest.

Irradiant had to admit: he'd been fooled. He thought he was getting a human! Would've welcomed it, really. But no. More of the same. Lots of substance. Itty bitty bit of accident.

At least this one had *juice*. Gunugg-sized juice, all wrapped up in tissue paper.

But just as Irradiant was adjusting to his newest host, receiving the usual dump of (mostly irrelevant) personal information that came part and parcel with every possession, who came charging up to his high stool but his own great-granddaughter, silver hook in hand and murder in her eye?

Not that she suspected a thing. *Heh*.

So he'd had his little joke on her, but, well, the joke was up now. Girlie was glaring at him from her puny position way down at the bottom of his stool, but he just ignored her in favor of doing a victory dance on top of it.

Never mind his twisted feet; they were just for show anyway. He did a little hop and heel click, then a bit of a butt wiggle. He swished his long green robes and flashed a length of saggy thigh.

His robes prickled with magic. Nettle cloth. Ubiquitous stuff. But never mind the itch—he'd won! He'd won! He'd won the second game against all gunugg-sized odds—and *how!* Easy as making candles from corpse wax.

The girl, as usual, was a poor loser.

"You just murdered a priest of Lan Satthi!"

"What do you know?" Irradiant sneered.

"I know that that god is going swallow you, chemically digest you, and cough you back up in pieces."

"How wrong you are, girlie. Lan Satthi should thank me! This body ate Her priest long ago, so it deserved whatever came for it—which was me! In fact, you *could* say I'm the embodiment of Lan Satthi's divine justice. And oh, this body's ripe—better than the bear!"

With a wild cackle, Irradiant launched himself off the stool. Robes flapping, he flew over his great-granddaughter's head, narrowly evading her hook, and smashed onto the floor on his host body's swollen knees.

Had the referee indeed been the human that she appeared to be, this maneuver would have shattered her.

But she wasn't. Not in the least.

Hearing his great-granddaughter rush up behind him, Irradiant grinned and kicked up onto his fingertips and toes. He scuttled away from her, roach-like, into the thunder of gunuggs who were stampeding toward him from the other side of the stage.

A flurry! A chaos! A maelstrom of limbs and teeth and claws.

Irradiant laughed as they closed around him. Gunuggs, he didn't mind so much. What could *they* do to *him?* It was his great-granddaughter who was the real danger. She just kept coming at him: grim-faced, mist rising from her wizard marks, dodging all those great, lummoxy feet to get at him.

That won't do, he thought. *I don't like the look of that hook of hers. Has the shine of Saint Death's own silver about it.*

Indignation rose in him. *Traitor god!* he thought. *Traitor girl.* Irradiant hoped the gunuggs *crushed* her by accident.

Which should he take down first?

Not the crab. Not yet. Save the priest for last. Avoid those choppy chelipeds at all cost. When the time was right, Irradiant would *demolish* him. Crab cakes for days!

But for now…

The bear was on his guard, so that was no good. The gorilla looked incensed. She was full of will, that one. Keen-eyed. Difficult to breach.

The rhino, though… The rhino was no warrior. Anxious. Panicked.

Perfect.

Giggling, beetling, dodging (but not very well), Irradiant reached for the long chain of office that swung from his neck: a fine steel stylus like a magician's pendulum, fully invested with the power of Lan Satthi. Rolling himself up into a ball, he tugged the chain over his head and clutched the stylus like a dagger, waiting…

Waiting for the moment that nervy bruiser of a rhino gunugg came trampling up to him like a runaway cart. As he took the hit, Irradiant reveled in the feeling of his fragile host body crunching under those three-toed feet. As he splatted beneath them, he raised his stylus and jabbed it into their thick ankle.

Bull's eye. Blood everywhere. That milk-glow stuff, luminous and viscous.

Of course, he was being smashed thin as a snakeskin in the bargain. Saint Death, this *accident!* Such flimsy, gluey material. His current shape was being pummeled out of all semblance, but the basic stuff was resilient enough to survive—at least, long enough for Irradiant's purposes.

In a liquid slither, eel-flat and featureless, Irradiant wriggled up one of the rhino gunugg's legs. He kept a grasp on his stylus, making sure it was still well-stuck in the rhino's thick gray flesh. As he crawled up the god-beast's body, he dragged the stylus up with him until the entire length of the leg was deeply gouged, white blood dripping everywhere.

But most importantly, the blood had soaked the steel stylus: body, base, and nib.

Using the stylus, then, as his piton, Irradiant climbed the rhino gunugg like a mountain right to the summit, until he was hanging off their back like a baby monkey. (A flattened baby monkey, but a baby monkey nonetheless.) About that size, too, relative to the god-beast's humongous body.

The rhino gunugg had lost their homespun robe in the scuffle and was shirtless. Their broad back made for a fine, blank parchment. Irradiant dug his cracked nails into their shoulder, and holding on hard, began to scrawl a new contract into their gray skin, using the god-beast's own white blood for his ink.

The stylus was a holy tool, and Irradiant was wearing the scraps of Lan Satthi's notary priest for his host. For a slim window of time, whatever he wrote with this stylus would be reckoned, in the god's eyes, a sacred contract, bound by blood oath. His words were Lan Satthi's law. But he didn't have long.

Addendum to the Instrument, he wrote in his rapid, spider-cramped scrawl: *this gunugg (thus inscribed) is requisitioned by Irradiant Stones for use in the Hastiludes. They will do as he commands, revoking all loyalty to country, queen, and gods.*

The rhino brute bucked and bellowed as Irradiant gouged them, trying to throw him off. But Irradiant would not be thrown. A skinchanger's body was light, mutable, and sticky withal. Easier to scrape a smashed beetle off the sole of a boot than get Irradiant off his mount's back now.

Finished writing, he dug his nib in unnecessarily deep, excavating his name near the base of the gunugg's spine with so much glee he thought his grin would peel his face in half.

The white-wet writing flashed a poisonous green upon the

gray skin, before black spurts of blood, the deep blood of a skinchanger's innermost wound, started leaking up through the cursive scratches. The black blood stained the blood oath into the gunugg's skin like tattoos, every letter of every wound gaping open like a screaming mouth.

The rhino gunugg let out a deep sigh. Then they stood very, very still.

Hooting, Irradiant clambered higher onto their back, wrapping the bone shards of his shredded knees around their waist.

"Charge!" he shrieked, and the gunugg obeyed. They smashed themself through the big crab's legs, cracked one off at the joint. The crab gunugg tottered, trying to maintain balance on his remaining legs.

Plastering his much-flattened body against the back of his war rhino's skull, clinging there like a lamprey, Irradiant shouted in their ear: "Ram that gorilla!"

Black oath tattoos pulsed black blood. The rhino gunugg rammed, their double horns goring the silvery gorilla-thing through her throat and jaw. The force of their impact drove the gorilla gunugg halfway across the stage, and right up against the jade barrier. The barrier slammed up, green and opaque, temporarily blocking the view of the audience.

That was all right. The audience was in a panic anyway. Many of them were fleeing, taking their infernal lights with them. The hypogeum was emptying, darkening, until the only light remaining was the cartulary hanging over the stage, and the mound of sand glimmering at the back of it, and the egg it cradled.

Irradiant shouted another command at his new pet, and sent a pulse of urgency through the blood oath on their back. Crusted wounds cracked. Scrawl-marks gaped. Black blood leaked.

And the rhino gunugg ripped their horns free, taking a chunk of gorilla throat with them.

A wettish thump as she fell to the floor.

Behind him, the clackety-click of crab legs. Reinforcements were coming.

Losing no time, Irradiant bounced his mount off the barrier's side, bringing the rhino down in a diving stomp atop the gorilla, who was flopping around on the floor, gurgling, struggling to rise.

Something crunched in her smoke-silver chest. White blood oozed from her mouth. Black blood spurted from the perissodactyl-shaped hole in her torso. The light in her topaz eyes faded, faded.

Heh.

One down.

Spurring his mount around with bare, broken heels, Irradiant shrieked, "Again!" and plunged his great gunugg right into the crab gunugg's spindly legs, breaking another of them clean off. Then the rhino skidded and stamped and flinched away, narrowly avoiding a sweeping cheliped as it waved over their head.

The duodecifold-damned crab meat was emitting such a disturbing scent of honeysuckle that Irradiant, who hated perfume of any kind, almost gagged.

That crab was up to something. Some kind of incantation, unless he missed his guess (which he never did). But he couldn't stop it in time. All he could do was sit there and watch as the crab gunugg's remaining legs—all but the two that had been damaged—plated over with some kind of molten-red shielding. He wouldn't be breaking any more of them.

Three Lovers' magic. That crustacean could be a real problem for him. Between him and the girl, they could keep Irradiant on the defensive. He needed to do some big damage, fast.

Where *was* the girl? Oh… There. Almost missed her. Little Miss Stones with her stubby human legs couldn't keep up with his gunugg mount. No sooner did she come within spear's length—breathing so hard, her whole body was heaving—but Irradiant spurred his galumphing gunugg on again, away from her and straight into the grizzly's back.

The grizzly—who had frozen when his girlfriend the gorilla fell.

So sorry. So sad. Shouldn't stop to cry if you don't want the ghost to get you.

Cackling, Irradiant puppeted his mount like a boy playing with a wooden soldier. "Grapple the bear," he growled out. "Cut off his air supply."

He was just about done with this rag doll of a body. Wanted a better one. A bigger one, with claws. He wanted the one he'd *originally* intended to possess, before that walking crab meat sandwich snipped him loose. Had to keep the grizzly's attention engaged, though. He was still on his guard, after fighting off Irradiant's first attempt.

Best, Irradiant thought, to let his minion do most of the work.

Enthralled by the contract on their back, the rhino gunugg slid both meaty arms around the grizzly's neck, tightening them in a terrible embrace. The grizzly reared up in surprise, distracted from his grief. Immediately, he reached up, his claw-tipped hands digging into the rhino's flesh until they screamed.

Irradiant smiled at the sound, and at the silence that followed: for the grizzly, his airways now cut off, made no noise at all. Just kept pulling and rending, bucking and riving, knowing that his strength wouldn't last long.

Sliding from his seat at the back of the rhino's skull, Irradiant slicked down their spine and smeared what was left of his host body around his mount's great waist, wrapping their ivory braids around his snapped wrists like reins. He pulsed power and compulsion through the blood oath—*strangle, throttle, choke*—and pondered his future.

Once he'd traveled to Skakmaht, and claimed one of the frozen wizard shells for his new body, and established his sky house, Irradiant would decorate it with trophies from today's great victories: a grizzly bearskin rug to replace the tiger-skin his great-granddaughter had stolen from him; a pair of chelipeds to hang above his mantle; rhinoceros ivory displayed under glass; and maybe a whole stuffed giant gorilla-woman hanging from the ceiling. Taxidermizing skinchanger accident would be a challenge, but he'd be up for it. Who better than a necromancer for that finicky work?

Saint Death's spawn, Irradiant thought, as his mount

suddenly jolted between his legs, screaming in pain. *That bear must have the lung capacity of an army bugler.*

He was beginning to doubt if his pet rhino could hold on long enough for the grizzly gunugg to pass out. Rhino's grapple was as inexorable as the blood oath on their back—but the grizzly was simply more powerful. Claws like a fistful of razors swiped up and back, aiming for the rhino's eyes. A few of the blows got caught on their horns, but the rhino's cheek meat was in ribbons, and their chokehold was beginning to loosen.

The grizzly also had a few tricks of his own in reserve. Flexing his air-starved body till it went completely rigid, he flung himself back against the jade barrier. But the rhino, still clamped about his neck, hit it first.

Actually, no, *Irradiant* hit it first. He was still piggyback on the useless ungulate, and didn't have time to bail.

SMASH!

The concussion squished his shattered body between jade dome and gunugg bulk.

SMASH!

As the weight of two god-beasts bore down on him, Irradiant shrank to almost nothing inside his host body. It squished and sloshed and squashed and splatted, until the green robes he was wearing were thicker than the sagging skin they clothed.

Ref was pretty much noodles at this point. All her juice squeezed out. Literally.

Time to jump.

GETTING IN WAS easy.

Getting where he wanted to go was harder: an act of pure will in a directionless dark.

Irradiant squirmed his way up and through the rhino gunugg's mucilaginous interior. For his ingress: the gaping black wounds of the blood oath. An embarrassment of doorways, and he'd used them all. Spreading his substance thin, he'd seeped through the rhino's lacerated back-skin like rain falling on mudcrack.

Given his druthers, his preferred ingress was through the eye. So much cleaner, and it gave him a good view besides. He was chewing his way up there now, eager to get out of the gooey middle.

It cost him precious seconds, but he made it through, and finally rooted himself firmly in the left eye socket, his throne of preference. Once there, he sent out his tendrils of substance to expand throughout his new host body like mycelium.

The rush of possession made him giddy; a flood of feeling and thought from his host came upon him like a sudden downpour. But Irradiant had grown adept at stuffing the main personality of his prey into his gullet and eating it first, where it would no longer bother him.

A big mouthful, but he gulped it down—and with it, all knowledge of the rhino gunugg Zerrinoa.

Huh, he thought. *So the beastie had a name, did they? Not anymore. It's my name now.*

Nice to have horns, anyway. And to be enormous. In life, Irradiant had been rather small in stature. And this large body was so filled with electric nervousness, with trembling readiness, with a desire to charge! The body was, Irradiant discovered, still hanging doggedly from the neck of the gigantic grizzly gunugg— Medyeved, his new knowledge told him—in an attempt to bring him to him knees.

No wonder Sosha loved big game hunting. Is this what he'd felt, every time?

"Down, boy!" Irradiant screamed, redoubling his chokehold on the grizzly. Then, borrowing a page from the grizzly's own book—*thanks a lot, Medyeved, old pal*—he wrenched himself sideways, off the wall and onto the hard basalt floor, capsizing his opponent along with him.

Like two mastiffs in a dog-fighting ring, Irradiant and Medyeved rolled and snarled and somersaulted. Irradiant tried to aim the epicenter of their battle in between the crab's— *Karramorra's*—legs, and beneath his massive belly, where the priest's super-armored, interfering chelipeds couldn't reach him.

But it was imprecise work, and Irradiant was both too busy and too dizzy to mark where they ended up.

It wasn't a fair fight. Medyeved was trying to murder him, but Irradiant was simply biding his time, siphoning off Zerrinoa's juices while keeping Medyeved happily distracted ripping his host body to shreds. All he needed was an opening. An opportunity.

He wanted *in*.

Irradiant had never felt so alive in all of his undeath. It was *enormously* satisfying to head-butt a god-beast in the face, to watch the double-holed wounds open up under his horns. Claws slashed. Fangs champed. Jaws clamped. Cuts opened up like chisel marks in his host body's clay-gray hide. White blood gushed from his flanks, his shoulders, his arms. More and more the black blood was spurting up and out. Leaky things, skinchangers.

But Irradiant was almost done taking what he needed.

Medyeved came at him with a huge downward stroke. He slashed right to left—beneath the breast, across the torso—and laid Irradiant's host body open, gullet to gizzard. In a human, he would've called this a liver cut, with adjacent damage to intestines, spleen, and stomach.

But Irradiant had chewed a path through the internal bits of this gunugg, and he knew firsthand what it was made of. Its material accident consisted of an outer layer of skin-stuff, then a thick layer of bright white goo, then, beneath that, a dense core of black tar-like stuff. Rivers of substance flowed through these materials like oxygen through the bloodstream, the invisible engine of its being.

Now that the innermost black stuff was showing up on the outermost skin-stuff, it was time to jump bodies again. Irradiant just needed to make the transfer when no one was looking.

Especially not the gunugg priest. Or the girl.

Where *was* the girl? He'd lost track of her again.

Bunching up his massive legs, putting all the force of his haunches into the movement, Irradiant kicked out, thrusting Medyeved off him. Medyeved staggered back, winded. In the seconds it took him to recover, Irradiant clutched his gushing middle and casting a furtive glance about for his true opponent.

There she was. Nowhere near him. Kneeling beside the felled gorilla, not even *looking* his way. She'd disappeared her misty guisarme, freeing both hands to press them against the gorilla gunugg's massive, caved-in chest. She was...

Irradiant goggled. *Is that infernal child* brinking *a soul-sucker?*

Brinking was for *humans*. Brinking was for special occasions—*state* occasions. One did not use one's necromantic powers to coax just *anyone* back from the cliff's edge of annihilation. One did not summon down Saint Death's dark lightning to succor *another* god's children! One did not *brink animals!* It was blasphemous!

This infuriated him—so much so, that Irradiant didn't notice the prodigious cheliped descending out of nowhere and almost clipping his head off.

He jerked back just in time, and reached behind his neck to close his three-fingered hand over the steel stylus jutting out of it, like a crossbow bolt stuck in his armored skin.

One tug, and he jerked it free. The stylus was barely bigger than a knitting needle compared to his host body's enormous palm. It lay inert; no endowment from Lan Satthi empowered it, now that Irradiant no longer possessed the notary priest's body, one with her flesh and her god-bond.

Heh. Ref was basically a sodden capelet sticking unpleasantly to his back.

Irradiant turned the stylus in his grip, just as Medyeved rushed on him with a roar of challenge. But when the grizzly gunugg crashed upon him, he bellowed in pain as Irradiant stabbed the stylus nib-first into his eye.

Didn't have much time to enjoy his victory, though. In the chaos of the scuffle, he'd lost sight of Crabby again. Didn't duck in time when that twelve-cursed cheliped came sweeping down from above, knocking the fighting gunuggs off each other, and sending them both flying in opposite directions.

Irradiant opened his eyes, discombobulated. He was lying on

his back, on the floor. Massive and alien, Karramorra loomed over him. Irradiant had the odd sense of being glared at, though he couldn't get a fix on which of the knobby bits and spines were the gunugg priest's actual eye stalks.

Anyway, he *refused* to be intimidated by an oversized bowl of bisque-to-be.

Accidentally speaking, there was hardly anything at all to the giant crimson spider crab. The gunugg was mostly legs and carapace, and brittle as a cicada shell—a mere thirty feet of air and nothing. Pah! Irradiant could knock him down with a grin and a handshake.

The thought filled him with feral, fey glee. The skin between his horns twitched. The raw tattoos on his back stretched and seared. The wound in his torso dripped and dripped.

Throwing back his head, he screamed in Zerrinoa's belly-big baritone, "I'll make *dip* out of you! I'll *dress* you! I'll *devil* you! I'll put you in my ice cream! You're not long for this world, spindle-shanks!"

Karramorra lunged for him. This time, Irradiant knew what to do. He had all of Zerrinoa's herd animal instincts at his disposal—and all of them were telling him to charge *toward* peril, not *away* from it.

He started the charge, staying with his host body just long enough for it to gain momentum, become an unstoppable force. Then, he flung himself out through the raw wounds of the blood oath he had carved into Zerrinoa's skin. His intimacy with Zerrinoa's blood, his sympathy with it, directed his flight from his former host body and into his new anchor.

Blood called to blood, became a bridge. The white and black goo running from Zerrinoa's wounds was the same stuff that coated the steel stylus he'd just plunged in Medyeved's left eye. A tightrope of sympathy.

Irradiant flowed across it, from one body to the next, this time in no danger of dissipating into the void, or bouncing from one jade wall to another like a fish in a bowl, waiting for that silver hook to jab him.

As he left the rhino gunugg's body, Irradiant tore their insides out. He took their gunugg-rich substance, kernel and all, leaving just enough in the outer husk to keep it nice and dense. He needed it heavy enough to do his intended work.

Which it did—beautifully! Zerrinoa's husk crashed into, and collapsed upon, the gunugg priest, then lay still.

As Irradiant slipped in through the puncture wound in Medyeved's left eye, he could barely restrain himself from yelling "*Timber!*" as the spider crab toppled like a titanwood in a lightning storm, knocked supine under the rhino's greater weight. He was massive, yes, but he was also nothing. Nothing!

And Irradiant was *everything*.

Or he would be, once he finished the girl.

Where was the girl? Still at her spellwork. Brinking away. The crash of the two colossal gunuggs did make her look up, briefly. She focused, wide-eyed, on the fallen god-beasts, but her gaze almost immediately snapped away from the pile of shellfish and rhino flesh to scan the rest of the stage.

Looking for *him*.

The gorilla gunugg—damn it, Irradiant thought he wouldn't have to worry about her anymore—was slowly sitting up, the wound on her chest closed completely. One mark remained, like a scar but chased in silver, running down the center of her chest.

His great-granddaughter turned her head, murmured something to the gunugg. Something stupid, probably, like, *Stay here*. Scrambling to her feet, she opened her left hand, and the next instant, her misty guisarme reappeared in it. Her head turned in his direction. Her body followed.

Damn it duodecifold. Had she spotted him *already*?

Maybe—but she seemed to change her mind about pursuing him. At the last minute, she veered toward the toppled crab gunugg instead. He'd fallen right on his shell, the heaviest thing about him. Hilarious to watch the big bug struggling to roll himself right-side up, legs waving in the air.

Medyeved bucked as Irradiant tunneled inside his left eye, still fighting—but not for long. Here, Irradiant reigned supreme. He'd started siphoning off the core of the god-beast's kernel the minute he had gained ingress.

Saint Death sucks eggs, but these gunuggs were packed with power. What a wallop! He was still reeling from trying to ingest all of Zerrinoa all at once, and now there was *this*.

Almost too much. Almost.

He glutted himself. He swelled with substance.

Pity there were only *four* gunuggs in all. Irradiant was developing quite a taste for them.

CHAPTER SIXTEEN
Reinforcements

As FAR AS her echo-wounds went, Lanie was more perforation than person. Her face and clothes were sopping—with tears, sweat, snot, other people's strange blood, her own, she didn't even know anymore.

What she did know: she needed to get Karramorra up and on all of his feet again.

She couldn't finish this without him. She might not be able to finish *with* him. But if she didn't get him back up, there wouldn't *be* a him anymore. There would only be the ghost, glaring from a pair of eye stalks, and grinning from a mouth not made for it.

But how to flip a spider crab the size of a house? How even to climb high enough to try and push poor Zerrinoa's husk off of him?

As she stumbled up next to Karramorra, Lanie felt a tug at her mind, like a cat batting at a string.

My lady, Stripes suggested to her (very much in the voice that Lanie used to use for him to entertain an infant Datu, both of them belly-flopped on the tiger rug in Stones Library and pretending his ferocious head could talk), *if I may be of service in this?*

Lanie eyed the cartulary uneasily. That green glow still emanated from its pages, the contract still active—despite the horrible husking of the notary priest. Lan Satthi yet presided in judgement over the Hastiludes. Which meant the outcome was still undecided: did Saint Death favor her or the ghost?

Which meant, according to the *Instrument to Compete in the Hastiludes*, Lanie couldn't accept any outside help, or use any other sorceries than her own death magic.

Ahem, Stripes coughed.

Oh, Lanie realized. *Right. Come on then.*

Tanned skin and stuffed tail flapping, Stripes shot up from the back of stage—Lanie caught a flash of Duantri's astonished face—and zoomed to her. He swirled twice around her before knocking her knees out from under her, sliding beneath her buttocks, catching her and lifting her aloft—right up onto Karramorra's abdomen.

Stripes wove through the obstacle course of Karramorra's segmented, straw-like legs, helpless as saplings in a cyclone wind, and zipped across the flat expanse of his pale abdomen, until he came the wreckage of the rhino gunugg. What was left of Zerrinoa was slumped over Karramorra's lower half, pinning him down.

"Now comes the hard part," Lanie muttered. But a moment ago, even getting this far had seemed the hard part, so she slipped an arm around Stripes's neck, hugged him hard, and kissed him twice on his whiskered cheek. "Thank you, thank you," she whispered, sliding off his back. He stayed close, hovering next to her, a source of heat and magic she hadn't known she'd needed.

It wasn't that they were dead. Lanie handled dead things all the time. It was that both Zerrinoa and the notary priest were recently, violently murdered, their durity violated, their pneuma devoured, and touching them felt like purposely peeling the skin of her palms off.

But she did. She reached out with both hands: one to lay upon Zerrinoa's spattered hide, one to touch the scrap of pulpy durity and green-dyed nettle cloth that used to be the referee.

Then, using no hands at all, she reached out for Saint Death, who was everywhere on Athe, and everywhere on this stage, and especially here, right here, beneath her hands.

Lanie's throat creaked like an old house settling. Her parched lips moved. She thought she was praying in her own language until she listened to the sounds she was making:

"Suriki, shallu, silili, suhm'sda, sejish, se'qa, setti, salal, sithisdi, suhf'sda, sihesh, sa. Suriki, shallu, silili, suhm'sda, sejish, se'qa…"

The twelve Quadic apologies. Over and over again.

Appropriate, Lanie thought, *that a priest of Saint Death can only pray in apologies.*

She tried to force her mouth to form other, more useful prayers, ones that could direct her substance into the dead matter, animate it into ectenica. She needed to hum the Maranathasseth Anthem, except she couldn't remember the melody. It took a great deal of sothaín to access an ancient spellsong. Recalling one meant coming at it sideways, like summoning the memory of a strong scent smelled only once in early childhood—and she just couldn't get her mind unmuddled.

She was too far up off the ground, which made her queasy. She was touching two murder victims with her bare hands, which made her queasier. Her whole body was wrung out like a dishrag used to clean a scullery's worth of platters after three consecutive feast days. Brinking Elkinzirra back from the chasm of death had taken all her strength, all her concentration—what little she had left after using all of those novel spells in the Game of Changes, and forging a guisarme out of death magic for the Game of Favors. She'd used so much of herself today, and felt as substance-less as these husks.

My lady, Stripes reminded her, giving her a nudge, *while sharing your substance with dead accident is the god's preferred method of making ectenica—it is how you made* me, *after all—it is not the* only *way of making ectenica.*

Lanie's brow wrinkled. Stripes was correct (or, the silly voice in her head that she was designating to Stripes was). There was another way. One she'd learned as a child, from Grandpa Rad. Her god disapproved of it, but it was easy. So easy.

All she had to do was bleed.

And since she was already bleeding from her echo-wounds—

all over the rhino gunugg and the referee, too—the thing was, in essence, already done.

The blood of a living necromancer. The material stuff of dead accident. The twain together: combining, interacting. These were the conditions to create the third of the three states: undeath.

Ectenica had kindled almost before Lanie realized it.

Both corpses—the massive gunugg and the pulverized remnant of the notary priest—liquified under her palms.

It was… a lot of ectenica.

Lanie found herself kneeling in a veritable pond of it. Fine stuff it was, too, beautiful stuff. With a quicksilver consistency, a color like melted lapis lazuli, and a low zizzle of lightning, the ectenica spread beneath her, coating Karramorra's abdomen in its slow tide. It laved Lanie's sore skin with cool, soothing licks, inviting her in, inviting her deeper.

For a tempting second, she considered diving into the ectenical pond, and letting herself go wherever it swept her. If she but asked it to, the ectenica would create a conduit for her through the solid stone of the scarp, just like the Witch Queen's sand had done to get her down here in the first place. It would make Lanie malleable, granting her a temporary liquid form, that it might bear her away on its current to wherever she bid it.

Within the ectenica, *becoming* ectenica, Lanie could enter the third of the three states herself, and be as one undead. Escape this life. Escape this place of death for good.

Clumsy and on the point of collapse, she swayed over the pond, peering into it like a child tottering unsupervised at the edge of a lake.

But ectenica was not water, nor reflective like a looking glass. It did not mirror her image, only rippled, and reached for her. Enticing her.

She wrenched herself back.

Don't nose-dive into your own ectenica, girlie, Grandpa Rad's voice rang hatefully in her head. It wasn't the ghost himself, just his memory—but it lived inside her skull as surely as if he had wormed his way in through her left eye. Even after she sent him back to Saint Death's cloak, Irradiant Stones would probably still be inside her head, yammering at her.

But the voice wasn't *wrong*, either.

Last time you covered yourself in ectenica, Lanie reminded herself, *it didn't work out too well*.

Stripes nudged her again, right between her shoulder blades. Somehow, he managed to transmit a purr through his nose. *My lady,* he admonished, the 'finish this' heavily implied.

At least she had Stripes's voice inside her, too, not just the ghost's. Stripes and Tanaliín and Duantri and Makkovian and Havoc. Enough voices to drown the hateful one out.

"Right," she grunted and glared with determination at the ectenica. Thrusting her arms out before her, palms flat, Lanie pushed at it.

"Off," she barked. "Get off of him. Help him. Flip him. Get him on his feet."

She didn't know where she found the strength, but she managed to dredge some up after all, and threw the lot of it behind her urging. She pushed the ectenica not only with her hands but with her whole will, driving it before her.

It was like trying to shift an entire fieldstone wall, or redirect an avalanche with her naked arms. A wave of gray dizziness hit her. She swayed.

But the ectenica *obeyed*.

The undead material coursed outward, pouring itself off Karramorra's abdomen like a pond overflowing. It splashed onto the basalt floor below in a cascade of ball lightning, exploding on impact, ectenica spraying everywhere, lambent and lovely, small cyclones dancing.

And then it gathered itself up again, beneath Karramorra's great red shell.

With a mighty heave, the ectenica geysered up, a waterfall in reverse, lifting Karramorra from the sandy stone floor and flipping him right-side-up in one joyous, buoyant heave.

Lanie went flying.

* * *

SHE MUST HAVE blacked out.

When she awoke, she realized she was somehow wedged between two of the giant, thorn-like protrusions on the back of Karramorra's shell, right behind his antennae. All her echo-wounds had closed. She was surprisingly warm and filled with wellbeing, as if she'd recently been ill, and someone she loved had been keeping vigil at her bedside, but only just stepped out of the room for a moment.

Her backpack, she discovered, was hanging within arm's reach, one of its straps hooked to another spike. Karramorra must have rolled over it at some point during the Hastiludes, and now it was smushed like a badly packed picnic sandwich. Lanie's deep senses reached out for the bones inside it, and received back a cacophony of fragmentary sensations.

Her heart panged for the poor hodgepodge, and her belly was full of a sick sadness. As a vehicle for death magic, crushed or powdered bone was almost as impossible to work with as ash. Lanie hoped she would be able to honor what remained. Bury the whole backpack, perhaps, or burn it. In some rite, later. If there was a later.

For now, she slung the pack over her shoulders, and opened her left hand—still shaking uncontrollably—before closing it again with renewed purpose. The shaft of the guisarme, lighter than caterpillar silk, formed in her hand, a physical presence only because she willed it so. Grasping it, she leaned forward between Karramorra's antennae, where his wizard mark winked up at her.

The triskeles of the Three Lovers began to turn, counterclockwise. Beast claw, striped stocking, spiral of smoke. The sigil burned a lambent lavender, smelling of wildflowers.

Lanie kissed the tip of her fingers and pressed them to his triskeles.

"Thank you," she murmured, for *Someone* had lifted her when she'd fallen from Karramorra's back, and healed her hurts, and set her in a place of safety. Yssimyss was the god of many mysteries, but her rescuer was not one of them; Lanie knew to whom she owed her reprieve.

Ahead of her, she saw Stripes diving—not for the first time, from the look of it—at Medyeved's face. She felt Karramorra's feet begin to move in that direction.

"We have to help him," she said.

"Yes," the gunugg priest agreed, and bore down upon his friend, the god-beast Medyeved, who was possessed by the ghost.

JOIN ME, GYRGARDU, said the Witch Queen in Quadic. *I would speak with thee.*

She was communicating with Duantri through the Bryddongard link, as only Tanaliín should be able to do—but right now, because of the nettle robe, could *not* do.

Duantri's head snapped up. She glared up at Tam, who was still squatting on her sand mound, brooding her half-buried egg.

Then free me from my chains, this nettle robe, Duantri blasted back through the link. *Return to me my kestrel and my bond, and then mayhap I'll deign to speak with thee.*

No nettle robe can cut thy bond from thee, Tam replied. *The cloth's a tool to bind the young and green, to hold them to one shape and keep them safe, protecting others from their tiny teeth. But* thou, *Gyrgardu, art no hatchling child.*

Duantri scratched her chest beneath the robe. The cloth still burned her, her kestrel inert, her tether to her gyrlady silent.

But though she could not feel that inner cord, and though she feared it was forever snapped, Duantri flung her thought along its length and screamed, in kestrel and in human tongue, one name:

Tanaliín!

From a thousand, thousand miles away, from just under Duantri's skin, there returned to her a startled silence—like a heartbroken baby, wailing alone in her cradle, surprised into a hiccupping happiness by the sudden appearance of a parent. The tears still flowed, the nose still ran, the breath came in bursts and bubbles, but the screaming was cut short, the baby's face wreathed in helpless smiles.

That was the feeling that flooded Duantri: joy—relief—recognition. And it was not her own. She heard the faint and far-off reply:

Duantri!

And inside her chest, an answering fluttering of wings.

There was no one at the gloomy back of the stage to share her gladness but the Witch Queen herself. Tam's impassive face conveyed so little—and yet Duantri thought she might be smiling.

Duantri hesitated, then surrendered. "I'll join you," she said out loud, in Lirian.

Immediately, a spill of sand slid down the side of the pile and mounded around Duantri's ankles. The next second, a wave of it swept up her body, coating her skin and robe, and entering her nostrils and ears. It turned the eerily lit stage prismatic as rainbow dust struck her eyes. The sand sifted through her flesh, into her body, as if solidity were no barrier. It rendered her as weightless as itself: a being of disparate dust motes, light as a puff of powder in an errant sunbeam.

For the second time that day, the sand sucked her up inside it, and thrust her into the heart of the mound. Only this time, instead of funneling her down from hatchery into hypogeum, the sand siphoned Duantri *up*, all the way to its summit, popping her out and setting her down to one side of the shining kernel egg.

Tam was already leaning over the curving shell, was nose to nose with her the minute Duantri turned. She did not flinch an inch when Duantri sneezed, spraying glittering dust everywhere.

"I am listening," Duantri said. "Why did you call for me?"

"Two of my gunuggs are slain," Tam hissed, her voice a piercing whisper, her gaze fierce. "A third would be dead, were it not for your friend's intercession. Lan Satthi is angry at the death of Her priest. My gods do not want Karramorra served up like a banquet to this severed shade. They asked, and were granted, permission from Their sibling that I may take my fableform and help him in this game. But I fear for my egg."

Her gaze intensified. She waited, her question unasked, for Duantri's answer.

It might have been Makkovian standing before her, begging protection for Datu. It might have been any of the guardians of the many young erophains entrusted to her tutelage in Quadiíb. That it was, instead, a centuries-old skinchanger begging her aid for the sake of an unhatched egg made, Duantri discovered, no difference at all.

There was only one answer. She was a Falcon Defender.

"With my life," she promised softly, in Lirian.

Tam's head retracted as she withdrew her scrutiny. Her impassive face, which was perhaps not so impassive after all, shone with something like gratitude, like trust. The faith she placed in Duantri shook her to her kestrel's soul—but she knew herself; she knew that faith was justified. In years past, Duantri may have done grievous injury to the skinchangers of Madinatam, but everything she had done then was in defense of her beloved. Those same skills would now be turned to protect Tam's own beloved: a reconciliation of sorts.

Delicate as a damselfly, the Witch Queen hopped down from her egg. She gave it a long, somber look, caressed it. Then, squatting on the mound, she scooped up two handfuls of sand, and brought her laden fists to her chest, next to her heart. She closed her bright and burning eyes, and bowed her head.

Duantri watched, knowing she was meant to watch. To cultivate a vigilant patience, she moved into a sothaín attitude from the seventh set: Engoloth's parade rest.

But even though her eyes never left Tam, when the Witch Queen did finally stir, her movement was too fast to follow. Her body seemed to blur, and then she was standing once again directly in front of Duantri, holding out both closed fists in an imperious gesture.

Allowing her surprise to shift her attitude, Duantri moved with fluid grace from the seventh set of sotháin to the fourth. She opened her arms, held out her hands, and turned her palms up, assuming Brotquen's gesture of welcoming.

Tam immediately moved her fists over Duantri's palms, as if to pour out the sand she carried.

But in her fists, the sand had turned to molten glass. It was as thick and liquid as honey, full of a forge-pale glow edged in black.

Duantri inhaled sharply. But she tightened her lips, held her hands steady.

Squeezing her fists, Tam compressed the molten sand through her grip until it took the shape of two glass daggers, one for each hand. The right-hand dagger was milk-white; the left, bitumen-black. Both were leaf-bladed, double-edged, and so sharp the edges cut the Witch Queen's skin as she dropped the daggers into Duantri's waiting palms, handles first.

She said nothing more. What else needed to be said? She was old and tired, and by this late hour had given away most of her words to her kernel egg. Tam did not look its way again, or at Duantri, but turned and jumped off her mound of sand, and onto the stage.

STRIPES WAS WINNING. He knew he was winning.

Yes, he was now missing an ear, there was a crack in his right eye, and he'd chipped two of his remaining claws on Medyeved's dense, oily fur. This was what winning felt like!

Stripes had the ghost by the scruff of the neck. Fur, blood, skin: none of that tasted like anything to Stripes. Hadn't for decades. All accident was mere dust in his mouth. But a gunugg's *substance*? His *pneuma*? (Were they the same? His lady necromancer seemed to think so.) Whatever this stuff was, it was *scrumptious*, flowing into his mouth, through white blood and through black. It lent Stripes strength, clarity, suppleness— the likes of which he'd never known in all his glorious undeath.

It tasted like... like...

Stripes wanted to smack his lips, but dared not, lest he lose his grip on the ghost's neck scruff. His lady had bid him bite and hold—so bite and hold he would and did. By the twelfth god, he champed down with gusto!

He kept expecting his fangs to meet a few neck bones, but his fangs kept sinking in, piercing pure goo. There *were* no neck bones. Disorienting. If nothing stopped his teeth, he'd soon bite all the way through, and there'd be nothing left to bite. Or hold. Which meant he would have failed his lady. Which wouldn't do.

But what ho! His lady necromancer was bearing down! Riding to his rescue! Mounted on her giant... crab steed? Creeb? Strab? Never mind.

How splendid she was, misty stick in hand, leaning between a thicket of antennae and eye stalks to screech, in her mellifluous and dulcet deep tones: *HOLD HIM STILL, STRIPES!*

Of course, my lady, Stripes said helpfully, and did just that. He held the ghost, who was currently in possession of a grizzly gunugg's form, by the neck, wrestling him in place while his lady bent down and thrust her big stick into his face.

It was a true tiger's strike—her silver fang thwipped through the left side of the gunugg's skull as if his flesh and bone were but sewn of silk. The blade passed into his face and *through* it, coming clear out the other side, like smoke through a vent. No blood, no wound. His lady's silver fang was not meant for the *living*.

Not great news for *Stripes*, actually. The hook's burning cold edge nipped just a *little* too close to his own whiskers for comfort. That ectenical silver would latch onto any undead being like a burr to wool—himself included.

So he spat out his mouthful of neck fur and skinchanger goop just in time to dodge.

The grizzly gunugg made a gurgling nose as the misty guisarme swiped the ghost clean out of his eye socket. No longer a host body, the gunugg dropped to the stage—knees-first, face-second—either dead or in a faint; Stripes couldn't tell. Anyway, the gunugg was no longer his concern.

Stripes's concern—first, last, always—was his lady.

Catching the updraft of the gunugg's collapse, the wind of it flapping beneath his flat belly, Stripes threw himself vertical, a kite on the wind. For a second, he hung in the air, fully upright, tail hanging between the stuffed stubs of his legs, eye to eye with his lady necromancer, who was perched high upon her mighty... creeb.

Like a chevalier in a ballroom, approaching his one true love for a dance, Stripes arrayed himself before her. His lady was wearing her 'death god help me, I'm way too far above the ground' look—which Stripes adored, because it was adorable. Almost a pity to rescue her and wipe that look off her face, but there you have it. It was his solemn duty to help her dismount that... that anomural mule... that decapodal destrier... that podophthalmian stallion... that *whatever* it was—*it* wasn't her proper mount; *Stripes* was!—and convey her back to the solid rock she longed for.

He reared up in the air, ready to somersault himself horizontal again, stiff as a board, safe as a...as an undead tiger rug (which, all right, was fairly perilous, but not to *her*), so that his lady necromancer might step her dainty foot upon his back. He twinkled his glass eyes up at her, signaling that he was ready.

She was staring back at him, wide-eyed, wide-mouthed, screaming.

But he couldn't hear her, because something blew through him.

Something big. Something rotten. Something that smelled of bad oranges.

Something...

LANIE HOOKED THE ghost. She knew she did. But it was like catching a shark on the sharpened edge of some driftwood.

She had wrestled with Irradiant's substance before. It had

always been immense, yes, but never more than she could manage. She'd always thought, with Saint Death's help and with the proper instrument, she'd be strong enough to take him out when the time came.

That time had come. She had her guisarme. Its silver hook went in, just like it was supposed to.

And just like *he* was supposed to, the ghost popped out of his host, hooked on her blade and wriggling with fury.

Medyeved slumped to the floor, but Lanie didn't think Irradiant had had enough time to husk him completely. The damage that Medyeved had taken from battling Zerrinoa's possessed host was extensive, however, and she might have to sit with his bleeding body and brink him back to life, just as soon as...

The guisarme jerked out of her hands, like a harpoon's dart when a whale dives with it...

Only Lanie's dart had found in the ghost no ordinary whale, but a sea monster huge enough to swallow the entire whaleboat—rowboats, crew, and all.

Her guisarme hung in the air, out of her reach, and out of Karramorra's reach too, hovering high above the floor, just under the invisible crest of the dome. The mist of its shaft and the silver of its hook crackled with the ghost's fell ectenica.

Rather than surrendering to her weapon, Irradiant had *entered* it.

He'd started with the hooked blade, and worked his way down the shaft, feeding on the weapon's substance, becoming one with it—as he had become one with all the skinchangers he'd possessed and murdered. But this time, it was *Lanie's* substance he was eating.

Irradiant the guisarme soared backward in the air, bending himself at the exact pitchpoling angle designed to cause the most damage at the end of a deadly arc. Then, fast as a flickersylph darting in for his flower nectar, he shot toward her.

Lanie didn't know what the guisarme might do to her, now that the ghost was entwined with it. She only knew that he was aiming for her heart. That was all she had time to know.

Everything happened so quickly. Stripes reared in front her, an aegis in tiger-skin, and Karramorra crouched low, tipping his body so that she slid halfway down his shell, receiving cover from it. The ghost lanced in.

Irradiant, anchored in the guisarme, swollen with the pneuma of a god-beast and three skinchangers, had become both blade and incendiary. He could cut through anything, and whatever he touched also erupted. He pierced Stripes through neck and jaw—through the wood wool and wire armature that gave his head its shape—and came out the other end, made of mist and silver and abominable ectenica, glistening with ill intent.

And then he *kept going*. He blasted through Karramorra's mouth parts. Mandibles, maxillae, maxillipeds, he skewered through them all, entering the buccal cavity and disappearing into his gullet.

Karramorra gagged on what he could not vomit up, choked on the guisarme's wake of eruptive fire. He shook so hard that Lanie tumbled off the back of his shell and onto the floor.

And Stripes…

Stripes hung headless in the air for just a moment, and then….

Exploded.

CHAPTER SEVENTEEN
The Dragon of Madinatam

STRIPES EXPLODED AND pieces of him went everywhere.

Excelsior wool fell onto Lanie's hair like snowflakes. Bits of wire whipped past her cheeks, leaving little cuts. Cracked glass eyes rolled like marbles onto the basalt. A fine fluff of buff and orange and black fur fell around her, getting everywhere, everywhere, and…

And the piece of Stripes that was really *Lanie* returned to her body, full of teeth and fury.

He killed me! Lanie screamed inside her own mind, an echo without origin.

But there was no time to mourn or rage, because Karramorra was rocking and wobbling above her.

His mouthparts exhaled a single, shocked whirlwind of breath, a summer wind scented with jasmine and lilac, and then all ten of his legs, chelipeds included, lifted up off the floor. He rose into the air as if scooped up by some enormous hand and kept floating until the back of his shell sparked off the suddenly opaque jade of Lan Satthi's dome.

Karramorra's underbelly pulsed, growing translucent. Lanie could see all the inner workings of his abdominal cavity. She watched, her neck flung back, her arms flung out, as the glowing ghost passed hook-first through Karramorra's center, anterior to posterior, mouth to anus, like a barbed laxative—and blew out the other side.

Covered in white and black gore, Irradiant righted himself, spun in the air, and reoriented his hook-end toward Lanie.

A little skip and whir—the guisarme's version of a victory dance—as he put himself again at the correct angle to lance down upon her with all the wrath of his substance and hers combined.

Lanie stripped off her backpack, lobbed it onto the ground, and launched herself on top of it, ripping it open and scrabbling among the shattered bones and crushed hornet dust for something, *anything* of use.

Too late—too late!

The guisarme was coming down on top of her, and Karramorra was on fire, he was toppling, he was crumbling, he was...

Silver sparked. The smell of ice. The falling woolen fluff became a snow flurry in truth. The next thing Lanie knew, two arms were closing around her, a hand coming up to shelter her head against a broad chest.

And a pillar of ice slammed down around her, the guisarme struck, and Karramorra collapsed.

ABOVE THE STAGE, the jade dome disappeared.

The glowing green veins crawling across the leather covers of the hanging cartulary snuffed out like a wet candle. The cartulary slipped from the ivy and slammed to the ground, spine broken, pages bent.

The Hastiludes ended, the hypogeum went dark.

IN THE DARKNESS, two things glowed.

The floating guisarme: gray as moonlight on mist, silver as starlight on water.

And Tam the dragon.

The Witch Queen's body had elongated, grown sleek and sinewy. Spikes erupted from her spine. The black half of her body was more luminous than the blackest pitch, her red half was as hot and bright as caldera coals, and all of it crusted over with jewel-like scales: jet and garnet, onyx and carnelian. The cord of her tailbone had burst from the bottom of her back, swelled to the size of a python, the size of an anaconda, and continued to expand and lengthen, coil and lash. Her thick neck, stretched long, was ringed with ridged muscle in alternating bands of black and gold and red. Her chest was broad and proud as a shield, her head an angular wedge. Golden tympana, round as cymbals, brightened each cheek. Bulbous golden eyes with black diamond pupils glared at the guisarme like it was her next meal.

From her shoulders flared a pair of massive wings, spread overhead like a canopy. Not quite the wings of a raptor, nor yet the wings of a bat, the membranes spanning the phalanges were translucent as glass, crackled with vein-thin cobwebs, and possessed of a nacreous sheen, like that of the kernel egg buried in its mound of sand. Insect wings. Dragonfly wings.

Ivy fell around her like a curtain, moving when she moved, separate and sentient but part of her all the same, like the arms of an octopus. Dragon and ivy: one and the same creature—just as Lanie and Stripes had been the same creature, discrete bodies sharing a twinned mind. Tam, the dragon of Madinatam, *was* Madinatam. She was the city and the scarp. Her pneuma inhabited it, and it was her: from the ivy, to the stones of Leech Keep, to the sands of the hatchery.

Out in the tiers, only a few skinchangers remained to witness the Witch Queen take her fableform. They were vague shapes in the dark, eyes gleaming. None seemed to be the younger coldfire forms. These were skinchanger elders, who had armored themselves in their largest predator shapes, ready to leap onto the stage at Tam's command.

Trapped behind a sheet of solid ice like an insect in white amber, beneath two hundred pounds of spiked red chiton, and held within the protective circle of Cracchen's arms, Lanie watched the double glow of weapon and dragon dance.

Tam stooped upon Irradiant like a falcon on a mouse.

The ghost had no time to react.

258

Possibly, he didn't see her coming from above, talons extended.

Tam grasped the ectenical weapon, as if she, like Lanie, could hold it as a solid thing, feel its edges, its boundaries, its boundless power.

And then she snapped it in half like kindling.

The silver hook flew off the end of its pole, sparkling with ectenica. Tam slapped it out of the air, onto the stone floor of the stage, and brought her talon down on top of it.

Lanie saw the blade shatter.

More than that, she *felt* it. It shattered something inside of her too—that part of her substance still connected to the guisarme, that the ghost had been feeding on. Severed, suddenly.

She waited for the relief of its ricochet, the infusion of furious energy returning to her, like that which had buoyed her upon Stripes's destruction.

It never came. Instead, a certain portion of herself, powerful and beautiful, drained away completely. Forever.

Lanie sagged in Cracchen's cold arms.

He cradled her skull close to his chest, like a secret hand of cards. His heartbeat was slow and large against her ear, the clapper of a cathedral bell. He said nothing.

On the other side of the ice, Tam the dragon smashed and smashed and smashed the guisarme. She splintered the mist of it into droplets. She powdered the silver of it into memory. She erased Irradiant Stones from existence.

And then she flung back her head and roared.

DUANTRI SAW A pillar of ice appear in the middle of the stage where none had been before. Where the pillar *had* been, on the other side of Tam's mound, there suddenly wasn't.

She saw Karramorra's crumpled, smoldering carapace heaped on top of the pillar, but she didn't know if he was alive or dead.

She saw one of the remaining gunuggs—Elkinzirra—rush up to the one on the ground—Medyeved—and run her hands over his body, checking to see if he was still alive.

She saw a crowd of skinchangers in their most terrible forms dash from the audience to the stage.

She saw the dragon, circling and pacing the pillar of ice, pausing once in a while to crush something invisible on the ground.

She could not see Lanie.

And she could not leave the kernel egg to go look for her. She thought—she trusted—she *hoped* that Lanie was in the ice. That Skrathmandan had protected her. She had not thought the sullen, broken man capable of such a rescue.

One of the smaller skinchangers, still wearing his yolkform, who had spent a few intense moments examining the fallen Karramorra, shouted to all the others: "Alive! He's alive! Clear the stage!"

The others glanced at him, from all appearances as bewildered as Duantri.

"Clear the stage!" he repeated, his voice rising. "I can hear him ticking! He's going to molt!"

This, at least, seemed to make sense to the skinchangers, if not to Duantri—enough to spur them into action. All of them, Elkinzirra included, with Medyeved slung across her shoulders, hopped off the stage and bolted away from the colossal wreckage of Karramorra's body.

Silent seconds passed—one, two, three—then, the back of that great red shell burst like a portcullis giving way to a battering ram.

A new Karramorra, huge and undamaged, but wobbly and vulnerable withal, his shell still luminous and tender, not yet hardened, emerged from his old collapsed carapace.

A pause, and then, in his high, sweet lisp, the gunugg priest shouted:

"Praise Yssimyss!"

"*O Mystery, we sing!*" the others shouted back from the safety of the tiers.

"Praise Wykkyrri!"

"*O Beast, we roar!*"

"Praise Amahirra!"

"*O Trickster, we dance!*"

In a much milder tone, as if stunned by the revelation, Karramorra muttered, "By the Three Lovers' grace, I am alive."

At his words, the skinchanger who had shouted warning about the molt—his yolkform a skinny, curly-haired, coral-and-brown-patterned figure—ducked out of hiding. Scrambling back onstage, he ran and hugged one of Karramorra's fragile legs.

"Three Lovers be praised," he sobbed, and kissed the leg over and over again. "Now, come home, my love. Come home, my beloved. You've done enough this day."

Karramorra bobbed his eight new walking legs in weary assent. His chelipeds waved in a helpless shrug. "Yes. Yes, I think I will. I could... rest now. If Tam has no more need of me?"

The dragon in the middle of the stage, still circling the ice pillar with sinuous curiosity, glanced at him, and nodded.

The skinchangers bobbed and ducked their many and various heads in her direction, and started streaming out of the hypogeum through the tunnels at the top of the tiers, carrying or supporting their wounded.

There was nothing left of the dead—of Zerrinoa and Lan Satthi's referee—but a sticky black ash of expended ectenica, mingling with the blood and bone fragments, and the detritus that had been Stripes on the stage floor.

Duantri hugged herself as the dragon whipped away from the ice pillar and prowled back towards the sand mound, the rich gold of her split-pupil eyes cold and unreadable.

She flinched as the dragon beat her wings, taking flight for the mound, but stood her ground next to the kernel egg, feet sunk ankle-deep in the sand. As she watched the oncoming dragon, Duantri told herself to step aside. Instead, she found herself stepping closer to the egg, putting herself fully in front of it, between it and the dragon.

Landing lightly, wings settling, the dragon cocked her head, as if to say, gentle as a spark to tinder, *Gyrgardu, your work is done.*

Duantri gripped her two glass daggers, slippery in her sweaty grip.

Tam the dragon set her front talon upon the kernel egg. She waited, doing nothing else, until Duantri swallowed, nodded, and stepped aside, sliding her way down the sloping sand. It carried her to the floor of the stage, where she stumbled a little before catching her balance.

High above her, Tam scooped up her egg in one great golden talon, and tucked it up against her chest. Turning around once on top of the mound, she gave a great flap of her massive, translucent wings, and rose into the air. From the back of the stage to the pavement at the front, she glided in a single movement. Then, ducking her wedge-shaped head, she slithered into the centermost of the three dark arches beneath the tiered seating.

Enormous, soundless, without a backwards glance, the dragon disappeared into the tunnels that honeycombed the lowest parts of the scarp.

Duantri stared after her, a strange feeling of forlorn dread sitting heavy in her chest. But her attention shifted back to the stage the moment Skrathmandan's pillar of ice suddenly sluiced away in a flood of pure water.

There she stood—"*Lanie!*"—drenched, bedraggled, shaking off Skrathmandan's embrace.

And there he was, clad in garments of clinging frost that gave off their own silvery light, staring down at the necromancer with the oddest expression on his face.

Duantri ran toward her friend. "Lanie!"

"Duantri!"

They started speaking at once.

"I was so afraid…"

"Where did he go?"

Duantri pulled back, but Lanie was already limping to the edge of the stage, holding her hand fast in a grim, cold grip, and dragging her along.

"What? Who? Lanie, where are we going?"

"The ghost." When Duantri just frowned at her, Lanie said, as if repeating herself, "The dragon."

Duantri stared.

Had another pillar of ice just fallen, this time on her, crushing and caging her at once? Perhaps that was why she could only stand there, frozen and staring, until something small and moth-light brushed her hair. It crumbled when she touched it, pieces of something crackling and falling to the floor.

Another piece of whatever it was fell from above. Another. Like rain, if rain were dry. Like dying moths.

Uncomprehending, Duantri glanced down to the mess that was piling up on the floor, and then, searching for its source, looked up at the ceiling where it was spilling from.

Ivy leaves.

Thousands of ivy leaves were dropping from the roof of the hypogeum, brown and shriveled, the great and ancient pneuma that had invigorated and sustained them for four hundred years, husked.

Intermezzo

VISITATIONS

The sky above Athe

Year 4826 of Higher and Lower Quadiíb
On H'za, 2nd of Anatha: the Third Month

18 Days till Spring Equinox

MAKKOVIAN'S PEREGRINE SHADE found his quarry in the night sky.

His quarry was currently speeding through the air in a sky house. Or... more like a... a sky cuddy? A small boat made of crystal ice, open to the elements, with an even smaller shelter cabin at the stern.

Standing at what passed for the cuddy's prow, like a carved figurehead, was Cracchen Skrathmandan.

He stared straight ahead in the direction of the flying boat's flight—due north—seemingly impervious to the elements. He was glittering head to toe with a diamond-frost of ice.

Makkovian decided to avoid him.

He slipped his peregrine shade into the shelter cabin through one of its icy walls (there were benefits to his shadeform; passing through solid objects was one of them), beyond which, his quarry lay.

Makkovian's connection to Mizka had grown stronger the closer he approached to her, but it was always with him. It had been with him ever since she had laid her spell of ice and mending upon him months ago, on their river journey to Quadiíb, when she reconnected him to his severed arm by the grace of several gods.

One of these gods, Mizka had warned him at the time, was the Skaki god Erre'Elur, who shared some aspects with the Quadoni god Doédenna. But even hinting at Their similarities in certain conservative circles of the Judicial Colloquium of Gyrveard would be blasphemy—and Makkovian was already in enough trouble with them over the death of his gyrlady, and the fact that he, her gyrgardi, had miraculously and through no fault of his own survived it.

In truth, Makkovian had been connected to Mizka long before that: from the day she had fused his late gyrlady's Bryddongard to his own arm, giving him control over his change from man to bird and back again. Giving him the sovereignty over his own body that her sister had stolen from him.

And, yes, even before *that*, they were connected. For he and Mizka had been trapped together in Stones Manor—her house, his prison—both of them living in fear of Amanita Muscaria Stones, and both of them raising his daughter, Datu.

He had not wanted to admit it *then*. He had thought of her as an abomination, a Stones, a monster, and her death magic as destructive and unnatural. He had thought that she bore a seed of aberrance inside of her, and that one day, without warning, she would turn on them all, a demon of nightmare, far outstripping her sister in power and terror.

But then, Makkovian kept receiving her magic—her god's *miracles*—into his own body.

And Mizka kept changing before his eyes—but *not* into a monster.

And *he* kept changing, too.

Most of all, it was the changes in his daughter that convinced him of Mizka's goodness, and of the virtue in their strengthening connection. Sacred Datura was far happier, and far more human because of her aunt—and even more so, because of her aunt's powers, which she had used to raise up a wolf pup from the dead, and bind it to Datu's life.

He owed Mizka Datu's happiness. He owed her everything.

Flying three thousand miles in the shape of a shadow bird

was nothing to his debt, or his gratitude. He was happy to do it.

"Makkovian!" Mizka cried out, the moment that his peregrine shade soared into the tiny shelter cabin to perch soundlessly on her cot.

The cot was a slab of ice. Everything on this flying sky cuddy was made of ice. Makkovian was glad his shadeform could not feel the cold, because just looking at Mizka and his beloved Duantri huddled together for warmth made him ache in sympathy.

They slept on top of their bedrolls, but beneath a heap of cloaks and blankets. His Duantri was asleep but shivering. Mizka had been awake, staring at the ceiling, until she caught sight of him.

At her shout, though, Duantri jerked out of her fetal curl and looked wildly about. She held two glass daggers, one white, one black, as if she'd been sleeping curled up with them.

"Where? Is he hurt? Is there a death? Is it Tanaliín? Datu?"

"No, no, Duantri—look! He's here! He's *here!*"

For some reason, Mizka was weeping and laughing and babbling at the same time, which Makkovian had seen her do on a surge day, but never when they were almost three weeks away from one. Scooting down towards the foot of the bed, Mizka held out her right arm to him. Her left arm hung at her side as if broken.

Makkovian cocked his head in scrutiny. Mizka looked... haggard. Too sharp. Angles everywhere. As if some cancer ate away at her from the inside.

She was waving an insistent hand at him. "Come! Come, Makkovian—talk to us! I can't believe you're actually *here*. How did you find us? Wait, *can* you talk in this form?"

Mizka grinned at him—and Makkovian would never tell her, but it was a ghastly expression, all bones. "I wouldn't put it past your shadeform to have learned new tricks since we left in Quadiíb. I know *I* have."

Makkovian sent his peregrine shade to hop onto her arm.

Her arm sagged like a branch laden with too much snow. He hopped onto her knee instead.

His shadow bird had no physical weight, but it did have *substance*. The warmth of sunlight. The whisper of wind. There was a slight change in pressure, Tanalíin had told him, when one held a palm against his translucid, smoke-sift feathers. And Datu had informed him that his peregrine shade had 'eyes like stars—just like Undies.'

Duantri scooted closer to him, making his heart well with happiness. She put her hand on Mizka's knee, right next to him. Ah, that comely, unparalleled hand! Makkovian wished to press her golden knuckles to his lips, one by one. But, at the moment, all he had was a beak—and even that would pass right through her perfect skin.

Mizka was muttering to herself, something about 'alternative methods of communication,' but must have realized she was making no sense to anyone else, for she stopped herself short. "Never mind. I'll keep thinking about it. Find a way to get that beak of yours speaking. Until then, we'll just tell you everything that's happened to *us*, so you can convey *that* to Tanalíin and—"

"Oh, please!" Duantri burst out in Quadic, bending her precious face to his. "Oh, please, Makkovian, my love! Tell Tanalíin I never meant to part! Bewitched was I, and bound in nettlecloth. But nevermore, in this life or the next," she added with a shudder, "shall I again return to that dark scarp: so sharp with appetence, so fair and fell."

Overcome, Makkovian hopped his peregrine shade onto Duantri's lap. Her face grew radiant with love, her volume dropped. She murmured, "And art thou also well, beloved own? So far from daughter, pilgrimage, and home? How cam'st thou here? How long hast been aloft? How oft canst fly in such a form while—"

"Duantri!" Mizka laughed at her. "My dear one, you know he can't answer your questions. Not yet. I have a few ideas about how we might be able to manage that—but first, let's make our report. He may not have much time with us." She glanced his way, eyebrows raised.

Makkovian did his best to ruffle his feathers in what he hoped approximated a shrug. His body had lain a full day in its dwalming ring, and more. Sacred Datura would be anxious. But he had only just arrived; he would not rush home now with no story to relay, no messages to pass on.

Duantri hovered a hand above his peregrine shade. She stroked the air above his feathers with the same idle tenderness with which she strummed a free etude on her guitar.

"We parted ways just outside the city of Madinatam," Mizka began. "Duantri flew on high, and Cracchen and I took the bridge on foot. And, oh, Makkovian, this *bridge!* It was made of *limestone* and…"

Makkovian listened closely as she and Duantri told their tale, occasionally talking over each other, or making small corrections to one another's narrative. One would take up the thread when the other grew too overcome to speak. Sometimes they held hands, or stopped to hug each other, pressed cheek to cheek, trembling. He wished he could be there in the flesh, to enfold them in his arms. They were cold and afraid and sad; he would warm them, and feed them, and sing poetry to them until they felt safe again.

But for now, he just listened, trying to remember everything. Tanaliín's curiosity and Datu's worry, he knew, would only be assuaged by a flood of narrative. He had to make it as comprehensive as possible, no detail too small. (Although perhaps he would leave out the part about Stripes—at least, until 'Auntie Lanie' came home to tell Datu about it in her own inimitable way. Mizka had a way of making the death of all things seem… friendly.)

When they had finished their tale—how the ghost had escaped Madinatam in the shape of a dragon, carrying away the Witch Queen's kernel egg; how Cracchen Skrathmandan had constructed them a ship of ice with the help of the sky wizards he carried in his body; and how they had been flying in pursuit of Irradiant Stones ever since—Mizka glanced over at the doorway.

"Cracchen," she called out, "join us."

Which was when Makkovian realized that there was another person in the room with them.

"Or, wait"—Mizka frowned, struggling, he thought, to sound friendly—"do you still *want* to be called Cracchen? Since you... well... since you... *changed?*"

The frost-coated glitter-wizard whom Makkovian had encountered on the prow now ducked into the cabin. Though everything in the room was already made of ice, the air grew colder the instant he entered. Though Makkovian's peregrine shade could not feel the difference, he noticed the way Mizka and Duantri shrank closer to each other, shivered harder. He watched a new layer of frost begin to form over every surface, another already beginning to build upon that.

"Our apologies," said the man, who did not sound at all sorry. "We did not mean to intrude upon your... reunion? Only, we heard you both speaking so animatedly about things we already know, and so grew curious."

His voice was low and slow, full of the calligraphic Skaki rhythms that Makkovian associated with a native speaker—not one who, like Cracchen, had been bred up in Rook, and then spent his adulthood living in other countries.

Makkovian recalled that Haaken, Cracchen's identical brother, spoke with a similar cadence—but Haaken was practically a recluse. He lived by himself in a tower in Liriat Proper, immersed in all things Skaki. His title was acting Skaki ambassador to Blood Royal Errolirrolin Brackenwild—though, from what Makkovian knew, Skakmaht no longer had a government to have appointed him to this position, nor a national voice whose interests he represented, nor any official mission he might serve. But Haaken seemed bent on making a reality of his fiction.

The frosty wizard paused, and smiled at Mizka with blue-cast lips. His skin was azure-pale, and his left eye, which had been carved of clear ice, held a strange, nocturnal glow.

Makkovian did not know if he liked the way this man was looking at Mizka. He could not help thinking that if this wizard really had not wished to intrude upon them, he would not now be looming in the doorway, pressuring Mizka to invite him in, making her colder, flashing his power around in a way that both discomfited and overwhelmed.

The wizard continued, "As for the mode of appellation by which you should address us—we thank you for inquiring, but we have no preference. You may call us Cracchen, if it pleases you. Or feel free to make use of any of our other names: Hrok; Lothgarran; Jegil; Fohr'ga…"

The man spoke perhaps two and a half dozen more names, and with each one that he spoke, his voice changed: sometimes deeper, sometimes lighter, some of the voices scratchy, some throaty or ringing or whispery, as if many different personalities spoke through his throat, his tongue, his lips.

"Perhaps," the man concluded, his gaze still fixed upon Mizka, his frozen mouth still smiling, "*you* will name us, priest of Erre'Elur. A Stones destroyed us; and a Stones has put us back together again. Who does our god say we are, when She whispers in your ear?"

Mizka answered sharply, apparently impatient with his games, "I am not your mother. It's not my job to name you."

The Skaki sky wizard—for that was what he was, Makkovian decided—laughed with pure delight.

"No," he agreed. "Our mother yet lives, does she not? Perhaps we will ask Sari Skrathmandan for our new name."

What *was* that expression in the sky wizard's eyes? Why did it ruffle all of Makkovian's shadow hackles? There was nothing of malice or spite in it. No intent to harm. No fear. But there was…. *reverence*. Desire. And power—so much power, and all of it so freezing cold. And Mizka, despite her acerbic words, was already so gray and shivering.

But here was Duantri, true to form, to fling her arm around Mizka's waist and gather her close in a protective hug, just as Makkovian had been wishing to do. In solidarity, he flew from

273

Duantri's lap and onto Mizka's shoulder, where he glared at the man, first with one eye, then the other.

The wizard laughed again. He had been watching the peregrine shade for its reaction, and seemed pleased with it.

"Extraordinary! And what, pray, is *that?*" He sounded amused, mildly interested, but Makkovian thought that, in truth, the wizard was deeply invested in how Mizka would answer him. Sorcery was central to this man's existence. He was mostly made of it, judging from the silver scars of ice seaming his skin. Any novel form of magic, like the shadow bird, would consume his restless attention until he managed to pin it in place and unravel its mysteries, performing his autopsies on the miracle until there was nothing left but rags.

"That," said Mizka, "is Makkovian Covan."

"And who is Makkovian Covan?"

"He is… family."

"Is he?" Cracchen stared into the shadow bird's eyes. "What is he doing here?"

"He came to help me."

"Do you need help? I could help you."

At this, Mizka cocked her head at him, as if she, too, were a Gyrgardu in her falcon form. (The Blackbird Bride, Makkovian recalled, had once tried to make Mizka her wizard lover, giving her the title 'Condor,' one of the four-and-twenty blackbirds of Rookery Court. But Makkovian had always thought that the bird of Mizka's soul was no kind of raptor at all, but something much smaller and more sociable. Like a salt-flat warbler, with her 'who-is-it?' call, and her fondness for flowers, and her tendency to build a home in other birds' abandoned nests.)

As her silence stretched, Cracchen smiled and coaxed her, "Do you have some task for us, Miscellaneous? Some favor?" Then, lowering his voice to a tone that Makkovian had only ever used in the privacy of Tanaliín and Duantri's esh, *long* after Datu had fallen asleep, he murmured, "You have but to ask."

Mizka half-smiled in reply, but shook her head. "What I'm thinking is… completely radical."

A gleam of speculation sprang to the wizard's eyes. Mizka could not have said anything more calculated to capture his interest. And she had done it, Makkovian thought, on purpose.

"Please," said the wizard, "ask us anything. No request too small. If it is in our power to grant it, we will. In Madinatam, we had to enter our chrysalis amidst a crisis. To ensure a chance for our mutual survival, we needed time to establish a common lattice between us. Thus, we were useless to you in the Hastiludes. This shames us. We would be most ecstatic to help you now."

"You weren't useless when you saved me from two hundred pounds of shellfish falling on my head," Mizka said, and the wizard smiled at her compliment, his glowing gaze full of a transfixed admiration.

She is egging him on, thought Makkovian. *And he is obsessed with her.*

"Do you really want to help?" Mizka asked.

"Oh, yes."

She turned suddenly to bump cheeks with Duantri. "And Duantri, my darling, you want to speak to Makkovian? Face to face, voice to voice?"

His beloved Duantri nodded, looking eager but confused.

"And, Makkovian—you have news to impart? Impossible to do in your shadeform?"

Makkovian cocked his peregrine shade's head, opening his beak in a soundless caw of agreement.

"Cracchen," Mizka gestured to the wizard. "You are no stranger to sharing your... vessel with"—she cleared her throat—"multitudes? If you are serious about helping us, may I ask—and it would be such a great favor to me—would you mind inviting another guest, um, in?"

The wizard was quiet for a long moment. She had, it seemed, surprised him.

So was Makkovian surprised. Even if he had a beak to squawk, he'd have been too shocked.

"Are you asking us," the wizard inquired with dawning incredulity, "to invite your demon bird into our body?"

"We really need to talk to him," Mizka opened her eyes very wide. "And it's not like it would be that *difficult*, spellwork-wise. The peregrine shade is a product of mostly Skaki magic— *Haaken's* magic, which you're already in sympathy with, by nature of your shared blood. And if there's one thing *all* of you"—she wiggled her fingers in front of his face—"*collectively* know more about than anyone else on Athe, it's Skaki magic. I think you could do it—easily! If you're willing. If you trust me."

She tilted her head slightly to the bird on her shoulder, her cheek brushing the outer nimbus of its wing.

"You'd have to agree too, Makkovian. Know this, I *truly* believe that you and Cracchen could share—for a time—um, Erre'Elur's protective umbrella, as it were. And it would be so useful, so wonderful, to speak to you in person?" But she ended on a questioning note, as if, in the lengthening silence, she had already begun to doubt herself.

"Lanie," Duantri began, with even more dubiousness than Makkovian felt.

But on the floor, the sky wizard was already easing himself into an alert genuflection. He lifted his arm and held it out, straight and strong: a perch for the peregrine shade. His face was confident again, his eyes alight—perhaps even greedy. Makkovian saw that he was eager to know this novel sorcery from the inside, and he believed himself mighty enough to quash the peregrine shade if it proved perilous to him.

"This," he said, "will be interesting."

ONCE MAKKOVIAN'S PEREGRINE shade slipped like smoke into the center of Cracchen's chest, and they'd all had a chance to converse for a few minutes, Lanie left the shelter cabin to give him and Duantri some privacy.

At first Duantri had been afraid to be alone with him, and had clutched Lanie's arm, holding her back. But as soon as Makkovian opened Cracchen's mouth to murmur, "My golden one, my dawn's own light, my love," in his unmistakable Quadic, with that southerly hint of a qasirate burr, she'd melted and flung herself into his arms.

Alone now, Lanie walked to the prow, shivering. She was thinking about vessels.

She thought about the vessel of the body, which housed the soul. Substance and accident. Pneuma and durity.

She thought about the vessel they were flying on now, that would carry them across the Taquathuran territories, and over Umrys-by-the-Sea, into Northernmost Skakmaht. She thought about what powered it.

The Old Skaki term for this kind of flying ice ship was called a 'vital-force fulmar,' a fulmar being a species of smelly northern gull. Cracchen (the integrated lattice of sky wizards now collectively known as Cracchen, *not* the Cracchen she had known before) had wrinkled his nose in distaste when telling her and Duantri about fulmar ships. He'd explained, very seriously, that in Skakmaht, such a vehicle was considered a far more inferior means of transportation than a sky house.

A fulmar ship was simply an extension of the icicles that overlaid every sky wizard's skin. One could, he told them, grow one's crystals out and adapt them into many useful structures— armor, pillar, ship, hut, steed: whatever was most convenient or necessary at the moment. A sky wizard used their own body's energy, their 'vital force' (or 'substance' or 'pneuma' as foreigners might call it), as the engine that powered the crystal structure's growth and movements.

A fulmar ship was *not*, as Lanie had first assumed when Cracchen invited them onboard, some sort of nascent sky house.

Oh, no, he had corrected her, most ardently, *a sky house is constructed of many kinds of crystal, stone as well as ice, and can grow to an enormous size. It connects to all other sky houses to make even greater structures, and is powered to flight not by the living wizards who captain them, but by 'our engine of ancestors,' which we also call 'the snowpyre-source.'*

In other words, had been Lanie's astonished reply, *you power your flying houses with the bodies of your dead? Ectenical fuel? But how do you stabilize it?*

And Cracchen had only smiled and said, *Not our dead. Our dying.*

At the very bottom of a sky house—which was not called a cellar but a 'sepulcher'—there was something like an enormous crypt, where the sky wizards interred their dying relatives. But instead of releasing them to their final death, the dying bodies were preserved in ice, becoming long-term magical fuel for the sky house that the ice itself siphoned off and used. This fuel was not ectenica—not an *undead* material—for the dying were not allowed to die. For many long years, sometimes decades, they lay upon their snowpyres, their lives extended by magic, the prolonged act of their dying feeding the power of the sky house.

Lanie found the idea of such lingering… disturbing. But she understood that her reaction might be a cultural, not a moral, one. Dying could take as long as it needed to take, as long as, in the end, Doédenna was able to gather all of those Skaki ancestors back into the hem of Her cloak. As long as the sky house didn't take everything—their memories, their names, their haecceity—and leave nothing for the god.

Are the dying people asleep? she'd asked Cracchen. *Are they comatose?*

He had only shrugged as if it did not matter, or as if he did not care to speak of it. Finally, he'd answered, *Later, we found a better way. Or, we thought it preferable at the time. In retrospect, we were perhaps overly excited and ambitious about the prospect of an alternative, and as a result, we behaved less than wisely.*

Both then and now, Lanie had thought that 'behaving less than wisely' was a mild way of saying 'stealing Taquathuran eggs to use for fuel and life-extending pneuma, and murdering anyone who got in our way.' But she'd felt conflicted about haranguing him on the subject, as they were stuck on an ice ship with him, and he was the one flying it, and Lanie's own magic was drained to the dregs. She was so sapped that she felt like crying, except her tears would freeze on her cheeks, and she'd be colder than she was now.

She had come so close, so many times, to taking down the ghost. But each time, he had escaped—only to murder, destroy, and swell in power. Everything the ghost did seemed calculated to make more enemies. Lanie knew she had the favor not only of Saint Death, but other gods besides—yet *he* kept triumphing, and *she* kept failing. Everything that had happened so far was her fault. Her failure. She was a flawed instrument.

"I'm not going to make it to spring," Lanie whispered aloud to herself. She needed to hear it, acknowledge it. Maybe, if she entered this next (and, she thought, final) battle with no hope of living through it, then she would not hesitate to do whatever needed to be done to the ghost—even if it killed her.

"Never say so, Mizka," came Makkovian's voice next to her ear. "Should you surrender to that thought and make it deed, it would break our hearts."

Lanie closed her eyes. If she just kept them closed, she could pretend it was *really* Makkovian there, standing behind her in his own warm body, with his worried frown, and his flame-bright hair, and all his scars.

"What are you doing out here, Makkovian?"

"May not a brother visit his sister?"

She smiled at that but asked, "Where is Duantri?"

"I sang my beloved a song of my love. I left her full sleeping, and dreaming of love." He was not speaking Quadic now—the language of Higher Quadíib—but the adjacent Qasirate dialect from Lower Quadíib, whence Makkovian's mother had hailed. All their years in Liriat he'd never spoken Qas even once, but ever since returning to Ylkazarra, he'd been reciting the poetry of his childhood to their esh, and also writing his own.

Opening her eyes, Lanie turned around and leaned her back against the prow. "Makkovian, I can't do this."

He stared out at her from Cracchen's face. "What do you need?"

She glumly rubbed her numb left arm, which hadn't been working properly since they left Madinatam. "Divine intervention? An undead army? An infusion of panthauma fit for a surge day?"

He grimaced, plainly frustrated that he could give her none of these things. Lanie regretted her words immediately. To take out her fear and distress on him after he'd come all this way was more than unfair.

"All right," she said, trying to come up with at least one practical strategy. "What I *really* need is to get a message to Haaken Skrathmandan in Liriat."

His focus sharpened. "The ambassador? Why?"

"We're heading straight for Iskald. No one alive knows Northernmost Skakmaht like Haaken."

"No one whom you trust." His voice very dry, Makkovian laid his hand against Cracchen's heart, as if feeling for the presence there that had effaced itself for his sake.

"Haaken's a known ally," Lanie said quickly. "A—a contemporary. And… my friend."

"Very well." His eyebrows lifted and drew in, a typical Makkovian look that she had never seen on Cracchen's face. "I will fly my peregrine shade to Liriat tonight, the moment I leave you. It might take the better part of a day. Perhaps two? Datu…" He shook his head. "Never mind. She will understand. Tanaliín will understand. It must be done."

The thought of Makkovian, pale as a corpse in his dwalming ring, taking neither food nor water for at least another two days and likely more, made Lanie shudder.

"You need to get back to your body."

"I need," he countered, "to courier your message to Liriat."

"No, no, I can do it," she blurted—and then sighed, because she knew it was true, and knew, furthermore, that it would be a simple thing to do—magically-speaking, anyway. "I'll take care of it. I was just… I was just being a coward."

"Mizka, you must let me do *something.*"

"Go home. Tell Tanaliín everything we told you. Maybe

between you and Datu and our genius gyrlady, you can all help me figure out how to defeat a ghost who just ate a *dragon*. I would be most"—she started laughing in a way that alarmed even her—"*most* grateful!"

Makkovian laid a comforting hand upon her shoulder. But Cracchen's touch was carved of ice, and she recoiled from it.

Instantly he withdrew, murmuring, "Suriki," as a delicate pink flush formed beneath his fine outer layer of frost.

"No, no, it's nothing." Lanie brushed away his apology. "I'm... I'm *indescribably* glad you came, Makkovian. Thank you. You interrupted your pilgrimage for us. You..."

Makkovian crossed his hands over his chest, thumbs hooked, fingers spread like wings. "Mizka. All my sorrows can wait. You and Duantri need me now, howsoever poor the offering of my shadeform. I hate—I *hate*—that I cannot be with you in the flesh, to stride at your side into Iskald, where danger awaits."

"Makkovian, this is for the best. Really." Lanie's eyes filled with tears. She dashed them away. "Because... there's Datu. And if we don't make it back, she'll still have you. She *must* have you."

"Mizka, she will have *all* of us. *All*," he repeated in the voice of avowal. "I swear it by Erre'Elur. I swear it on my own right arm."

That was when Lanie surprised both of them by throwing her arms around him, frost and all, and crushing the bird of his hands against his chest. Extracting his arms, Makkovian returned her hug, at first carefully, and then so powerfully that all her breath was squeezed out, until she pushed back from him and wiped her eyes.

"Now go," she sniffled. "Get back to... where are you all right now anyway?"

"Just outside of Nurr."

"Get back to Nurr, as fast and safely as you can. Tell Datu that her Auntie Lanie will talk to her *soon*, through Undies. Thank her for the loan of her didyi. Remind her about Thrice-Digested Stones—that we have precedent in our family for

281

fighting dragons. I'll send my message to Liriat tonight, and then I'll sleep. And that will… that will make me stronger. Although"—she rolled her watery eyes—"I have no handsome shade to sing me lullabies of love."

"This wizard wishes to sing you something," Makkovian muttered, rubbing at Cracchen's chest again. "Be wary of him, Mizka. He looks on you with untoward longing."

Lanie held up a hand. "Makkovian. You *know* he can hear you, right?"

"I am counting on it, my sister." Makkovian tapped Cracchen's chest twice, sternly, like he was knocking on a door to deliver an injunction, and switched to Quadic: "Thus ever shall thy suitors be fair warned: thou hast a brother who will not be charmed by devious manners and a courtly air. Though no gyrgardi, still I stand as guard and friend to thee, my sister—*evermore*."

Shrugging off her shivers, Lanie hugged him again, and replied in her scolding, too-halting Quadic: "Fly swiftly through the midnight, brother shade. Thy sister is no weak and trembling maid, but lo a *mighty wizard of Saint Death!*" She switched to Lirian. "I'll be fine. I promise."

Makkovian grinned, and twined his fingers with one of the dark braids dangling beneath her hat, tugging it and letting it loose again. "You *will* be fine, Mizka, come spring and after—when we meet again in Ylkazarra."

Her eyes flash-flooded again, but Makkovian did not see it, for he had bent to brush her forehead with a kiss. Cracchen's lips were cold, but Makkovian's kiss was dawn's own light, and Lanie thought that she smelled a hint of the fragrant frankincense he sometimes wore at night, for Makkovian loved nothing so much as perfumed oils and soaps, and candles that cast scent as well as light.

The peregrine shade burst out of Cracchen's chest in a cloud of night-clear wings. The glint-motes of its eyes shone at her. Then he was gone.

It was Cracchen who stared down at her now, his glacier-colored eyes strangely warm, a small smile playing at the corners of his lips. "That was... illuminating. Thank you, Miscellaneous."

"You're welcome." She knew she sounded smug. But she couldn't help that.

"*You*," he replied, "are welcome."

Flushing, Lanie realized she should be thanking him instead. But he shushed her, frozen fingers pressed to her lips.

"Miscellaneous. It was our pleasure and honor to offer you aid. We wish to be your ally. Your *trusted* ally."

Lanie moved out from under his touch. "That will come. In time."

"In the meantime"—Cracchen let his hand fall—"is there anything else we might do for you?"

Lanie was still shivering. "Can you make your fulmar ship a little less duodecifold-damned cold?"

He smiled suddenly. "We can certainly," he said, "help you feel warmer."

AFTER CRACCHEN DID his 'frostwork' (as he called it) on her and Duantri, filming their skin with a lace of insulating ice that left them, if not precisely warm, then no longer freezing, Lanie went to crouch on the lee side of the shelter cabin. As this was at the stern of the fulmar ship and Cracchen remained on vigil at the prow, she felt somewhat concealed from his hungry scrutiny. She wanted no witnesses to what she had to do next, not even Duantri. Certainly not the entity that was Cracchen.

She oriented herself in a southerly direction, towards Liriat, and from the bottom of her battered backpack, removed a small but heavy iron box. It had weathered the worst that both gunuggs and ghost could offer, surviving everything that her collection of bones had not. When she unlocked the iron box, the smaller, black-lacquered box inside of it was still pristine and undamaged.

From this box, Lanie withdrew a bejeweled reliquary pendant on a long golden chain.

The pendant was pediform, carved of black walnut, with hammered copper details and a fitted sandal of blue enamel set with rubies and sapphires, such as Lirian Blood Royals were known to have worn in days of old. It nestled in the palm of Lanie's hand. Compared to the wide winter night that was pressing around her on all sides, the reliquary felt warm to the touch. The little crystal window at the top of the walnut foot allowed a view of the relic contained within: the left hallux of the Founding Queen of Liriat, Ynyssyll Brackenwild.

Lanie closed her hand over the pendant, releasing her substance into it. Just a tiny bit, hardly a thread. It moved through the crystal window and into the toe bone, filling the relic with Lanie herself, with her will and her memories.

She awoke the substance of the dead queen who was slumbering inside the bone with the barest whisper of the Maranathasseth Anthem.

Ynyssyll—or the shadow of Ynyssyll—remembered her. The toe bone knew her. It recognized her and loved her, and inside the reliquary, it jumped for joy.

A few seconds later, Lanie felt the exact moment when, two and a half thousand miles away, in Liriat Proper, Ynyssyll's *right* hallux also jumped—inside of an identical royal reliquary.

The question is, she thought, *is anybody wearing it? Is anyone listening?*

Lanie made the bone jump once. Twice. Thrice.

Twelve was all she would give herself. Just twelve, and then she would come up with another solution. Maybe she shouldn't have sent Makkovian away so precipitously... and yet, it would have been *unconscionable* to send his peregrine shade all the way to Liriat. Unconscionable and cowardly.

On the ninth jump—for the ninth god, Sappacor—a whiff of white pepper incense stung her nostrils.

Lanie's eyes smarted, started to water. (*Definitely the incense,* she told herself. *And the wind. And the cold. Nothing more.*)

A second later, a blood message popped out of the darkness in front of her.

Usually, a message sent this way was small, about the size of a single peppercorn, ruddy with blood and flickering with flame. Any fire priest of Sappacor might make such a message by pricking a finger on one of their own long nails and casting the spell.

But this message was much larger than any of the beads that Lanie had seen before. It was a vivid splash against the starry dark, as if whoever had let their blood had done so in a hurry, in a fervor, not caring how deeply they cut. Hovering and flickering, unsteady as candlelight, the blood message danced a few inches from her face.

The skin of Lanie's right palm split in sympathy, splashing a like-sized amount of echo-blood onto the icy floor, before her hand quickly knit itself to rights again.

She bit her lip, swallowing a cry of pain.

"Lanie," the blood message ventured, trembling in the air, "I'm here. Tell me. What do you need?"

Ah, Lanie thought in surprise, *they answered.*

So Blood Royal Errolirrolin Brackenwild—Lanie's former best friend and once-lover—still wore their reliquary, twin to the one they had given her. She hadn't known if they would. She had never tried knocking at that crystal door, not since Errolirrolin had banished her from Liriat. From her home. From *them.* Forever.

She rolled her shoulders back. *I'm here for one thing,* she told herself. *Nothing more.*

"Hello, Lir." She pushed her voice through the hallux, across the sky, into its sibling bone. Much like when she spoke through Undies, she knew her voice would resound out of that reliquary in Liriat. Hopefully, Lir wasn't sleeping next to their spouse, the Blackbird Bride, who doubtless, would be startled to hear from Lanie.

"Sorry to contact you like this," she went on. "I need a favor. A... a temporary loan of an asset. It's for the good of Liriat, I promise... and of Athe... so you needn't worry that—"

"Anything." Errolirrolin's blood message flickered like a

far red star. The scent of white pepper incense intensified. "*Anything*, Lanie. There is no need to… Just tell me. What do you need?"

Wiping her tears—only to find them frozen to salt-frost on her face—Lanie told them.

Part Three

THE WOE-LANDS

Skakmaht

CHAPTER EIGHTEEN
The Dragon of Iskald

Year 4826 of Higher and Lower Quadiíb
On T'rahb, 3rd of Anatha: the Third Month
17 Days till Spring Equinox

THE DRAGON FLEW over the ruined city, and took pleasure in its white wreckage.

Centuries ago, Iskald had been a trading post. As more people settled there, it became a port city, and eventually a center of naval power, though the only ships the ancient Skakis had built in those days were the seafaring kind.

Coal-cutters, whale-lancers, cod-eaters, the dragon thought irritably. *Drowning in blubber. Coughing up slag. Languishing a quarter of the year in the Always-Night of an Iskald winter. How did such a people ever grow to power?*

But he already knew the answer. *That frosty-dugged winter elemental, Erre'Elur. That's how.*

When the cult of Erre'Elur began to prevail over all other forms of worship in the north, and Her priests became ascendent, Skakmaht rose in more ways than one. Sky houses, piloted by wizards, ascended from the permafrost to fly far and wide, expanding Iskald's import and export markets, and infusing the capital city with untold wealth. The sky wizards set it as a jewel in the crown of Skakmaht: Iskald, Pearl of the North.

North of the capital were only ghost towns, old mines, and abandoned hunting settlements. Beyond those, nothing permanent could be built upon the moving ice. Beneath the ice, feeding it and being fed by it was the Kratakkan Ocean, which extended from the tip of the Drathhal Peninsula at the north-most point of Northernmost Skakmaht all the way to the Kratakkan Pole.

Iskald made for a striking landscape, if you liked things like fellfield and icefall and three months of total darkness out of every year. The dragon didn't. The pissy yellows and dead browns bored him. The drifting mosaic of pack ice on the Kratakkan was an endless tedium, gray on white on gray, or else an array of lapis and aqua and indigo and turquoise that so dizzied and dazzled him, he felt sick to the stomach. He, who in a skinchanger's fableform had no stomach to think of, still less bile and stomach acid, and *yet!*

He made slow, circling swoops over the slopes of the Fiellharth, its crags eternally clad in white winter garments. The slopes showed the dark striations of avalanche barriers, stark against an immaculate canvas. To the dragon, they looked like the steps of a giant's staircase, or terrace farms built to harvest the color of snow. But the barriers were just there to protect the tiny, once-colorful houses that squatted at the mountain's base.

No one lived in them anymore. There was no one left alive in Iskald to cower the winter away, waiting out the Always-Night for the first rays of spring.

And *that* was due to Irradiant Stones.

The dragon surveyed his new domain, hating it as he had hated it in life. But there, just ahead, was the one thing in Iskald that he hated most of all.

The mountainous blot of the Guilded Council.

It hung in the sky, a hazardous heap of dark stone, crystal, and ice. Its edges were irregular—a mix of crevasse, serac, moulin, battlement, parapet, and tower—as if someone had come along and plucked a section of the Fiellharth range from the permafrost, upturned it to depend peak-down in the snot-freezing air, and then carved a hundred castles into it.

The dragon studied it.

Did the Guilded Council hang lower now than it had when he'd left it over a century ago? Surely the kernel eggs powering its snowpyre engines had degraded over these last, long, hundred years. Even with the connected sky houses suspended in stasis, using none of the energy reserves stored in their sepulchers, all of those kernel eggs, once rich with fableforms and fat with potential, must be due to fail soon. Any minute now.

But the dragon didn't think it would be *this* minute.

He landed, his claws slipping on, then gripping a section of shaped ice near the top of a jutting tower. At the center of the tower was an ingress into the rest of the Guilded Council: a perfectly round hole like a maw, just waiting for him to dive in it. It would conduct him into the Mistral Atrium—the crystal heart that connected all the sky houses to each other. And then the Guilded Council would be his for the taking.

Time enough to explore the lot, and choose his new sky house from the best of the best.

Time to fill its rooms with a hoard of treasures looted from other, lesser houses.

Time to furnish and refurbish his lair, and stick that witch-bitch's kernel egg down in its snowpyre, and start siphoning off its juices to power the house and make it fly.

And then—*Heh!*—*then* he'd finish it.

He would blast the other sky houses, one by one, out of the air, and watch the Guilded Council fall like a meteor storm onto the city below.

He would smash the Pearl of the North to scree, using its own 'bastions of indestructible power' for ordnance.

The dragon would make this city a monument to his first death, his rebirth, and his great victory.

CHAPTER NINETEEN
Sky House Skrathmandan

Year 4826 of Higher and Lower Quadiíb
On Balah, 5th of Anatha: the Third Month
15 Days till Spring Equinox

IN THE LIBRARY at Stones Manor (back when there was a Stones Manor), in one of the many moth-eaten travelogues she had devoured during her childhood, Lanie had read that during Wells, the third month of the year ('Anatha' in Quadic), it was possible to glimpse the Blithe Dancers in the night skies over Skakmaht. But for tourists who didn't want to miss this extraordinary sight, it was best to visit during Umbers or Vespers at the end of the year, when it was 'night all day, and night all night, for weeks on weeks, and months on months!'

Better still, the travelogues suggested, the tourists should remain in Iskald for the entire duration of Vespers ('Edenna,' to the Quadoni, 'Elurra' to the Skakis), the last month of the year, a dramatic time to experience the remote beauty of the north. It was during Vespers when the sky houses and merchant royals co-sponsored Dark Festival, a month-long celebration of Erre'Elur: Woe-Woman, Winter-Crowned, Night-Outlasting-Day, the Frost Queen of Skakmaht.

Dark Month featured snowshoeing, sledding, skiing, ice-skating, and ice-carving. Competitive baking abounded. Fierce rivalries ignited between the hot-chocolate vendors and the mulled-cider vendors. There were knitting competitions to win awards like 'The Coziest Scarf of the Year' and 'The

Warmest Socks in Skakmaht' that were so cutthroat, even the death-defying champion snow-riders shied away from their grandparents until it was over.

And above these festivities, way high up in the Always-Night, would dance the Blithe Dancers, celestial ribbons of opalized light, a sure sign that Erre'Elur walked among Her people.

At least, that was what Lanie's books had said.

Another name for the Blithe Dancers was 'Vixen's Nimbus.' Lanie used to imagine that Erre'Elur sometimes appeared to Her worshippers in the guise of a snow fox: white and gray, with the absolute fluffiest tail, and the darlingest fur-poof of a body. But instead of a furry little face, Erre'Elur's fox head would be a delicate, bare-bone skull, cocked curiously at living passersby as her fur reflected the glow from above.

As a child, Lanie had been utterly *sure* that, should she ever make it so far north, she *would* see such a sight—the god in Her vixen furs, walking by the light of the Blithe Dancers. And Lanie would crouch down, and open her palm, inviting the god to sniff her. And Erre'Elur would come into her arms, rank and wild and trusting. She would fall asleep against Lanie's chest, and Lanie would hold Her, and love Her, and keep Her warm.

Now, there was no Iskald to visit. No Dark Festival. No celebration of the god, whatever Her appearance. There were no humans left alive in the ruins of the capital city to wait out the dark and lend meaning to the lights in the sky.

But the Blithe Dancers danced on.

THEY HAD BEEN flying for three days, north and northwest from Madinatam, occasionally alighting their fulmar ship on some likely looking patch of land. They stayed put from late morning to late afternoon, so that Duantri might hunt and Lanie cook, and Cracchen could rest and regain the 'vital force' he was spending to keep the ship aloft.

It was a little warmer on the ground than in the air—at least, it was when it was sunny out—and Lanie was grateful for a few hours to have nothing beneath her feet but dirt. The further north they traveled, however, the more it seemed like they were traveling backward, out of approaching spring and into the heart of winter. Cracchen's layer of frostwork on their skins kept the worst of the cold at bay, but Lanie was forgetting what it was to be actually *warm*.

On their fourth day in the sky, Cracchen announced that they had officially crossed the boundary line separating Umrys-by-the-Sea from Skakmaht. They were flying Skaki skies now, and when night fell—early—upon their fulmar ship, Lanie beheld the Blithe Dancers for the first time.

She stood at the prow, Duantri's arm tight around her shoulders. The lights appeared out of nowhere, a fanfaring flare of viridian ribbons falling in handfuls from the heavens.

Both of them gasped at the same time, and started pointing in every direction at once. Their smiles were so wide that their stiff faces ached, and they wept frozen tears for the All-Marvel of it all. The lights of the Blithe Dancers reflected off the frosted tracks on their faces.

When the lights in the sky showed signs of fading for the night, Duantri excused herself to use the pot in the shelter cabin, confessing that she'd been 'holding it in' for the last hour because she couldn't bear to leave the display.

"That's terrible for your bladder!" Lanie scolded her. Duantri just laughed. When she was gone, Lanie turned back to the sky, watching for any last vanishing wisp of light, hungry for it.

"Miscellaneous."

Shaking off her reverie, she turned to Cracchen. He had appeared at her elbow, in the place Duantri had vacated. Perhaps he had been standing there for many minutes, not watching the lights but her face. His smile was partly pleased, partly proprietary, as if he owned the skies, the Blithe Dancers, and Lanie's delight in them.

"What?" Lanie didn't mean to snap the word, but she wanted to bite that look off his face.

"Look south," he advised her in his lazy way.

She turned around, glanced toward the stern of the ship.

In the southern skies, a tower. Flying through the air.

Not only a tower—not only *flying*—but one that Lanie *recognized*. She had even visited it twice before, but had never, in all her unchecked daydreams, expected to see it—the entire *Ambassadorial Palace of Skakmaht*—uprooted from its tree-lined boulevard in Liriat Proper's First Circle neighborhood, and turned into a *sky house*.

But the creamy travertine stone was unmistakable, as was its idiosyncratic architecture: seven octagonal stories, each stacked on the other in a series of tapering tiers. The roof was copper, aged into graceful verdigris and adorned in ornamental acroteria. Lanie had always hypothesized that the acroteria, which she could never make out clearly, depicted some kind of dragon—but dragons as designed by someone who had no idea what dragons looked like. Now that she had seen a *real* one, Lanie thought that the renderings might not be dragons, but highly hyperbolic, exceedingly unrealistic swans, perhaps mixed in with a bit of wolf. It was all very stylized and bewildering.

The tower sped up until it flew just before them, descending to take the lead. At her side, Cracchen snorted, "Show off."

"I love it," Lanie breathed. It was so upright, so unlikely, so weirdly aerodynamic for something so *vertical*, as if it moved through a shimmering other-medium than air, and could ignore inconveniences like climate, altitude, and wind resistance.

The tower began to turn in the air, rotating until the front of it faced them. Cracchen's hands closed on the prow of the fulmar ship. He leaned forward. The ship bent to his will, and veered, aiming straight for the double doors standing wide open at the base of the Ambassadorial Palace.

At least, Lanie *thought* that was what he was doing.

Everything was happening too fast.

Shoving her spectacles down her nose, she tracked their inevitable collision. "C-Cracchen—just how unbreakable is the unbreakable wizard ice your ship is made of?"

Cracchen laughed.

As they swooped toward the tower, Lanie glimpsed a face in one of the windows of the seventh floor. The topmost room was almost all windows: one full glass door for each of the eight walls, opening onto its own little balcony. She recognized who was standing there, watching them approach.

Lir had come through, after all. They had sent her Haaken Skrathmandan.

CRACCHEN NAVIGATED THE fulmar ship into the bottommost level of the tower, slipping it between the boxes and casks and barrels that had been stacked against the walls in anticipation of the tower's new cargo. The ship glided in, the doors of the tower shutting behind it. The rush of wind, which for the last four days had been blowing perpetually in Lanie's ears, even when she was huddled in the shelter cabin, fell blessedly silent.

Bloodlamps, in their intricate iron cages, lined the tower's creamy walls, casting a rutilant hue about the space. *Is that Lir's own blood?* Lanie wondered. *A gift from the Blood Royal to their Skaki ambassador?* Bloodlamps lasted all year when sparked off a Brackenwild's veins—but even a minor fire priest's bloodlight still lasted a full quarter year, the catch basins only needing refueling every High Holy Fire Feast. Only public street lamps were lit for free; private ones could save a household an annual fortune in coal and oil, but only if you could afford the large lump sum donation of golden monarchs, deposited directly into Sappacor's church coffers at the beginning of the year. Only the very wealthy, therefore, could afford to keep their bloodlamps going year-round.

The rosy light was pretty, though. Like cuddling skin to skin with a lover fresh from a steaming, scented bath.

Duantri ran up to stand at Lanie's other side, panting from her sprint. In Quadic, she echoed Lanie's thoughts. "Twelve gods! Please tell me this is not a dream. My flesh doth soften and my blood doth heat! Is't possible this tower is truly warm?"

"Methinks our coats of frost are melting, friend." Lanie held up her arms to examine them. Cracchen's frostwork was indeed evaporating off her skin in little swirls and whorls of mist.

With a happy hum, Duantri handed Lanie her backpack and her bedroll, and shouldered her own, holding her hand as they disembarked the fulmar ship. Cracchen didn't follow them except with his gaze, watching until they were clear of the deck. Lanie peered over her shoulder to where he stood at the prow. Their gazes locked.

When he was sure she was looking, Cracchen made a sweeping with his arms.

The fulmar ship folded up.

One second it was there, slim and small, sparkling white from prow to cabin to stern, their home in the high winds. The next, it was gone. Cracchen stood straighter, appearing invigorated.

"One always forgets," he said, walking towards Lanie and Duantri at a brisk clip, "how much one's vital force can be absorbed by trivialities—until it all returns at once, and one feels oneself refreshed and whole."

A sharp click in Lanie's throat, as she remembered Stripes: the part of her that had animated Stripes returning to her, and filling her with a furious heat, with snarls and teeth. She pushed the thought away and tried for some courtesy instead, sorry that she had snapped at him earlier for pointing out the oncoming tower.

"Thank you, Cracchen, for all your efforts and… your hospitality. Your ship was an unlooked-for boon. We've made up so much time, and seeing the Blithe Dancers was a dream made real. And"—her mouth crooked—"once I stopped freezing to death, that shelter cabin was cozy. If I could make a fulmar ship out of my own substance," she added wistfully, "I'd never crave a sky house."

Cracchen bowed like a Rookish courtier currying favor with the Blackbird Bride. "We promise you, once you fly a sky house, you will never degrade your feet by setting them upon a fulmar's deck again. You have noticed this tower is heated?" He gestured around them. "Atmospheric management is but one of many amenities in a sky house. A fulmar ship is not quite so sophisticated."

Lanie opened her mouth to retort that she'd rather live rough off her own vital force than exploit the moribund for fuel, or rob another country of their next generation for it, but the sound of footsteps on the stairs interrupted her. Also, Duantri's hand, still clasping hers, gave a warning squeeze.

"Our host comes to greet us." Cracchen smoothed his hands over his frostworked robes in a quick, nervous gesture. His train swept the floor, stitched from thousands of small silver feathers that tinkled and chimed when he moved. The robes were open at the front, displaying glittering ice mail beneath.

They had all taken the opportunity to bathe the last time they had landed the fulmar ship. A small, icy stream ran near their esh site, and after several applications of Duantri's strong soap, Lanie not only felt human again, she was also reminded that Cracchen was a blond. He had been so filthy, so crusted in frost and dirt and the dried blood from his wounds, that she had forgotten this fact. He had used a piece of sharpened ice to shear his overgrown mane close to his skull. Frost clung to the fine pelt of it, the crystals ready to grow out into a spiked helmet at need.

But it wasn't until his identical brother walked down the spiral staircase and into the storage room that Lanie understood how much Cracchen had truly changed.

When first she'd met the 'Scratch triplets'—as she'd known them then—Lanie hadn't been able to tell them apart. In those days, she'd not yet learned to direct her deep senses beneath the skin's surface, to scan the deep accident of a person and taste the singular nature of their substance, which could never be mistaken for another's. After spending some time in their company, though, Lanie had identified Cracchen as the nasty one, Scratten as the dewy one, and Haaken—or Hatchet, as he'd been called at the time—as the enigmatic one. (Actually, back then, she'd thought of Haaken as 'the bovine one,' but that wasn't *her* fault. Haaken... made himself difficult to read.)

But anyone who was meeting the two remaining Skrathmandan brothers for the first time today would never be able to guess they had been born identical.

The ghost had broken Cracchen, inside and out. Where Erre'Elur and the storm of souls had seamed him up in ice, Cracchen's physical repairs were idealized recreations of the craggier original. Before, when he was a creature made entirely of flesh, Cracchen was, by most societal measures, considered a handsome man. But now, more ice than flesh, he was beautiful: perfect and uncanny. Hundreds of new thoughts and memories overpainted his previous palette of expressions, such that the original work entitled *Cracchen Skrathmandan* was barely a pentimento peeking out from the thick layers of new pigment. He was the Wizard Skrathmandan now.

His palate was silver and blue, from the tint of his lips and ears to the shadows under his eyes and cheekbones. The glow in his mismatched left eye rivaled the Blithe Dancers.

Haaken, on the other hand, Lanie observed, though he was as pale as ever—practically diaphanous, really—when compared to his brother, was practically *ruddy*. Seeing them both so close together, in the same moment, brought all their new differences into sharp relief.

Haaken seemed struck by the change as well. He stared at Cracchen, mute and immobile, until his brother moved to fill in the breach. Approaching the steps, he reached up and offered Haaken his hand.

"Mykkha orkessa, buhror." The words Cracchen spoke weren't Old Skaki, a language which Lanie had been given command over by Erre'Elur Herself, but a contemporary dialect, which she didn't know at all. She cast Duantri a hopeful glance, but the Gyrgardu only shrugged and shook her head.

Haaken's face showed a flash of shock before retreating into its 'least interesting cow in the herd' expression. He'd had years to develop it over his childhood in Rookery Court, where his mother had indentured him to Bran Fiakhna for an unknown quantity of time, and to what purpose Lanie didn't know. She guessed that the Blackbird Bride, having sensed Haaken's bright potential for Skaki ice magic, had wanted to collect him and bind him to her court. That Haaken had *not* ended up as one of her espoused kin—her snowy-winged egret amongst four-and-twenty blackbirds—was either a testament to his untold power, his hidden cunning, or some compromise he had made with Rook that Lanie feared to imagine.

After a moment's hesitation, Haaken took his brother's offered hand in both of his.

"Mykkha orkessa, buhror," he replied. Stepping down from the staircase that wound up the inner wall of the tower, he joined them on the floor of the storage room, never releasing Cracchen's hand. They were still standing quite close to each other when Haaken suddenly sank to one knee, and pressed his forehead to Cracchen's knuckles, murmuring, "Mykkha orkessa, anuraki."

A light, loving hand fell upon Lanie's left shoulder. She knew the instant it touched her that the hand was not Duantri's. A sweet breath whispered against her ear, the sound of it like smiling.

Lanie's nostrils pinched with a pang of lemon as Saint Death bent from Her utmost reaches and whispered the translation:

"*Evensong to you, my brother. Evensong to you, my ancestor.*"

Lanie's tongue drank in the bright zest of her god. She was filled with a longing to hold a sweating glass of Havoc's limonana in her hand, cold from the cellar; to be flushed with happiness and in good company; to feel safe and warm and relaxed enough to nurse a single drink for hours, the citrus tart and cool, with a hint of muddled mint mixed in.

The hand slipped from her shoulder. The sweet breeze left her ear. Lanie blew out a breath of regret; she always wanted to go with her god, whenever her god left her.

Duantri, who did not sense Saint Death's presence but who could read Lanie's moods like sheet music, brought her hand, still clasped in fierce tenderness, to her lips, and kissed it. Lanie leaned her head against Duantri's shoulder and passed on the translation.

"Haaken returned Cracchen's greeting first as a sibling to a sibling, then as a descendent to a forebear."

Cracchen seemed as stunned at this as Haaken. Then he barked a humorless laugh and removed his hand from Haaken's grip. His tone, when he spoke, was one Lanie hadn't heard since before Madinatam, before the Hastiludes—mocking, hard-edged, with more than a hint of sarcasm but none of the Skaki burr that had laced his voice ever since his integration with the storm of souls.

"Good to see you, Hatchet, you old stage empress. Get up, jackass; you're making a fool of yourself in front of our guests."

Silently, Haaken stood.

"Well?" Cracchen prodded him. "What's new? What does Mother say about your escapade North? Jealous she couldn't come?"

Duantri's elbow thumped Lanie's ribs. "Who is that talking?" she whispered.

"That's... Cracchen. Like he was last year. You didn't know him then."

"Yes, I did," Duantri countered. "I fought him when he tried to shoot you in the face. I did not remember that was how he spoke." She shook her head. "The change in him is startling."

Lanie frowned so hard she feared her forehead would cave in. "I think he's trying... to put Haaken at ease? Or maybe distancing himself from what he's become because, because...?" she trailed off, shrugging.

Duantri's expression softened. "Meeting his brother has exposed his vulnerability."

"Maybe." Lanie shrugged again. "At least this means... Cracchen's still in there somewhere. He didn't get... eaten." Not entirely anyway.

Rising from his knees, hands now clasped behind his back, Haaken regarded his brother with a somber expression. "Mordda did not stay behind in Liriat Proper, buhror." He was still standing close to Cracchen—perhaps too close, for Cracchen took a few steps back, laughing.

"Oh? Is she traveling? The Nine Baronies perhaps? Back to Rook for a spell? Or did she hie herself to Bran Fiakhna's holiday court at Damahrash, where winters are mild and entertainments prolific?"

Haaken, as usual, took his time answering. Lanie studied his face in its thoughtful repose. The Skrathmandan brothers were tall men, past six feet and going on seven. But where Cracchen's body had been honed by a warrior's regimen, then whittled down to skin and bone and ice, Haaken's slimness was softer. He was probably not sedentary—*not walking up and down seven flights of stairs every day,* Lanie thought—but neither was he a professional soldier. The white gold of his hair fell past his shoulders, combed smooth and braided behind his ears, bound back in a series of leather bands. His clothes, layered for height and flight, were wool and leather in various shades of smoky gray, with that strange cygnine-lupine knotwork of Skrathmandan heraldry pyrographed in black over his breast. He looked... closed off. Tired.

Lanie didn't realize she was staring with an intensity usually reserved for skeletons until his gaze flicked sideways to meet hers. Just as quickly, it moved back to Cracchen.

She let out a breath, silent but explosive. Her belly was suddenly full of... mouse skeletons. Tiny, adorable, skittering little mouse skeletons. With sweet little metatarsals like little glass beads.

Duantri's elbow soft-nudged her in the ribs again. When Lanie turned to look at her, she mouthed "*Haaken?*" her face full of glee.

Lanie bugged out her eyes and mouthed back, "*What?*" with a vigorous wag of her head. "*No!*"

Duantri smiled and waggled her eyebrows.

"*Duantri! No! Shh!*"

"Mordda is here," Haaken finally answered, so softly that Lanie had to strain to hear him. "With us."

"Oh?" This time, Cracchen did not laugh. His facade of hard fraternal joviality cracked, revealing... apprehension? "Why did she not..."

"I... I did not have time..." Haaken hesitated. He turned, his gaze meeting Lanie's again. This time, he spoke directly to her. "Mistress Stones. Welcome to Sky House Skrathmandan."

"Thank you?" Lanie said faintly, wondering at the 'Mistress Stones.' *At least*, she thought, *it isn't* Miss *Stones*.

Haaken's gaze moved to include Duantri. He greeted her in accented but melodic Quadic: "Gyrgardu, House Skrathmandan welcomes thee."

"My Lord Ambassador, I greet thy house"—Duantri hooked her thumbs together and made the sign of wings at her breast— "and thank thee for thy hospitality."

He addressed all three of them now, each in turn. "Blood Royal Errolirrolin came to me two nights ago with your call for aid. They said the matter was most urgent. We left yesterday at dawn, and have been flying since. But I... That is..."

Lanie had never seen Haaken at such a loss for words. His turquoise-pale eyes connecting with hers again, he asked with some urgency, "Do you understand the nature of a sky house?"

"They have been briefed," Cracchen said, at the same time that Lanie said, "Sky houses have sepulchers that bind with the terminally ill. Your snowpyre engines transform their substance—vital force—into fuel for flying, and other things that have to do with... house maintenance. The process prolongs their dying but delays their deaths. Sometimes, if I understand it correctly, for years."

Haaken looked relieved. "Yes. Yes, that is accurate."

"Sometimes thy snowpyres also bind with eggs, and suck the pneuma from skinchanger babes," Duantri added, when Cracchen opened his mouth to speak again. Her gray eyes, usually so limpid and lovely, flashed like edged steel. "And what is *thy* house fuel, Ambassador?"

Shoving her hands into her pockets, Lanie ducked her head. She was glad Duantri had asked it, so she didn't have to—but they *had* to know.

Haaken hesitated a fraction of a second before answering, his somber voice even quieter, "Mordda—that is, our mother,

Sari—has been ill a long time now. Yesterday morning, she volunteered herself as source for our snowpyre, so that I might fly this house to you. But I was not… we were not… entirely prepared. Mordda was still settling her affairs. There were so many of them. She always wanted—always intended—to be the snowpyre-source for our first sky house. It just… came early." He had been studying the floor. Now he lifted his head and looked at his brother, who was staring at him in dismay, lips parted, eyes wide as a child's.

"Mordda wants to see you as soon as possible," Haaken told him. "She is still somewhat aware. Come. We will situate our guests in their quarters, and then go up to visit her."

"Up?" Cracchen asked, gesturing to the bottom of the tower where they stood. "But shouldn't a sepulcher be…"

Haaken was already shaking his head. "The idea of residing the rest of her years in a low, lightless place, with the bustle of deliveries always coming and going, and visitors and staff— even if we walled off the sepulcher and set it apart as sacred— did not please Mordda. So"—he began leading the party up the staircase—"we decided to set her snowpyre on the seventh floor. Mordda always liked that room best. Now she will never leave it. There, the sky shines in from all directions, and light will always fall on her. You will see. It is good. As good as it can be, under the circumstances."

Haaken led them past the servant's quarters on the second floor, the kitchen on the third, and up to the guest bedrooms on the fourth. There he stopped and turned to Duantri.

"I believe this one is yours."

For just a second, Lanie saw his strange eyes glint with warmth. There was a kind of quiet gladness in his expression that she had never seen before on his face. He opened the door.

"Duantri!" cried Tanaliín idden Fa'nim'wai, and threw herself through it, into her Gyrgardu's arms.

CHAPTER TWENTY
Snowpyres

IF LANIE WERE given her druthers, she would have lingered near the enfolded knot of gyrlady and Gyrgardu, peripheral to it, drinking them in as they basked in each other. Eventually, they would open up their embrace to her—they always did—and then she too would be entwined in their generous love. She wanted to hug Tanaliín for twenty years and never let go.

At her side, Haaken did not put a hand on her elbow, nor in any way herd her up the stairs again, but something fraught in his gaze, some weighty summons, compelled her to turn away from her friends and towards him.

"Lead on," she said, and left Tanaliín and Duantri to their kissing.

Haaken took the next flight so quickly, Lanie was barely able to keep pace. Her thighs burned with the effort, her lungs ached, and she was wheezing before she was halfway up the next story.

Cracchen, bringing up the rear, was moving even slower than she was, though Lanie suspected this was not due to physical weakness. When the sound of his footsteps stopped entirely, she turned around on the staircase and called down to him, "Are you all right?"

"We hardly know."

Lanie hopped down a step and leaned against the wall. "I promised her, you know. I *promised* Sari I'd bring you home to her. Don't make a liar of me, Cracchen Skrathmandan."

He stared up at her, unmoving. His forlorn expression

reminded her of Datu in one of her despairing moods, so she smiled encouragingly and held out her hand. "We'll go up together. We've come this far."

Cracchen's freezing fingers closed over hers. Where he touched, he also frostworked, protecting her skin from himself. He took one reluctant step up, and then another, until he was just a single step beneath the one she stood on. He still towered over her.

"Ah, Miscellaneous Stones. Strange, the things that bring us low. But a mother's love"—Cracchen's voice held an edge of his old mockery—"is complicated."

"Sari has complicated sons."

"Are we still her son?"

Lanie pushed up her spectacles and squinted at him for a long, thoughtful moment. "I believe your mordda will recognize her Cracchen," she said, and waited until he gave a slow nod. "Now, son of Sari—do you really want her to suffer your absence one second longer than she must?"

Cracchen's breath blew out through his icicle teeth, a cold draft that funneled up the staircase. He squeezed Lanie's hand, almost crushing it, before letting it slip from his fingers.

She had not wholly withdrawn it, however, when he caught it up again, bent his head, and brought his lips to her wrist for a quick, fervent kiss.

Lanie tugged her hand away. "You're stalling."

"Are we?" Cracchen wasn't laughing at her, she thought, but something of his swaggering confidence had returned, along with the possessive light in his eye that she was coming to loathe.

"Yes," she said firmly. "And I don't appreciate being the object of your procrastination. Go on. Go ahead of me. I'll be right behind you."

His steps on the stairs were quicker this time, hers much slower, and Lanie was glad for the distance between them.

* * *

WHEN LAST LANIE had met Sari Skrathmandan, the woman had been weeping on the floor of her ruined gallery, holding her son Scratten's mangled body in her lap and blaming Lanie for his death.

But even before that, Sari hadn't looked well. Translucent, tired. She had lost most of her hair, Lanie recalled. Her face, the one time she had seen it without a thick mask of cosmetics, had a chalky pallor, with permanent shadows and creases of pain.

Now, on the seventh floor of Sky House Skrathmandan, Sari lay upon her snowpyre. This was a catafalque of gray quartz or perhaps ice crystal, enclosed in a clear glass dome. (*Or, if not glass*, Lanie thought, *likely it is Haaken's miraculous, immaculate ice, so pristine you feel like you could walk through it.*) Sari wore no clothes or any other adornment, her nakedness encased in a fuzz of frost. More ice was crawling whitely over her body even as Lanie watched, sealing her to the surface of the catafalque. Soon, the entire space between catafalque and dome would be a solid block of ice, with Sari trapped inside it, dying but not dead. Alive, but not living.

This is not necromancy, Lanie told herself. *It's more like brumation. But there's no waking up from this late winter dormancy. There's nothing at the end of this for Sari but Saint Death. And not for a long, long time.*

She watched as Cracchen walked straight over to the snowpyre at the center of the room. Haaken stepped back from the catafalque, ceding the padded chair placed near the head of it. Next to the chair, on a small table, was a heap of familiar river rocks.

Seeing them, Lanie stopped in surprise, standing in the doorway. There were twelve rocks total, all of them plain and gray, worn smooth by rushing water.

"Are those *dwalming* stones?" The words blurted out of her, but at least she managed to keep her voice hushed.

Haaken walked across the room and leaned against the wall by the door where she stood. "Yes," he said.

Lanie posted up on the other side of the door, and they both silently observed Cracchen, as he flattened a hand against the dome covering his mother, and frostwork flared from his fingers. Tendrils of ice moved through the dome's vitreous surface, and unfurled on the other side, reaching down to Sari's face, where they lay like fingers against her cheek.

Inside the dome, Sari's pale-drained, ice-furred mouth twitched in a smile.

"Um." Lanie cleared her throat, turning her head to Haaken. "Is that... common?" she whispered. "In a sky house? To use a dwalming ring on your sepulcher-source?"

She had been under the impression—and would be humbled, even indignant, to discover she was wrong—that a dwalming ring was her own innovation. Hers and Makkovian's and Tanaliín's, all together. They had invented it most *particularly* to help Makkovian focus when he cast himself out of his body and into his peregrine shade. As far as she knew, none of them had even written about it yet. Lanie was planning to co-author a paper with Tanaliín for the Judicial Colloquium of Gyrveard just as soon as...

Haaken was shaking his head. "Gyrlady Tanaliín and I have been corresponding for some months. She suggested the dwalming ring as an experimental sedative and focusing agent. As far as I can ascertain from my research, our primogenitors in Skakmaht did not use anything like it in the old sky house sepulchers. But..."

"Wait... you've been writing to each other for *months?*" She'd had no idea. Lanie had never imagined she could simply... send a letter to Haaken. Maybe even receive one in return. She used to write letters to Lir all the time. She currently had several correspondents in Liriat Proper, Havoc chief among them, but maybe she and Haaken could...

"She wanted to keep me apprised of Makkovian Covan's injury, and his recovery, since... She said... she thought I would want to know."

"Oh," said Lanie, chagrined. "Of course you would. Of course! Your magic preserved his arm in the first place. *And* helped to reattach it. Why didn't I think of telling you?" She was ashamed of herself, and was sorting through her Quadic apologies for the appropriate one—suriki, probably, but it *felt* like salal—when Haaken held up a hand, forestalling her.

"I am just glad," he said, "to help."

She grinned at him suddenly, whispering, "It's an All-Marvel, isn't it? The peregrine shade? Did you have *any idea* that such a thing would happen?"

"None," he said quickly, his face igniting in excitement, an answering grin flashing across his face like sunlight lancing through ice. A thrill of shared triumph passed between them, intimate as a secret.

Lanie had always liked Haaken Skrathmandan (well, not *always*, but ever since she'd started *noticing* him, the real *him*, and the silver secret of his magic, not the stolid brick facade he slammed up for all to see). Somehow, she trusted him completely, the way she had trusted Karramorra in Madinatam from the first moment she saw him. She'd known that Haaken would come to her aid if she called. She would never have broken her months-long silence to Lir elsewise.

Does Haaken know? she wondered as they beamed at each other. *Does he know I'll always help him if he asks?*

She shook her head at her own fancy, and glanced away. "So, how does Tanaliín come to be here? Did you just, you know, sort of swing by Quadíib on your way north?"

"It was not *precisely* on my way. But"—Haaken folded his arms—"this house travels quite fast."

"How fast?"

"We reached Zadiqai—or, rather, a stretch of the Caravan School Road between Zadiqai and Nurr—in eleven hours."

"From *Liriat Proper?*" Lanie squeaked. "That's more than a thousand miles!"

"It was not... easy. And it was my first flight," Haaken confessed. "Tanaliín insisted I rest when I arrived. She said she would not dream of stepping foot in a flying house captained by"—he cleared his throat, and quoted the Quadic directly—"'a

Skaki fledgling who has never flown, whilst wielding wizardries so long unknown that most is guesswork and the rest, a test.'"

Lanie blinked, her heart thudding hard at his fluency. She barely had time to recover before he was speaking again, this time in Lirian.

"When I awoke, Makkovian Covan came to consult with me about dwalming rings. He made me a gift of his own river rocks, assuring me he would find more. His shade had only just returned from its visit to you, and he was full of tales both strange and wonderful—which, of course, Tanaliín needed to hear in full before she left with me. I was glad to hear them, too." He lowered his voice. "On some of those matters... might we speak more later?"

"Of course," Lanie assured him, assuming he meant to ask more about his brother's fate, the storm of souls, and the shared vessel of his body. "And you can tell me all about your snowpyre. How you set about creating it from... from scratch. From stories."

Haaken looked haunted. "In Liriat, when I first laid Mordda on the snowpyre, it... she cried so, and writhed. Then, when the ice began to take her, she grew so still—as you see her now—but she still seemed aware of everything. Everything," he repeated, "her own body, and what was happening to it, and how the snowpyre was draining her. Her eyes were wild, shocked. When she talked, she muttered of walls and windows, how she could see in all directions, how fast she was moving, how she wanted to stop and rest. Those first eleven hours were..." He shook his head.

"I'm sorry," Lanie whispered.

"But... later, in Quadiíb, when Tanaliín came aboard the house and we tried the dwalming ring on Mordda, she... the pain seemed to leave her. The house flew more smoothly. She did not weep, or cry out. At night, when we removed the dwalming stones to check in with her, she reported that it was much better with them than without. That she thinks she might enjoy being a house, after all. This morning, when we removed them again, she did not speak at all. She... seemed bewildered to be back inside her body."

"Without dwalming stones or *any* kind of trance-inducing anodyne," Lanie asked, "did the sky wizards of old just... leave their sources to suffer?"

Haaken crossed his arms and shook his head. "I do not know. So much was lost when Iskald fell. Everything I have built—snowpyre, sepulcher, sky house—has been all by guesswork, from haphazard years of research, and a guiding instinct from..." His gaze fell, pale lashes sweeping his cheeks. Lanie knew, without him saying it, that he meant Erre'Elur. It was as if, having kept his god a secret from so many, for so long, Haaken could trust no one with Her name. Not even Lanie, even now.

So she just said, "For guesswork, this is *miraculous*."

His sun-dazzle smile returned, though briefly. "We do not know if... if the dwalming ring will alter the fundamental magic of the snowpyre. From everything I have read, a snowpyre-source—in this case, Mordda—once it is rooted in the sepulcher, becomes the heart of a sky house."

"Her accident lies in the catafalque, but she casts her substance out of herself, into the house. Like Makkovian and his shade," Lanie surmised. "Or, like a haunting. Except, she's still alive."

"Or, at least," Haaken corrected, "not dead. And, unlike shade or ghost, a sepulcher-source, once it is on the ice for long enough, no longer remembers who it once was. As their vital force is purged from their bodies, and sent through ice into the house, it is purified of its identity. It cycles out of the source, through the sky house, and back into the source in an economical loop of energy. This can last for years before the source runs down. But there is no..."

"No memory, no will," murmured Lanie. She leaned her head against the wall and looked up at the ceiling, thinking over the ramifications of the magic. "So... so you and Tanaliín think, with the dwalming ring, that the sepulcher-source might behave differently?"

"Tanaliín believes," Haaken said carefully, "that because of the dwalming ring, something of Mordda's... *essence*... will remain. In old Skaki sky houses, perhaps they let their sources suffer so that they would voluntarily flee their bodies—the panic, the discomfort, the endlessness of physical being—shedding their shades quickly into the house, and entering into a blessed emptiness. But in a dwalming swoon, there is no pain. Her shade will still be intact, more or less, so..."

"So it *would* be more like a haunting!" Lanie exclaimed.

"But not by an *angry* ghost. I hope."

"Less a poltergeist," she supplied, "and more like a... a happy genius of a place. A household spirit."

"I would like that, Mistress Stones," Haaken murmured. "It is what I profoundly hope for."

For a while they were silent, as Cracchen whispered to his mother through the ice. Then Lanie took a deep breath, reached across the threshold and stuck out her hand. "Haaken. I think you should call me Lanie. Don't you?"

His eyes narrowed. He slipped his hand into hers, but released it just as quickly. "Lanie."

"Miscellaneous," Cracchen's voice called to her from across the room, "Mordda wants to talk to you."

Removing his hand from the dome of ice, he stood and offered her his seat. Lanie took a fortifying breath, crossed the room, and sank into his proffered chair to contemplate the snowpyre before her.

Cracchen asked, "May I?" taking her hand before Lanie had time to respond. He placed her palm, as he had done his own, against the glassy ice, sending a wave of frostwork through her flesh. Ice to ice, flesh to dome, Cracchen bound her.

Like licking frozen metal, Lanie thought, irritated, testing her fingers. And like the proverbial tongue, they were stuck fast. On the other side of the dome, a stalactite of frost grew down from her fingers to touch Sari's cheek.

Pale aquamarine eyes opened, and rolled to look at her.

"She can't speak," Cracchen said, "but through the ice, she can send her intent..."

Lanie nodded, but she was already speaking in her deep voice, that the dead and the undead—and sometimes, the dying—could hear. She didn't even need to open her mouth to do it.

I have brought him home to you, Sari Skrathmandan.

Sari's response pulsed back through their conduit ice, a single throb of bone-deep satisfaction. More than just her intent was conveyed in that moment; a sense of Sari's entire body-being, both deep and surface, washed over Lanie. She learned several things at once, the lump in her throat like a chunk of ice too large to swallow.

It was good that Sari had given herself to the snowpyre when she did. If this was truly what she had wanted, what she had been planning for years, then she had almost left it until it was too late. Had she known how sick she was? Or did she think—hope—she still had time? Months, maybe? Possibly years?

From the state of Sari's bones, Lanie guessed it would have been more like weeks, if not days.

To her deep senses, the skeleton of a healthy, living animal was a vibrant, rosy color, like peering at the sun through a conch shell. A living bone blushed with life—unlike the bones of the dead, which glimmered for Lanie like pale pearls. The bones of the undead, quickened by the Maranathasseth Anthem, took on a spectral, ectenical hue. Lanie loved *all* bones equally: living, dead, undead; pink, pearl, and blue.

But Sari's bones were a dull, dim yellow, riddled with red holes. These ragged and angry-edged perforations were particularly concentrated around Sari's ribcage, but when Lanie peered further into the woman's deep accident, she perceived that the holes had spread throughout her entire skeletal structure. There was a deep smell to her too, that Lanie could perceive in her heightened state: the heated, yeasty, curdled-cream reek of cancer-eaten marrow. She had never smelled it before, but she knew what it was.

But brittle as they had been, Sari's bones were now undergoing a transformation. Haaken's ice was reaching up from the catafalque's surface and down from the dome, and moving through her skin, into her bones. They were becoming one.

Another pulse of Sari's intent thrummed up through the ice to Lanie, but she quickly realized that this was not intended for her, but for Sari herself. She was reassuring herself, staving off panic and discomfort and dread of the unknown with a ritual repetition of thought, like a chant.

It is good. It is for my boys. My bright boys. The two survivors of my triple suns. You can take this. You can do it. It is for them. For our house.

Lanie spoke in her deep voice again, trying to comfort her, *Your sons will lay you in the dwalming swoon again. Then, this pain will be but a memory.*

And maybe not even that, she thought but did not say. None of them knew, after all, if Tanaliín's theories about snowpyres and dwalming rings would prove true, or lasting. Not even Tanaliín.

Sari's silence pulsed again. *I will endure any pain.*

I wish, Lanie whispered, *we could have been friends. I wish the world were different. That you had not lived through several hells to die like this.*

But Sari's answer was scornful, an intent that seemed to say: *I regret nothing. I would endure it all again—and more—to lift my boys to the sky. To give them back their birthright.*

To this, Lanie could think of nothing else to say. She herself did not wish the Skaki sky houses unfallen. She wasn't even sure how she felt about the Skrathmandans lifting one up again. Nor did she regret the loss of the sky wizards a hundred years ago—who would otherwise still be terrorizing Taquathura to this day, arrogant and unchallenged, taking what they wanted, lording it over all the other realms.

And she could not—could *not*—wish Cracchen Uthpansel Skrathmandan as he had been before the ghost possessed him. Lanie didn't even know what she wanted for Sari now, except for peace. She didn't know what she wanted from Athe, either— except that those who lived on it be kinder to each other during the brief span of their lives. She did not think her wanting this would make it any likelier to happen.

She would not say any of this to Sari Skrathmandan, in any of her voices, deep or surface. So she asked instead: *Do you want me to sing to you as your sons dwalm you down?*

But from the woman on the ice came vigorous dissent: Sari wanted only her sons, only their voices.

Lanie asked, *Do you need anything more from me? Anything at all?*

No response. She waited a minute, then another, just in case Sari's thoughts had turned sluggish with snow, and required more time to formulate answers. After about three minutes, Lanie felt it: a clear and final dismissal.

Farewell, then, Sari Skrathmandan. She hesitated, and added, *May your life pass into legend. I will not forget you, as you lie all your long years upon your snowpyre—and neither will my god.*

STANDING AT THE head of the snowpyre, Haaken placed the first dwalming stone upon the catafalque. "I remember," he told his mother, "the day you taught me how to lace my shoe. You punched holes in a piece of leather, and strung it with a cord, and said I must practice every day."

At the foot of the snowpyre, Cracchen placed the second stone. "I remember the day you took me for a walk in the gardens of Rookery Court. Just me, not my brothers. You pointed out all the flowers, and called them by their Skaki names."

Haaken placed the third stone, near Sari's left shoulder. "I remember the first day you brought me before the Blackbird Bride. She commanded you to leave me with her, and you did. When we were alone, she cupped my face in her hands, and told me that one day, if I was good, I would become her own Egret. Later, when I awoke from a nightmare of white wings, you told me to stop weeping, that she meant to honor me, that I should go back to bed."

Cracchen placed the fourth stone, at Sari's right ankle. "I remember when you bought me my first practice sword. You introduced me to the Master of Arms at Rookery Court. He said I was a natural—'a monster with a blade.' Scratten called me a natural monster, and you spanked him and put him in a corner."

Haaken placed the fifth stone. "I remember when you purchased our first property in Liriat Proper. *Having fallen so far*, you said, *this is our first step into the sky*."

The two living sons of Sari Skrathmandan laid the dwalming ring around her, remembering their mother as they had known her—which was not all of her, or even a large part, but it was what remained.

And the beautiful ice, the sacrificial snowpyre to the god Erre'Elur, began to build upon itself.

It branched and split, divided and multiplied. It entered Sari and enclosed her. It filled the empty space between catafalque and dome, between muscle and bone, between blood cell and blood cell and blood cell, packing itself ever tighter, ever more densely, absorbing the body's memory. Sari's sons told no lies as they circled her in twelve river rocks, hoping that these would ground the shade that would soon be flying out in all directions, through the ice, into the walls and windows and floors. Hoping the rocks would be the solid anchor she could return to, and not lose herself completely to the house.

They were not sure if Sari heard them, suspended as she was in crystal and ice and her dwalming swoon, alive but not living, dying but not dead. But before the frost completely closed over her face, Cracchen and Haaken saw that she was smiling.

Soon enough, it was done. The walls of the tower began to hum more strongly. The wizard sons of Sari Skrathmandan stood side by side, shoulder to shoulder, wearing identical expressions of sorrow, carrying identical silences in the hollows of their throats.

And Miscellaneous Stones, necromancer, Saint Death's daughter and Her doorway, found herself with nothing more to do here today. So she slipped quietly from the sepulcher, and left them to their grief.

CHAPTER TWENTY-ONE
Vital-Force Kestrel

**Year 4826 of Higher and Lower Quadiíb
On Mahluin, 6th of Anatha: the Third Month
14 Days till Spring Equinox**

"THRUST, THUS. I stop you. Hook right. Rip clear. There. Yes. Now, slash across. Thrust. No. More circular. Yes. Then—jab, jab. Rip through. Again. Thrust. Hook. Slash. Thrust. Double jab. Again."

Duantri wiped the sweat pouring off her face and took a large step back from her opponent, letting Tam's witchglass daggers fall to her sides.

"Maximum strength grip," Cracchen reminded her. "Use all your fingers. Wrap your thumb around them like a band. Hold hard. Don't want that glass to slip."

Blowing out a breath, Duantri readjusted her grip yet again.

"Need a break?" Cracchen's expression was midway between a scowl and a sneer. "Too bad. In a real fight, there won't be time. Fly at me again, birdie."

Birdie. Scowling, Duantri dove into another of Cracchen's drills, putting a burst of speed into it.

She had always excelled at sports, at dance, at any of the martial arts the Gyrgardon Academy offered its fledglings. She knew that she would excel at double-knife fighting, too: one more tool for the Falcon Defender to use in defense of those she loved. This was not the first time she had set herself to learn a skill from a teacher she did not like. She would learn from Cracchen Skrathmandan, too.

Last night, as they sat down to a funereal dinner on the sixth floor of the sky house, Cracchen had asked Duantri for permission to examine her witchglass daggers. Reluctantly, she had allowed it, but he only looked them over, and upon returning them, asked if she had any idea how to wield two blades at once.

The truth, which Duantri had confessed, was that though she excelled at improvised weapons (since, coming naked out of her kestrel form, any nearby object might be a tool), she was out of practice when it came to knife-fighting. Cracchen offered to drill her. When she agreed, he even cleared the tower's first floor of its casks and boxes, and transformed it into a sparring room.

Cracchen had been a soldier, she knew, before taking the post of Royal Assassin to the Blood Royal Brackenwilds in Liriat Proper. And all of that was before he'd become several dozen other people as well, each of whom brought to his body a plethora of talents she could only guess at, since Cracchen was not forthcoming about them. He was a resource, potentially rich in skills she wanted and needed.

And doing dagger drills was better than sitting still and fretting through their last days of travel.

An hour into their first training session, and Duantri had come to several insights.

Cracchen knew many tricks and moves. He could impart his knowledge clearly, both verbally and physically. But Duantri was a teacher. She lived amongst teachers, most of her closest friends and lovers were teachers by trade *and* inclination, and many a student who had grown up under her tutelage had gone on themselves to teach. Despite a wild youth on the streets of Ylkazarra, where education had been the last thing on her mind, Duantri was nevertheless a proud citizen of Higher Quadiíb, where the Judicial Colloquium of Gyrveard—a body of *educators*—constituted the highest circle of government.

In her considered and informed opinion, Cracchen Skrathmandan was, to put it mildly, a terrible teacher.

He refused her request to conjure practice knives from his

frostwork, blunting their edges to make sparring safer. He had spurned her idea to make a practice post, that she might drill without fear of injuring him. And, while teaching her, he reinforced all of his lessons not with praise and encouragement but with jibes and insults. He had shouted at her, demeaned her, and mocked her every move, like his words were a second pair of knives to slice her with.

Duantri understood that Cracchen himself (and several of the people who went into the making of him) had probably been taught this way. She understood that, having once been possessed by Irradiant Stones, Cracchen knew every method of manipulation and abuse that the ghost would employ to distract, distress, and damage whoever might contest his right to live forever. But...

Birdie?

Slash up. Slash down. Pop up. Slash over. Cut down. Pop. Thrust. Thrust.

As they fought, and Duantri's anger swelled, a grin broke out on Cracchen's face. It was not a warm expression, but it was full of a sharp understanding. Like he knew what she was thinking, and reveled in it.

Or perhaps he simply enjoyed sparring. Duantri did, too. It was a *relief*.

...until she went for a wide slash to his quadriceps, and missed laying his flesh open by barely an inch when he was a little late jumping back.

She stared at him appalled. Cracchen's grin just widened.

"Awful," he said cheerfully. "Just sloppy."

At least—Duantri adjusted her grip on the witchglass again— *if he is grinning at me, he is not smiling at Lanie. None of us want him smiling at Lanie.*

"Again, birdie," he demanded. "Faster. Each second counts. Can't wait for our foe to bleed out. Even if he's dying, he still has time to kill us. Shred his muscles. Sever his tendons. Forearm— slash. Upper arm—slash. Above the knee, slash, slash." Cracchen demonstrated each cut in the air. "Incapacitate him."

Duantri gritted her teeth and practiced the moves. Again. And again.

"This is not *sothaín*, birdie. We don't take five minutes to bat an eyelash. Faster."

Duantri was just beginning to contemplate taking her falcon form and plucking out his remaining human eye just like the *birdie* he said she was, when she heard Lanie's voice on the staircase:

"Quick, Tanaliín, stop her. She's thinking about eating his eyeball."

"Duantri is not a *seagull*, Lanie," her gyrlady replied. "She will do no such thing. But *you* should probably back up a few steps. Look away from their playtime. Your own eye is starting to twitch from an impending echo-wound."

Knowing that her gyrlady was present energized and calmed Duantri. Her movements smoothed out. She felt silk-limbed, swift. She wanted to show off her newfound skills. Impressing Tanaliín with the feats of her body was an evergreen pleasure.

In response, Cracchen redoubled his efforts to criticize, distract, and beat her down.

"Gah," Lanie muttered from somewhere above, on the stair. "He sounds *just* like Grandpa Rad! Uncanny."

"It is a miracle you turned out as well as you did, my dear," Tanaliín complimented her. "That sort of punitive pedagogy is limiting and illiberal."

Lanie laughed. "Before I send Grandpa Rad to Saint Death's cloak, I'll inform him that he really should have worked harder on his educational methodologies. He'll love that."

At this point, Cracchen intensified the drill, upping his flow of insults and quickening his pace, so that Duantri could pay no attention to aught else but him.

Then Tanaliín lifted her voice and started cheerleading her on in Quadic. "How wondrous well my Kestrel flies her knives! All ghosts should go in fear of their un-lives. The razors of her witchglass flash and shine—but no less sharp than Kestrel's amber eyne."

Duantri grinned. Sweat stung her eyes, and her muscles ached, but her heart lifted. Through their Bryddongard bond, Tanaliín was pouring love enough for Duantri to live on for days. She needed neither bread nor water, nor warmth, nor light, nor air—just her gyrlady's love, which gave her strength enough to slay a thousand ghosts!

Lanie, matching Tanaliín's pitch, encouraged her as well. "And if Makkovian were here, he'd say, 'Thou blazing bright-best star amongst the stars, come take me now—sans pillow, blanket, furs—and I shall be as putty in thy hands.'"

"Putty?" Tanaliín exclaimed in Lirian. "That's hardly flattering to Makkovian."

"Metaphorical putty," Lanie amended. "With a cock of iron."

Duantri guffawed—and to her surprise, she broke through Cracchen's guard. With the un-blunted tip of her witchglass dagger, she slashed a long line down the right side of his face, from the hollow of his temple near his hairline, across his right eye, into his cheek. The blade bit deeply, and the wound welled with blood.

With a gasp, Duantri jumped back, as if with distance she could take back her blow. Cracchen stared at her, hatred in his eyes, and Duantri knew that her own held more blame than guilt. *If you had blunted our blades with frostwork!* But saying so would be of no use.

Lanie cussed and excused herself, muttering something about cleaning up her echo-wound. Hearing this, Cracchen's gaze flickered towards the stairs, watching her go as his red blood turned silver, and a new seam of ice stitched over his wound, cinching it closed.

Wiping off a crust of crimson frost, he told Duantri, "Good work today," and turned away.

Stunned, Duantri watched his back as she sheathed her witchglass daggers and toweled off her face. Perhaps feeling her gaze like a shiv between his shoulders, Cracchen whipped around, snapping, "What? Keen for another round?"

He does not like that Lanie left, Duantri thought, then,

making her words as tranquil as the first attitude of the second set of sothaín: *The Lizard Suns Herself Upon a Stone,* she said, "The ghost."

"What of him?"

"When last we saw him, he was a dragon. Lanie thinks by now he will have jumped bodies, to walk in a sky wizard's skin. What if I may cut him and cut him with my dagger, and yet— like you did just now—he patches all his hurts with ice? What then?"

"Why then, Gyrgardu," said Cracchen, infusing such sweetness in his voice that it bewildered her until he finished: "your death will have bought the rest of us time to either finish him or flee. May we thank you for this favor now," he inquired even more sweetly, "since you are likely to perish on the morrow?"

Duantri rolled her eyes.

Cracchen seemed to approve of this reaction, and relented enough to say, "Ice is slow. Ice takes practice. If Irradiant Stones dares to put on a sky wizard's husk, he will not have the benefit of absorbing that body's mind as well—for *we* are all *here*." He touched his chest. "There will be no memories attached to that body, nothing to teach him that body's magic, or the skills to use it. He will not know how to establish a common lattice with the crystals in his skin. He will be overconfident and arrogant—"

"—doubly so, if a sky wizard born anew," Duantri muttered.

"—and he will not be your primary concern."

Her eyes narrowed. "Will he not? Who are *you* to—"

"Of course he won't, my love," Tanaliín interrupted, joining them on the floor. "Irradiant Stones falls under Lanie's mandate. He always has."

"But—" Duantri swallowed the words, *Three times and more hath she already failed—and through her trials didst grow so gray and frail, so burnt-out meager in her face and frame, that if she tries again, I fear she'll die.*

"You are no necromancer, Duantri," her gyrlady reminded her, with that intense gentleness she reserved for complex negotiations, difficult conversations, and news of bereavement.

"The worst you can do to him is incapacitate his new host body so injuriously that he jumps into *yours*. That will not help Lanie. It will distract her when she needs most to focus. No," she concluded, "while these wizards three deal with Irradiant, you and I, my Gyrgardu, have work elsewhere in the Guilded Council—"

Cracchen interrupted her to say, "Or you could stay behind and do nothing—as you did in Madinatam," with that hard light in his eyes that Duantri now understood was his way of teasing. Probably.

She understood it—but still did not like it. It reminded her of the Ylkazarran street gang she used to run with as a child. Among the Viper Queens, the more comfortable you felt with someone, the quicker you were to roughhouse with them, the crueler your tongue when it cut them. They had been like feral dogs, Duantri included. Until the Gyrgardon Academy had recruited her. Until she had met Tanalíín.

She turned to her gyrlady, holding onto her sothaín with an effort. "What is our work to be, gyrlady mine?" she asked in her most formal Quadic.

"The egg, my love! The egg!" Tanalíín said in Lirian. "Our job is to steal back the Witch Queen's kernel egg and—no matter what happens to the ghost—ensure its safe return to Madinatam."

"But—"

"Lanie told me you swore to it, Duantri. She sets the kernel egg as your first priority, above all else, including her own safety."

"But, Tanalíín!" Duantri broke in at last, "thou hast not *seen* Tam's egg. I cannot bear its weight in kestrel form; it makes a solid armful for me now! And how, with egg attained, shall we then flee—with such a burden and from such a height? What if"—her gut was sickening with every anxious question—"yon wizards three should fail and fall, who then shall steer this sky house safely south? I do not think the tower flies for aught but that which bears Skrathmandan's name and blood."

What if, she continued in her private thoughts, *by wraithlike magic, Lanie's slain? For all we've done, and all the miles we've come, the bonded friendship of our esh and quest—does it mean nothing in the end but this?*

Yet, the memory of Tam's hand resting on her kernel egg did haunt her.

Tanaliín slipped her fingers through the crook of Duantri's elbow, shaking her arm with bombastic enthusiasm. "Fear not, my kestrel, but take soaring heart! Bright miracles abound inside this heart of flying ice and wintersong and woe. Our Lanie hath a plan in hand, and more: a Haaken who will help her spin the spell." She switched back to Lirian again, and asked Duantri with a broad wink, "How would you feel, my darling, about being the test subject of a *very* innovative magical experiment?"

HAAKEN STOOD AT his workbench on the seventh floor of Sky House Skrathmandan, with Tanaliín and Duantri perched on stools to either side of him. His hand lay lightly upon Tanaliín's Bryddongárd, which she was wearing, the silvery lines of his frostwork just beginning to overlay the silver-traced leather.

Lanie sat on the floor, cross-legged, her back against the wall by the east-facing window, her head tilted up to contemplate the ceiling. Her job was to hold sothaín and augment Haaken's frostwork with her prayers, since, magically-speaking, she wasn't good for anything else right now. This was Haaken's show; Lanie was just here for support.

But stillness was elusive. Sothaín could be anything from a regimen of one hundred-forty-four full-body attitudes to a wholly mental meditation, wherein one concentrated on the twelve gods and each of their twelve aspects, but needn't wink so much as an eyelid. Lanie was performing a fingers-only modification of sothaín: moving through the tiniest of gestures with a special attention to her breath. As her fingers formed the attitudes, she thought:

Why do our great miracles spring from such ugly

circumstances? Why must they be born out of our direst need? Shouldn't beauty's sake be need enough? Instead, we make magic to thwart the perpetuation of cruelty, or deliver tardy justice after a crime is committed.

Her fingertips faltered. She thought wryly that she had been wise not to attempt any prolonged physical contortions, sothaín-wise. She just didn't have the wherewithal today.

She tried again: each gesture deliberate, every flick of the finger keeping her focused on the gods whose attentions she desired.

First Kantu, Flying God of Thunder.

Attitude one, four fingers upright, split by the thumb: *Whose wings are thunderstorm, be with us now.*

Attitude two, middle and ring finger upright, others folded with the thumb: *Whose brow is crowned in light, be with us now.*

Attitude three, pinkie and index upright, others folded with the thumb: *Whose hornéd head brings rain, be with us now.*

A diamond spark flashed, straight ahead and just to the left, from the southwest window of the tower. An answering flush sprang to Lanie's cheeks. She knew not to look too directly at impending divinity, not while her thoughts were still so unstable. No, she must keep sothaín, and keep going.

As her thoughts began to slow, they turned in a lazy arc toward deeper stillness, like a flock of songbirds wheeling to watch a raptor the size of a storm pass by. The first god was close. She was right outside the window.

Hello, Kantu. God, you're huge!

Her fingers moved unhurriedly, forming the ninth attitude of the second set, belonging to Ajdenia: *The Lizard Huffs and Puffs and Grows in Size.*

Ajdenia, she prayed to the second god. *Lizard Lady. God of prey, of small things. Hear me, a small thing. O devourer of fiends, there is a fiend in our midst. O helper of the helpless, help the unhatched kernel egg he holds in his clutches. Help us now.*

Immediately to her left, in the southeast window, a sinuous emerald glitter twinkled in her periphery, like sunlight glancing off the plated tail of a bejeweled reptile. Lanie's thoughts calmed, warmed like lizards lazing on a rock.

Her fingers flowed into ever more measured movements: the sixth attitude of the sixth set (*the Trickster wagers all for love—and wins*); the ninth attitude of the ninth set (*Bird am I, that never of egg was hatched*); the eleventh attitude of the eleventh set (*Whatever thou expected: guess again*).

Amahirra, Wykkyrri, Yssimyss: Three Lovers of Taquathura.
Amahirra, Wykkyrri: Bryddongard gods of Quadiib.
Your friends Tanaliín and Duantri call you.
Your friends Miscellaneous and Haaken call you.

A slight movement at the work bench as Haaken, his face canted toward the western window, straightened from his concentrated slouch. He kept his palm on Tanaliín's Bryddongard, but Lanie would wager her own gray left hand that all the hairs on his body were standing on end—just like hers were.

Haaken knew. He could feel the Three Lovers approaching from the west.

How did They appear to him? Did he see what Lanie saw—straight ahead from where she sat: the Taquathuran triskeles, now of a stupendous size and translucent as stained glass, the great wheel of Their legs turning like a windmill in the sky?

Lanie blinked and looked away before she lost herself in the sight. She glanced right instead, towards the northwest window, and thrust her whole hand upright, blade-like, like the dorsal fin of a shark in the first attitude of the third set, for Aganath: *O god of sailors, do not let us drown.*

Aganath was an unpredictable god, a hungry one. But Anatha *was* Her month, and every day of this month was Her feast day, including today. It wouldn't do to leave Her out. Always better to invite the Bone Shark's charity than to risk Her wrath. Not to mention, theologically speaking, Aganath was a fierce protectress of the young. Particularly, the orphaned young.

Which, Lanie thought, *Tam's hatchling will be. If it hatches.*

Across the northwest window now, a lethal shadow came swimming up: pale on the bottom, gray on top, a crescent-shaped tail with a sharp caudal keel, heart-puncturing jaws rimmed with teeth bigger than Lanie's head, thick fins, and pig eyes. The bone shark blotted out the blue of the sky.

Heart pounding, hand cramping, Lanie relaxed her fingers, turning away from the northwest window to await the god they were to invoke next.

There was no sothaín attitude appropriate for this god. Instead, Lanie stared intently at the back of Haaken's neck, at the heavy, ghost-gold twist of braid that lay against it.

His hair looked very soft. Pettable.

Not that Haaken was pettable—he was barely approachable. And yet…

Shaking her head, Lanie rattled away the thought, telling herself, *Concentrate, Miscellaneous Stones.*

And then she began to pray.

Erre'Elur. Woe-Woman. Winter-Crowned. Vital-Force Source. God of sky wizards. God of Skakmaht. There was a war. Your miracles were misused. Ours, too. Help us set that crooked path aright.

The north-facing window to her right frosted over with abrupt ice. Lanie rolled her head that way, her gaze fixed on the glass. Not a scrap of blue shone through it.

Haaken had gone utterly still, staring where Lanie stared. The expression on his face was too private, too intimate; she should not look at it. She *wanted* to look at it. How familiar it was…

Inhaling deeply, Lanie forced her head to turn again, this time towards the south. Left, toward Liriat.

Come, my Saint Death, she thought. *Last and greatest.*

And then She came, stepping through the south-facing window, dragging Her cloak of bone behind Her. She smiled at Lanie, Her teeth white and charmingly uneven in a wry brown face.

I am yours, She said. *As I belong to all things, so do I belong to you.*

Lanie stared and stared and stared some more. Of all the gods in the room, she could not get enough of this one. *This* one.

"Lanie."

Not her god's voice.

Lanie shuddered her attention back to mortal things, and, with a powerful reluctance, turned once more towards Haaken's workbench. He and Tanalíin and Duantri were all watching her now with identical expressions of expectation.

She smiled at them. Even her lips were languid with sotháin.

"Are you ready, Lanie?" Haaken spoke her name like a foreign word that his tongue did not quite wrap around.

Silently, she held up her left hand, showing him the twelfth attitude of the twelfth set fixed in her fingers: a full circle. *Who is my doorway that the dead walk through?*

But the gesture was not enough. She had to force her mouth to speak words, not prayers.

"They're here." Her deep voice slid just beneath her surface voice, twinning it.

"Yes," Haaken breathed, his pale face like a glass filled with pure panthauma.

How he gleamed! How gleamed this whole glass-paneled place! This timeless space, this seventh-story tower, this sepulcher, where eight gods deigned to gather! The bouquet of Them. The brine of Them. The wildflower-ice-and-feather, lightning-and-petrichor, mineral-citrus smell of Them!

Haaken cleared his throat but even so, his voice when he next spoke was rough. "Gyrgardu Duantri? Are you ready?"

"I am ready."

Duantri slid off her stool to stand beside Sari's snowpyre. Its clear dome had gone utterly opaque, showing nothing now but crackled gray crystal. She moved her body into Kywit's fifth attitude, one of waiting: *Bones of child are buried in the tree roots.* Her posture steady, her expression relaxed, and her witchglass daggers left in Tanalíin's keeping, Duantri kept her focus on her gyrlady's newly bewitched Bryddongard. The sparkle of silver frostwork on its tracings was almost too bright to look upon.

"Tanalíín?" Haaken asked. "Are you ready?"

"More than ready, sweet boy!" Tanalíín replied cheerfully. "Your frostwork is so wonderfully interesting! Let us submit a paper on comparative and collaborative theology for the Annual Summit of Deep Learning next fall. Duantri and I would be pleased to sponsor your badge. Our scrape has room enough for one more esh. Even more room"—she grinned—"if you park your sky house right above us, instead of roughing it on the ground with the rest of us."

Haaken's glacier-ice eyes glinted at her in amusement, but he did not answer. The gods at Their windows were restless, pulled in every direction at once, and Aganath especially so. Lanie's eyes tracked Her as She circled the tower unceasingly, sometimes in front of the window glass, sometimes behind it, Her dorsal fin cutting through the copper roof like it was a wave of the sea.

"Tanalíín," he invited the gyrlady, his voice sure and slow, "if you would please activate your Bryddongard at this time. And you, Gyrgardu—"

"I know what to do," said Duantri, and flung off her robe.

Lanie looked on as the eight gods—massive and diaphanous, too incredible for the heavens to contain, an empyrean horde of snow and lightning, scales and teeth and tails, wings and radiant eyes and colored smoke, and so many, *many* bones—turned as one to watch Duantri, now naked, backing up as far as she could against the southwest wall. Then, taking a running leap, she sprinted across the tower room and through the open northeast window, vaulting over the little iron balcony that separated the topmost chamber from the rest of the sky.

Only silence, only stillness, as she plummeted like a stone dropped from the stars.

One second per twelve gods, Lanie thought, *till terminal velocity*.

On Tanalíín's wrist, the Bryddongard flashed like a sun exploding. Her gasp was so loud it was almost a shout.

Lanie, breaking sotháin, clawed to her feet and stumbled to the open window after Duantri.

The wind rushed in at her, freezing and thin. She hardly felt it. All she saw was the Gyrgardu, a speck in the air far below them, as she burst into her kestrel form.

Her kestrel's *fableform*.

Duantri had become a *vital-force kestrel*, born of Skaki ice magic, and mingled with the more familiar mysteries of seven other Quadoni gods. She was tremendous—enormous!—big as a gunugg! Her feathers were frosted over with silver ice, her amber eyes were the size of bucklers—no, of millstones!—and her talons were like scimitars cut from crescent moons!

And when she gaped her great beak to call the kestrel's *killy-killy-klee*—a clap of Kantu's thunder pealed forth.

Warmth enveloped Lanie from behind as Tanaliín rushed up to hug her. The gyrlady pressed her wet face to Lanie's neck, and even her voice was incandescent when she cried, "Oh, Lanie! My Lanie! The marvel of it all! The All-Marvel! The All-Marvel!"

Lanie's deep senses flashed out as wide as the sky for exactly three heartbeats, rippling out from the tower in all directions for miles and miles. Her perceptions pulsed through Duantri, counting every one of her gargantuan feathers—down, semi-plume, filoplume, contour, and bristle—analyzing the silver-white magic of each singular snowflake that clung to her like dew. Her senses found and brushed against the tether of her Bryddongard magic: a braid of fluid fire-opal that ran from the center of Duantri's feathered chest all the way back into Tanaliín's right arm, into her Bryddongard.

But to Lanie's surprise, what her deep senses discovered was that the tether no longer stopped at Tanaliín. Now it moved *through* the Bryddongard, up her arm, through her heart and out from behind her right shoulder blade, where it continued its burning path through the air into *Haaken*, coming to terminus in the hollow of his throat.

There, in the notch between his clavicles, a drop of perfect crystal ice began to form. No chain or thread held it there. But it shone like a pendant, suspended against his skin. It was their fableform spell preserved in ice, for as long as they all needed it.

Some amongst the Gyrveard would say that what they did today was sacrilege. An abomination. A bonded Bryddongard pair, to share their connection with a third party? And one who was not even a worshipper of the Twelve, but a Skaki heathen who prayed to wintry Erre'Elur, instead of to Her right and proper aspect, Doédenna?

But Lanie's deep senses, which were like an inrushing tide sweeping the tower room on their return journey to her body, brushed against the gods, and knew that their work today was no sacrilege. The gods had made it possible. This was Their miracle.

And now, miracle made, the attending eight began to wisp off one by one, disappearing from the windows and sidestepping into elsewhere. And all of Them were smiling—even Aganath.

The flat disks of the Bone Shark's black eyes contemplated Lanie for an eternal moment. Lanie thought, *Havoc's god. And the Blackbird Bride's*, and smiled at Her tentatively.

In response, Aganath jutted forth Her lower jaw to flaunt an amphitheater of fangs. Twelve times twelve rows of serrated, triangular teeth returned Lanie's smile twelve-fold, and then Aganath, Queen of the Sea, swam off into an underwater gloom somewhere just adjacent to the sky.

Last to leave were the gods of Death.

Doédenna's back was to Lanie as She passed through the southernmost of the eight tower windows, into the dimming afternoon light. Her cloak of bone dragged behind Her, filling the tower with its chattering, clattering, curious rattle. Lanie stared after Her hungrily, and Doédenna seemed to feel her gaze, for She turned slightly to glance over Her left shoulder.

Soon, Her brown eyes promised, full of sadness and hope. *Soon*.

I know, Lanie replied. *I know and I'm ready, sweet friend*.

She would have said more, would have stayed that way forever, and forever, and ever, watching Saint Death—Her quiet brown face, the bird of wind and flame cupped to Her heart, Her ever-trailing cloak of bone—but a murmur distracted her, pulling her gaze away for a fraction of a second.

There was Haaken, standing at the northern window, speaking in such pleading-sweet Old Skaki, urgent and low. She knew his words were meant for his god alone. But she couldn't help eavesdropping a little.

> *Sovereign of Saxifrage, our Lady of Lychnis,*
> *what is Your will in this wind-blasted waste?*
> *Source-sundered sorcerers, sullen with secrets*
> *sink in their scathe-sea, and widen old wounds.*

Standing before him, stooped over him, holding his hands in Hers: Erre'Elur.

All Lanie could see of Her skin was Her bare hands: the color of a late-midnight sky, with stars at the bottom of a depthless black, and a freckling of snowflakes atop it. Her hair was the swirling halo of the Blithe Dancers—a polar corona of green and pink and purple. Her enormous coat was of caribou fur, its deep hood lined with snow-fox fur. Her trousers were of silver sealskin, and Her socks were of rabbit fur, and Her boots of ring-seal skin were lined with loon feathers, that She might stride the length and breadth of Skakmaht, from its highest peaks to its deepest snowdrifts.

Her face was the skull of a narwhal.

A long tusk jutted from the center of Her bone mask, at least eight feet long, pale and helical. It rested on Haaken's shoulder like a knight's lance as She bent Her head to hear him.

In that moment, perceiving Lanie's fixed attention, Erre'Elur lifted Her head, and pointed the bone mask of Her face in Lanie's direction. The coronal night fires that crowned Her head also illuminated Her eye sockets.

Lanie and the Woe-Woman faced each other across the tower. Noticing each other. *Knowing* each other.

Lanie lost time.

A few seconds? Minutes? Maybe longer.

Once there was a god. Then there was a window.

Glass. Sky. Nothing.

Lanie stared into the north, waiting, shocked at the emptiness the gods had left in Their wake. If she waited long enough, patiently enough, perhaps Erre'Elur would return, and notice her again.

But as she re-surfaced from her deep senses, Lanie found that the gods had left not *only* emptiness behind Them.

Her body was electric with energy. When she held her hands in front of her face, her fingers, in their mittens, sparked and fizzed with the sunshine-yellow citrus of her god. The wizard mark on her left hand had deepened to an especially dense gray, with a sheen on it like quicksilver, as if she had dipped her hand in some metallic paint. She was so stuffed with panthauma that her aching weariness had fallen from her body like a kestrel plummeting from a sky house. She hadn't felt so refulgent, so indomitable, so *plenipotent* since... since... last year's High Holy Fire Feast of Midsummer?

Maybe not even then.

Eight gods had gifted her with an early surge, it seemed.

Later, on the High Holy Fire Feast of Spring Equinox, Lanie would set Them a banquet. She would eat every delightful thing and offer her fullness up to them. She would dance for Them, barefoot, wearing garlands of silk flowers. She would drink only the finest fruit juices and sweetest wines, tasting everything twice-twelve times, in gratitude for the gods' generosity. And then she would rest, at last.

She did not think that she would feel her surge on that future day, or for several fire feasts to come. But that was all right—more than right—because this was Their gift *now*, when she needed it.

Lanie's hovering heels slammed back down to the floor. She must have been floating about three inches in the air, and never noticed till she landed. Looking around her, startled, she saw—just in time—Tanaliín, leaning a little too far over the iron balcony. Dashing over, she grabbed the back of her jacket. Tanaliín squirmed into a slightly less precarious position, but otherwise remained absorbed in the sight of her Gyrgardu giantess flying below.

A fingertip touched Lanie's elbow, a breath-light warmth, there and gone. She glanced up to see Haaken standing beside her. His pale hair and eyes still reflected the green and purple lights of the Blithe Dancers, though none shone now in the afternoon sky, and his skin seemed so translucent, she could see midnight in his depths, an infinite black, burning with stars.

But Haaken was not looking at her. He was gazing across the ocean of air to where the vital-force kestrel hovered, and smiling.

Lanie leaned sideways, shoulder-bumping Haaken's arm, and murmured, "Well done."

DUANTRI, IN KESTREL's fableform, glided on the updraft till she paralleled Sky House Skrathmandan.

The late afternoon sun was everywhere upon her. She smoldered in that slanted gold like a great and gorgeous kite.

Miracle, retrieval, rescue, flight, and future—none of that mattered in this moment. For now, she existed for one reason and one alone: for the pleasure of delighting one Tanaliín idden Fa'nim'wai, whom she knew to be watching from the window of a flying tower.

Look! she flirted her tail. *Kestrel as a fulmar ship!*

See! she flourished her wings. *Kestrel as a feathered steed!*

Observe! and she rode the wind like she was surfing the crest of a giant wave. *A reversal of our roles! Kestrel as* perch *for her gyrlady!*

And Tanaliín laughed and clapped and hollered down loving words at her, her Duantri, at play.

CHAPTER TWENTY-TWO
Citadel Irradiant

Year 4826 of Higher and Lower Quadiíb
On Amahtar, 7th of Anatha: the Third Month
13 Days till Spring Equinox

IRRADIANT PEERED IN the full-length looking glass. How long he'd been standing there was anyone's guess. All the clocks in the Guilded Council were long stopped, daylight here so brief, and today's skies overcast. Hard to tell time in this duodecifold-damned place.

Smelled like snow. But then, when didn't it, in benighted Skakmaht?

Irradiant stroked his beard. Turned his head this way, that. Turned all the way around, twisting to examine his broad shoulders and his sculpted (if perpetually horripilated) backside.

He liked his new body... fine. It was just fine. Not too old. Not too young. Tall, which he enjoyed. He'd never been tall himself, in life. Too pale, of course, but that was Skakis for you.

And he couldn't tell the color of his eyes. Milky gray? Blue? Kind of a cold-water agate, perhaps. Irradiant didn't quite admire them, but he had to admit they were striking. The kind of eyes that would smite absolute terror into the hearts of anyone he glared at. *And that*—as Sosha would say—*is what eyes are for.*

Strange to be seeing out of two human eyes again. Not having to burn one out on his way in. He'd made ingress into his new body with the precision of a pin, piercing the tip of a single finger, careful not to damage it, as from that moment the body would belong to him and him alone, for as long as he desired to occupy it.

No one inside this shell to fight him. Flesh without anima. Accident without substance. Waiting for him.

And the beard! There was *something* about his beard. Something familiar.

Irradiant found himself constantly compelled to stroke it, from his chin to his chest. It stopped at the center of his solar plexus, splitting into a neat fork: a reddish, dried-blood color much darker than the coppery blond hair on top of his head. Certainly darker than his eyelashes and eyebrows, which were almost white. Individually, his beard hairs were wiry, but taken as a whole pleasurably soft on the downstroke. There were little braids in it, with crystal beads and bits of shell tied in. Gray streaks, here and there. Enough to be dignified. Enough to be taken seriously.

Where have I seen this beard before?

Irradiant's new body, beard and all, had been completely frozen and frosted over when he had slipped inside it. An unpleasant shock, like pouring himself out as water into a pitcher of frozen meat. But, ah! The fit of it! The ease! The relief! The *humanity*.

For the first time since abandoning his shattered padlock on the Sarcophagus of Souls to possess Cracchen Skrathmandan, Irradiant didn't need to gouge out a space to situate himself. Here he was no parasite, latching onto a host body until he could consume all that was most useful inside it. Here, there was no host body. This was no possession. This was... *reclamation*.

...reclaimed by Irradiant Stones, the very man who'd husked this body in the first place, a hundred years ago during the Northernmost War.

He'd thought, upon admitting himself to his new body, that his triumphal entry alone would be enough to thaw it out. He'd thought that, once incarnate, his powerful presence would melt the ice magic preserving this fleshly framework from decay. And then his new body would start *working*. Like *normal*.

Not so. The ice magic was tenacious. A few hours of Irradiant pouring the better part of an entire *dragon's* worth of enfolded substance into it, and all he'd managed to do was thin down his thick outer layer of frost to a gelid slick.

However, he did feel himself growing a little less stiff. He was able to swing his limbs more freely, crack the icicles from his incredible beard, and arrange for himself a change of clothes.

He wanted to be moving faster. He had things to do. *Agenda* items.

All of that, it seemed, would have to wait while he hobbled around his new bedroom, growing accustomed to a body not only stiff with ice, but unused to moving in the way he wanted it to move. This body's muscles had memories of their own, although the meat of the brain itself was a pure canvas that Irradiant's substance could rewrite.

At least he wasn't freezing. Chilled, yes, unpleasantly so. But this ubiquitous slick on his skin seemed to be also insulating him from the worst of the weather—which, he supposed, was its job. He would rather by far get a fire going in that huge marble fireplace that took up half the bedroom wall. Why have a fireplace if you couldn't enjoy it?

At the moment, however, kindling, tinderbox, and cordwood were all incapsulated in solid ice.

So, pacing it was to be.

Irradiant pressed on, perambulating, rubbing his hands together to keep them from stroking his beard, and then forgetting and stroking his beard. A few rounds about the room, and he stopped again in front of the looking glass to admire himself.

His face looked funny. Not just alien—odd. More so than before.

Irradiant squinted. What was on that on his...?

He sagged with relief. Frost. Just more frost, forming on the mirror's surface, which he'd scraped clean not an hour ago.

Cursing, he reached out to scrub at the stuff with his sleeve, but the frost merely transferred itself onto the fine, thick-quilted silk, and immediately started branching out and multiplying.

There was no *working* with this stuff! Soon it would be all over his new robes. Even now, it was creeping across his hands like the little lace gloves Irradiant's wife used to wear, even though he'd told her time and again that they looked ridiculous on her, because everything did. A ridiculous woman.[19] Irradiant stared at his frost-covered hands, enraged.

All around him, the twilit room throbbed with silence. Ice everywhere, on everything, like mildew in a house gone feral: not only on the looking glass, but on the walls, the carpet, the furniture, the curtains.

And now, in the mirror, he saw that the clear, flexible slick on his skin was again covered in a new white crust, like the bizarrest case of middle-age acne a man might contract.

For what seemed like the hundredth time, Irradiant scraped a long, manicured fingernail through the thick frost on his cheek. He scratched and scratched, rasping off as much as he could. Took some skin off, too. To no avail—the raw grooves just refilled with more remonstrative ice.

Snorting in disgust, he flicked a fleck of frozen flesh to the floor and stepped back from the mirror, smoothing the watered silk of his robes. They were handsome garments, even crystal-clung with ice cubes as they were.[20]

The room was growing darker by the minute.

Night is falling, he reminded himself, *even though it was* just night *two seconds ago. Get to work.*

Irradiant forced himself to turn away from the mirror and the reassuring fork of his beard. Plenty to do up here in the

---

19 The 'ridiculous' Phantosmia Stones ("Fancy" to her friends) had the sense to survive thirty years of marriage to her husband, and against all odds, outlive him. At the end of the Northernmost War, she left Liriat Proper, changed her name, and passed out of history, which, one surmises, was probably her dearest wish.

20 In fact, the beadwork on antique Skaki garments of that era, particularly those worn by sky house elites, suggest patterns fashioned to show off any frostwork that formed upon them to best advantage.

Guilded Council, even if he had to grope about in the dark to get it done.

One thing a sky house was good for was its windows. They were everywhere: panes of every size in every possible placement, and doors, too, of clearest glass or ice. Even the walls had been grown out of semi-translucent crystal to let in plenty of natural light. The moon tonight would provide him with sufficient illumination—until he could figure out how to work those duodecifold-damned crystal lanterns he kept finding.

Ice and crystals. To make *light*. Not bloodlight nor olive oil nor whale blubber nor anything else so civilized. He hated them.

For now—leaving the lanterns out of it—Irradiant would start by sorting corpses. He could sort corpses anywhere, in pitch blackness or high noon's light. Corpses he knew. Corpses he could *use*.

He just needed to get his pretty, snow-laced fingers on a sharp knife, or better yet—a syringe! There was much a living necromancer—which he now was—could do with a corpse, a knife, and the hot, human blood that was running through his own blue veins.

Did Skaki blood even run hot? Didn't feel like it.

Well, he'd find out soon enough.

The thought made Irradiant smile—then chortle—then chuckle—then laugh out loud.

His laughter was the only sound in Iskald.

ALL IN ALL, Irradiant was as pleased with his new house as he was with his new body.

He'd done his housecleaning all throughout the night, sorting any of the wizard husks he found in the hallways from the regular, non-magical corpses—servants and the like—who'd been stuck up here when the war ended, and had starved or frozen to death, unable to make their way down from the Guilded Council. These, he could store away and use for his ectenica.

He kept a few wizard husks for himself, as trophies—but only the ones whose faces he recognized from the war. The rest, he merrily defenestrated, and watched them drop all the way down till they splatted. Very satisfying. As Sosha used to say, *Nothing's as funny as bodies falling out of windows.* The ones he kept, he would store down in the sepulcher, where they could keep the witch-bitch's kernel egg company. Much later, if he ever happened to tire of his new forked beard and striking eyes, he could step into one of their frozen shells like a new garment.

He had yet to insert the egg into his snowpyre; Irradiant only had the one, and didn't want to waste it. Wanted to study up on it first. Look through the library for any hints and bits about snowpyre engines and sepulcher magic. Examine the old, much-degraded kernel egg currently in situ before attempting to replace it. That, too, was on his agenda.

But now, in the bright morning light, Irradiant decided to explore his tidied sky house, sepulcher to skylit tower. The one he had chosen for himself was not the largest house in the Guilded Council—but it was the *second* largest, and by far the finest. No haphazard outgrowth of quartz and spontaneous reproduction of icicle, this! It was obvious to Irradiant that an architect with some elegance of mind had been responsible for its design: someone with vision, and acuity, and a firm grasp of the principles of proportion, balance, emphasis, hierarchy, and contrast.

...someone with sense enough to include an *entire library* in one of the wings—something none of the other sky houses had, barring a few bookrooms here and there, or shelving for a private collection in someone's study.

The library was all picture windows and long, cushioned window seats. The bookshelves formed maze-like, meandering paths through the large chamber, some of these ending in little reading nooks that were fitted with couches, or graceful chairs with matching footrests, or well-appointed desks meant to be lit by those unlightable crystal lanterns. The whole place was a treat, or it would be—once Irradiant removed the frost from everything, and augmented the space with all the treasures he culled from the other sky houses.

Other than the sepulcher at the bottom of the house, which could be accessed from the kitchen by a trapdoor near the central fireplace, the lowest rooms were the laundry, still room, wine cellar, an array of pantries, and the long kitchen, where he had decided to store his human corpses—at least until he set up a workshop area for himself—so that he would have easy access to supplies like knives, cauldron, lye, that sort of thing.

The knives were… *Yes, more infernal crystal*. Irradiant sighed. *At least they aren't prone to rusting.*

There was also a quantity of accumulated snow in the kitchen that had drifted in through one of the propped-open windows. Which was good—he'd need water for his next project.

Heaping the non-wizard corpses next to the enormous hearth, he dragged one of them onto the grate itself. Then, business-like and with more than a little relish, he nicked his forefinger and spilled three drops of blood onto it.

The ectenical bonfire that this kindled was all he'd hoped for. His new sky wizard blood—which was now infused with the death magic of his own substance—took to the frozen flesh like flame to kindling. His ectenica caught immediately and began to spread into a low, slow, crawling blue flame.

"Splendid!" Irradiant crowed. "Just splendid! Burn hot!" he commanded it. "But don't burn all at once. I have a large pot I want you to bring to bubbling. There's a heap of frozen meat I want boiled down to the bones."

The ectenica did as it had always done, and obeyed him.

He set his cauldron over the fire, and filled it to the brim with snow, letting it come to a simmer while he did other work.

Work was such a *pleasure* after years of imprisonment. Padlocks were tedious. Possessions were draining. Work was *life!* You knew you were alive if you were busy, all the time. There was so much to do!

First, he worked on the defective crystal lanterns.

By the fungal glimmer of his ectenical bonfire, Irradiant stood at the large butcher block counter with five lanterns in front of him, and a set of five small egg cups he'd found in one of the kitchen cabinets. Drawing inspiration from the bloodlamps of Liriat, Irradiant affixed an egg cup to the bottom of each lantern with a bit of frost from his fingertips. These would be his catch basins! Only, instead of bloodlighting it (which would require abducting a fire priest of Sappacor to perform the ritual), he cut off a chunk of frozen finger flesh from one of his corpses, set it in the egg cup, and sprinkled it with a drop from his still-open wound.

Bone dust, of course, would be a much tidier way of doing all this. (His great-granddaughter had never learned the way of working with bone dust, and he'd never bothered teaching her, enjoying watching her struggle). Bone dust he'd have, and plenty of it, once he got that water and lye up to boil and disintegrated all the meat off the corpses. The bones that would be left over would be fragile, friable, easily powdered. He'd dump the ancient, blackened leaves out of the large tea caddy on the counter and fill its wells with powdered bone instead. Scooping powdered bone into the egg cups whenever he needed a light, or anything that required small portions of ectenica, would be much less messy, and much more economical, than chopping up bodies.

Besides, Irradiant had never liked tea.

Inside the lanterns, in his improvised catch basins, his ectenica caught right away, just as the bonfire had—but with an additional surprise. As the chunk of frozen finger collapsed to ashy black sludge in its egg cup, the ice-crystal panes of the lantern *retained* their light, each facet reflecting an azure glow, as if the ectenical fire were still captured there.

Irradiant yipped in triumph at the sight, lifted the skirts of his robes, and danced around the kitchen.

Lantern problem solved!

He was beginning to change his mind about boiling down all the corpses too. He should keep a few out of the cauldron, preserved in their ice. The ice that encased their flesh seemed to be making his ectenica last longer—which would prove useful if he needed to raise a few undead servants and puppet them around. His great-granddaughter had found a way to stabilize her ectenica in clay; Irradiant would do the same—but do it with magical ice instead!

"Take that, girlie!" he sang to himself. "Who's the best living necromancer on Athe *now*? Heh."

When he was finished celebrating, Irradiant sat down and ate an actual lunch: something he'd not done for himself in a century. (Making his host bodies eat didn't count, since he couldn't taste anything when he was possessing them.) He'd been wondering why he was feeling so lightheaded, why his belly was cramping, why his hands trembled as they held the crystal knife as if he were afeared—when suddenly, he realized he might be hungry. He'd not eaten a meal since entering this body yesterday morning.

Now it was alive. And it—*he*—wanted feeding up.

Humming to himself, Irradiant thawed a frozen loaf of hundred-year-old bread and a jar of equally frozen hundred-year-old meat in a double boiler that he hung over the cauldron. Didn't taste like much, but there would be time for fine cuisine later. He'd fly his sky house to Liriat Proper, where he would feast on decent food.

After lunch, to his shock, he fell asleep. He was so tired he couldn't even drag himself to his fine, frost-covered bedroom, so he dropped right there in the kitchen—on an old dog bed, no less! (He'd boiled the dog bones down with the rest of them.)

His eyelids drooped closed, his pale lashes fluttering like ghosts. The last time he'd felt so tired—dog-tired, ha!—he had been with Sosha, somewhere in the ruins of Iskald, just below…

DURING THE NORTHERNMOST War, he and Sosha used to play darts every night, using sketches Sosha had made.

Sosha was an artist. The Brackenwilds generally were, one way or another; it was one of many endearing traits they shared in common with the Stoneses, and the Regent Sinister was no exception. He had all the Brackenwild charisma: the inexorable charm, the performance readiness, the blood magic in his veins. But he was also master of a quieter set of skills, with his fine eye and delicate hand for drawing.

His favorite medium was popularly known as 'the two-gods approach,' or sometimes 'Lirian crayon drawing,' so named because it used chalk pencils in only two colors: the sanguine (for Old Sparks) and the black (for Saint Death), usually on a mid-tone paper.

Sosha may have cut swaths on the battlefield with his heirloom axe Drjōta. He may have slain dozens of courtiers (metaphorically, of course) (mostly) with his raffish beauty, his lightning-flash grin, his dark eyes and arrogant swagger.[21] But it was for Sosha's drawings that Irradiant loved him best.

In his little tent on the permafrost, leaning over his folding field desk, Sosha scribbled away at his work. From time to time, he had to pause and swing the *hilarious* garland of severed hands that he always wore out of his way, so that it didn't disturb his febrile sketching. (Irradiant had bewitched the garland so that its grisly charms never rotted, never withered. Each one was as dewy as a fresh-plucked chiranthodendron blossom, the blood upon its flesh still bright.)

He stood just behind Sosha's shoulder, so tired he was swaying on his feet. But he wouldn't sleep until they had played their game of darts, and Sosha declared it time for bed. Sosha was notorious for the late hours he kept.

"Ah," Irradiant observed, leaning over to leaf through the finished pile of sketches as Sosha continued to work on his newest. "I do believe I espy the faces of our honored enemies: the august members of the Guilded Council of Skakmaht." And he spat, delicately, over his shoulder.

"Someone has to capture their likenesses," Sosha murmured, "before we wipe them off the face of Athe."

"That falls to you, does it? You are your own court portrait artist?"

---

21 Not to mention his enormous coercive power as Blood Royal of Liriat, unethically wielded in his own favor.

Sosha paused in his sketching to grin up at him. "The last set I made is perforated beyond all recognition. And I am owed a victory after our last game. You and your unerring left hand."

Irradiant paused as he came to the last of Sosha's pasteboard portraits. It depicted an old woman with deeply carved lines in her face, the white of her hair rendered in the spaces between the lightest lines of sanguine and black. "Who's she? I've never seen her before."

Sosha carelessly handed off his newest sketch, just finished. "Her? That's Lothgarran. One of the contingent who flew down to camp yesterday to sue for peace. You missed it—you were still resting up after raising up all those corpses, lazybones." Sosha squeezed Irradiant's arm. His hand, always hot with blood magic, burned with a far more terrible fever. "I hated to wake you. Why bother? We both knew already what the outcome of that meeting was to be."

Irradiant waved the portrait in Sosha's face. "I'll pin her up. The usual place?"

The portraits, affixed to the hide walls of Sosha's tent, all in a line, made for a row of fine targets. There they were, the sky wizards of Skakmaht, all rendered in red and black crayon, staring back at them. A pile of rusted steel darts glinted on the folding table next to Sosha's cot. Irradiant's fingers itched to snatch one up. But he would wait for Sosha. This was *their* game, after all, not his alone.

Sosha sauntered over to fling an arm around his shoulder. "Well, Irradiant Radithor? Want to wager on the winner again?"

"Think you'll beat me this time, Regent Sinister?"

"I always beat you, Raddy." Sosha smiled as he lied, the dimples crimping his lean brown cheeks. He smiled so charmingly that Irradiant started laughing, which made Sosha laugh—laugh and laugh and laugh, until his laughter turned to deep, racking coughs that bent him double. He buried his face in his elbow as Irradiant fumbled for a handkerchief he did not have. When Sosha finally did come up for air, the corners of his mouth were as bloody as the last sketch that fell from his spasming fingers.

Irradiant bent to pick it up.

"And who's this one?" He only asked to give Sosha enough time to sop up his blood. Sosha hated being babied.

"That," rasped Sosha, clearing his throat in vain, "is Aadar Skrathmandan. Powerful bastard. Demon-lover. Favored, they say, of Erre'Elur. Have to admit, he dresses well. He was the brains behind the"—he coughed again—"the whole egg thing in Leech."

"Ah, yes"—Irradiant nodded—"that one. I like his beard."

"I'll make you a present of it," Sosha promised, "when I cut his face off. Now, stop stalling, you coward—as if I'd let you win by forfeit. Shall we play?"

As each dart hit its mark, Irradiant and Sosha declared the downfall of another sky wizard.

Thus falls Hrok son of Kaork, of Sky House Ka'ha!

Thus falls Lothgarran, daughter of Lothgirran, of Sky House Othralska!

Thus falls Jegil, scion of Merilda and Mattam, of Sky House Bassahb!

"Thus Aadar Skrathmandan!" Sosha hooted, hoarse with glee and coughing, as his dart landed right between the sky wizard's alien-pale eyes. (Black chalk, but shaded to the lightest gray.) "Your beard is ours, old man!"

Irradiant laughed so hard he swooned. He'd been swooning a lot lately, as the winter deepened, and the nights grew longer and colder. Sosha tried to catch him, but the Blood Royal was himself barely strong enough to hold his own weight. Irradiant's head struck the corner of the desk as he went down.

Red splashed gray. Gray, gone black.

Knocked out cold.

IRRADIANT AWOKE IN his dog bed, his living heart pounding in his chest. "What was that?" he muttered blearily. "Did I just *dream*?"

Not something he'd done in a century. Wasn't sure he approved. And what had woken him?

Then it happened again: a noise from below.

It came from beneath the trapdoor by the fireplace—the one leading down to the sepulcher.

Someone, he thought, *is in my house.*

CHAPTER TWENTY-THREE
Sepulcher

Year 4826 of Higher and Lower Quadiíb
On Lasaqi, 8th of Anatha: the Third Month
12 Days till Spring Equinox

THERE WERE AT least two dozen sky houses composing the current iteration of the Guilded Council, Cracchen informed them, and therefore, he proposed, they should all split up to search the structure for the kernel egg. Wheresoever they found the egg, he argued, there they would find the ghost.

Practical Tanaliín countered his proposal with one of her own: *none* of them should go off by themselves like nincompoops. If they had to split up, they should do it in groups: she with Duantri, and both the brothers with Lanie.

Cracchen was all amiability, all agreement—*then*. But as soon as Tanaliín and Duantri had set off down the vitreous corridor leading to their designated quadrant of the Guilded Council, he turned his slight smile at Lanie, ignoring Haaken entirely.

"The truth of the matter is," he said, "when we are with ourself, we are with a group already. The two of you should pair off and explore the middle houses, and we"—he gestured to himself—"will go on and explore the upper houses—not alone, but together, as one. It will be much faster this way."

Lanie narrowed her eyes at him, her spectacles slipping down her wrinkled nose. Haaken had bespelled her lenses so that they didn't fog up every time she breathed the cold air, so she had a crystal-clear view of Cracchen's guileless face.

Guileless, she thought. *Right.*

Her voice as mild as his face, she asked, "What are you up to, Cracchen?"

His smile widened—that new, blazing, sky-wizardly smile of his that held a force in it like thundersnow—and stepped forward to cradle her cheek in his fingers of sculpted ice.

Lanie jerked her face out of reach. Cracchen's hand landed on her shoulder instead. She shrugged it off, rolling her eyes at his brother, who watched, bovine and placid, as if he had nothing better to do all day than chew cud.

Never play bluffing or social deduction games with Haaken Skrathmandan, she reminded herself. *He could convince anyone to buy realty on an avalanche pathway.*

"Miscellaneous." Cracchen sighed happily, wagging his finger in front of her nose, half an inch from booping it like a kitten's. "Miscellaneous, Miscellaneous. Do you not trust us yet? After our long journey together? After all you have done for us, and we for you? Are we not fast friends and allies?"

Lanie was strongly tempted to bite his finger. "Sure. I'll ask again. What are you up to, *friend?*"

When Cracchen tweaked one of her braids, Lanie slapped his hand away, light but fast, like waving off a fly without wanting to crush it. The echo-wound softly stung the top of her own hand, but that was bearable.

Drawling his words, Cracchen said, "We have a daunting set of tasks before us, do we not? Rescue the kernel egg. Destroy the ghost. And, though we may not have bothered mentioning it to that *supremely* inquisitive gyrlady, we also have a vested interest in finding the rest of… of our bodies." He ducked his head, swallowed, and said in a lower, far more earnest tone, "We know, of course, that there is no possibility of returning our sundered vital forces to their original sources. We made that decision in Leech, while in chrysalis, to net ourselves together in a single lattice. There is no reversal now, not without shattering all of us. And yet…"

He turned, appealing to Haaken for the first time. "Last

night, buhror, we flew over Iskald in our fulmar ship. There were... bodies. Below us. Lying atop the snow, freshly fallen. As if someone... had recently pitched them from the windows of the Guilded Council. We searched them. We know their names. We know, also, who among them is missing. We must find the rest of us before *he*"—his voice was colder than the air outside—"further desecrates them."

Haaken bowed his head, murmuring respectfully, "As you will, anuraki."

'Anuraki,' Lanie remembered, was the Skaki word for ancestor. Not 'buhror,' brother.

She looked from Haaken to Cracchen, compressing the outrage in her lips. Cracchen should *not* go alone, whatever his argument. Wrathful as he was, powerful as he was, still, alone, he was vulnerable. And he *was* up to something—something he wasn't telling her—and no, she *didn't* trust him, not completely, even though he had saved her life, and brought her safely to Skakmaht, and had even helped train Duantri with her witchglass daggers. Even though he smiled at her like he... like she... like they were some kind of...

Anyway.

Even if she didn't trust him, she *did* trust Haaken, whom the beautiful god Erre'Elur loved so well.

And Haaken, Lanie sensed, was also up to something.

She crossed her arms. "Fine, then. Go. Alone, if you must. You're an adult, after all. Several."

Nodding his fond approval of her unnecessary permission, Cracchen pointed down one of the dark, glassy corridors that branched out from the Mistral Atrium. "I'm off that way then. Miscellaneous. Buhror. Meet you back here at moonrise?"

Haaken nodded. "Very well. Mistress Stones, do you accompany me? Or shall you, too"—he waved a listless wrist—"wander off alone?"

Cracchen cuffed his arm, hard enough that Lanie felt hers twinge with the echo-bruise. "Never let her, brother! Protect her with your life—or I'll have yours when next we meet."

Then, too quickly for her to dodge out of his way, he did, in fact, boop Lanie on the nose.

Her left hand flashed up between her body and his, hard and upright, a quicksilver glimmer in the dark. A dorsal fin. "Don't."

"Do not *fret* so, Miscellaneous. You are in the north now," Cracchen advised, "and your face might freeze like that. Do you not know that your countenance is our daily delight? We have so few."

Lanie rolled her eyes again. "Enough of this. You have your periapt, in case of…"

Cracchen withdrew the small amulet from his collar, a droplet of Haaken's unmeltable ice with a silk string threaded through it. He jiggled it at her.

"Here is our leash, Mistress Stones. We will come running when you whistle, your faithful wolf."

Lanie pointed at the periapt. "And *you'll* call for *us*, too—through the periapt—if you come across the ghost first. You *won't* try to take him on alone."

They were not questions, but Cracchen countered with one. "Do you doubt me?"

Which is not, Lanie thought with a glare, *an agreement*. Nor did he wait for her to reply, but turned and trotted down his chosen corridor. Lanie eyeballed Haaken, who was not looking at her, but after his brother.

"Well?" she asked, her voice as dry as the ashes in a lone golden urn.

Instead of answering, Haaken stretched out an arm and laid his hand flat against one of the clear, dark walls of the Mistral Atrium. Under his long fingers, marks began to etch themselves across the ice, in the dancing iridescent colors of the Blithe Dancers. The marks became a map, the map spreading out over the wall until the entire Guilded Council was laid out for them like a blueprint, lighting up the glassy corridor. Five flaring dots appeared near the bottom center of the map: two moving off in one direction; one speeding away in the other; and two hovering in one place, still.

"You. Me." Haaken pointed to the latter dots.

Lanie wanted to jump up and down. She wanted to squeal. She wanted to pepper Haaken in questions and speak in exclamations points. But that would have to keep till later. If there was a later.

"And this," she asked, pointing to the area surrounding them, "is the Mistral Atrium?"

Haaken nodded. "We are in one of its several sub-levels, but yes. It"—he tapped the map—"is the heart of the Guilded Council, where all sky houses converge."

"And those"—Lanie pointed at the first two dots, still on the same sub-level as they were, but moving towards an area where the sky houses started spiking and spiraling out from the center. "Those are..."

"Gyrgardu Duantri. Gyrlady Tanaliín," Haaken provided. "They appear here on the map because their periapts are linked to mine, and I... I am linked to this ice." He tapped the wall again.

"Haaken," Lanie asked, impressed, "are you... in an integrated lattice with *all* the ice in Skakmaht?"

The corners of his lips curved. Or she thought they did. The wyrded light of the wall map made all expressions tricksy and unsure. Especially his, which were hardly shadows in the first place.

"Not *all*," he replied. "But Sky House Skrathmandan is infused with my vital force. Our snowpyre is powered by my own... ancestor. I am, therefore, connected to it. And *all* sky houses are created to connect back, in some way, to the Guilded Council. Since I scraped the ice for our periapts from the walls of our sky house, the ones we are wearing are looping us together—and thus, to this place as well. Do you see?"

"I see." Lanie was more impressed than ever, just burbling over with admiration. "And that dot right there, Cracchen's dot, is it... wait. What is he *doing*?"

The last dot, which had been darting in the opposite direction to where Duantri and Tanaliín were headed, now began moving a few layers up in the blueprint, out of the sub-corridors and into the vast central hall of the Mistral Atrium. There, the dot turned and doubled back at great speed, taking a path that aimed in the same direction as the first two moving dots. Cracchen was paralleling Tanaliín and Duantri's movements, but using the upper halls of the sky houses so that they would not notice his presence.

"I think," Haaken said, "the anuraki knows *exactly* where he is going."

"Well," Lanie retorted, "I don't think he should find it first—for his own sake, and for…"

"For the sake of anyone who gets in his way," Haaken finished.

His hand traced a third path through the blueprint: a convoluted series of quick turns, subtle shortcuts, and secret passages that should move both him and Lanie in the same direction as the others, but without detection from either party.

He glanced at her, eyebrow raised. She nodded.

Haaken removed his fingers from the wall, and the map flashed out of existence, back into his hand. For just a moment, his palm smoldered like a fistful of fireflies.

"Come." Haaken offered his greenly glowing hand to Lanie's silver-dipped one. She grasped it, surprised to find his skin as rough and warm as Cracchen's was smooth and cold.

They ran.

IN THIS LATEST sepulcher they had entered, another endless undercroft of ice-brick and quartz and darkness, there was something new: a shifting sort of shimmering, light where there should not be light. It tricked Duantri's eyes.

The glimmer gradually took on texture, too, something like overlapping ivy leaves, but with the rich gleam of gemstones. She did not realize what she was looking at, until…

"Oh."

She stopped short, standing in the threshold between the sepulcher and one of the many conducting corridors that branched out from the bottoms of the sky houses like glass tubes. (Duantri, for all she was used to height and flight, was finding the tubes, with their views both *out* and *down*, to be strangely dizzying. Tanaliín, of course, adored them.)

Following on her heels, her gyrlady did not see Duantri stop in time, and bumped into her back. She peered around her and into the sepulcher. When she glimpsed what Duantri had beheld, she gave a low cry.

"Beloved mine—what is that awful nest?"

"Those are the dragon's scales. The... husk he left," Duantri whispered, dry-mouthed, "when jumped the ghostly tick, that parasite, from Tam of Taquathura's fableform."

The dragon's corpse spiraled around itself like an enormous snail. Its scarlet, gold, and black scales reflected light but emitted no glow, though something in its hollowed skin must have retained a memory of heat, for this sepulcher was much warmer than any of the outer hallways, and the source of warmth seemed to be the dragon.

In the precise middle of the coils sat the kernel egg— the source of light. It was half-buried in the hot scales, just as it had been in the warm sands of the hatchery. The egg was as fulgent and fulsome as it had been in Madinatam, sending out its play of colors across the room. All the other sepulchers that Duantri and Tanaliín had explored prior to this one were empty and dark and cold, the old kernel eggs in their snowpyres giving off only the faintest, if any, radiance through the opaque domes enclosing them. In this chamber, the ancient kernel egg still shone brilliantly under the cracked gray dome of its catafalque. The radiance that pulsed from its degraded shell was scintillant, but also wildly flickering—as if by proximity to the Witch Queen's egg it had been somehow reactivated, and at the same time, destabilized.

Tanaliín set a hand on Duantri's shoulder.

"Step forth, my love," she urged her, "take heart and seize the egg. I have the cradleboard Haaken hath made, and furs to wrap yon kernel kindly in. We'll stuff a sack with scales to keep it warm, in memory of Tam who lent it life. A keepsake for the hatchling, by and by."

Nodding, breathing, nodding again, Duantri strode forward—

—and tripped over a corpse.

That was when it all went wrong.

"WELL, WELL, WELL," said the ghost. "What have we here? Two Quadoni thieves, come to steal my egg."

He dropped down on them from nowhere—from above like a spider. On either side of him stood two frost-bitten, blue-skinned children, their eyes seamed shut with ice. Their little faces were tilted toward him like obedient dogs, and he, the man with the sausage treats.

"Hello, birdie," he greeted Duantri. "Shucked your nettles and found your hag, did you?"

The ghost may have been wearing a body Duantri had never seen before—tall, bearded, pale-eyed, pale-skinned—but his grin was instantly recognizable. She had seen it time and again at the Hastiludes.

And... *birdie*.

At knife practice, Cracchen had imitated his former parasite's intonation perfectly. She had heard that word, oozing derision, so frequently and so recently, that it sparked no outraged indignation in her now, no fiery desire to destroy him at the cost of her sense.

She was ready for him.

Duantri stepped in front of Tanaliín, as Irradiant Stones snapped his fingers at the undead children. They whipped about to fix their attention on Duantri: two puppets hanging from invisible sinews, with one puppet master to put them through their paces.

At that point, she also glimpsed the dark staircase behind them, leading up to some kind of trapdoor. The stairs had been obscured by the snowpyre's opaque dome and the... *dozens,* (she now saw, appalled) of frozen bodies that were piled in front of it. She had tripped over one of them on her way to the egg, which was probably what had alerted the ghost to their presence.

As the children stepped closer to the kernel egg's light, she saw that they both bore bright red marks on their foreheads: four stark fingerprints where the necromancer had anointed them with his blood. Lining each fingerprint was a thin line of ectenical blue. This made them—Duantri knew, from her months traveling with Lanie—the necromancer's ectenical constructs. And ectenica was a formidable opponent. It could do anything, *be* anything, that the necromancer willed.

The children moved closer to her, and Duantri drew her witchglass daggers from their sheaths.

She did not want to hurt children. Lanie would not; Lanie would find another way.

But part of her (Kestrel) also recalled that Lanie was not here. That these children were not alive. They were only the dead dreaming they were alive.

Behind her, there was a rustle of movement as Tanaliín took advantage of Duantri's cover to drop down to the floor. Duantri would wager that she was already stuffing the kernel egg into a sack of dragon scales, and securing it to the cradleboard, ready to make their escape. Tanaliín would set about accomplishing this task with an unswerving focus, ignoring undead children and resurrected necromancers alike, until it was no longer feasible for her to do so. She trusted her Falcon Defender to defend her.

But because she was Tanaliín, she could do more than one thing at a time, and started humming a tune under her breath as she worked.

Duantri recognized it as one of the old Quadoni spellsongs that Tanaliín had made special study of for her doctoral thesis. While Duantri had occasionally set about trying to learn the spellsongs too, she could never quite manage to recreate their melodies on her own, either with her voice or on her cavaquinho. But she could harmonize well enough with her gyrlady whenever Tanaliín sang them.

This melody was neither the Lahnessthanessar Lullaby nor the Maranathasseth Anthem, spellsongs Duantri had come to know intimately since meeting Lanie. The song that Tanaliín was humming now, if she recalled it correctly, belonged not to the death god Doédenna at all, but to Aganath, Queen of the Sea. It was the Karkryklys Hymn, Canticle of the Bone Shark.

After all, Anatha was Aganath's month—and Tanaliín, as a gyrlady, was (among other things) a priest in balance with the twelve gods, each in Their times. In this month, in Tanaliín's mouth, the Karkryklys Hymn was no idle tune, no desultory prayer, but a true enchantment.

Doubtless her gyrlady knew what she was doing, so Duantri would let her do it. In the meantime, she adjusted her grip on the knives, widened her stance, and softened her knees.

Tanaliín had warned her that she could not bring down this necromancer with martial arts and two witchglass daggers. Their duty was to the egg. Duantri must just hold off the undead long enough for Tanaliín to escape with it—and hopefully, for Duantri to escape as well.

The ice of Haaken's periapt burned against her throat, and she said loudly and clearly so that he might hear her through it, "We need help."

She hoped help would come soon, for even now, the ghost in his new sky wizard skin was growing an armor of plate as impenetrable as Cracchen's, the plate starting to form great spikes of ice, like a porcupine's quills...

"Ah ha!" Irradiant cried, glancing down at the barbed shards protruding from his inner wrists like rapiers, as if delighted by this development. "*That's* what the damned frost is for! And here I've been scraping it off this whole—"

Duantri darted in and sliced at one of his quills.

To her surprise, the witchglass snapped it right off and the spike clattered to the floor. *Just* like porcupine quills, Irradiant's ice spikes were barbed on one end, and detached easily from his armor, all the better to stick into the skin of an enemy. But they were also fragile and hollow—which was helpful to know.

His pale gray eyes flashing a familiar yellow, Irradiant snarled something in words she could not hear. He was not speaking to her, Duantri realized, but to the children—a command, in his deep voice.

One of the undead pair, a little girl with yellow braids that sparkled under a rime of hoarfrost, barreled into her like a snow-capped battering ram. The other, a little boy with dark brown hair stuck forever in a frozen cowlick, went straight for Tanaliín.

Duantri flowed aside with the first blow, slashing out with both daggers as she spun to take off two more of Irradiant's long, translucent quills. Irradiant spat out another command. The girl came at her again, drawing from her apron pockets a meat mallet with one hand, and a little crystal paring knife with the other. Duantri rolled behind Irradiant, putting him between her and the child.

And the girl's inexorable little body, eyes still seamed shut, blundered right into his quills.

Ice pierced ice. The child hung, twitching, from three barbed spikes, until Irradiant shook her free of him in a paroxysm of rage, breaking off a few more of his spikes in the process. When the undead girl made not so much as a whimper, Irradiant cursed again, and lashed out at Duantri with one of his wrist rapiers.

But she was no longer where she had been. She was already circling him, slashing, and slashing, and slashing again.

Irradiant Stones, she was beginning to perceive, was no warrior. Just as Cracchen had predicted, the armor of ice that grew from his new body, that protected him, also made him heavy, clumsy, and uncertain of his center. She was grateful for any incompetence on his part. Warrior or no, he had evaded Lanie's magic for months. Lanie! Whose god stood behind her at all times, with other gods looking on.

Duantri thought she was prepared for any shock, any cheat,

any cruelty from her opponent. But when Irradiant bent down to heft the undead girl into the air, with his barbed spikes still jutting from her neck and chest, to use her as a shield against Duantri, she fell back a few steps and looked to her gyrlady for counsel.

But where Tanaliín had been kneeling was only a watery darkness.

It was as if a vertical pond, limpid and clear, had dropped down from the skies to curtain Tanaliín off from the rest of the sepulcher. But the water, so placid it barely rippled, showed nothing of the room behind it, only an endless ocean.

"What are you waiting for?" Irradiant shrieked at the undead boy when he hesitated before the wall of water. "Go after the hag!"

The icy little corpse thrust his hands through the curtain, but pulled them out immediately; where it touched him, the water had washed away the thick layer of ice on his skin.

Irradiant snarled again, this time in his deep voice. Duantri could not hear what he commanded, but it was obvious when the boy plunged through the vertical pond, submersing himself. But instead of breaking the spell, instead of fighting his way to Tanaliín—wherever she was—the boy entered into the vast ocean realm beyond. The ice that had been encasing him vanished. The bloody fingermarks on his forehead disappeared. His eyes opened, sightless. He began to drift, a floating corpse, pale and dead once more.

From the far depths of those dark waters, much further back than the sepulcher walls of the sky house, a shadowy shape was swimming towards him. Duantri was afraid it was coming to rend him apart, to take off his head in a single bite, and incarnadine that curtain of water until it flowed like crimson velvet.

Instead, the Bone Shark delicately took the back of the boy's jacket in her fang-fringed jaw, and swam off with him, into darkness.

They disappeared.

And so did the wall of water.

Tanaliín was standing behind where it had been, completely dry, the straps of the cradleboard firmly attached to her back. Her lined face was shadowed with sorrow. She was no longer humming the Karkryklys Hymn.

Irradiant screamed in outrage—something about *his* work, and *Quadoni bitch*, and *Saint Death will eat you all*—right before he chucked the undead girl in his arms at Duantri as if she were a sack of flour.

The cold dead weight knocked her back against the wall. One of the barbed quills shaved a slice of skin off her flank. Another skewered a chunk of flesh from her arm, above the elbow. The girl wrapped her frozen arms around Duantri's neck, legs locking around her waist like a parody of a tired child wanting her big sister to carry her home.

The bloody mark on her forehead flared blue. Ectenica ignited, and the top of the girl's head melted into liquid blue flames. The flames licked quickly down the rest of her body, which… *unbodified*. Became strand-like, sticky. Ropy webs of undead material broke off to wrap Duantri's limbs in a thickening cocoon, binding her tighter and tighter, constricting her. The only objects the webs could not seem to cling to were the witchglass daggers. But since Duantri could not move her arms or hands, these were useless.

Irradiant began to laugh. He advanced, the spikes on his wrists preceding him.

Duantri met Tanaliín's gaze over his shoulder before the ectenical webs closed over her eyes.

Tanaliín raised her Bryddongard to her mouth. She kissed it.

The dim sepulcher flashed with the whiteness of sheet lightning, and Kestrel, huge as the dragon husk that coiled in the center of the room, burst from the sticky strands of ectenica like a butterfly from chrysalis, screaming out a single clap of thunder.

Every solid piece of ice in that room, from the dome of the snowpyre to the ghost's spiked armor, shattered.

Kestrel stomped forward. Not much room to maneuver.

Kestrel was large. Sepulcher was tomb-small. But room enough to bite off one *little* necromancer's head…

"Duantri!" her gyrlady shouted. "Stop! STOP!"

But Tanaliín did more than shout. A second flash of sheet lightning swept the sepulcher, snapping Duantri out of her fableform and back into her human body. She staggered forward, away from the wall, away from Irradiant.

Her ears rang. Her nose bled. Her sight was full of the opposite of light: bright shapes became shadows, and shadowy shapes were too dazzling to look upon. She was not sure, for a moment, where she was, or who she was, or what was happening.

And then, her gyrlady spoke. "Forgive me, love, my darling own, my heart." The whisper sounded panicked, breathless. "Come toward my voice, nor from this path depart."

Bewildered but obedient, Duantri stumbled towards Tanaliín's voice. She blinked rapidly, hoping to clear her vision, and with every blink, a puzzle piece of either color or sense came back. The jigsaw began to take form: Tanaliín, standing before the snowpyre, her right arm thrust out before her, the Bryddongard still sizzling with electric tendrils of light. She was staring in the direction Duantri had come from, a fearful expression on her face.

Confused, Duantri glanced over her shoulder. Kestrel's concussive shriek had knocked the ghost in his stolen body all the way across the sepulcher's chamber and dashed him to floor.

Looming over him now was Cracchen Skrathmandan.

"You cannot finish this, Gyrgardu," Cracchen reminded her, not sounding anything like the snide, irritable knife instructor who had called her 'birdie' and mocked her fighting form. He was not even looking at her, but standing over the sprawled necromancer like an executioner at the stump. "Go to your gyrlady. Take her off this Guilded Council ere it falls to Iskald with you in it. Bring the kernel egg to safety. You have a promise to keep.

As he spoke, Irradiant began slithering to his knees, searching the ankle-deep ice powder on the floor for a shard large enough to cut himself with. But all of his ice had been atomized by Kestrel's thunderclap. Even his skin held only the flimsiest sheen, like rain that had not decided if it yet wanted to freeze.

Duantri croaked, her throat hot and raw, "Are *you* to finish this fight, Skrathmandan?"

"I am no necromancer," Cracchen replied, never looking away from Irradiant Stones. "But I am yet a sky wizard of Skakmaht. I can hold him until Miscellaneous comes to do her god's work."

Duantri glanced at Tanaliín, who looked as doubtful as she felt. "We will stay with you..." she began.

"Look to the snowpyre!" he barked. "*There is no time!*"

With the dome shattered, the old kernel egg was now fully exposed, flickering like a guttering lamp on its catafalque. There was a buzzing about it, and a miasma that arose from it, indicating that a long-delayed hatching into dust and decay was imminent.

"When that shell breaks," Cracchen warned, "this house falls. It is the *last* egg; it is holding the rest of the Guilded Council aloft. Do not risk your lives, or the hatchling's, out of a misplaced concern for me! Go, Gyrgardu. You *know* I have my own means of escape."

He was right—Duantri knew that Cracchen could fly out of here on his fulmar ship at any time. He could erect it around himself from the ice on his skin and his own vital force, even if the Guilded Council collapsed around his ears. Cracchen should be able to flee the wreckage, or weather its fall, safe within his protective ice.

She stepped closer to Tanaliín, wrapping an arm around her shoulders. Warmth from the sack of dragon scales simmered up from the cradleboard like a banked bonfire. The Witch Queen's kernel egg, snug within its wrappings, glimmered and gleamed.

"Let's fly, my Tanaliín," Duantri murmured, "and let him be. The ghost we'll leave to him, whilst we three flee."

And if her words tasted bitter on her tongue, and if she felt a coward to her core, then she would accept that as her sacrifice.

Hers would not be the deciding strike that felled a ghost reborn. If she tried, she would only fail Tam of Taquathura yet again. And if she failed, she would also fall, giving the ghost herself. Which meant Tanaliín would fall too.

Tanaliín's sharp black eyes searched her own. Then, finally, she drew in a deep breath and nodded, agreeing without speaking. She threaded her arm around Duantri's waist, and matching her steps, walked them out of the sepulcher, into the darkling glass corridor.

They were but a few steps out the door when Cracchen shoved it shut behind them.

There was the snick of a chain. The clunk of a drawbar sliding into its slot.

The sepulcher was shut and locked.

Duantri immediately turned back to the door and tested it. It would not budge. She pounded on it. No answer.

"But," she whispered, "then how will Lanie find—"

Narrow-eyed, narrow-lipped, Tanaliín shook her head. "If that sly boy believes a bar will work, he does not know our Lanie as he should. But come, my love, let's you and I away. Methinks this whole place is a sepulcher."

CHAPTER TWENTY-FOUR
It All Falls Down

CRACCHEN STARED AT the necromancer who wore Aadar Skrathmandan's face.

His face... one of them.

The rest of Cracchen's bodies—all the wizard husks whom Irradiant hadn't yet dashed upon the broken stones of Iskald— were present in this sepulcher, blank and frozen. Receptacles waiting to be filled.

But not by Cracchen. Never by him again. He had made that choice when the only likely alternative was execution at the hands of the Witch Queen of Leech. He did not regret it.

But he would be *damned*—damned to wither like a mummy on the permafrost; damned and eternally embalmed in ice; damned and condemned by Erre'Elur to live in the endless slow decay of vacuum cold—before he let *Irradiant Stones* keep any of his previous bodies for his trophies. For his... *wardrobe*.

That he *dared* to wear the body of Aadar Skrathmandan, the very wizard to whom this sky house once belonged, was enough to make Cracchen want to flay the ghost where he lay. He wanted to unspool his flesh, strip him skinless, reave him of his protecting ice; pluck out his eyes and scalp him; disembowel him; quarter him; make him an unrecognizable pile of sentient viscera. Reduce him from this mockery, this simulacrum, this cuckoo of the man whom he, Cracchen—*Aadar*—had once been.

With the enlivening presence of the Witch Queen's kernel egg now removed from its orbit, the old egg's guttering light flickered even more erratically, growing dimmer and dimmer on its catafalque.

Cracchen eyed it with extreme distaste. He remembered the day, over a hundred years ago, when he—Aadar—had flown his sky house—*this* sky house—over the accursed lands of Leech. He remembered House Skrathmandan's raid on the Witch Queen's hatchery: all of those glowing kernel eggs, all smelling like a garden, singing in their crystal voices.

There had been *plenty*—more than enough to power all the sky houses of Skakmaht for years and years. The soul-suckers could always make more. Was the petty thievery of a few embryos really worth a war? A city in ruins? The fall of a nation?

They were *only eggs*.

And now it had come to this.

His sky house—the *true* Sky House Skrathmandan, not some paltry excuse for a flying tower, hardly more than a fulmar ship with pretensions, built by a young fool who knew *nothing*—was rumbling in its foundations. This sky house had been built by Aadar's ancestor *two thousand* years before the founding of Liriat.[22] But now its crystal bricks were shifting in the walls, and the floors were trembling, and the ice spalling, and every vitreous connector between House Skrathmandan and the Mistral Atrium starting to fracture. It was all so fragile, all on the verge of falling apart.

But Cracchen could fix this. *His* sky house, at least, if not the rest of them. Right now.

The necromancer, leaving off his scrabbling in the powdered ice, was scrambling to his feet and slipping his way up the slickened stairs, heading back towards the hatch that led to the kitchens. There were more corpses up there, probably, to summon for his minions.

It amused Cracchen to know that this self-proclaimed

---

22 The oldest sky houses were erected after an incident known as the First Elurran Apparition: the earliest recorded encounter between the Woe-Woman and the Skaki people in Athe's religious histories.

almighty necromancer could not use his own vital force to power the undead from a distance. and make them dance for him—as his truly indomitable great-granddaughter quite easily could. He smiled, opening his arms and leaning as if into a buffeting wind, and shouted, "Irradiant Stones! Come back here!"

All the powdered snow in the room lifted off the floor at his words, and swirled, rushing up the stairs. It wrapped around the necromancer's legs, propelled him off his feet, and spun him around, yanking him back down to the bottom of the steps and into Cracchen's waiting grip.

He lugged Irradiant upright by the collar of his robe (Cracchen remembered Aadar being fitted for that robe; consulting on the beadwork, the cut, the fabric; he was to have debuted it at the Masquerade of the Blithe Dancers, at Dark Festival, right before the war interfered with all such celebrations), and hauled him over to the snowpyre, shoving him down on top of it.

Irradiant's spine crunched against the catafalque. The old kernel egg shattered like spun sugar beneath him. Rotten yolk spewed out, black mucus that smelled of unturned mulch. The snowpyre's vestigial ice magic froze the ooze immediately, adhering it to Irradiant's robes, gluing him to the catafalque.

Shivery little frost pellets burst from Irradiant's skin—*Aadar's* stolen skin—trying desperately to rearrange themselves as weapons. Cracchen slammed a fist down on the center of Irradiant's chest, knocking the breath out of him. All nascent ice powdered down to particles once more.

"You know *nothing*," he snarled, leaning close. "You take and take but *you never learn*."

To Cracchen's amazement, Irradiant grinned up at him. His beard was full of snow. Spittle and blood flecked his mouth, where he had bitten his tongue, either when being flung across the room or down the stairs.

"Who's taking what now?" he sneered. "*You're* not Cracchen Skrathmandan. *That* gony couldn't string a sentence together—except to beg pardon for pissing himself. Ate him, did you? Like I ate your friends?"

Cracchen slapped him hard across the face. "I'm still here. There's just more of me now."

Grin never faltering, Irradiant opened his fist and tossed a handful of bone dust into his face, then spat blood at him.

Cracchen felt the ectenica ignite immediately, like a line of fire ants crawling into the seams of ice that scarred his cheek. It started working its way into all the places where his flesh met the magical ice, loosening the spells bonding them together. The ectenical ants crawled up his nose, into his left eye, surrounding the icy orb that had replaced the eyeball Irradiant's possession had melted from his skull.

He screamed.

Darts of ice shot from his skin, puncturing Irradiant in a dozen places. But Irradiant didn't stop laughing.

"Afraid I'll take you again? I could do it, but you're so ugly now. No, I think I'll just take Athe instead. Maybe, after that, all the planets beyond it... Ah, hello again. Enjoying the show, are you, girlie? Looks horrible, doesn't he? That's his real face, you know, without all that fancy ice tying him up with such a pretty bow. Like a freak at a carnival! So glad you finally decided to drop in. Who'd have thought that wall opened up like that? Lots of tricks and turns I'll have to learn about my new house!"

If someone murmured an answer, Cracchen couldn't hear it for the terrible ectenica now burning in his ears. He stumbled back from the catafalque, his boot sliding against something on the floor. Stooping, he snatched it up, squinting out of the one eye not under ectenical attack.

It was not ice he had slipped on, as he had hoped—but glass. One of the witchglass daggers, let fall when the Gyrgardu had burst into her fableform.

His grip closed over the handle, just as he had taught Duantri to hold it. Knife fighting he knew. Execution he understood. It had nothing to do with ice magic or death magic, with stolen husks or crystalskins. This training was embedded in Cracchen's body, and his body understood what to do next, no matter the pain. He had endured worse—far worse, a lifetime of worse—and had battled through it. This old hatred, with its acid tide of anger, had been with him for far longer than either the ghost or the Skaki souls. It filled him, spurring him to action.

Because if *she* was here, then Cracchen was out of time.

Leaping at the snowpyre, he drove the witchglass blade through Irradiant's throat. He knew what the choked cry behind him portended, knew what the echo-wound would be doing to her if she was standing too close. But that couldn't be helped.

Ignoring her pain, Cracchen began chanting the Formula for Investing a Snowpyre. Though this was not an enchantment he had spoken in many generations, and though the icicles of his teeth were loosening in his gums as he spoke it, the formula sprang readily to his lips—modified somewhat for the circumstance:

> *Body-blood binding, dim-dying as dome-fuel*
> *Inspirit our snowpyre with sepulchral source*
> *From witch-wreck of wizard who hex-hurt this high*
>   *house—*
> *to smoke-heart and stone-flight, horizon-bound home.*

The moment Cracchen invoked the formula, Irradiant started gagging.

Blood bubbled from his throat as hundreds of slender, hollow needles, made of ice but hard as steel, jabbed up from the surface of the catafalque and stabbed into his skin.

His blood ran down, into the snowpyre, and the snowpyre extracted from it the substance it needed to power the sky house. Once the blood was stripped of its substance, the needles would redirect it back into his body. This cycle would continue, for years and years, until the last of Irradiant's substance was leeched out of him.

But the snowpyre was an efficient spell; it took only what it needed and no more. So long as Irradiant had a spark of life left in him as he lay upon the catafalque, bleeding from the wound in his throat that would never close, the ice would sustain him.

Not only sustain him, Cracchen hoped, *but keep him aware*.

This was something useful he'd learned from Haaken and the interfering Quadoni gyrlady in the past few days. If Cracchen set a dwalming ring about the snowpyre, Irradiant Stones needn't be graced with oblivion as the sky house drained him. No, for within a dwalming ring, Cracchen might keep his prisoner conscious. So that he would suffer. And keep suffering. For years. Decades, maybe.

Leaning over the catafalque, he spit his loosened teeth upon it, and murmured a new formula over them. The crystal ice of molars and incisors grew until they were the equivalent of palm-sized river rocks, rough and cold and gray. He quickly placed twelve of them in a circle around Irradiant's body, smiling all the while with his bleeding gums—even though his face felt like it was melting off, even though he feared the rest of him would fall apart at the seams.

Worth it.

It was worth it—to have silenced Irradiant Stones at last. To have him, now, here, under his power.

"Now I lay thee down to dwalm, thou asshole," he spat in toothless Quadic, giving credit where it was due.

The pain, now everywhere, all throughout his body, spiked—becoming so intense he almost fell face-first onto the catafalque. But hands pulled at him, large and warm, dragging him away from Irradiant and the snowpyre, where a new dome of ice was, so very slowly, starting to close over the necromancer's bleeding body.

A silvery-cool sensation washed over Cracchen's skin, easing the ectenical acid that was eating away at his face. It was like someone had taken a handful of snow and packed it into his wounds. Strong arms supported him, held him upright. He heard Haaken's voice, murmuring another of the ancient formulae, the spellprayers to Erre'Elur, adjusting it as needed for the present situation.

Ken me, O Kin-wright, Quietus and Kith-seed!
Before You, my brother, spell-scored and sore-seeping
Tend to his tear-wounds, repair him of rupture
I beg and beseech of You, Frost Queen, Your favor.

Even before Haaken finished speaking, the burning-itching-invading agony in the seams of Cracchen's face had ceased. He raised his hand to touch the places where the necromancer's ectenica had sunk into his skin. His fingers came away blackened with an acrid wet sludge. His gums tingled, tore. New icicle teeth started to form at the root. His skin prickled as his torn-open scars refilled, once more, with ice.

Slumping against his brother, Cracchen almost wept for relief. Haaken held him close, cradling him, until he felt well enough to push himself away and straighten up again.

Turning back to the snowpyre, Cracchen took in the satisfying sight of all the blood still pouring from Irradiant's—from Aadar's—*Irradiant's* throat, soaking his beard a darker sanguine. Irradiant bled and bled, and the catafalque pulsed, and the walls of the sepulcher hummed happily, the ice and crystals in the foundations bustling to repair themselves.

A few more seconds, and the trembling and rumbling in the floor stilled and calmed.

Cracchen clasped his hands behind his back and walked closer to the snowpyre. He did not look up, did not look around. Did not look for *her*, though he knew she must be there, somewhere in the sepulcher with him. After her cry when his witchglass slipped into her great-grandfather's flesh, he'd heard nothing. Perhaps she had passed out from the pain and blood loss.

But she would recover. He was sure of it. She'd recovered from worst at the Hastiludes.

Over his shoulder, he tossed a question. "How did you two get in, buhror? I barred the door."

"You are not the only sky wizard in Iskald, anuraki. I know the ways of this house."

Cracchen twitched. It annoyed him that Haaken referred to him as 'ancestor,' as though they were no longer brothers. No doubt Haaken understood that it annoyed him, and that was why he did it—*because* he was his brother. He played with one of the dwalming crystals on the catafalque, smoothing the rough ice under his fingers.

After what felt like a hundred years, he asked, "Is Miscellaneous all right?"

Haaken did not answer.

Cracchen was afraid to turn around, knowing that he would see her there, imagining her large brown eyes, wide and shocked behind her spectacles, her throat wet with the blood of her echo-wound—the echo-wound *he'd* opened by his violence against her great-grandfather.

"A few more minutes, after the dome has closed over him, the gore on his neck should no longer affect her," he said, trying to sound insouciant. "The snowpyre protects its source from ready access at the hands of outsiders, including magical interference. But its muffling effect works on both sides of the dome."

Now he could hear, from much further back in the sepulcher, the sound of her breathing: harsh, wet. Cracchen sighed in relief, but still did not turn around. He wanted to tell her what he'd done, so that she would understand, approve, admire him.

"From everyone he has gorged on, the necromancer has more raw vital force inside him than any one body—than any one *kernel egg*. He is enough to power Sky House Skrathmandan for generations to come."

Cracchen turned his head slightly to catch Haaken's expression in his periphery. "You will have to invent a new name for *your* house, buhror. Sky House Skrathmandan has been taken for over a millennium, I'm afraid."

"I only wanted," Haaken said carefully, "to rebuild what I thought lost, anuraki."

"It was *not lost*," Cracchen snapped. "It *is* not. Not yet. Not ever. Just call your tower what it is, boy. We will make good use of it, and you, for diplomatic purposes in the south, whilst we remain here, in the north, and begin rebuilding Iskald to its former glory."

"Cracchen."

Not Haaken's voice this time. *Hers.* A bit rough, a bit phlegmy, like she was convalescing from a lung disease, but girded with steel.

"You don't get to use Irradiant Stones for your fuel. I'm sorry." And she did sound sorry, a little. But also inflexible.

His shoulders stiffening, he spun around and sought out her face in the dark of the sepulcher.

Miscellaneous Stones.

How could he have ever thought her plain, scrawny? How could he ever have scoffed at her spectacles, sneered at braids, her bony shoulders, her gray left hand? All of his previous faulty opinion had been mere callowness, sheer ignorance on his part.

Cracchen knew better now. He knew what Haaken had always known. That she was devastating. That he could gaze at her forever and never grow bored.

Her face, dust-streaked and chap-lipped, couldn't hide an expression if she tried. Those clear dark eyes, just now gone pollen-yellow with impossible power. Her sternness. Her earnest entreaty.

Ah, this flower of death magic. This supernova masquerading as a young woman.

Stepping toward her, Cracchen held out his hand. She flinched back half a step, and he realized that he was still holding the witchglass dagger. No blood clung to the edge of the magical blade, but his entire hand, up to his elbow, was sprayed with Irradiant's blood.

He slipped the dagger into his pocket and showed her his bare palms, saying fondly, "Miscellaneous Stones. You rare thing. How excellent an ally you have been to Sky House Skrathmandan—indeed, to all of Skakmaht—as we rise together from the ruins Liriat has made of us. I include *you* in this ascent, Miscellaneous—you, whom Liriat stupidly cast aside. But," he advised, gentling his tone at her stricken look, "do *not* stand against me in this. My gratitude and admiration are twin rivers running swifter and deeper than the Fet and Fragor. But they are not infinite."

For reply, Miscellaneous just sighed a sigh that seemed to come from the very soles of her feet. She gazed at him for another long, stern moment, looking for all the world like someone's exasperated auntie, before her gaze flicked over to Haaken. Some unspoken agreement passed between them.

Cracchen wanted that. He *craved* it. Whatever that thing was moving from Miscellaneous to his brother and back again, that was his by right. It *belonged* to him. He, too, would have such an intimate, unspoken communion with her one day. Soon, he hoped. Just as soon as he finished this.

Out of the corner of his eye, he caught his brother's subtle shift. Haaken said something, spoke a single word, in a voice so deep that it seemed to reach into the very walls.

And then, every single husked wizard body in the sepulcher exploded into chunks of empty ice.

CHAPTER TWENTY-FIVE
Last Auspices

"WHAT HAVE YOU done?" Cracchen demanded as the ice settled.

Lanie did not answer him but turned to ask Haaken, "You can hold them?"

"For a while."

"They won't hurt y—"

"Lanie."

Her name, in Haaken's low northern burr, was all she needed. It wasn't that he was trying to *reassure* her exactly; he was just reiterating what needed to be done. And he was right.

So she did it.

Lanie closed the distance between herself and Cracchen, and took both of his blood-soaked hands in hers. His attention, which had been ranging over the shattered husks—all of his former bodies—now veered back to her, wild with grief and rage.

"*What have you done?*" He tried to pull his hand away, but her left hand closed fast about his wrist, a shackle forged of star metal. No breaking that hold; Lanie clung to him like Saint Death Herself.

"Cracchen," she said, speaking as evenly as her ravaged throat would allow, "your other bodies are gone, their accidents sundered. Your awful, suspended unlife is truly ended. Now, at last, the sky wizards of Skakmaht are dead. What *you* are now, my friend, is a living man who is sharing his body with a horde of hungry ghosts. And I"—she slid her silver-gray hand up his arm, never breaking contact, and laid it against his cheek—"am here to sing them out of you."

Cracchen yanked away from her, his expression horrified as he realizing the hum he was hearing beneath her spoken words was her deep voice. Lanie was singing to him in a voice that only the dead and undead could hear—and *he* could hear her.

The truth was, she had been singing this whole time: all the while that she and Haaken were racing through the sepulchers and corridors of the Guilded Council, through secret doorways and access panels, and crawl spaces. She had kept singing when her throat was torn open, while her blood was pouring out. She sang while her echo-wound was knitting itself closed again, and she was singing now.

She didn't even need her throat. This was the Lahnessthanessar, the Great Lullaby, oldest of all Quadoni spellsongs but one.

And when it was done, she stopped.

Cracchen's eyes rolled up in his head. He would have fallen to the floor, but Haaken was there to catch him. He stepped up right behind his brother, slipped his arms beneath Cracchen's armpits, and eased him to floor.

After that, Lanie didn't pay much mind to the Skrathmandans. *They* were still alive. They were not, therefore, her concern. Her attention was all for her left hand.

The last of the legendary sky wizards of Skakmaht swirled in the quicksilver palm of her hand, a cyclone of angry snowflakes. This was the storm of souls. Who had admired her. Who had called her their ally. Who had wanted her to trust them, and be their friend.

Lanie sighed again, deep voice and all.

But friends do not let friends torment their prisoners in perpetuity, she thought. *Not even if that prisoner is Irradiant Stones.*

Haaken stood up from the floor, his brother still pallid and unconscious at their feet. Cracchen's ectenical repairs were all still holding, for this time his silver scars and elegant prosthetics were of Haaken's making, and owed nothing to the sky wizards who had been rooted inside his skin.

Now, pressing his palms together, Haaken breathed upon his

hands, and drew them apart again. Where he had been holding nothing, now he cradled a sphere of ice the size of a child's bauble, smooth but opaque.

"It is ready," he told her. "But… it is a temporary container only, Lanie."

"It won't need to last long," she assured him, with more optimism than empirical evidence. He crooked an eyebrow at her, letting her know that *he* knew that *she* had just about as much experience with this sort of thing as he did. A lot of theory, and very little practice. She smiled back, hoping to convey a spirit of enthusiastic, but not *frenzied*, improvisation—one thing that she did have practice in.

Stepping closer to him, Lanie laid her left hand atop the sphere, tipping it so that the storm of souls sifted down from her palm. The snowflakes passed through the surface of the ice crystal, wrathfully swirling all the while. Once they were about halfway through the sphere, Haaken closed his hands over it, and breathed on it again, sealing them in.

From the enclosure of his hands came the sound of crystal cracking.

Haaken loosed a light hiss, both his eyebrows hitching up. He opened his fingers, and he and Lanie quickly peered at the sphere. Flaws were already beginning to fracture the depths of the ice, but they had not reached the surface. Not yet.

Closing his hands over it again, Haaken breathed once more. Another layer of ice formed over the sphere, reinforcing it.

"Will you be—"

"Go," he interrupted her. "I will hold them. Until…"

"Be ready. As soon as I'm done with—"

"Yes."

Nodding at him, Lanie shook out her left fist, which still prickled painfully, and walked over to the snowpyre. The ice crystals forming the bottom of the dome had been growing at a steady rate. Already they had created a barrier several inches high all around the rim of the catafalque.

Lying on the catafalque, stuck to it, was Grandpa Rad, his

pale eyes wide and staring. The blood pumping out of his throat wound had slowed, now that the catafalque was feeding him back the blood that he had lost. But still it burbled lowly, a pulsing outflow.

His lips moved soundlessly—cursing, of course. But also, Lanie knew, praying.

She could hear Irradiant's deep voice, calling out for Saint Death. *His* Saint Death, who had always come for him before, whenever he needed Her most.

"It's me," Lanie informed him. "I'm here. She sent me instead."

His eyes rolled to look her over briefly, then rolled away, dismissing the sight. His mouth gasped for air that would not come. Lanie felt her own throat squeezing shut in sympathy.

But she breathed in. Held her breath. Breathed out. Held her breath.

Where is breath?
In the stillness.
What is stillness?
Sothain.

As she inhaled, held, exhaled, held, Lanie pondered her particular conundrum. She knew, without a doubt, that Grandpa Rad would rather remain bound to this snowpyre— tormented for decades, but still *aware*, seething, biding his time till he could free himself and steal some other vessel for his host—than return to Doédenna's cloak. He knew—they both knew—that if Lanie tried to rip his substance free of his newfound flesh, Irradiant would fight her all the way.

She also knew, without a doubt, that she *could* rip him free—willy nilly—and force him to go where he so desperately, murderously, heel-diggingly did not want to go.

And she would, if it came to that. But the thought made her impossibly sad. She still had to live with herself, after.

So, once again, she had to improvise.

Unlike Ynyssyll's toe bone in its bejeweled reliquary, Lanie didn't keep a piece of Sosha Brackenwild's skeleton upon her person. There had been nothing left of it for her to keep. When, at the end of last year, Errolirrolin had taken off Sosha's skeletal head with the great axe Drjōta, Sosha's entire undead skeleton had fallen to dust with it.

But what Lanie could do was recall the late Regent Sinister down to his tiniest ossicles. She could remember the spark of blue undeath that had lit him from within—the spark that *was* Sosha Brackenwild—in all his rambunctious, joyous, courtly arrogance.

After all, it was *Lanie* who had called him awake with her Maranathasseth Anthem; Lanie, who had been watching through his own eye sockets as he battled the Blackbird Bride to her knees; Lanie, who had borne witness to the ungentle death of his undeath.

More than that, she knew Sosha's face. His portraits and statues abounded in Liriat Proper: on walls, in courtyards, and on coins. But many, many more intimate and informal sketches could be found in the journals that Irradiant Stones had kept— all of which Lanie had read diligently. Over and over again. Memorized, paragraph by cramped paragraph.

Irradiant had never listened to anybody but one man in all his life.

Perhaps he would listen to him now.

Therefore, although Sosha Brackenwild's accident was dust, Lanie reached deep within her own memory, and recalled that blue spark that went by so many names in so many different languages (*substance*) (*pneuma*) (*vital force*), the star-like flame that was Sosha's and Sosha's alone.

She breathed in. Held her breath. Breathed out. Held her breath—

—and invited the Regent Sinister into her skin.

IRRADIANT HAD FORGOTTEN that living hurt, and that dying hurt worse.

He'd forgotten how much he hated feeling—actually *feeling*— the cold.

He was cold to his marrow.

Always one to pride himself on his cleverness, Irradiant was kicking himself now. All he'd needed to do once he'd made it to Iskald was pick out a sky house, replace its kernel egg, and get the whole duodecifold-damned edifice moving along. Nobody could've caught up with him in a sky house! They flew even faster than dragons!

Instead, he'd lingered at mirrors, preened over his library, done a little experiment with lanterns. Lanterns!

And that nap in the dog bed! *Unforgivable!* It had only *delayed* him.

And now, this.

This dome of ice, rising all around him, but never numbing him. No darkness to overcome his senses. He remained bristlingly awake within the ring of twelve dwalming crystals, aware of the blood draining out of his body, leaving his every limb nerveless and his heart a weak, thin strain, and then returning to him so that he could *keep bleeding*.

Curse all Skaki demon-worshippers! He should have studied the snowpyres! All he knew about them had to do with kernel eggs. But now he recalled some other bit of gossip... something about how snowpyres, at some point in history, used to be powered via a kind of spiritual cannibalism of the aged and useless and infirm? A way to recycle one's ancestors, or something like that.

And here he was, in Aadar Skrathmandan's skin. In *Aadar Skrathmandan's sky house*. He had become, in a sense, Cracchen's ancestor, and now Cracchen Skrathmandan (or, in any case, the storm of souls that was possessing his useless meat shell) was going to use *him* to power the sky house—*Irradiant's* sky house!

He cursed again, soundlessly.

All right, then. He'd just have to bide his time.

Soon enough, his great-granddaughter would stop yammering at him and let the dome close over his head. He'd been stuck for a hundred years in an iron padlock; he knew how to wait.

Sooner or later, some young Skaki teenager with frosted-over acne and bigger balls than brains would venture down to this sepulcher, exploring where he wasn't allowed—and then, oh, then, Irradiant would *pounce*.

"Raddy," came a voice he'd almost forgotten—it had been so long, so long since he heard it.

Irradiant rolled his eyes this way and that, searching for the source. He tried to speak—"Sosha!"—but the name came out only in his deep voice, for his vocal cords had been severed by witchglass, never to grow back again.

But—thank Saint Death!—his Sosha heard him.

A tall, thin shadow stepped up to the snowpyre, leaning over it curiously to peer inside. Two deep dimples bracketed a wide, full mouth. Dark skin. Dark eyes. Curling black hair, bound in a lopsided silver circlet that was decorated in flourishes of the Triple Flame.

"Irradiant Radithor, what have you gotten yourself into this time?"

"Never mind that, Sosha—get me out of here!"

Sosha laughed down at him. "Certainly! Where do you propose we go?"

"Anywhere!" Irradiant grinned back, stretching his neck wound. "Sky's the limit. We have this flying house. Have to rid ourselves of a few pesky meddlers, then we're golden as gods."

"This house?" Sosha glanced around, his slashing black eyebrows winging high. "Raddy, really… it's falling down around our ears. And Skaki architecture"—he shuddered— "leaves much to be desired."

"Back to the surface, then—to Iskald," Irradiant cried glibly. Hard to speak glibly in a deep voice, but Sosha had always had that effect on him. "Plenty of ice fishing down there. We'll eat all the polar bears and go tobogganing and live in a hut. Can't complain about the architecture if you're living in a hut. Say what you will, it's better than an army tent."

Sosha shuddered again, with such hyperbolized vehemence that his silver circlet tilted over his brow. It gave him a rakish aspect, but no more so than the deepening of his dimples, the flash of his black eyes.

"You know I could never live in a hut, Raddy. The thatch—the insects—the lack of sycophants. No one would attend my grand levee in a hut. What's more"—he rode roughshod, like he always did, over whatever protestation Irradiant was about to attempt—"I don't have a body anymore. Huts are bad enough when one is *corporeal*, but as it is..."

"What do you mean you don't have a body anymore?" Irradiant demanded. "You're right here!"

He had always harbored some tender hope that, once he had his sky house up and soaring, once he had studied up more on stabilizing ectenica, he would return to Liriat, dig Sosha up, put him back inside his bones and *anchor* him there. Certainly wouldn't do it till he could be *sure* Sosha wouldn't collapse to ash when the ectenica burned off.

"Oh, didn't you hear?" Sosha asked with a casual shrug. "My great-grandniephling—my sister Moll's brat's brat... Perhaps another brat in there? Lost count. Anyway, last year, Vespers I think it was, whatever their name is—something with ever so many vowels—cut off my head with my own axe! Your own great-grandbrat had raised me up to fight some Rookish birdie with a spear two sizes too big for her. I almost had her too, but then... Drjōta dropped. Could've knocked me over with a, well, with an axe. I was so astonished! The gall!"

"They didn't!" Irradiant gasped. "Errolirrolin! That little ingrate. What is Liriat coming to? After all you sacrificed for the Brackenwild legacy! You wiped *Skakmaht* off the mat for them! You gilded Liriat in war gold! You made the other realms fear ours above the rest—and Errolirrolin Brackenwild just... *beheaded* you?"

"Scandalous, I know!" Sosha agreed. "But I comfort myself in the knowledge that, by banishing your great-grandbrat for her *heinous* crime of saving Liriat, the little twit basically slit their own throat, politically speaking. So I got my vengeance posthumously." He cocked his head. "*Post*-posthumously? Hmn."

They were silent for a blissful while, contemplating each other with the delight of friends long parted, now reunited. But before too long, Irradiant noticed that, for all his humor, for all his *hereness*, Sosha was making no move to liberate him from the snowpyre.

It would only take one sturdy yank. The needles would tear his back up a bit, and Irradiant would have to stuff his entire throat full of magical ice to patch it up, but...

"Why are you just standing there, Sosha?"

"Well, Raddy, I'm in something of a quandary," the Regent Sinister sighed. "You see, at present, I have the dubious honor of sharing a body with your great-grandbrat. Try as I might, I can't take it over. I can only allow her to wear my aspect, use her as my mouthpiece. She wants me to urge you to come along with me—to Saint Death's cloak, or whatever she's calling it. It's not like that, though," Sosha confided, lowering his voice to a whisper, "where I am. There is no cloak of bone." He scoffed. "I don't think there ever was one. It's just a metaphor priests make up to ease a coward's passing. What I can tell you is this: there I was on my deathbed, hacking out my lungs while Moll waited for me to kick it in the other room. Then, nothing. Then, it's a hundred years later, and there I was on Ynyssyll's Tooth, not a scrap of skin or muscle on my bones, but otherwise hale and hearty. Then, the axe. Then, nothing. Then, months later, this. That's all. And that's good enough." He shrugged. "You know I've always preferred being alone—saving your company, of course."

"So..." Irradiant's thoughts seemed to be as slow and cold as his pulse. "What you're saying is, Sosha... all this time... you've been alone in the dark?"

"It's not dark," Sosha insisted. "It's not *anything*. There's this." He gestured around him. "And then there's *not*."

"But you're alone," Irradiant pressed him.

"*Gloriously* alone," Sosha said. "Although, I have to say— even when I'm alone—even when I'm nothing—I think... I think I still miss you."

Heartbeats: faint, spaced-out, thin. Otherwise, silence. Irradiant stared up at Sosha. He was so thin he'd disappear if he turned sideways. He wore a shroud of shadow for his robes, and his crown was beginning to blacken with tarnish—yet *still* he exuded that same warm vibrance that Irradiant held sacred in his memory.

He wanted nothing more than to stay like this, forever. Just looking at Sosha's face. Just like this.

But that damned dome of ice kept growing up all around him, faster now, ever faster, the crystals of frost piling upon each other, crisscrossing, braiding, interlocking. A few more seconds, and Sosha's face would be lost to him forever.

Well.

Irradiant could bear an eternity of solitude—who better? Nothing would suit him more! He needed nothing, nobody. He could bear dying forever, biding his time, waiting for a vessel of his rebirth to come along and be eaten from the inside out. He could even bear being entombed in ice in order to fuel his lifelong (and deathlong) enemy's sky house. Of course he could.

But what he found he could not bear, could *not*, was the idea of Sosha's solitude. He couldn't live (or even go on dying in perpetuity) knowing that his friend would return to nothing, alone.

"If I join you, Sosha," he asked, "will we be nothing together?"

"Something like that," said Sosha, looking mysterious and mischievous. "Or maybe—nothing like that at all! Ha!"

"Heh!" said Irradiant, and thought about it for one moment longer, then muttered, "Damn it duodecifold. Give it here, girlie. You've won."

When Sosha reached out a familiar quicksilver-covered left hand to him, Irradiant lifted his substance out of his stolen accident, and took it.

"QUICKLY," SAID LANIE. "It's done. He's gone. Fit them in."

But Haaken was right there already, efficient and precise,

the stormy crystal sphere in his hands showing fractures all throughout the ice.

And then he was placing the sphere into the wounded throat of the empty body in the snowpyre, before the last pulse of its blood trickled out and froze to purple frost…

And then…

A new pulse, light as a moth wing.

A bright-dark trickle of blood fluttered from the throat wound, down the side of the body's neck, onto the catafalque. The entire snowpyre pulsed in reply, sending the blood back into the body through its array of needles.

The body shifted, resettled, sighed without breath.

The storm of souls opened their pale gray eyes, and glared at both of them from Aadar Skrathmandan's face.

Words without a voice thundered in Lanie's mind. *What have you done?*

Lanie shrugged. *Not me*, she replied. *I did my work for the day. This is between you, Erre'Elur, and Her priest. Good luck.*

"Anuraki," Haaken told his ancestor. "You have a choice to make."

Lanie left them to their decision, and went to sit right in the middle of the dragon's corpse, where it was warm, where she could be alone.

To think. To pray. And not to weep.

CHAPTER TWENTY~SIX
The Wizards Skrathmandan

Year 4826 of Higher and Lower Quadiíb
On Ishnaq, 11th of Anatha: the Third Month
9 Days till Spring Equinox

DUANTRI FOUND LANIE on the sea shore, squatting to stare at some bones. "Because," she said aloud, "of course you are."

Lanie lit up at the sight of her, and pushed herself to her feet. She was moving much more slowly now that her early surge had come and gone, and her left hand was merely gray once more. But she had been sleeping well and long, ten or twelve hours at a time these past two days, and eating heartily. The hollows of her face were no longer so bruised with care, and her eyes were clear and brown as woodland brooks.

"Duantri!" she exclaimed, tugging at her hand. "Look what I found!"

Duantri obligingly allowed herself to be led over to whatever new treasure Lanie had found. It might be anything. It might be sticks. But it was probably...

"A whole *narwhal* skeleton! Picked clean, too!"

"Bones," Duantri sighed, and shook her head.

"Just look at the tusk on it! It's almost twice as long as I am! And that perfectly scrumptious spiral! Oh, it's so beautiful! I'm *almost* glad"—Lanie lowered her voice to a whisper—"that all my *other* bones got pulverized in Madinatam. I think I can fit all of this into my backpack. Well, maybe Haaken has an extra bag for me. Or two. Except for the horn. I think I'll just carry that. Maybe I'll use it for my walking staff if I can reinforce it somehow. It's a very sensitive material. It... it *feels* things... about its environment. And when I'm sharing my substance with it, I feel them too!"

Duantri smiled into her shining face. When Lanie was happy, only a monster could scowl in her presence. "As if thou needed sensitivity in any more abundance than thou hast."

Lanie laughed, and babbled on as Duantri shivered in her quilted jacket and furred hood. In Skakmaht, even her tolerance for the cold was being tested to its limits. She was grateful that, between them, Tanaliín and Haaken had provided them all appropriate attire for the north. She was surprised that Lanie herself was not already blue as glacier ice, but these narwhal bones of hers had her ablaze with an inward sun. So Duantri shrugged inwardly and listened to her friend wax ectenical about her plans for the narwhal bones.

She wanted, Lanie explained, to use the skeleton's accident to construct a 'vital-force vehicle'—much like Cracchen's fulmar ship, except out of bone, not ice. A land-and-sea vehicle, but *not* an air ship, because Lanie did *not* like flying.

She'd been, she said, chatting with the narwhal bones, learning all about them, and *did Duantri know* that "narwhals are the most darling blubber-de-bloop mammals, capable of keeping themselves warm in the coldest water? Even now, their bones retain the *memory* of heat, like Tam's dragon scales. Can you feel it, too?"

Duantri couldn't, but Lanie didn't give her a chance to say so. She was too busy explaining how, because of this temperature-regulating quirk of narwhal anatomy, she thought she could make a vehicle that was able to maintain a comfortable internal atmosphere when she was riding around inside it.

"Not to mention," she added, "that narwhal's blood is *loaded* with oxygen to help them stay underwater for enormously long periods of time. So even if I seal off my vehicle against the cold— *with me inside it!*—I think I'll get pretty good air circulation, so long as my substance remains in contact with the narwhal's accident. And, of course, I can always vent the vehicle at night. Isn't Datu going to love it? I'll host overnight parties inside it once I get back to Quadiíb. Duantri—it's my very own esh!"

Lanie was almost certain that she could manipulate the narwhal bones into a more malleable material, creating a state somewhere between accident and ectenica that was both uniform and plastic enough to stretch into four thin walls, with four thin legs, and a roof overhead. And whenever she didn't want the hassle of storing or parking such a vehicle—and if she didn't want to live in it *always* (but why *wouldn't* she? she asked, with such enthusiasm that Duantri didn't have the heart to answer)—Lanie would be able to revert the bones back to their original form, or even perhaps fold them up into some kind of puzzle box, and keep them as a decoration until she needed them again.

"Either way," she concluded, "the good news is, with this narwhal skeleton at hand, and after my lovely few days of rest, I can get myself all the way back to Quadiíb. Haaken, as you know, has his duties back in Liriat. Much to report to... to the Blood Royal. And Cracchen, from what Haaken tells me, wants to stay here in the old Sky House Skrathmandan. Cracchen..." Lanie paused, reflecting. "I don't think he's quite sure *what* he is yet, or what he wants to be, now that he's no longer host to the most powerful and cruel minds of Skaki history. He remembers much of the magic he learned in his lattice with the storm of souls, but Haaken says it's like he dreamt it, or learned it long ago. He wants to stay near the anuraki in the snowpyre and learn from it, since it has elected to remain within the dwalming circle, and keep its memories. It can't speak directly with him now that the dome is closed, but you can feel its vital force throughout the whole house! It seems to be learning how to communicate with Cracchen by means *other* than words. Like the sky house itself is haunted, but not by anything malicious. Or, at least, not meaning any malice towards *Cracchen*..."

She started laughing. She was talking much too fast, too hectically, and Duantri thought she understood why.

She asked gently, "Does Cracchen still refuse to speak to you?"

Lanie hesitated. "Cracchen... doesn't want to see me. Understandable, I think."

"Because he is still in love with you?"

Lanie ducked her head, flushing. "He's not! He never was. Not really. Before all this, Cracchen didn't think of me at all. It was a mixture of the circumstances that brought us together, and the other things in his mind that were... were attracted to power. It happens to me too," she confessed. "Every time I meet a wizard whose god loves them very much. They're so bright with it. Hard to look away. Anyway"—she shrugged— "hopefully, Cracchen will soon forget all about me, and whatever... whatever he thought he felt."

"Hmn."

"Hmn?"

"And what if," Duantri pressed, "*Haaken* forgets all about you too? Would you be quite so careless of that?"

Lanie's head ducked even lower, her flush deepening. "Duantri," she confessed, "I have a crush the size of a *gunugg*. It is my pleasure and my torment—my crushes always are—but it's also... mine. I'm not sure what Haaken thinks of me. If he thinks of anyone in that way. He's very much... a creature of the mind. Maybe he was born like that. Maybe it's a part of how he survived his vassalship in Bran Fiakhna's court. I don't know. None of my business. I don't mind."

Duantri arched an eyebrow at her.

"I don't!" Lanie insisted, a bit too loudly. But outdoors, even her loudest voice was swamped by the sky and sea. "I'm just glad—*glad*—to be his friend. His... colleague. That's special, you know? It's enough. Besides, he lives in Liriat. And I'm banished forever from Liriat. It's complicated enough, just being friends. I'll have to start writing him letters, like I do with Havoc. I can't believe," she muttered, "that *Tanaliin's* been writing to him this *whole time*."

Lanie's gaze lifted again, and suddenly her eyes were welling with unexpected tears. "And that's *another* thing. Tanaliín. You. Oh, twelve gods, you're going to leave soon, aren't you? You probably came out here to say goodbye, and I've been talking the whole time. Oh, Duantri," she moaned, "why am I *like* this?"

Duantri wrapped Lanie in her arms and rocked her, right there on the snowy shore.

"But say the word," she whispered in Quadic, "and Tanaliín and I shall stay with thee, and bear the egg on foot. We needn't rush our voyage on return; Tam's kernel egg will keep—or else, will hatch! And if it hatches—then, we'll feed it up, and swaddle it in love till we part ways."

Grimacing, Lanie pulled away, but not completely, from the embrace. "Oh. Well. I'm... I'm not sure it's safe for you and Tanaliín to be the first living creatures a baby skinchanger sees."

"Dost think the infant will imprint on us?" Duantri teased. "And follow us, as duckling, to Quadiíb?"

"No-oo. I just think it will eat you. And then become you. And, while that's *fine*, it's *natural*, it's just..." She clasped Duantri's upper arms, squeezing them with a healthy fervor that meant the strength was returning to her limbs. "It's just I love you both. As you are. Yourselves. Alive. Right now. In your current bodies. I mean," she added thoughtfully, "if we came down to it, I'd also love you and Tanaliín as two darling strata in a new hatchling's pneuma. But... don't. Don't get eaten. Take your fableform. Take Tanaliín. Get the kernel egg back to Madinatam. Enter the city on the scarp as the heroes you are, forgiven for your past crimes. Make friends with the gunuggs, so that Tanaliín can write some scholarly papers on the Taquathurans, like she's always wanted to. Let the egg hatch safely among its own people. And by *safely*, I mean with you and your gyrlady *far away* from it."

Her eyes were still unhappy, but no longer streaming. Duantri hugged her again, for longer this time, and harder. "What if I carry Tanaliín *and* thee...?"

Lanie shook her head. "You'll fly faster with only one human on your back—you big, beautiful Kestrel. Tam's egg is *not* an insignificant weight. And I hate flying. No"—this time, she shook her whole body, shedding her melancholy like a winter coat come spring—"best we part ways for now—just for a little while. I have a lot to… to think about. Probably best I do that alone. Well, alone except for… my *narwhal esh!*"

At the thought, her sadness vanished entirely, and once again she was beaming down at her newfound skeleton. A second later, and without warning, Lanie seized Duantri's wrists, and swung her around in a wide circle. Duantri burst out laughing, leaning her weight into the swing. Their boots scuffed the snow. They spun and spun until they collapsed in a dizzy heap, laughing.

Lanie rolled around in the snow until she found her knitted hat, which had flown off, and popped it back on, wet and sparkling, over her dark braids. Propping herself up on an elbow, she said, lips still smiling, but otherwise as serious as if she were performing a death rite: "Truly, Duantri, you're one of the All-Marvels of Athe. Thank you. Thank you for everything you've given me. For your dear companionship. For all the times you saved me. Saved my life *and* made it better."

"Beloved Lanie!" Duantri leaned in to kiss her soundly on both cheeks, on her forehead, on her lips, and on her lips again for good measure. The kiss did deepen, mutually but only briefly, before she shot out a hand to tickle Lanie in the ribs, making her shriek and bounce away.

"As for being an All-Marvel of Athe," Duantri called after her, "*you're* one to talk!"

DUANTRI AND TANALÍN left late that morning with Tam's kernel egg, and Haaken was to leave within the hour.

Last night, by the lights of the Blithe Dancers, they had all watched—Cracchen from a window of Sky House Skrathmandan, the rest from Sari's seventh floor sepulcher in Sky House Secundus—as the great mass of the Guilded Council split apart and fell in chunks of rock and ice onto the ruins of Iskald.

Over the past few days, there had been enough time to remove what was precious and necessary from the other sky houses into Secundus and Skrathmandan. Books, mostly, and art, some artifacts of archeological antiquity, a few curios and collections. But the bodies that fell with the houses were buried in the rubble. Iskald itself would be their monument.

Now Lanie watched as Haaken rode down to the shore from Secundus on his fulmar ship, landing it on a smooth stretch of shore nearby. He disembarked, and sauntered slowly over to watch Lanie as she worked.

She was low on magical reserves, but her communion with the narwhal bones was more like a conversation than any perilous act of death magic. Working with them was hardly any harder than sitting there and breathing. It felt more like playtime. really—and a great privilege.

She breathed in; the bones became a thin, almost rubbery material.

She breathed out; the material re-shaped itself as she desired.

A tiny hut—just big enough to stand upright in, or lie down comfortably at a full stretch. It stood on four bony legs, and the walls were warm to the touch, translucent as membranes. The sunlight shone through them, golden-amber. The air inside the hut was fresh but heated, circulating through vents in the membrane, and held the faintest zing of citrus.

"That," Haaken said, "is remarkable."

"It's my vital-force narwhal!" Lanie explained proudly. "Like your fulmar ship!"

"Yes. I can see that."

The narwhal's tusk, which she kept distinctly itself, was currently slung across her back on a wide strap. It lay like a shaft of sunlight against her skin, dreaming its dreams of the deep, deep sea, and filling her mind with the oddest underwater thoughts.

Lanie could not remember the last time she had felt so

contented. She smiled at Haaken, and he smiled back. That shadow. That glint.

Then he cleared his throat. "Lanie."

"Yes, Haaken?"

"Do you… need money?"

She blinked at him. "Um…?"

Of all the questions she had expected him to ask, *that* was not one of them. *Did* she need money? Why *would* she need money?

"For your journey back to Quadiíb?" Haaken clarified.

"Oh! Right. Right. Supplies. And things." Lanie thought about it. Tanaliín was carrying just one of the saddlebags that had initially been strapped to Stripes, as well as the egg in its cradleboard. Duantri could only bear so much weight, but she could always hunt enough food for the two of them.

Lanie was planning on taking the rest of their bags, filled with whatever Haaken could spare from his larder, but *that* wouldn't last her the whole journey back to Quadiíb, and she… she could *not* hunt.

Maybe she could scrounge? In winter? In the far north?

"Oh," she said again. "Hmn. Well."

Haaken was unslinging a bag from his shoulder. "There are many settlements to the south who will sell supplies to you. I have made a map for you. Here, in this bag. There is also money."

Lanie bit her lip. "Oh, but—"

"I must tell you, it is not from me," Haaken said. "It is a… gift. From Blood Royal Errolirrolin Brackenwild. They wished"—he cleared his throat, and when he spoke again, she knew he was quoting Lir directly—"*to contribute to your heroic efforts to cleanse Athe of an undead Lirian fiend.*" He added contemplatively, "I think perhaps they felt responsible for Irradiant Stones's continued existence, though I do not myself know why."

"Because," Lanie muttered, "claiming responsibility for something justifies any action taken over it—whether or not it's yours to act upon."

"I told you about the money, Lanie"—Haaken's voice slowed

and deepened—"so that you would know there is no debt between us."

At his words, she glanced up swiftly, and then almost staggered at the sight of him. How tremendous was his magic. How snowblind-deathdazzle-silverwinterwhite it was. And how soft his hair looked. How silken pale gold. And his eyes, like secret glaciers lit from within by the Blithe Dancers.

Whatever he saw in her face seemed to startle him in return. They looked away from each other simultaneously.

And since Lanie knew she had to say *something*, she said exactly what she felt.

"Thank you." She hefted the sack. "For this. For everything. When you see them, tell Errolirrolin—tell Lir—thank you from me, too. This money will keep me from starving on the tundra."

He smiled at that, his there-and-gone, sly-as-a-snow-weasel smile. "No," he said, "Thank you—for ridding Athe of a murderer, and ending the Northernmost War. It was kind of you to include me." And he gave her a little Rookish bow.

Lanie snorted. "Yes. Right. I'm the kindest necromancer on Athe—and don't forget it."

"It is not likely."

Before they could allow the next silence to grow awkward again, Lanie began patting down her pockets, then digging in the right one to bring out a tangle of leather cords. "Before you go—I have something for you. Two things. Well, three. First: did you want this back?"

She untangled one of the leather cords, the one dangling Haaken's periapt: a tiny droplet of perpetual ice through which he could communicate with whomever wore it.

He shook his head. "That is for you, should you have need of it. Please feel free to lock it away with your reliquary. But if it remains on or near your person, I will be able locate you directly and come to your aid—wheresoever on Athe you be."

Grinning, Lanie pocketed it. "Great. Thank you. Absolutely keeping it. You're still," she noted, "wearing your Bryddongard droplet, I see."

He touched the droplet of ice at his throat that connected him to Tanalíin and Duantri's bond. "I must—for however long they wish to keep the Kestrel's fableform."

"What if they never want to give it up?"

He shrugged, and smiled. "I do not mind if they do not."

Something to ask Duantri and Tanalíin about when I get home, Lanie thought.

Finally, she managed to untangle the other two strands she was holding. Like the periapt, both were small amulets. But these were ones that she had made, from two of the vertebrae in the narwhal's spinal cord.

"This one is for you. And this one"—she dropped the second amulet into his palm—"is for Cracchen. If he wants it. I can talk to you through the bone, and you can answer—"

"—through the ice," Haaken finished. He looked deeply interested and pleased.

"Exactly! So now *you* may call *me* at need." She gave him an encouraging nod. "And I'll be able to find *you*—'wheresoever on Athe you be.'"

"What if... what if I merely want to talk?"

She blink-blink-blinked at him. Eyelids fluttering half-shut, she looked down at the sun-on-snow beneath her feet, for it was far less bright than he. "Anytime."

"Good."

"Good."

Haaken gave another of his bows. "Then, until we meet again, Miscellaneous Stones."

"Please tell Cracchen—" Lanie stopped. Haaken waited. "Just... if he ever needs, or wants, to talk. I'll listen."

Nodding, he turned to go, making his way through the snowpack back to his fulmar ship.

"Haaken Vikanthar Skrathmandan!" she called after him.

He leaned over the prow to look at her.

"You're absolutely *wonderful!*"

Haaken smiled. His fulmar ship twinkled. It rose up, and he was gone.

Epilogue

THE FEAST OF
THE BONE SHARK

Caravan School Road, Higher Quadiíb
Nurr, Waystation 3

Year 4826 of Higher and Lower Quadiíb
On Balah, 19th of Anatha: the Third Month
The High Holy Fire Feast of Spring Equinox

Quadoni Feast of the Bone Shark, Sea Queen's Festival, Aganath's Crowning Day

NURR WAS ABUSTLE in festival finery, and every street rang with music. Music on every corner. Music from rooftop stages, from pavements and alleyways, from tavern courtyards, and from the flung-wide windows of private residences. So many songs all playing at the same time should have been a cacophony, tuneless and terrible, but somehow it wasn't. It more like a great spellsong, every melody at once, never again re-creatable or re-playable, but so mighty it could rend the fabric of the universe with its splendor and let the gods pour in.

On the outskirts of Nurr, Lanie folded up her narwhal vehicle into its puzzle box, and placed it tenderly at the bottom of her ratty backpack. Her new collection of bones was growing, but ever since she had invited Sosha's substance into her skin without having to touch so much as a scrap of his accident (and without his accident even *existing* anymore in heterogeneous form), she wasn't sure she *needed* to collect bones anymore. She just... loved them.

If she could share her accident with the substance of any dead thing that was weighting the hem of Doédenna's ethereal cloak, then... then... Lanie could take *any* shape, remember *any* memories, from *any* creature who had *ever* lived on Athe. She could...

But there her mind always fizzed out in a blissful little blitz, and she found she couldn't even *imagine* it. And maybe she shouldn't, not until necessity compelled her to... improvise.

She had been able to do what she did with Sosha's substance because, she thought, the gods had given her an early surge. And Saint Death had given her a job to do. And *that* work had called for a specific tool in order to complete it. But it was a borrowed tool, not for everyday use. Not even for every surge. Like the one-off, specialized spells of Yssimyss of Mysteries, who, Her priests said, always granted prayers sideways and from around corners, what she had done with Sosha's substance might have been a miracle for that moment alone. Like this unrepeatable music of Nurr, and its grand mosaic of many songs, playing right now and never again.

Grinning at the thought, Lanie skipped up to the nearby line of stalls and tables that were selling all sorts of wares, from pastries to pottery to dipping pens. Lir had sent her more than money in that bag Haaken had given her. They'd sent her letters too—an entire packet of them. She had read them all over the long nights of her journey from Iskald to Nurr, safe and warm inside her narwhal.

She had yet to reply.

But a short postcard from Nurr, Waystation Three, Quadiíb, on this, the Feast of the Bone Shark, and the High Holy Fire Feast of Spring Equinox? *That* she could manage.

Dear Lir, Lanie wrote as she stood at the table, the vendor having been more than happy to sell her pen and ink for the amount of coin she'd poured into her hand, *You'd love it in Nurr. I've never heard so many different sea chanties sung in so many keys by so many voices in all my life. Nor did I ever imagine merfolk to be so anatomically complex. Nor how picky some sailors can be in their selection of a fishy spouse. Hope you make it to Quadiíb someday. —M.I.S.*

"Thank you," she told the adorable vendor, who had freckles and hair done up in triple puffs like ice cream. "Is there some sort of post office or courier service nearby, or..."

As she asked the question, she selected several more painted postcards to purchase, all desert landscapes or sketches of urban life in the Quadoni Waystations, done in wax crayons or colored ink or graphite. She planned on sending them to her friends in Liriat Proper: to Havoc Dreadnaught at the Lover's Complaint, to Eidie at Eidie's Unparalleled Breads and Pastries, to Gyrveard Viquar at Waystation Thirteen, and to Lord Ambassador Haaken Skrathmandan at Sky House Secundus, Skaki Ambassadorial Palace, First Circle.

The vendor grinned and gave her directions to the local courier service, as well as a necklace, gratis, strung with shark-teeth-shaped candies. Whereupon Lanie gave *her* an enormous tip, courtesy of the Blood Royal Brackenwild of Liriat.

After wandering the streets of Nurr to her heart's content, Lanie found an open-air tea house and settled in, setting her backpack at her feet, and leaning her narwhal tusk between her knees. She had to navigate around it in order to eat her way through a plate piled high with sandwiches, and little custards, and flaky, buttery, sugary pastries, and also drink an entire pitcher of rose hip tea that her bladder would have *stern words with her* about later. But for now, Lanie was so blissfully happy she thought she might swoon.

With each bite, she offered up praise to the Queen of the Sea, one hand holding her food, one hand forming each of the twelve modified sothaín attitudes dedicated to Aganath.

All attitudes completed, but her dish not yet decimated, Lanie started on Havoc's postcard:

"*Basically, Nurr in springtime is all about Aganath, all the time. Like it was made for you. I keep expecting to turn around and see you here. Let's meet in Nurr next year and celebrate the Sea Queen together—we'll share a room, wear nothing but strategic strings of shark-teeth candy, and eat our way through the stalls. Tits and pickles, Havoc, there's this pastry I'm stuffing my face with RIGHT NOW that's all pistachios and honey and dough, and I'm about to faint for the deliciousness! Also, remind me to tell you about my narwhal in the next letter — M.I.S.*"

Her handwriting had gotten very cramped and tiny towards the end, until it looked like something Grandpa Rad might have scribbled in his diaries.

Lanie flinched from the thought.

Then, cautiously, she returned to it. Prodded the memory of his final moments.

Irradiant, laid out in his snowpyre. Lanie, cautiously watching him from behind Sosha Brackenwild's eyes.

His last words to her: "*Give it here, girlie. You won,*" before his substance cracked loose of Aadar Skrathmandan's accident and floated up to rest in the palm of her hand.

The poor, mangled bird of his soul. How it had hunched, sullen, glaring at her: wings torn, beak broken, one eye missing, feathers the color of void, smelling of rotten citrus.

In the bustling teashop in Nurr, Lanie stared down at her empty palm, remembering the acidic un-weight of her great-grandfather's ghost. She thought, *What do I want? To remember you always, Grandpa Rad? Forget you entirely? Or, maybe, just remember you enough—and move on?*

She came out of her revery when a very dry tongue licked her hand. It was like a dog's tongue, if that dog never needed another drink of water, because that dog was undead. And was also a wolf.

"Undies!" she exclaimed in surprise. "How did you find me?"

"Auntie Lanie," her niece replied from behind her chair, "Undies can *always* find you. You helped *make* him, remember? What are you doing, sitting here all alone? I have been waiting and *waiting* for you. Can I have one of your pastries?"

LANIE, IT APPEARED, was the last one to return safely home to the family esh. When Datu and Undies towed her back to their scrape in the campgrounds outside of Nurr, not only was

Datu's and Makkovian's esh erected there, but Tanalíin and Duantri's as well.

"They're back! They're back from Taquathura! Why didn't you tell me, Datu?"

Datu smirked. "Because. You squeak when you are surprised."

"Sacred Datura Stones!"

As they approached their rented scrape, Datu bellowed, "Hoozzaplo, naked people! Sacred Datura incoming—scrape-bound with Mister Underwear Stones and Auntie Lanie Stones. So put some *clothes* on already!"

In just seconds, Tanalíin, Duantri, and Makkovian all spilled out from the larger esh, all three of them in a state of adorable deshabille.

"I *told* you," Datu groaned, slapping her forehead, "*clothes!* Not *lingerie!*"

"No wonder you were wandering Nurr alone, Datu!" Lanie murmured to her niece.

Datu nodded, aggrieved. "They can get *loud*. Also, I like the festival music."

"Me, too, Datu."

And then, Lanie was being hugged and bussed and grasped and handled from all sides, and everyone was passing out more shark-teeth candy, and there were more kisses, and breathless explanations, interrupted only when Undies, who had disappeared into the esh, trotted back out again, with a scrap of silk in his mouth.

"Underwear Stones!" everyone exclaimed together.

"Is that your lingerie?" Lanie asked Duantri as Datu sat on the ground and tried to wrestle the silk away from her wolf cub.

"No, not that…" Duantri began, but her niece interrupted, "It is *Didyi's*. And Undies"—she grunted, yanking—"*knows* he is *not* supposed to *eat* it! We always buy him his *own* lingerie from the rag-and-bone stalls in *all* the Waystations we go to! But"—she brandished the silk above her head, as Undies leapt and snapped for it—"Undies likes everyone else's lingerie better."

Makkovian murmured, "For an undead hellhound of adolescent age, Mister Underwear Stones has quite expensive tastes."

"Like father like son," Tanaliín said.

Lanie snorted. "You should talk, Tanaliín."

"Ah," cried Duantri, "That reminds me! Come inside the esh, our Lanie. We have a surprise for you!"

"Two, actually," said Tanaliín.

Datu slipped her hand in hers, gave it a warning tug. "Auntie Lanie, I *tried* to talk them out of buying it." Her nose wrinkled. "It is *very* pink."

"Oh, goody!" said Lanie.

The first surprise was a dressing gown of lace and silken brocade, with a pattern of repeating peonies. It billowed like a bell around Lanie's feet, the color of a gorgeous cloud: specifically, the sort of fat-bottomed, top-heavy, cumulonimbus cloud that is as plump and fruity as the inside of a ruby grapefruit, and festoons Quadoni horizons during monsoon.

"After all your adventuring," Tanaliín told her, "you are *not* to dress in anything practical or durable for the rest of the month! This dressing gown is to facilitate a period of sartorial abandonment."

"Makkovian picked it out for you," Duantri put in. "He purchased dressing gowns for all of us while we were gone, specifically for this festival day."

Lanie met Makkovian's smiling gaze. "I told you, Mizka," he said, "that you would live to see the spring. I knew we would meet here again."

"*My* dressing gown is black," Datu announced. "Because it is the best color. And there is no lace. Or pink."

"Pink," Lanie announced grandly, quickly wiping the tears from her eyes, "helps me concentrate on raising the undead. The more expensive and froofy a pink thing is, the stronger my magic becomes. You should try it sometime, Datu. I'll buy you a dressing gown to match mine, and you'll be a necromancer in no time. We can be twins."

Her teasing sent Datu right into a high dudgeon. "We will *not* be twins. I will *never* be a necromancer, Auntie Lanie, because I will never, *ever* wear pink. Not over my dead body!"

Laughing, Lanie hugged her dressing gown close to her chest. She loved it like she loved her narwhal vehicle. Like she loved Nurr. And music. And bones. And her beautiful family.

"Well, you know," she told her niece, "I can always resurrect your dead body and dress you up like my little doll in all the pink dresses I want. That's what's so fun about being a necromancer!"

"And on that subject," Tanaliín said, "here is your second surprise."

THE SURPRISE WAS Stripes.

Rather, it was the mound of fluff, claw fragments, toothy bits, and two cracked glass eyes that *used* to be Stripes, all stuffed into a large sack.

"The gunuggs gathered him up for you," Duantri told her softly. "The big one, the spider crab—Karramorra—insisted that not a piece be left behind. He said you would want them."

"I wish I could thank him," Lanie said, then remembered she had another blank postcard, and resolved to write to him in… "Wait," she said, "if Tam is dead, is the city still called Madinatam? Has the kernel egg hatched? If so, does that mean there's a new Witch Queen, or…"

Tanaliín explained that the three god-beasts who had survived the Hastiludes were dividing governing duties between them at the moment—and they were now calling the capital *Madina*—which meant, merely, 'the city.'

"They do not know if they want to live under a Witch Queen's rule. That was a human perception of how things were anyway. But as the city grows its human population, the gunuggs are thinking about forming a joint government of skinchangers and humans, by election. Can you imagine?" Tanaliín was shining with satisfaction. "I provided our Ylkazarran address at the university to your splendid Karramorra, in case the gunuggs desire to consult with the Colloquium about precedent for organizing human governments. We are looking forward to a long correspondence."

Lanie sat quietly, the sack of Stripes in her lap. It had weight and heft, but no warmth. No spark. It was… homogeneous, like bone dust, or columbarium ashes. It was no longer *Stripes*.

Tears pricked her eyes again, but not the happy kind.

The back of her neck also prickled. She looked up to see Datu's green gaze fixed on her.

"You can put him back together again. Right, Auntie Lanie?"

"Hmn," said Auntie Lanie, not sure how she should answer.

"Sacred Datura," Makkovian said gently. "There comes a day, for all of us, and for all things, when we must release all those we love the most with our best grace."

"But not today," Datu insisted. "*Right*, Auntie Lanie?"

"Well—" Lanie contemplated the sack. She bit her lip. Tanalíin and Duantri were carefully looking elsewhere, but Makkovian gave her his calm contemplation, ready to support her as she navigated this difficult conversation.

Finally, she turned to Datu, who sat opposite her on a cushion on the floor. Her didyi had painted her face like the Bone Shark: labial furrows curving like parentheses around her mouth; huge circles around her eyes, colored in with black kohl; dark gill-slashes on the sides of her neck. He had even stitched and stuffed a dorsal fin accessory, which Datu wore on straps over her shoulders like a backpack. There were ten candy necklaces looped around her throat, dozens more on her wrists and twisted through her red-gold hair, which was as thick and curly as Lanie's, and which she wore in two pompoms on the sides of her head, a bit like that stationary vendor.

Lanie was suddenly, ravenously envious of those pompoms. She wanted to put her own hair up in pompoms.

"Tell you what, Datu," she said, feeling reckless, speaking without thinking, "let's go into my narwhal esh, you and me. We'll have our own private slumber party while your didyi and his darlings have their own. My narwhal," she added persuasively when Datu raised a dubious eyebrow, "is *soundproof*. If *you* do my hair just like yours… and maybe give me one of your candy necklaces, then… then *I'll* see what I can do about Stripes. But not today. We'll do it first thing tomorrow, whenever we wake up."

Lanie wouldn't be performing any magic today, on this the High Holy Fire Feast of Spring Equinox. She'd had her surge already, when she'd needed it most. Today was for resting. For celebrating.

Datu beamed at her, her worried brow untightening with relief. Until she relaxed so completely, Lanie hadn't realized her niece was on the verge of breaking down in wailing tears.

Datu was… sensitive about some things. Easy to forget that when she was barking out orders, draped in teeth, and dressed like a shark.

"Let us go to your esh right *now*, Auntie Lanie," she insisted, standing up. "I will bring my cavaquinho, and play you all the songs I made up while you were gone. May Undies come too?"

"Sure. But I'll have to hide my unmentionables."

Datu grinned at her. "But then, what will he eat?"

THE FIRST LIGHT of dawn found Lanie shaken awake by a most upright and insistent Sacred Datura Stones, while her face was being licked half off by Mister Underwear Stones who, lacking any undergarments to feed upon, had to content himself with other displays of affection.

Blearily, she peeled out of her sleeping roll, stumbled out of the narwhal to empty her bladder at the campground privy, and then returned to find Datu already laying out a circle. It was much like her didyi's dwalming ring except, instead of river rocks, the circle consisted of Stripes: his fur, his skin, his teeth, his claws. The amber glass eyes Datu kept a hold of, rolling them in her hand like nervous marbles.

"You sit there," she directed Lanie.

Rubbing her eyes, Lanie plopped down in the midst of the scraps. She picked up one of the pieces of fuzz and balled it between her fingers, watching Datu straighten everything out again until the circle was *just* right.

"Why are you staring at me, Auntie Lanie?" Datu demanded, never looking up from her work. "You should be raising Stripes like an undead army."

"Tell me, Datu," Lanie said in a sleep-roughened voice. "What do you remember most about Stripes?"

Datu frowned. "What do I *remember?*"

"Your favorite memory," she clarified. "It can be more than one, if you like. In fact, it should be. We're gathering up his memory, you and I, like flowers that got scattered in a storm. We need as many pieces of it as possible to try and put him back together again. *I* have some memories of him, but *you* have your own. I want him to be as complete as possible."

"Hmn," said Datu, in a manner so familiar that Lanie had to suppress a smile.

"It's all right, Sacred Datura. Take your time."

After a series of heavy, world-weary sighs, Datu began, very reluctantly, "We always sat on him. In front of the fireplace at our house. You told me stories about the other Stoneses. But when I told them to Mumyu, she said..." Datu hesitated, licked her lips, her breath going shallow as she spoke of her mother. "Mumyu said *none* of those Stoneses you talked about really existed. That you made them all up. Like Thrice-Digested Stones and the dragon. She told me some stories about *real* Stoneses. The ones whose pictures hung in the gallery. But..."

Her chin lifted. She said suddenly, fiercely, "But I liked yours *better*, Auntie Lanie! And, sometimes... when you went down to the ossuary to work with your dead people, I went back to the library, and I sat on Stripes, and I told *him* your stories. So I could remember them. And I played pretend with him... that I was a famous Stones...that I rode on Stripes's back into battle. And we fought a dragon—the same dragon that ate Thrice-Digested Stones. But he did not eat me. I won! And the dragon and Stripes and I became friends. And we started a zoo."

She fell silent.

Lanie cleared her throat. "That's… a good story, Datu. I didn't know any of that about… about Nita. Thank you for sharing your memory."

Still fingering her piece of orange fluff, she imagined a very young Datu, perhaps aged two or three, still wearing her daytime diapers but trying every day to use the privy like a 'big girl.' She imagined this young Datu lying alone on Stripes's back in Stones Library, babbling stories at him in her toddler argot, while her mother punished her father by keeping him in his falcon form, and her aunt escaped the gloomy house to go underground and play with her bones.

She sighed, regretting much, unable to change anything.

Datu scooted closer to her, and put a hand on her knee. Undies belly-crawled an inch closer and laid his head on her other knee. Both of them looked up at Lanie with identical expressions.

"I know you think you cannot do this, Auntie Lanie," Datu said. "But you can. I *know* you can."

"I appreciate your confidence, Datu. And… I do *want* to do this, even though… I don't know how. I miss him, you know. So much. Stripes saved me. He gave up everything for me. And I never got to… to thank him."

Datu sniffled, hiding it by pretending to cough. She turned her face away to wipe her nose on the black sleeve of her dressing gown, leaving streaks. Lanie politely ignored this, deciding to share her own memory now. This was work they both had to do, together.

"Stripes talked to me in my head sometimes. His voice was just like I thought it would be—loud—declamatory—but also courtly, like a Bright Knight from a Lirian tale of romance and chivalry." She cleared her throat. "*My lady! But bid me take on some noble quest—and I will do it! Anything! But preferably make it a quest that involves my incomparable tigrine skills, my apex-predatory instincts, and, if it could please somehow necessitate me flying at the speed of light as you cling shrieking to my neck, my gratitude would truly exceed all seemliness…*"

"Stripes *talked* to you?"

407

Lanie scratched Undies behind his ears. He whined in bliss. "The problem was getting him to *stop* talking!"

Datu also reached over to scratch Undies, who immediately rolled over and showed her his belly, waving his paws in the air. "I wish *Undies* could talk. In his own voice," she added, "not yours. Although that… was all right. I liked when you talked to me in his mouth."

Lanie patted the lopsided pompoms of her hair, wreckage from Datu's ministrations the night before.

"Undies may yet learn. Early days for that undead cub. We don't know anything about how he will develop from here. It's a novel spell that binds you two together. There's never been anything like it."

"We do not know how *I* will develop either," Datu muttered gloomily.

Lanie swallowed. She'd had no idea Datu had been fretting over that. "So far, so good," she said carefully. "You look fine to me. Your studies are progressing. You've grown a few inches. You've composed a concert's worth of new music on your cavaquinho." She lowered her voice to a confidential whisper. "But I have to ask—and it's all right, by the way, Datu, however you answer this—have you developed any strange cravings for undergarments?"

Datu made a face. "*No*, Auntie Lanie! *Ew!*"

"Then," said her impenitent aunt, "there's hope yet for you— you and your undead rascal. Speaking of hope…"

And with a slyness that would rival Haaken Skrathmandan's, Lanie flourished the scrap of fur she'd been worrying at.

"Why… what do we have *here*, Sacred Datura Stones?"

The scrap wasn't a scrap anymore. It was a long, thin tube of striped hide. It looked, rather, like the beginnings of a tail. As she flicked it in front of Datu's face like a limp wand, Lanie breathed in, held her breath, and breathed out.

And on her exhale, she made the bits of fur and claw and teeth that Datu had set all around her rise up and contract into a tight circle. Knitting itself into a continuous loop of buff and orange and black, this ouroboros of tigerish bits girded her like the ring of a distant planet, turning and turning and turning.

Datu, watching every move that Lanie made with eyes as big as spinning tops, did not seem to be breathing.

Lanie reminded her, "Where is breath?"

"In the stillness," Datu gasped in.

"What is stillness?"

"Sotháin!" she gusted out the word.

"Perfect. Keep doing that. Breathing. Thinking of Stripes. We must both remember him as hard as we can."

As she spoke, Lanie took her little tube of a tail piece, and placed it atop the rippling circle of conjoined fur. It melted in with the rest of it.

A silver mist was rising, not just from her left hand, but from all of her wizard marks. Undies whined, his own plumy tail sweeping the narwhal esh's bone-thin floor. His unblinking eyes gleamed like two distant stars.

"Auntie Lanie," Datu whispered, "your eyes are bright like Undies'—only yours are yellow and his are blue."

"That happens, Datu," Lanie replied calmly. She was speaking in both her voices, deep and surface, for a part of her was calling out to Stripes, calling him back, singing the Maranathasseth Anthem. *Awake! Awake! Awake!*

"I know," Datu said, like it was obvious.

You owe me nothing, Saint Death. You have done everything I have ever asked. But... if You would grant me one more gift today, I ask for Stripes. Stripes as you would have him. And this time, with a voice Datu can also hear...

The zesty, sparkling, always-fresh air inside the narwhal esh breezed in a little stronger, and separated into several citrus scents. Grapefruit. Yuzu. Lemon. Bitter orange. Lime.

Her god was near. Her god was coming closer. A great tigress, black as void, striped in bone.

And riding on her forehead, a tiny figurehead at the prow of a massive ship, was an orange-and-black striped tiger cub.

Welcome, Lanie called out to her god. *Welcome, Doédenna,*

Great Tigress! Welcome, Stripes, bone of Her bone, fang of Her fang! Come home! Come play! Come pounce!

Out loud, she whispered, "Don't be afraid," to Datu and to Undies. "You mustn't be afraid."

"I am not afraid." But Datu's voice was shaking, and Undies had crawled into her lap like he was still a newborn cub and not the quite large cub he had grown to be since his undeath.

"BE TERRIBLY AFRAID!" roared Stripes.

From the contiguous ring of fur surrounding Lanie, a small, kittenish-shaped head reared up. The shape was indeterminate, unspecific. No separate features like nose or whiskers or ears or eyes distinguished themselves in its face. Nevertheless, the little head swung from side to side, as if searching the room for something.

Lanie brought up her left hand and chopped down in a rigid motion. It split the ring of fur into a single, long ribbon, with the kittenish head at one end. The rest of the ribbon's striped length rolled itself up, furling like the end of a fern, until it was just a tight, tiny, sweet, little ball of fluff—which fell, out of the air, onto the floor.

The cat-shaped thing landed, feet-first, in front of Lanie. The tip of his little tail flicked. His little paws contracted, shooting out tiny, needle-like claws that scratched the bone floor of the narwhal. He was still mostly orange and black and buff fluff, with a blank face and a vague body, and a small mouth the color of void when he opened it and roared:

"TREMBLE! FOR IT IS I, STRIPES, REBORN!"

"Hello, darling," Lanie said. "Welcome back."

"Thank you, my lady." Stripes instantly modified his voice to a much meeker tone. "My lady... If you don't mind me asking... where did you put my eyes?"

Datu leaned forward, cracked amber glass eyes in hand, and placed them carefully, if a little lopsidedly, in Stripes's face. They were much too large for his tiny face.

"I CAN SEE!" Stripes bellowed, no longer bothering to modulate. "And the world is... YELLOW!"

"Auntie Lanie," Datu whispered, smiling like springtime, "I *told* you you could do it."

"You were right, Datu. Absolutely right. But," Lanie said, "*we* did it."

The End

KEY TO QUADONI TERMS

Quadoni Days of the Week

Balah (*Flameday*)—a day to begin new projects, a day for
baking and preparing for feasts, a day for government
announcements, family meetings, naming ceremonies.

Mahluin (*Brineday*)—a day to grieve, to keep a journal of
your intimate thoughts, for reading and reflecting, to
keep quiet, to cure meat, to collect keepsakes, to write
letters to old friends.

Amahtar (*Rainday*)—a day to nurture what is before you, a
day for culture, for poetry and music, a day to bring food
to the sick, or enact deliberate kindness upon loved ones
and strangers alike.

Lasaqi (*Rimeday*)—a day to make hard decisions with
cold logic, to balance your accounts, to have a difficult
conversation you have been avoiding, to do the least
agreeable chores, a day to tally your deeds and assign
yourself hard tasks.

H'za (*Luckday*)—payday! a day to pay court to the person
you admire, a day to interview for jobs, a day of
wagering, a day to take risks, a night for pleasure.

T'rahb (*Dustday*)—a day to bury your beloved dead, a day
of rest, a day of forgiveness and indolence, a day for
cleaning and organizing (if such tasks seem pleasurable).

Ishnaq (*Hangday*)—a day of execution and death-by-
intention, a day of divorce (or of marriage), a day for
seeing your grown children off to their new esh, or
moving your aging parents to an esh where they can be
cared for more thoroughly in their eld.

Months of the Quadoni Calendar Year

Winter: Edenna (*Vespers*), Antua (*Squalls*), Jdeni (*Barrens*)
Spring: Anatha (*Wells*), Quena (*Broods*), Wita (*Sporings*)
Summer: Hirra (*Flukes*), Loth (*Stews*), Satthir (*Drubs*)
Fall: Yrr (*Chases*), Acora (*Embers*), Myssa (*Umbers*)

The Twelve Gods of Quadiíb

Kantu, Flying God of Thunder

Ajdenia the Lizard Lady

Aganath, Queen of the Sea

Brotquen, Four-Faced Harvest Goddess

Kywit the Captured God

Amahirra Mirage-Shaper, Trickster God

Engoloth, God of War and Time and Pepper

Lan Satthi, the Notary God

Wykkyrri Who Is Ten Thousand-Beasts

Sappacor, the Many-Gendered God of Fire
(Lirian: Old Sparks)

Yssimyss of Mysteries

Doédenna, God of Death (Lirian: Saint Death)

The Twelve Apologies

suriki: *I sorrow for my small but blundering transgression.*

shallu: *I sorrow for all those whom I kill on the hunt, whom we take so we can eat.*

silili: *The teacher apologizes to the student for moving too quickly and impairing understanding.*

suhm'sda: *I sorrow for this necessary crime I must commit, and commit as well to appropriate reparation in the future.*

sejish: *I sorrow for your sorrow (but not the part I played) or (in which I played no part).*

se'qa: *I sorrow for myself, mired in this mess of my own (or another's) making.*

setti: *I sorrow for my cutting word, flashed in fire, regretted in ash.*

salal: *With all the best intentions, I acted in ignorance and without nuance. Knowing a better way, I sorrow for my past actions, and set myself to better actions in the future.*

sithisdi: *I apologize to my community, from whom my actions have alienated me, and to whom I long to return.*

suhf'sda: *I regret my long neglect of you, my slow forgetting, and my letting go without acknowledgement or ritual farewell.*

sihesh: *I sorrow for the systems I am caught in, for these cycles I inherited from my forebears, that harm you and harm me, and harm us all, yet we cannot seem to break from.*

sa: *the most abject and final sorrow. The sorrow of the prisoner on the gallows, the tyrant on their deathbed, the warlord undone by war: those who have committed consciously to the worst of crimes, who regret, only at the end, the suffering they caused.*

ACKNOWLEDGMENTS

I WANT TO start by thanking Zig Zag Claybourne—my most wonderful friend Clarence—who was writing Book 2 of *The Khumalo Trilogy* as I was writing *Herald*. We were constantly texting each other "Words I Like Today," and sending care packages and letters. He commissioned for me a *crocheted* Stripes the undead tiger rug! I knew from the start I'd be dedicating *Saint Death's Herald* to Zig Zag; it was my happy fuel throughout the drafting process, knowing that this work must be made worthy of his name.

This was also perhaps the most *social* book I've ever written. Sometimes I'd ride the subway from Queens to Brooklyn to work in my best friend Mir's apartment as she graded papers. Sometimes I'd meet Delia Sherman at a cafe as she worked on *The Absinthe Drinker*. I was in Cassandra Khaw's apartment for several work sessions, sucking up the fluffy cat vibes and excellent finger food. (Cass asked to read my first draft *before* I cut 90,000 words, then rewarded me with sneak peeks of their own latest work.) Thank you, friends, for your spaces, your hospitality, your offices away from home.

I owe many thanks to my writers' group RAMP—Ellen Kushner, Delia Sherman, Joel Derfner, Carlos Hernandez, and Liz Duffy Adams—who also read that big behemoth of a first draft before it went off to my agent and editor. I had many months to mull over their suggestions and combine them with my editorial letter when it came.

Thank you to my editor David Moore, for the clarity and concision of that letter, and for all of the encouraging words in it. Thank you, Markus Hoffmann, for the incredibly exciting and nuanced behind-the-scenes agenting work you do for me! Thank you, Kate Forrester, for the kind of cover art that readers go over with a magnifying glass, ALLCAPS, and exclamation points! And thank you to my copyeditor Donna Bond for her careful work.

I spent days on end in silent Zooms, body-mirroring other writer friends as we all drafted like a pack of cyclists. I owe much of my concentration and stamina to the hours I spent with Kyle Kratky (darkly gorgeous micro shorts), Patty Templeton (monster trucks in space), Jessica Wick (swashbucklers and devil's bargains), Christa Carmen (she turned in her third novel a week after I turned in *Herald*), and Amal El-Mohtar (she was expanding *The River Has Roots* from novelette to novella).

I texted a lot with Sean Elliot, who sent me small chunks of his beautiful novel-in-progress, and encouraged me with many *EXCELSIORS!* along the way. I attended the Carterhaugh School of Folklore and the Fantastic's intensive writing sessions, led by Dr. Brittany Warman and Dr. Sara Cleto. I traded Skype readings with my friend Caitlyn Paxson (she'd give me chapter-by-chapter narrations of her forthcoming *A Widow's Charm* in exchange for sections of *Herald*). I read to my mama, Sita, as she gardened and played with her new grandson Hermes Asunción. (Mama fondly calls this book "Harold," like it's another grandson.)

All the love and encouragement that has come pouring in from friends and family and readers—from Facebook, Instagram, my Substack, and my blog—has been such a golden joy to me. To every book club that has read my book: thank you! To every artist who made art from my characters, thank you! To every convention that had me as a guest and reader: thank you! To Randee Dawn, who hosts the monthly reading "Brooklyn Books and Booze" at Barrows Intense Ginger Tasting Room, and to the kind hosts of Fantastic Fiction at KGB, thank you! You are all community-makers and genre-celebrators, and I salute you!

I want especially to thank Anthony John Woo for setting his 5e D&D campaign in my world, and for encouraging me online with all those "grabby hands" GIFs. I shared a *Saint Death* Google doc Lore-book with him to help inspire play, and also with my darling Phoebe Leung Ashcroft—an artist and book reviewer. Not only did Phoebe draw fan art of Lanie, not only did she draw *three* different versions of Doédenna, Saint Death (the woman, the wolf, and the Doe-Her-Mother), but, over the time I was drafting *Saint Death's Herald*, Phoebe also drew all *twelve* of the Quadoni gods! (My mother is planning to make a calendar out of them even as I write this.) The fan art that came my way in the wake of *Saint Death's Daughter* is so stunning, so astonishing, it makes me want to cry to think about it.

The effervescence of gratitude has buoyed me all throughout these choppy waters of drafting, and it sometimes came from unexpected sources. I was so surprised and moved to hear about people's experiences listening to the audiobook of *Saint Death's Daughter*. I always write to read aloud, but learning how my voice accompanied people on their way to work (this is how my darling papa and stepmother listened to it), to funerals and final visitations, or just going grocery shopping or cleaning their houses, just fills me up. What an utter realization of a vocation: to tell you my stories—to be a part of your lives—to spend such time with you, so intimately. Thank you. I wrote *Herald* for your ears as well.

Most of all, I want to thank mi esposo Carlos Hernandez. Again, always. I read him every draft—every single draft— of *Saint Death's Herald*, right up to the very last polish. We spent many, many, many hours—days—weeks—months— working and writing together these last two years. He wrote three different Marvel comics, several short stories, a novella, an RPG *and* a LARP in the time it took me to write *Herald*.

Our life in art is so luminous, so challenging and tender, and so beloved. Whatever else life is—and it is all the darkness that ever was—it is this bliss, too.

I look out my window right now, over our neighborhood in Queens, on this holy October afternoon, and my heart overflows.

C. S. E. Cooney
October 19th, 2024

ABOUT THE AUTHOR

C. S. E. Cooney (she/her) is the World Fantasy Award-winning author of novel *Saint Death's Daughter* and collection *Bone Swans, Stories*. Her other work includes *The Twice-Drowned Saint*, *Dark Breakers*, *Desdemona and the Deep*, and poetry collection *How to Flirt in Faerieland and Other Wild Rhymes*, containing her Rhysling Award-winning poem "The Sea King's Second Bride."

Her short fiction and poetry can be found in such places as Jonathan Strahan's anthology *Dragons*, Ellen Datlow's *Mad Hatters and March Hares: All-New Stories from the World of Lewis Carroll's Alice in Wonderland*, Rich Horton's *Year's Best Science Fiction and Fantasy*, and the forthcoming *Storyteller: A Tanith Lee Tribute Anthology*, edited by Julie C. Day.

Cooney is also a voice actor and game designer, who has narrated over 120 audiobooks, as well as short fiction and D&D actual plays for podcasts. *Negocios Infernales*, a TTRPG she co-designed with her husband, writer and game designer Carlos Hernandez, is out now from Outland Entertainment.

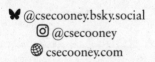

🦋 @csecooney.bsky.social
📷 @csecooney
🌐 csecooney.com

FIND US ONLINE!

www.rebellionpublishing.com

/solarisbooks   /solarisbks   /solarisbooks

SIGN UP TO OUR NEWSLETTER!

rebellionpublishing.com/newsletter

YOUR REVIEWS MATTER!

Enjoy this book? Got something to say?

Leave a review on Amazon, GoodReads or with your
favourite bookseller and let the world know!

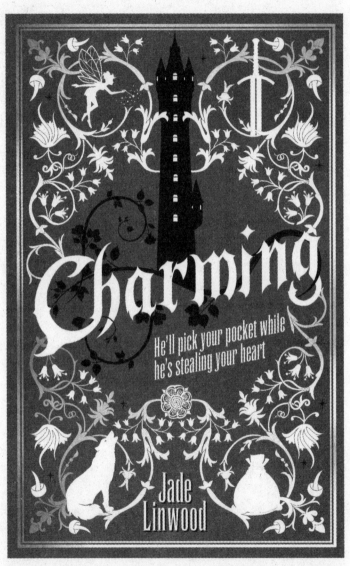

Charming

He'll pick your pocket while
he's stealing your heart

Jade Linwood

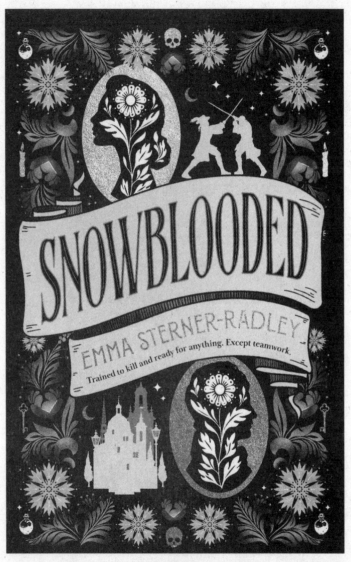

SNOWBLOODED

EMMA STERNER-RADLEY

Trained to kill and ready for anything. Except teamwork.

SOLARISBOOKS.COM

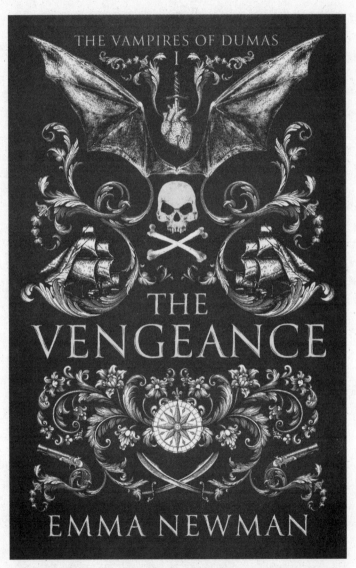

THE VAMPIRES OF DUMAS

I

THE VENGEANCE

EMMA NEWMAN

⊙ SOLARISBOOKS.COM

HERESY IS POWER
CHAOS IS DIVINE

REDSIGHT

MEREDITH MOORING

"A VISCERAL, REALITY-WARPING JOURNEY"
— RYKA AOKI